I0761068

ALSO BY KIM HARRISON

BOOKS OF THE HOLLOWS

DEAD WITCH WALKING

THE GOOD, THE BAD, AND THE UNDEAD

EVERY WHICH WAY BUT DEAD

A FISTFUL OF CHARMS

FOR A FEW DEMONS MORE

THE OUTLAW DEMON WAILS

WHITE WITCH, BLACK CURSE

BLACK MAGIC SANCTION

PALE DEMON

A PERFECT BLOOD

EVER AFTER

THE UNDEAD POOL

THE WITCH WITH NO NAME

THE TURN

AMERICAN DEMON

MILLION DOLLAR DEMON

TROUBLE WITH THE CURSED

DEMONS OF GOOD AND EVIL

DEMON'S BLUFF

THE SHADOW AGE

THREE KINDS OF LUCKY

ECLIPSED EVOLUTION

FIRST CONTACT

TOTALITY

EMERGENCE

SECONDHAND LUCK

KIM HARRISON

ACE
NEW YORK

ACE
Published by Berkley
An imprint of Penguin Random House LLC
1745 Broadway, New York, NY 10019
penguinrandomhouse.com

Book design by Daniel Brount

ISBN: 9780593437490

An application to register this book for cataloging has been submitted to the Library of Congress.

Printed in the United States of America
1st Printing

The authorized representative in the EU for product safety and compliance is
Penguin Random House Ireland, Morrison Chambers, 32 Nassau Street,
Dublin D02 YH68, Ireland, https://eu-contact.penguin.ie.

For Tim

Secondhand Luck

1

THE COFFEEHOUSE WAS A FAMILIAR MIX OF SHOPPERS GRABBING A QUICK BITE and silent, focused people working on their laptops, gazes fixed and lukewarm cups of coffee beside them. The Chicago River was only a few blocks off, and I stifled a shiver when the wind drove pellets of snow against the wide windows, pattering like rain. It felt good to be out of St. Unoc—even if my thin Arizona blood couldn't handle the cold—and I hunched deeper into my admittedly lightweight coat as I waited for Lev to come back with coffee.

All the better to fit in with, my dear, I thought as I scanned the café for our target. Chicago had a decent-size mage population, which meant glittery dross hung in the corners like bits of straw paper and discarded stirring sticks—and my nose wrinkled in disgust at the waste created by magic use. Unlike mundanes, mages, sweepers, and Spinners could all see the latent, dangerous energy to some degree, but only sweepers and Spinners could physically handle it without issue.

It wasn't illegal for mages to discard their dross at the point of magic; in fact, I harbored the belief that most mages did it for the amusement factor, getting a kick out of watching an oblivious mundane step in it like dog doo, where it invariably fractured into bad luck. I'd always thought the practice criminally risky. Too many accidents might break the silence of our existence and expose us. Everyone was supposed to work to keep the silence. Most mages equated that with sweepers cleaning up after them.

I wasn't a sweeper anymore, having found my true potential as a weaver, but it was hard to let go of the feeling of passive discrimination, and I risked a glance at Benedict sitting with a smiling woman at the far end of the store. He was the bait in this bad-mage trap—clearly the most affluent of our four-person team. It was a good bet that, as innocuous as the woman seemed, we had found our target.

Lev's militia intel hadn't included a description, other than it was a woman who had been magically mugging both mundane and mage alike for the last three months. Three months, and all they had was that she was an ether mage, stealing everything in her take's wallet, both physical and phone. She blotted out the incriminating memories, leaving her victims oblivious until after the fact. All we had was that she tended to pick up her marks around here. Sloppy.

But I suppose if you could magic the memory of yourself right out of someone's mind, you could afford to be a little sloppy.

The door chimes rang, and I pulled my collar closer when two men came in, coats open as if oblivious to the cold. *So unfair,* I thought when the draft hit me. "You okay, Pluck?" I whispered as I fingered my lodestone, safe around my neck.

A deeper cold tingled against my fingertips, the sensation somehow carrying a feeling of mirth. *I am the cold,* sifted dryly through my mind, and I smiled as I tucked the rough, semitransparent, greenish-black crystal behind my sweater, where it made a cold spot against me. Living shadows did best in the dark, and though Pluck could tolerate light if he took a form, a sleek hairless dog the size of a Doberman would attract a lot of attention. His snake aspect would be even worse. I usually discouraged him from hiding in the wire-wrapped chunk of moldavite, but the longer he was in it, the more dark matter accumulated in it—and the stronger my magic was.

I was pretty sure that was our coffee sitting at the take-out counter, and still Lev chatted up the barista, either to make sure she wasn't the mage we were looking for or, more likely, because the trim woman was very much his type. Lev was the lead on this, being mage militia—our clandestine police force in a world where magic wasn't supposed to exist. His recent promotion put him as Master Ranger Lev Evander, but bunnies would lay eggs before I'd call him that, especially when the promotion had been so he could better babysit Pluck and me.

Agreeing to work with—not for—the militia had been the best of my bad choices, and until I found a way out of my agreement, I was splitting my time between the militia and working for St. Unoc University, one of a few mage schools of higher learning. Both the university and the militia wanted to know if a living shadow could overpower ether magic—which was why I was here, freezing my toes off in Chicago in November.

And where I went, Dr. Benedict Strom, my boyfriend and one-time darling of St. Unoc University, pulled strings to find a reason to follow. If we were lucky, we'd snag the thief this afternoon, giving Pluck and me time to check out the local high school for a possible weaver hiding among the sweeper population. Catching a badly behaving ether mage would put some money in my pocket, but finding a weaver was my true goal. That, and a really good pizza.

This is taking too long, I thought as Lev finally gathered our coffees and headed over. St. Unoc had an artificially high ratio of magic users to mundanes. Though still covert, magic was an everyday occurrence at the university. Here, in downtown Chicago, any blatant show of the paranormal would get everyone in trouble. We had to be fast and subtle. Fast I could handle. Subtle . . . not so much.

"The barista is clear?" I asked when Lev set a coffee in front of me, and the young man with his intentionally too-long hair nodded. Cold, I wrapped both my hands around the paper cup to try to warm them. Steam rose between me and my view of Benedict and the possible suspect.

Jealousy flickered, soothed by Pluck's confident thoughts twining about mine. Once, sharing mental space had given me a migraine. Not bad considering anyone else but a weaver would be driven insane by it. That had been months ago, and now all that remained was a faint sense of fizzing, the cold of pure energy diving deep in my mind whenever we touched.

Lev dragged a stool closer to the high table, the slim, shorter man easing himself onto it with a casual hip shift. He was wearing a tatty cloth coat and worn knit hat, but he still looked military to me, even slouched as he was. It was something in the eyes, the walk: steady, observant, not a flinch when a crash came from behind the counter. A lodestone glittered from one ear, the glass more precious than the diamond it was trying to mimic. He was a mage, obviously, but I'd never felt slighted in his presence, not even once, and I trusted him, *had* trusted him, with my life.

"I got some of those little scones," he said as he unwrapped the brightly patterned paper. "You want one?"

I shook my head, too nervous to eat. "To better blend in?" I guessed, and his smile widened into a grin.

"Because I'm hungry," he said as he shoved an entire scone into his mouth. "Don't look at them," he said, his words garbled.

I grimaced, knowing he was right. Much to my surprise, Pluck ghosted out of the moldavite lodestone. The shadow was careful to remain in a near pure-energy state that would be hard to see, his hazy, tingling wash of presence slipping down my arm like an icy aura until he coalesced into a wispy snake wrapped around my wrist. Large dog, small snake: the living energy was what he wanted to be.

"It's got to be her," I said, annoyed at how close their heads were when Benedict showed the pretty brunette something on his phone and she giggled.

An unexpected wave of amusement hit me. Pluck's, obviously. *If you want him to do more than kiss you, you should mention it. Good men require an invite,* the shadow suggested.

Oblivious to our silent conversation, Lev nudged his plastic cup lid to the floor to use the excuse of picking it up to glance at them. "It's her." Lev resettled himself, his arm wrapped protectively about the bag of scones. He had shifted position, though, and it only took a slight tilt of his head to see them. "The barista says she's a regular."

I sipped my coffee, eyes almost closing as the nutty warmth slipped down. "She didn't show any interest until Benny added two hundred dollars to his coffee card."

"You noticed that, too?" Motions languid, Lev stretched, the small man ending the motion by taking the phone from his pocket. "Hey, her intel came in." Brow furrowed, he scrolled. "She's a Ms. Fawn Nates. Works in retail a few blocks down. Mage, but it doesn't say what she specializes in. Ah! Here it is. Her father was a professor of ether studies out on the East Coast." His eyes met mine. "Deceased."

A quiver ran through me, making ripples on the coffee in my hand and pulling Pluck's hooded head up from my wrist. Most magic users learned from their parents. St. Unoc went beyond, teaching the skills to use magic in your mundane job for better effect and not get caught.

I snuck a glance, not liking that she saw Benedict as an easy mark. Lev wadded up his empty bag, clearly amused. "You want to hold hands? Make him jealous?"

Pluck's interest snapped to my forethoughts from where he'd been watching the electrons haze the overhead lights. *You do and I'll freeze his fingernails off.*

"Ah, no," I said, adding a mental rebuke: *Pluck, relax.* I'd known Lev for a few years, but until recently he'd been the neighbor down the hall, fixated on my roommate with a sweet, puppyish attraction. That he'd actually been surveilling her as a suspected separatist mage had come as a nasty shock. Now that Ashley was in mage prison, Lev and I occasionally spiraled together to bust our respective boredoms. Benedict had been giving me more space than I needed or wanted. I think he was worried he would come between Pluck and me, but Pluck was my shadow, and Benny? Benny was the best thing since smartphones.

I snuck another glance at Benedict over a sip of coffee, grimacing when his hand touched that woman's shoulder for a telling second when he stood. "He's moving," I said softly, and a small noise slipped from Lev. "She's not. He's going to the register."

"Uh-huh." Lev chuckled. "Don't look at her. She's spelling."

The sensation of Pluck around my wrist grew icy cold. It was all I could do to not turn.

"Nice tidy field," Lev murmured, head down as he pushed a drop of spilled coffee into a spiral. "Her lodestone is in a ring. Right hand."

"Right hand. Check." I stared at my coffee. If we snagged her lodestone, she couldn't spell anyone into forgetting anything. That is, if she only had the one. Ashley had usually carried three, but she was a separatist mage hell-bent on exterminating weavers—which had really put a crimp in our friendship when we realized I was one. *Pluck?*

Pluck's thoughts fizzed sourly in mine. I knew he didn't like Benedict, but I did, and the whole point of us being here was because Pluck said ether magic didn't affect shadows.

"Curious." Lev shifted in his chair. "She didn't throw the spell. She's left it on his chair."

"Like, for him to sit on?" *Pluck,* I tried again, only to get a sensation of obstinate defiance. The shadow snake wasn't interested in helping Benedict, only in keeping me safe. "Can you tell if it's ether magic?"

Lev shook his head. "Not by looking." His frown deepened as his eyes met mine. "She made a shitload of dross, though. Hey, is that shadow dog of yours ready?"

Pluck, if you don't show your value, they won't let us leave St. Unoc again.

Immediately his fizzy, icy presence sharpened in mine. *It's a memory charm. It will take a few moments to mature after contact. Once it does, he will not remember the afternoon.*

I took a slow breath, nervous. I was used to handling problems no one else could, quietly and with a practiced precision. This covert stuff was not my go-to. "It's her. Pluck says it will erase Benny's memory."

You want to see her without turning your head? Pluck asked, and before I could answer, his cold presence slithered deeper into my mind as if it were his own. I blinked at the table, dizzy with a confusing double vision until I submitted and Pluck's awareness took precedence.

With a subliminal *whoosh*, every single haze of dross in the room brightened into a threatening sparkle. It was how Pluck saw the world, and his fear of the unstable energy drifted about my thoughts as our minds became one. My entire outlook became crystalline almost, older, sharper, slower, and having a lot more complex feelings.

That said, Pluck moved on emotion, not logic. Most shadows did, or at least the few I'd talked with. It made them unfortunately easy to manipulate by those who knew. 'Course, if you did a shadow wrong, you'd likely end up driven insane by something alien and subversive in your brain.

This, though, was marvelous, and I relaxed as Pluck filled my mind. It was like training your brain to decipher a stereogram, and suddenly I was seeing both my coffee before me and Fawn Nates halfway across the store. Such finesse would have been impossible even a few weeks ago, but Pluck was getting better at working with my senses and I was getting better at trusting him. The scintillating cold carrying the scent of the universe felt almost comfortable.

Lev was right. A huge drift of dross hazed under the table like a heat distortion, and the prim woman pulled her feet in to avoid it. "Bizarre," I whispered, letting Pluck settle deeper into the folds of my brain.

I saw most spells as a glow or aura-like haze. Pluck, though, saw the charm waiting on Benedict's chair as a glittering lacework of potential energy, far more organized than dross. The latticelike pattern was more complex than I could see with my mundane eyes, and for a moment, I simply stared, fascinated. *This is amazing, Pluck. How do you know what it does?*

His flash of pleased amusement raced through me. *You can read a menu, can't you?*

"Grady."

I started as Lev gripped my arm, but the man let go when Pluck flattened his snakelike head into a cobra hood and hissed at him.

"Sorry," I said, absently soothing the shadow. "Should we warn him?" If I pushed my knitted stocking hat off the table, Benedict would leave.

Lev fingered his hip, clearly missing his usual sidearm. "No. We need more proof than Pluck's say-so or she walks. We have to let it invoke." Exhaling, he slouched over his coffee, his almost-hidden tension prickling through me. His lodestone earring glinted as he inhaled to make a tiny field between his hands. A spell hazed within it, powered by his glass earring. It was something I'd never been able to do and never would. A weaver's magic came from a darker source, and I touched my moldavite lodestone through my shirt.

"Grady, could you . . ." Lev prompted, and a flash of Pluck's ire flickered through both of us when Lev nodded at the small drift of dross he'd created along with his spell. Yeah, I was all for keeping our working area clean. And sure, I was the logical choice for taking care of the waste, seeing as out of the ten or so people in the shop I was the only one the dross wouldn't break on. True, Pluck could use the dross to make himself stronger once I cooled it off. But the ability to handle dross had been perverted over the years into a menial task designed to separate magic users into a have, have-not society. It rankled that Lev assumed I'd take care of it. Like the maid.

And yet . . . I dutifully flicked a small wand with an attracting core from my pocket to twirl the glittering, hard-to-see ribbon of dross up like cotton candy. The latent energy sizzed, threatening to break and give me bad luck. Any mundane watching would assume I was fidgeting with a pencil, which was the entire point of the exercise. Exhaling, I settled a field of thought over it, feeling the shock of connection before the dross cooled in a tingling wash. Inert.

You want it? I asked, but Pluck had already thrown a wispy tendril of essence out to take the now-safe energy. Tickling pinpricks eased through us both as it became a part of him, but his satisfaction quickly tarnished when Benedict returned to the table with two cookies. Yes, Benedict had agreed to help, but I wasn't happy with him losing his memory.

Pluck, as soon as you can, I want you to break the spell on Benny, I thought, and a wash of irritation flowed up like an acidic barb.

I'm not here for him. I'm here for you.

Yeah? I touched my lodestone and my fingers became numb with cold. *Then do it for me.*

Fawn smiled at Benedict, the pleasant expression vanishing when Benedict sat down and burst the spell. With an almost unseen flash, the energy she'd left in it ran straight to his neural system. My gut hurt when Benedict's focus went distant. He'd been spelled.

"Wait for it." Lev put a hand on my wrist and Pluck fizzed darkly. "She needs to . . . Yep, she's going for his phone." His grip on me tightened. "Don't look. This will be when she's at her most attentive, most wary."

Gut hurting, I stared at the table and watched through Pluck's eyes as the woman took Benedict's phone from his pocket, unlocked it with his face, and began scrolling through his apps.

Benedict's expression looked as empty as a keg after a fraternity party. An ache throbbed in my hands, and I unclenched my fists. "Do we have enough evidence now?"

My breath caught when Lev let go of my wrist and stood. "Yep.

Stay clear until I get her ring." His gaze was fixed on Fawn as the woman emptied Benedict's electronic wallet. "She won't do anything here. She can't risk breaking the silence of our existence."

I wasn't so sure. She'd been working this corner of the universe for weeks. *Go,* I directed Pluck, and a wave of disorientation made my stomach flip-flop as he lifted from my thoughts and the bright dross under the table dulled to its usual heat-distortion haze. Worried, I watched through a window reflection as Lev approached the table. Fawn looked up from Benedict's phone as Lev sat down on her other side, his hand falling to pin her palm to the table. Lodestone ring glinting, she jerked out of his grip.

"Hey, handsome," she said to him, an ugly smile on her face as she glanced directly at me. "Why don't you have your *friend* join us. I'm all for doing this quietly. She and her shadow need to die. No need to make a news story out of it."

Petra . . . A winding shadow of gray tightened about my ankle with the icy cold of winter. *She knows you're a weaver.*

Which wasn't anywhere near as troubling as her wanting both Pluck and me dead.

Until with a sudden implosion of thought, I realized why. She was a separatist mage. She wasn't kidding. She wanted me dead.

Lev turned to me, his eyes telling me to run. I jerked when Fawn's lodestone flashed. A scintillating cloud of haze exploded from her, spreading throughout the entire shop. It filled my lungs on a breath, and Lev sprang to his feet only to fall back down, gaze empty. Cries rose, then cut off into a frightening silence.

I tried to stand, slumping on the stool when a winding pattern of threads moved from my lungs to my mind, numbing me. Unable to fight, I felt myself sink into a haze of dreamy nothing . . .

Until a cold spike of anger jammed itself between me and the fuzzy allure of peace.

Pluck! I exclaimed as the scintillating threads of the spell pushed from my mind just enough for Pluck to slip in. Fawn's spell snapped into place, but this time, an uncomfortable itch crawled between it and me. It was Pluck, and I watched as the shadow sent a hazy ribbon of dark matter to cleave to the invasive magic. Once there, he shifted it, changing the resonance of Fawn's spell, pulling it beat by beat out of alignment.

Like an uneven load in the washer, the forget spell began to thump and wobble until it shook itself apart and broke entirely.

Thank you, I whispered into my thoughts, sure I hadn't lost any memory when I looked up to see the coffee shop the same as I'd left it. That is, apart from the people silently staring at nothing, the piped-in music sounding alien and wrong as they all sat or stood like statues.

She spelled the entire store. Pluck's thoughts fizzing through mine held a harsh accusation. *The longer they're under the influence, the more memory they will lose.*

Then we break it. My head lifted, and Fawn's attention snapped to me in shock. My own anger grew as I stood, and she went ashen, her fingers white-knuckled around her phone.

"Shit, she's awake," she whispered, and a frantic, demanding voice on the other end of the connection began yelling at her: "Get out! She's got shadow with her! Get out!"

"Sit!" I demanded as she pushed to her feet and Pluck swirled to the floor as a half-seen shadow. "I said, sit!"

She bolted. Dross trailed from her in a glittering, dangerous ribbon. Until I cooled it, it would burn Pluck . . .

Torn, I froze—watching when the dross from her own spell broke on her in a tinkling wave. The door jammed in a wash of bad luck . . . and she slammed face-first into it. Trapped, she spun to me, her expression ugly.

"Benny, wake up!" I shouted, but both he and Lev were dazed and unresponsive. The door chimes rang merrily as Fawn finally got the door open. Damn it all to hell. If we lost her now, we might never find her again.

Desperate, I turned to Pluck, surprised to see he'd swirled himself into a slim, sleek dog with pointy ears and a cord-like tail. "Pluck, can you wake them . . ." Fawn was already across the street, that glittering ribbon of dross trailing her like toilet paper stuck to her heel.

It will take time. I'm unfamiliar with their minds. I'll tear them if I'm not careful.

I took a step to the door, hesitating. "Get them free, then catch me up."

Petra, she knows who you are. This is a trap!

But Fawn's silhouette was getting smaller. "That spell would have depleted her lodestone," I said, pulse quickening as she hustled down the busy, snowy sidewalk. "I won't engage. I'll follow her. See where she goes." My brow furrowed as he pinned his ears, clearly reluctant. "Pluck, I need you to wake them up!"

His anxiety was obvious, and when his entire being hazed, I knew he realized our emotions sprang from the same place. As desperate as his fear was for me, it was equaled by my worry for Benedict.

Go, he thought bitterly. *I will wake them.*

"Thank you," I whispered, then shoved the door open.

Cold slammed into me. I hunched, squinting through the driving snow, looking for Fawn. Traffic moved, and pedestrians wove around me in the early dusk. The sudden squealing of tires pulled me into a jog. She'd been trailing dross. Dross caused accidents. The colder it got, the faster dross broke—and it was icy out here.

My shoes weren't meant for this and my hands were cold. My breath came in and out, chilling me. At the corner, two men argued over a dented fender, the stoplight above them flickering as it shifted from red to green. I slid to a halt, listening.

The sound of a horn drew my attention. There, a block down, I spotted her.

"Got you." I broke into a stiff jog. Pluck would find me. He could find me anywhere.

As if sensing me, Fawn began an awkward run. I ran faster, not caring that I was freezing my lungs. She had spelled Benedict and Lev. She used her magic to harm, risking all of us if she broke the silence of our existence.

Angry, I didn't hesitate when she darted into an alley. I'd seen her fear. She ran because she didn't have anything left in that ring of hers. "You have scammed your last take, sweetheart," I said when she halted before a chain-link fence halfway down the alley and spun to face me. Wary, I scuffed to a stop, feeling the cold dive deep into me with each breath. "You're done."

It was just her and me. She didn't have to worry about the silence here, and her fear tightened into something worse as her chin lifted defiantly. "Done? Hardly." Her gaze went to where the buildings met the sky. "Now!"

2

I GASPED, DUCKING WHEN TWO LIGHTS SLAMMED INTO EXISTENCE, A FLOOD OF bright glare pinning me between the cold walls of the alley. "Hey!" I shouted when Fawn shoved me, knocking me off-balance. My butt hit the filthy cement, then my back, but the surprise went almost unnoticed when my head followed, stunning me.

Cold hands pushed against my face, followed by a tug and sudden give as Fawn yanked my moldavite amulet from around my neck. *Pluck* . . . He needed it. It was his. Hell, I needed it. It was the source of my magic.

"Got it!" she crowed, pushing herself off me. "I got her lodestone!"

I sat up, frightened. She wasn't alone. I'd made a mistake.

My head hurt, and I could hardly see straight. But she had Pluck's amulet, and my breath caught when I saw the glint in her eye. "No!" I cried out as she flung the glass to the snowy pavement and stomped on it. Shards flew, glinting in the overhead light, green among the falling snow. I stared, shocked.

Any fear Fawn had once had was gone. Overflowing with confidence, she circled me, blocking my way out.

Okay, she'd busted my lodestone, but why the oppressive light? My gaze flicked to the roof as I put one hand on the cold pavement and stood, angry when I realized the only reason for the light would be to drive Pluck into my lodestone. *And then she broke it?*

Fawn stood dead center of the alley, coat open and her hands clenched into fists. In her grip was a new lodestone, brilliant in the bright light, but it was her ugly, vindictive smile that scared me. "No stone. No shadow," she mocked. "It's almost too easy."

My lips parted. She broke the lodestone to kill Pluck? It didn't work like that. Did it? Shadow spit. They had known who we were. Who had been hunting who?

"You're a separatist," I whispered, my gut twisting at the voices echoing down from the rooftop. Fawn was part of the very group that had spent centuries ridding the world of shadow and weavers . . . and I had walked right into her trap.

"Now you get it," Fawn mocked. "Just in time for the end. Filthy weaver."

Okay. I was alone. I was drowning in light. Pluck's amulet was busted and she was between me and any escape. But that didn't mean Pluck was gone or that I was helpless.

I let my anger flow, yelling as I ran for her. She stupidly did nothing, and my shoulder slammed squarely into her gut, sending her pinwheeling backward into the wall.

She cried out as she hit, and I stiffened as my aura sparked. She was casting a spell.

The golden threads of her magic laced into a hazy field, settling over me as a second lodestone brightened, releasing the stored energy of the sun to fuel her spell. Suddenly I couldn't breathe.

I hunched in pain, panicking as my lungs refused to work. Shocked, I froze when her foot slammed into me. The last of my breath escaped me in a pained groan, and I hit the ground hard.

Inches before my eyes was a shard of Pluck's amulet, the glass a dark green amid the slushy gray of snow. As Fawn crowed, I reached for it, desperately pulling it closer until a sharp stab of pain when it cut me told me I had it. A little drop of red squeezed out from between my fingers as I held it tighter, struggling to make a field to break the spell.

Stars spotted my sight. I could sense the dark matter within the shard, twisting like black threads in my mind . . . But I couldn't focus. I was slipping. It wasn't my memory she was going to take. It was my life. *I'm so sorry, Pluck. I should have waited,* I thought. *Benny . . .*

"She's down!" the woman shouted up to the lights. "Give me a second to finish this. First round is on me." A toe nudged my ribs. "Kill your shadow, and you're nothing."

"You sure the shadow is gone?" a voice called down as my forehead touched the cold pavement.

"Yeah, I got it. It was in the stone when I broke it. They're nothing but shards now," Fawn said; then louder, to me, "Bet you didn't know that, did you, weaver bitch? You break a stone when a shadow is in it, and you kill the shadow."

No, I hadn't known that. No wonder Pluck didn't take refuge in it very often. It was both sanctuary and death. *A tiny little church,* my oxygen-starved brain said, stringing nonsense together into pseudowisdom.

Except that Pluck hadn't been in there when she'd broken it.

And then the lights beating down on me exploded with a sodden pop.

Sparkles fell like rain, hitting the cold pavement in a sudden patter. Fawn's shriek echoed, followed by a masculine grunt and a soft and certain thud.

"Petra!"

Warm hands pulled me from the stones and turned me over. *Benedict.*

"Pluck! Over here!" he shouted as the last of the sparks faded and were gone.

Shadow spit, I couldn't die. I had stuff to do yet.

"You're going to be okay," Benedict said, panic furrowing his brow, and my heart broke as I heard the lie. "Petra, you're going to be okay." He looked desperately into the new dark. "Pluck!" he called in agony.

A sharp, familiar thought skated through my mind, breaking Fawn's spell with the shock of a sudden slap. Gasping, I sucked in the frigid air as Pluck's horrified presence twined frantically through mine. His thoughts were too chaotic to realize, but his emotion was clear enough. It was hard to say who he was more angry with—himself or me.

Benedict yanked me closer, a hand pushing my hair from my eyes as I shook. "Thank God. Are you okay?" he whispered. The alley was blissfully dark again, but stray bits of dross lit the night and I could see him. Pluck fizzed in my uppermost thoughts, the fear behind his anger almost frantic . . . until he realized I was sensing everything he felt and he hid his emotions from me with a soul-shaking snap.

"You're bleeding!" Benedict said, and I looked at my hand in a numb haze.

"It's from a shard of Pluck's lodestone. I'm fine." I hadn't meant to worry either of them, and it was heady knowledge that they both cared for me that much. Almost . . . I could smile. I opened my hand to show him the ragged shard of glass, black in the low light and shining with my blood. It was all that was left of Pluck's very expensive, very old chunk of moldavite.

Ryan is going to be ticked . . .

Another shout sounded from the roof, followed by the flash of a spell. Clearly Lev was up there, risking the silence to catch Fawn's cohorts. If anyone saw it, he could blame it on a blown transformer. "It was lucky you got here when you did," I rasped, my gaze dropping to Pluck. The shadow was sitting before Fawn, pinning her against a rusted door. He was the size of a small pony, and drifts of dark matter lifted from him in black curls, hissing when they found the iced pavement. His massive shoulders and powerful haunches gleamed in the glow of the dross and the streetlight, and the snow, I realized, was falling right through him.

Dross littered the alley, glowing like lava as it dripped from the rooftop. The big lights on the roof might be busted, but I could see better in the dark and the leftover energy from mage magic burned like little suns. Both annoyed and relieved, Pluck flicked an ear. The splat of dark matter hit the pavement inches from Fawn's foot, hissing evilly until it dissipated.

"Don't touch me!" Fawn shrieked as she pressed against the door. "Someone help! I'm being mugged!"

But no one ventured down the alley to investigate, and whoever had been manning the lights was gone or in cuffs.

"Careful. She's too mean to go down easy," I said as Benedict helped me stand, his hand cupping my elbow. My hip hurt, and I wrapped my arms around myself and longed for my Arizona sun. "Thanks, Pluck." I limped forward to put my hand atop his head, but he was misty and it simply fell through in a wash of cold tingles. He clearly wasn't happy he had needed to save me. Or maybe it was Fawn. Or his busted amulet. "Ah, we'll get another lodestone. No need to kill her over that," I joked.

Why not? iced through me when he twined a ribbon of ice about my ankle. And if the truth be told, I kind of wondered that myself as the back of my head throbbed in tomorrow's bruise. *I'm too fast to be caught in a breaking lodestone, but her aim was to kill both of us.*

Too fast? I asked silently, and a flush of his annoyance wove about my confusion.

I know my way through a lodestone's lattice, he fizzed, soothing my worry. *Another shadow would have to hold me there while it broke to be effective. Even so, I don't like that she knew it was possible.*

His amulet wasn't a death trap. Relieved, I dabbled my fingers in his quasi-solid state, feeling his fear and anger swell my own until his abiding hate trickled through me and I pulled my hand from him. Without his touch, my thoughts and emotions became solely my own again.

"I don't remember anything after breakfast," Benedict said, his brow creased with worry. "You were gone, and Pluck's charades made it very obvious he knew where you were. What happened?"

"We found her. Confronted her. She spelled the entire shop." But as I took a breath to tell him we'd gotten more than a badly behaving mage, the woman pinned against the door lunged for the pavement.

"Lodestone!" Lev called out from the roof. "She's going for another lodestone!"

She's got three? I reached out as Pluck darted to intercept the bauble of glass glittering in the snow. It had to be Fawn's. If she got it, no telling what she'd do.

I had no time to think, and I clasped that tiny shard of my amulet in one hand to draw on the dark matter still within it. Other hand extended, I inhaled to make a small field. Dark matter stored in the crystal's lattice rang with the echo of the big bang. With a practiced flip of thought, I brought my personal energy field in line with it. The two echoes synchronized, and the stored energy was suddenly mine.

"Benny, down!" I shouted, filling the small field with everything the shard had, exciting the energy to a higher level dangerously fast.

My class-five field ripped apart from the assault, the backlash raking my mind like little daggers. A silent boom flung me against the wall. Even expecting it, I hit hard, dizzy as I tried to keep my feet. Benedict was on his knees, eyes wide. Fawn, too, had slammed into the wall and was gasping in pain, trying to sit up.

Pluck was misty, glowing green from the charged energy passing harmlessly through him. Making a little doggy huff, he sat on the woman's second lodestone, tongue lolling. She could still see it, but no way was she getting it now.

"You okay?" I said as I rolled my shoulders, and Pluck flicked an ear, clearly amused. Yeah, maybe I'd overdone it, but I hadn't wanted to be spelled back to the Stone Age. "Ma'am, are you okay?" I added, not really caring. "Lev! You good up there?"

"Good!" he shouted. "Don't let her spell herself. She's going to tell us who her friends are. Ben, meet me at the top of the alley in case they return for her. I've got the van coming, and Grady and Pluck have her."

Yeah, we had her, and I tucked the depleted shard into a pocket as I limped to Pluck. My entire arm tingled with cold when I reached through him to get Fawn's lodestone. The piece of glass was unremarkable on the outside, and I handed it to Benedict. He couldn't use it as it was tuned to Fawn, but I wasn't about to take it anywhere near her when I cuffed her. "She's a separatist," I said, and his expression hardened. "She knew who I was. This entire thing was a trap."

Again Pluck huffed as he stood and stretched, reminding me of my dog so much it almost hurt. *Never happen,* he thought as he wrapped a cold tendril around my ankle so I could hear him.

Benedict's lips moved in a silent swear word. Angry, he dropped the lodestone into a pocket. Fawn could make a new one with any bit of glass, but not when the sun was down. Light powered mages' magic, and shadow powered mine. "We didn't even know there was a separatist cell in Chicago," he said. Brow furrowed in concern, he jogged to the head of the alley. Silent, I watched him, remembering his desperate worry when he found me unable to breathe.

"You will all rot in hell for this," Fawn said bitterly, and I turned to her.

"Ah, hands out," I said as I wrangled the cuffs from my coat pocket.

"Like hell!" Suddenly angry, she focused on Pluck. "Don't touch me!"

She gave me a shove, but I'd had enough, and I shoved her right back as Lev had coached me, using her own momentum to twist her wrist against itself and force her face against the door. "Fawn Nates,

I am detaining you for suspicion of confidence schemes involving ether magic because that's what the warrant in my pocket says, but it's your crimes as a separatist that will get you a nice, cozy cell." Awkwardly, I pulled her other arm around and cuffed her hands. I had like zero practice. This wasn't my day job. "Let's go."

"Hands off. Hands off!" Fawn's eyes went from the empty roof to me when she spun around. "I know people. I know people who can make you disappear."

Pluck sat on his haunches, his indulgent yawn ending in a little yip. The friendly sound was at odds with his demon dog aspect, but Fawn paled, clearly knowing if he cared to slip into her mind, he could scramble her brains like eggs in a pan. Actually, it had been remembering how *not* to scramble my brains that had been the trick. Which was probably why he and I were at the top of the separatist mages' most-wanted-dead list. But just because you could do a thing doesn't mean you will.

"Move. Now!" This anger wasn't me, but she *had* tried to kill Pluck. *Shadow spit, Ryan is going to be mad I broke a lodestone,* I thought as I rubbed the dried blood from my palm. Unlike mage amulets, which could be any chunk of glass, mine had to be made of moldavite to withstand dark matter under stress.

Head down, she began to walk to the top of the alley. Her coat was open, and she looked cold. "You're going to wake up dead," she muttered. "I'm important. They need me. Let me go, and they might ignore you for a while."

The adrenaline was long gone, and I gave her a shove to move faster. Two hunched figures were making their determined way through the snow toward us, but Pluck was relaxed, and I trusted him. "You are dead! You hear me?" Fawn shouted when she saw Benedict and Lev.

Lev was grinning, the somewhat short man giving me a satisfied nod after checking her cuffs. "Ma'am, you need to glory in your right to remain silent."

"Van is here." Benedict's head drooped as Lev shoved Fawn into a faster pace. "Petra, I don't think I'm cut out for this. I . . ."

Smiling, I sidled closer to him until his arm went over my shoulder and our sides touched. "It's okay," I said, and Pluck made an annoyed huff. Amused, I tried to tug the dog to my other side—until he went utterly misty and all I got was a cold handful of nothing. Ears flat, he padded after Lev and Fawn. He left no footprints in the new snow. *I couldn't have done it without you, either, Pluck,* I thought, but he was no longer touching me and couldn't hear.

The van at the top of the alley had opened its side door with a familiar rumble, and two militiamen in street clothes got out. Motions brusque, one took Fawn by the shoulder and yanked her in. It was done—badly, but done—and I bumped into Benedict as we scuffed to a halt at the curb.

"Hey, at least now we can concentrate on interviewing students for St. Unoc scholarships." Because that had been both our cover and my original intent. Working with the militia was from my ill-thought promise, not any real desire.

Benedict took a long, slow breath, his eyes on Fawn and Lev in the van. "I'm sorry, Petra. There won't be any weavers in Chicago. Not if there is a separatist cell here."

"How about Naperville?" I said. "It's on the outskirts."

He bobbed his head, his smile holding little hope. "I'll call them tonight."

His hand gave mine a squeeze, but even I knew it was a thin chance. We'd been looking for weavers among the sweeper population for over five months and hadn't found any. Once you knew what to look for, weavers were easy to suss out, which was probably why there were so few of us left. Pluck's cold touch returned to my ankle. *Pluck, remind me again why I didn't let you drive her insane?*

He turned, one green eye finding me. *It's not too late,* iced through me, the reminder of his terrifying past chilling me more than the snow falling through him. Mages had once hunted them and their weaver caretakers almost to extinction—and in return, shadows became the threat the mages said they were in order to survive. But without shadow, magic had become unbalanced until our society was threatening to collapse under the waste it left behind. Pluck and I were trying to bring balance back, but no one liked change, especially when it meant knocking mages from their high-and-mighty seat.

That Pluck had restrained himself was a testament to how smart shadows really were. And yet, as I looked at Fawn slumped and cuffed to a seat, I couldn't bring myself to get in. "Hey, you think we could take a different vehicle?"

Benedict pulled his hand away from the van, smiling as his gaze went from Lev to me. "I could do with a walk. It's what? Six blocks?"

"Great." Lev slammed the side door shut. "I'll see you both at the hotel." He paused. "Sorry, the three of you," he added, his attention going to Pluck sitting at my heel like the dog he wanted everyone to think he was.

Benedict tugged me closer as the van crept into motion. The snowy dusk was beautiful, but I could hardly enjoy it. Sure, we had captured Fawn, but no one had expected her to be a separatist—much less the bait in a trap set for Pluck and me. Fawn would never see the inside of a mage courtroom. No, she was headed for a militia cell and interrogation. They'd have to keep every shard of glass from her lest she spell herself into forgetting everything.

Though forgetting might be a blessing.

3

THE TEACHERS' LOUNGE AT NAPERVILLE'S LARGEST HIGH SCHOOL WAS A SAD MIX of old upholstery, lavender, and cheap coffee. I slouched in the folding chair behind the battered card table, tired, hungry, and disillusioned. The fabric cushion was stained, probably new in the early 2000s, and the Scotchgard had long since been rubbed off by polyester slacks and knit skirts.

Benedict sat beside me, his brow furrowed as he studied his tablet while we waited for the last student. The buzz of the class bell was faint through the cinder-block walls, and I smiled when his breath quickened in anticipation at the rising sound of students. This was the first time either of us had done scholarship evaluations, and whereas Benedict had earmarked a few good candidates for the mage program, I was beginning to lose hope of finding a talented sweeper, much less a weaver.

On the plus side, the vice principal was a sweeper, which meant we could talk freely in private. Most public schools had one or two magic users on the payroll, doing both what they were contracted for as well as their second, unpaid job of helping to cover up magical mishaps. But when had being a teacher ever been a one-task job?

It might have been the noise in the hallway, or the cold tile floor, or possibly the smell of old coffee, but I smiled as the memory of Benedict and me playing paper triangle football surfaced. It was bittersweet, still tainted with the heartache Benedict had inadvertently heaped on me despite the acres of time between then and now.

Real friends don't dump on you to impress the in crowd—but real friends also make mistakes. He had been afraid, I had been naive, and it was scary how fast infatuation could twist to a childish hate—especially in high school. *And back again,* I thought, lips quirking. I understood now where his insecurity had come from, and with understanding came forgiveness. The real and heartfelt apology had helped, too. He had stood up for me more times than I could count, and I trusted that.

Not that we always got it right, I thought, starting when a cold tendril wrapped around my ankle and Pluck's presence blossomed in mine.

If you don't tell him how you feel, he won't know, Pluck sizzed in my mind, and I frowned. He was a solid half of our partnership. He shouldn't be hiding under a couch.

I thought you didn't like him, I thought.

Pluck's annoyance frothed against my question. *I don't,* he fizzed. *But you do. Move forward. Your uncertainty is straining my certainty.*

"Sorry," I whispered, and Benedict looked up from his tablet.

"For what?"

Crap. I had said it aloud, and I flushed in embarrassment even as Pluck's icy grip tightened until my entire foot went numb with a demanding cold. "I, ah." I tried to pull my foot from Pluck, but he only stretched until his energy sparked in the added stress, chilling me. I took a breath. Held it. Let it out. *Pluck . . . I'm not going to tell him how I feel in a teachers' lounge,* I practically whined as his cold shot through me. "Um. Thank you for being there with me last night," I added, and Benedict smiled. "It means a lot that you want to help us find weavers."

Pluck's dissatisfaction was a quick flash. *I'll tell him later,* I thought, and it subsided into a frothing grumble.

Benedict beamed. Tablet in one hand, he pulled me into a sideways half hug with the other. "Petra, I wasn't there just to help you find weavers. I was there because I care about you."

Alight, I took a breath to say how important he had become to me—teachers' lounge or not.

"You do some of the dumbest things sometimes. Honestly, taking on a separatist cell by yourself?"

I hesitated, my emotions a sudden slurry. The anger was mine; the annoyance was probably Pluck's. "I wasn't alone," I muttered. "Pluck was bringing you. And how was I supposed to know she was a separatist? You want to call someone dumb, call Lev dumb. It was his intel." God! It was like we were in high school, and I slumped in my chair.

Benedict's brow furrowed as he studied his tablet. "You're right. Lev is dumb. Mace Handon is the last student. Mage, not mundane. Pluck, you want to come out?"

I leaned to look under the couch, seeing only his glowing eyes. There were five of them at the moment. We had needed to talk to the mundane kids interested in St. Unoc as a matter of course, but the only way to get into St. Unoc was an invite, and only the magic users made the cut. "Pluck?" I encouraged, and three of his eyes vanished.

No, I do not, the sullen shadow grumped as his grip frosted my ankle.

Benedict's lips twisted into an apologetic smile when I shook my head, clearly out of sorts. "Petra, I'm sorry. I know you were hoping to find a weaver," he said, completely misreading the situation.

I forced myself to smile. *You should be out here, Pluck.* "We have a few schools yet to visit. Maybe we'll get lucky."

And it would take luck—good luck. This far from St. Unoc, the ratio of magic users to mundanes was its typical one in a thousand. Trying to find a weaver in that would tack on another zero. Perhaps I was doing this wrong. If there was an active separatist cell in Chicago, I might do better investigating unsolved murders and talking to their surviving kids.

We're never going to find another weaver, I thought, not surprised when a feeling of comfort and support rose through me with an icy clarity.

I found you.

My lips curved up when the cold sensation on my ankle ebbed and his thoughts vanished. He'd been alone, subsiding on the inert dross given off by a rez, or ghost, as mundanes called them. He had recognized the inert dross I'd accidentally used to make my long-sticks, tearing one apart to get to it, starving. I'd captured him, then almost destroyed him in the university's vault, as was protocol at the time.

It had been my mentor, Darrell, who had stayed his execution. Ryan was the one who had recognized that dross I handled spontaneously cooled to where shadows could absorb it. The ability made me a weaver, not a sweeper. I had been unknowingly attracting shadow like moths to flames.

I'd never been more scared in my life, but Pluck and I figured it out. Well, mostly Pluck. He'd been here before, had watched his partner murdered by jealous mages . . . had mourned.

But that was thousands of years ago, and I couldn't help but wonder if there was someone out there right now, scared as they realized they were a living, breathing shadow magnet. Finding them would likely only exchange one fear for another. Most of my sweeper friends worked hard to avoid me, worried that Pluck might drive them insane.

"Benny, I'm so glad you're not afraid of me," I whispered.

Benedict made a soft grunt of surprise, his eyes wide as they lifted from the tablet. He reached out and held my hand. "Where did that come from?"

I shrugged, nervous as the hall noise began to abate. "Just thinking how terrified I was before I knew Pluck wouldn't hurt me. And then how everyone got scared of me when I stopped being afraid to be who I was."

His expression shifted, and my heart gave a hard thump. "Petra, I could never be afraid of you."

I can fix that if you like, Pluck interjected.

Jealous much? I thought, then drew my hand from Benedict's at the hesitant knock.

Another new mage. How wonderful, Pluck fizzed, vanishing deeper under the couch to leave only the thinnest threads of presence tangling about my ankle so we could talk.

Benedict leaned closer, whispering, "You may wrangle shadows, but the light in you is amazing." He nodded sagely at my wince, then shouted toward the door, "Come in!"

I sat straighter when the door opened and a young face, brown and innocent, looked in. "Hi," the kid said, awkward and gangly as he came in at Benedict's gesture. "Ms. Maple said I should knock."

"Mace Handon?" Benedict said with a smile. "Right on time. Come on in. Have a seat."

I stifled a sigh. I was here for the sweeper students. That was it.

Now you know how I feel, Pluck interjected with a wash of cold tingles.

Benedict cleared his throat and set his tablet aside. "I'm Professor Benedict Strom." Smiling, he extended his hand.

Mace hesitated, his brown eyes widening. "You developed the way to freeze . . . dross." He practically whispered the last, which was par for the course. We were in a mixed setting, and breaking the silence took a lot of diligence to clean up.

"It was a team effort." Benedict knocked my elbow to get me to say something.

"Ah, I'm Ms. Grady." I extended my hand over the table. His fingers met mine briefly, not a tingle or wisp of dross to mar them. *Point on his side,* I thought. A mage willing to take responsibility for his magical waste would be an asset to the university, but Pluck's faint grumble told me he wasn't impressed.

Benedict pulled his tablet closer. "Ms. Grady was highly instrumental in making the process safe."

"Safe" was a relative term. Benedict's new spell basically fixed magic waste into an artificially frozen state, its molecular structure as tight as if it were still active. Living shadows could release the pressure—in essence, explode the waste. That was how the large auditorium at St. Unoc University and the vault under it had been destroyed. The only "safe" way to get rid of dross was to encourage it to naturally dissipate as bad luck, or to turn it inert and give it to a shadow—incidentally making the shadow stronger.

Which was probably why several thousand years ago a faction of mages labeled shadows and weavers as evil. They targeted the weavers first, and when their human voices were gone, they attacked the sentient shadows without mercy, spreading the lie that shadows were malicious and to be destroyed on sight—until the shadows themselves believed it.

Pluck and I were more than ambassadors, we were innovators and reluctant soldiers.

"It's nice to meet you." Mace gingerly eased back onto the chair. "Um, I haven't actually put my app in yet. Guidance won't let me until next year."

I smiled encouragingly. "That's okay. We're talking to anyone who might apply in the next four years. We don't get out this way often, and if you do decide St. Unoc is a good fit for you, you can skip the psi assessment portion of the app. We'll keep today's evaluation on file."

Mace glanced nervously at the small tabletop dross trap at Benedict's elbow. The three crossed sticks had been designed to look like unsharpened pencils, but these had a core of dross, and when arranged as they were, they not only kept dross from wandering about to break shoelaces and cell phones, but actually attracted it. At least, that was the idea. Getting mages to put their waste in the "can" was another story. "Ah, my mom went to St. Unoc," Mace said.

Benedict looked up from his tablet. "As long as the grades stay where they are, there should be no problem."

"Did you bring a lodestone?" I asked, wanting to see the kid in action, and Mace flushed.

"I'm not allowed to take one to school."

Because he'd use it and someone might notice. *Can't lie convincingly,* I thought in satisfaction. *Point two in his favor.* From the instant they learned how to break light into its components so as to use the energy that released, every mage had a lodestone on them. Always.

"That's fine." Benedict's shoulder touched mine as he searched his pocket. "We need a demonstration of where you are. Making one will suffice."

The hall was now silent, and the click of the glass marble meeting the table was loud.

Mace grinned as he took it. "This is so weird. I spend every day hiding what I can do, and you ask me to make a lodestone."

"The room is secure," I said, and Mace nodded.

"Mrs. Brans is a sweeper," the kid said, his caution melting away worrisomely fast. "She calls dross dust bunnies and gets on our case if she sees any. You won't tell her, will you?"

"She knows we're testing everyone," I said wryly. "You're rated on time and mistakes, so when you're ready . . ."

Mace's grip on the marble tightened, and I felt the distinctive pressure of a psi field form as he inhaled. A heat-distortion mirage flickered over the kid's hands as he reorganized the glass at a molecular level, both to bond to it and to store energy. It was something I couldn't do—but Pluck could, and an icy sharpness came over my thoughts when the shadow began to take an interest.

Mace's brow furrowed in concentration. His psi field was typical for a student—about a class one or two—and the dross began leaking out long before he was done with the spell. That didn't bother me as much as him utterly ignoring the haze of sparkling bad luck on the table, and my smile froze when he casually flicked the heat-like distortion away from him before it could break on him in bad luck.

Suddenly nervous, Mace set the lodestone down for Benedict to inspect. If he'd done it right, the glass would—when exposed to sunlight—passively separate the particle portion of light from the wave, storing the wave energy for later use. Once a stone was depleted, it could be recharged by the sun. Spinners could do the same thing, but they used the energy from the particle portion of light. In both cases, dross was the resultant waste. Weavers didn't use light at all, but dark matter. It was everywhere the light wasn't, but it only gathered in sufficient quantities to power magic where shadows, living shadows, rested. Thoughts full, I fingered my collar, missing Pluck's amulet.

"May I?" Benedict asked formally, and when Mace nodded, Benedict put a tidy field around the lodestone, setting it resonating with a thin trace of energy to gauge its quality. "Nicely done," he said, and Mace exhaled in relief. "Good use of energy. Little dross residue. Have you given any thought as to what you want to focus on if you are accepted at St. Unoc?"

"Ah, I'm good with fire magic," he said, gaze flicking up in pride. "My dad has me boil water for him when he makes dinner and I've warmed up my little sister's bottle. But I'd really like to explore water studies. Maybe combine it with a criminal science degree so I can find lost people or solve crimes."

I stifled a smile. Everyone wanted the high-profile jobs—until they found out how hard it was to become proficient in the rarer disciplines. Still, using one's magic to assist in their mundane job was common. Those proficient in air studies tended to become doctors, nurses, or paramedics, where their hard-won ability to move objects through other things could save lives. It was the rarest ability, and with a degree in that, a mage could go anywhere. Magic users specializing in earth magic tended to go into security, where being able to cause things to attract others could freeze a fleeing person to the ground. Water studies was sensing when something was out of place—also useful in the police force—and ether, of course, was being able to modify a person's perceptions or memory. It was probably the most desirable skill after fire magic as it was imperative to helping keep the silence.

Water mages were rare, and he'd have a steep hill to climb, especially with his class-one psi field. As much as mages didn't want to believe it, it was the field strength that equated magic strength, not how big your lodestone was. Mace had a long way to go.

"As long as your fields are strong, any aspect of magic is powerful," I said, and Mace shrugged. I was sure his mom saw that look six times a day, and though it raised my eyebrows, it wasn't half as bothersome as the dross still on the table. He hadn't made one move to put it in the trap. And that, of course, was the real test. I didn't care if he could make a lodestone; I wanted to know how responsible he was. Right now, I wasn't impressed.

"And your dross-handling skills?" I prompted.

Benedict cleared his throat in a subtle warning and extended a dross-cored wand mimicking a sharpened pencil.

Mace flushed as he took it. "I thought that's what you were here for."

And there it is, I thought dryly, too familiar with the sentiment to be angry. We were probably a generation out from breaking the stigma of being a sweeper. *Who am I kidding. We're going to be lifetimes fighting this,* I thought, and Pluck sizzed a sour agreement.

"Mr. Handon," Benedict said formally, and Mace squirmed, knowing he'd messed up. "Ms. Grady is not here to pick up after you. She's here looking for weavers among the sweeper population. You haven't noticed any unusual shadow activity, have you?"

Mace looked up from where he'd been wrangling the dross. He had a nice technique, managing to hold on to everything as he paled. "Sh-Shadow?" he stammered, gaze darting to me.

My lips quirked in a smile. *Pluck, you want to scare the shit out of some mage?*

No, iced through my thoughts, but I could feel his irritation as well. *He's just a kid.*

Despite Mace's distressingly familiar beliefs, I agreed. *Fine. The bird, then.* If it was going to take generations, no time like the present to start.

Pluck slipped out from under the couch as a black haze, swirling counterclockwise to take on the form of a sleek, raven-like bird at my elbow. Green eye fixed on the boy, he flapped his wings once and a single feather broke free, dissolving with a hiss when it hit the floor.

Mace went ashen as I dabbled my fingers in Pluck's icy presence. Once, his bird form had been ragged, ugly, with twisted feathers falling out to show pus-bubbled skin. But his image was a reflection of how I saw him, and now all I saw was grace, splendor, and above all, power.

"Th-That's shadow. You're touching shadow," Mace whispered. "You're not insane?"

Benedict smiled with half his mouth. "That depends on who you ask."

"It's only when a shadow enters your mind that you go insane," I said. "If it wants, shadow can touch a person to no ill effect." I was trying to be comforting, but I think it failed, as the kid went paler yet. Still, he was doing better than the last candidate I'd thought had enough potential to give the hard truth to, and both Pluck and I shared a feeling of positivity. Knowledge was strength, and Mace Handon had the drive and potential despite his tiresome views. He deserved the chance to grow.

A cold ribbon of Pluck drifted onto the table, and I played with the strand, winding it around my finger as if I were a seer of old. *He's handling this pretty well,* I thought, and my entire hand went numb with cold.

I'm not a circus animal to be paraded out to impress children.

No, you are my partner, I responded immediately. *You should have been sitting next to me when he walked in, not hiding under the couch. If Mace ever does run into shadow, I want him to remember a smart, intelligent presence who can be reasoned with, not the raving monster he's been taught.*

Pluck was silent, and then warmth returned to my hand in a wave of painful pinpricks. *Benny may touch me to prove shadow can be reasoned with. Not Mace.*

Fair enough, I thought, then tore a small drift of dross from the desk trap, lip twitching at the heated jolt of connection. The painful shock was one of the tells that I was a weaver, but I hadn't known that when I was growing up. I'd only thought I was different.

The heat vanished when I formed a field about it, my mind instinctively shifting electrons from shell to shell until the energy expressed was completely different and yet utterly the same. I'd made the dross inert, and I handed it to Benedict knowing Mace could see the heat distortion—knew what it was.

"You want to . . ." I prompted, and Benedict jumped, his nervousness a quickly hidden flash.

"Sure." Benedict extended the dross to Pluck. They weren't exactly friends.

The things I do for progress, Pluck complained, head tilting to angle his razor-sharp beak and miss Benedict's fingers as he took it. *I am not a toy,* he grumbled.

Then you should have been out here from the knock on the door, I thought. *Pluck, nothing will change unless we change it.*

Perhaps. And with that, Pluck evaporated, his structure utterly collapsing to leave a wash of tingles where his hazy presence touched mine. The sentient energy flowed in a sparkling, icy stream to vanish into my shirt pocket, spiraling down to the size of an acorn.

Mouth agape, Mace stared.

"Mace, I'd never touch a shadow that I've not bonded with," I said, and his wide eyes flicked to mine. He looked half a breath from fleeing the room. "The wild ones will still fight back when cornered. They're only defending themselves after centuries of persecution."

The kid swallowed. "Like when they brought down the auditorium at St. Unoc?"

I nodded, not proud of how badly the university had handled the situation—how badly I had.

"That was an accident." Benedict tucked the discarded wand into a shirt pocket. "Self-defense. It was our mistake."

Mace looked ready to throw up. I could understand why. Up until recently, it was standard practice to destroy captured shadow not retained to use for instructional purposes. That a handful of desert shadows had taken up residence under the shattered auditorium had not gone down well with mage or sweeper. It only took two weeks of footing the bill to ship the dross created by an entire university of mages out of state for disposal before plans for a new vault had been finalized. In response, the desert shadows had taken to the streets after sundown wearing the images of those who died in the explosion. It was an eerie yet effective protest, leaving Pluck and me to find the middle ground between mage tradition and the reality of an even older, intelligent magic faction surviving a supposed extinction.

Fortunately there was one thing both parties could agree on: there were too many mages in St. Unoc to not have a place to put the dross they made. The construction of St. Unoc's new vault had begun and no-vaulting-shadows legislation was put into effect, coupled with the promise that existing vaults nationwide would be retrofitted with shadow escape valves for accidental incarcerations.

The desert shadows weren't entirely happy, but they didn't want the dross hanging around, either, seeing as it was like living next to an active volcanic field. The desired end point of a no-vault society would take time. Shadows we had, but trained weavers were in short supply. Until Pluck and I found more, we'd be handling our waste as we always had: shoving it into a thick glass-walled hole in the ground.

I couldn't let Mace walk out of here scared, though, and I cleared my throat. "So," I said cheerfully, "dross-handling skills are important. I suggest you practice them along with your fields. Not to mention it never hurts to test out of a semester or two of required dross studies."

Mace took a shaky breath. "Okay."

"Thank you, Mace." Benedict's voice held the same "we're done" tone. "You did good." Smiling, he stood to indicate the interview was over. "Keep those grades where they are, and I don't see a problem in your future application. We'll be sure to let guidance know."

Mace stood up. "Thank you, sir," he said as he shook Benedict's hand, then, after a telling hesitation, mine. It was cold, but we'd dumped a lot on him. By the time he showed up on campus, he might have found a clue or two. *I hope.*

"Ma'am," he added, hesitating for a moment before turning and walking out.

And you wanted me to play nice, iced up through my thoughts. *He's a yeth.*

"So was I," I whispered, remembering how scared I'd been.

Benedict chuckled as he sat back down and touched his tablet awake. "He took the lodestone." He started to scroll, looking up when I didn't say anything. "Hey, I know he's got some growing to do, but I was just as bad as a freshman."

"Freshman?" I chuckled. "You didn't lose your 'shit don't stink' mentality until someone rubbed your nose in it."

Benedict's hurt expression flashed across his face . . . then he bobbed his head, chagrin replacing it. "Yeah. You're right. But isn't that what college is for?"

Relenting, I touched his hand to ease my harsh words. "You weren't that bad. I never felt as if you thought I was a trashman," I lied. His fingers were warm in mine, and he gave my hand a quick squeeze when I added, "How many more schools left?"

He moved away from me, good mood restored. "One this afternoon, and then we've got . . ." His words faded as he stared at his phone. "Ryan is trying to get in touch with you."

I reached for my phone. I kept it silenced during the interviews so I could stare at the students when theirs hummed. "He probably wants to find out how I managed to destroy another priceless antique moldavite lodestone," I muttered, but in all honesty, the man would be far more concerned about me than a piece of glass Pluck could replace ad nauseam if he wanted. My hip was still hurting, but even as I realized it, Pluck sent an icy drift through me, numbing the ache.

Thanks, Pluck, I thought, frowning when my phone connected to a tower and two messages—including one from Ryan—dropped in. I didn't bother reading them and hit the call icon while Benedict folded up our interview table.

Ryan was more than my university boss, and it still hurt that I'd lost the camaraderie I'd once had with the entire sweepers' guild that he managed and I had once been a part of. They were scared. I didn't blame them, seeing as I was joyfully cheek-to-jowl with shadow, the terror they'd been told to fear their entire lives.

We will find weavers, Pluck thought, the chill in my pocket growing. *You will have kin.*

But my friends' fear still hurt. I might never find that easy companionship again.

I took a breath when the phone connected. "Hi, Ryan," I said before the older Spinner could say anything. "Sorry I didn't call last night. Lev has already left with that separatist mage. She gave us a list of names and they will be picked up. We're fine and there's no reason we can't finish out the interviews. They're going great, by the way. Only one fainted at Pluck."

She'll be the better for it, Pluck muttered, his embarrassment a quick, cold wash.

Ryan cleared his throat, the dry sound cutting my babble off clean. "You haven't looked at your messages, have you."

It really wasn't a question, and I glanced at Benedict gathering our stuff. "Ah, no. Let me put you on speaker." Worried, I opened up my messages. Clearly this wasn't about me breaking another lodestone. *Cameron Owens? Who is that, and how did they get my number?*

"I'm sorry to cut the interviews short, but I need you and Pluck here," Ryan said, his gravelly voice rumbling. "Now."

Benedict looked up from shaking out my scarf. "We have a few schools—" I started.

"Someone cracked the new vault and we're getting a lot of unusual shadow sightings," Ryan interrupted. "We think they might be looking for you."

Benedict came close, his brow furrowed in concern. "Intentionally? It was supposed to go on line next week. What are we supposed to do with the dross in the meantime?"

"I suppose what they are doing with it now," I said as I clicked open the first message to find a shortly worded text asking for an appointment at my earliest convenience. "Who is Cameron Owens?" The second text, from Ryan, was even better, telling me about a mandatory meeting tomorrow morning to introduce said person.

"She's a mage marshal," Ryan said, and my eyes jerked up to find Benedict's. "I suggest you get in touch with her before she decides you are avoiding her and puts out a warrant."

"A marshal?" I whispered, and Pluck's interest grew, fizzing through my worry with a confidence I had no right to feel. She'd be a mage, obviously, the courts' muscle able to cross state lines and given a lot of latitude in fulfilling her assigned duties. Lev had originally studied to become one, only to take a step back and remain militia. "What does she want with me?"

Benedict pinched the bridge of his nose and sighed. Wide shoulders hunched, he clamped his hand around the tabletop trap, the disguised wands clicking as the dross left behind squirted out and oozed to the floor. Obviously he thought it had been empty, and I mentally marked the hazing energy to get later.

"She's not being up-front, but by her questions, I think she wants to discuss the shadow age you started," Ryan continued, and I frowned at the obvious ire in his voice. His anger wasn't at me, but the bureaucracy behind the claim.

"I didn't start a shadow age," I said, and Pluck bubbled softly to himself in the quiet regions of my brain that we had—or would, given half the chance.

"Technically, you did. Or Pluck did, which in their eyes is the same thing." Ryan sighed. "The courts also want to talk to you about the cracked vault."

"They think I did it?" I said, and Benedict's shoulders slumped. "I wasn't even there," I complained. "Will you remind her that I was instrumental in convincing the city shadows that we needed a vault until we found enough weavers to start a balance?"

"I did. She thinks you egged them into destroying it."

I huffed out my breath, not believing we were having this conversation.

"Petra, the vault can be fixed, but the repairs will delay its opening another three months. It's costing the university five times more to ship dross off-site than store it here. The mages are calling bullshit, but what dross pits we do have easy access to are all dangerously overfull."

"Then maybe everyone should use the microwave to warm their coffee."

Benedict stood with his head down over his phone as he checked something.

"I told her it's not you and Pluck," Ryan was saying. "It didn't help. She thinks you used your absence to give yourself an alibi while the shadows at the memorial do your bidding."

I pushed my fingertips into my temples to drive out the coming headache. "That is stupid," I said, but inside, I was cringing. "I don't control them."

"Well, I strongly suggest you don't tell Marshal Cameron Owens that when you meet her," Ryan said. "Right now, she thinks you do, and whereas it puts you in her crosshairs, if she thinks the shadows are acting on their own, it might be open season on them. Everyone knows the reinstatement of vaults was not their first choice."

Pluck bubbled and fizzed, his anger sliding between the cracks of my frustration to make my stomach knot. Benedict's brow was creased in worry. It was bad enough trying to convince the magical public that shadows could be reasoned with. To say they were actively working to keep a new vault from going on line would not go down well.

"Grady, relax," Ryan said, misreading my continued silence. "I'm not going to let her make you her scapegoat. Just get back here and set up an appointment. Maybe go down and talk to the resident shadows and find out why they are out and about. It's obvious that the shadows are in St. Unoc because you are."

"The shadows are there because of that huge inert-dross nugget Benedict made," I grumbled, and Benedict winced.

"Then get your and Pluck's collective asses on campus and convince her," Ryan said.

"Fine. I'll text her," I grumbled. "We'll be home tomorrow for the *big meeting*."

"Thank you. Oh, and good work on bringing that separatist in."

The phone clicked off and I sat there, unhappy and fatigued. Pluck's thoughts sparking through me were too fast to be realized. He wasn't happy, though. That much I could tell.

"Lev's military flight is gone." Benedict's expression was concerned as he fiddled with his phone. "We'll have to fly commercial. I've got a flight booked, but we have to be at the airport in like two hours."

I nodded, motions slow as I shrugged into my coat. A mage marshal wanted to talk to me about having started a shadow age? A handful of shadows taking up residence over ten years' worth of inert dross might be pushing the definition, but if they *were* interfering with vault construction, technicalities wouldn't matter.

And by Pluck's cold presence in my pocket, I knew he agreed.

4

THE FLIGHT HAD BEEN QUIET, DARK, AND FRUSTRATING BECAUSE THE PLANE HAD been full and I'd been unable to talk things over with Benedict. Who knew who might be listening? It hadn't been a red-eye flight, but it was close, and the gates to the restaurants and shops were down as we made our way from the terminal to ground transport. No one spoke, and the entire planeload of people moved at the same tired pace, roller bags making a familiar plastic-on-tile hum.

Benedict and I each had one bag, and if not for me having been requested to check my three-foot-long dross-cored staff—tucked within a case to house a fishing rod—we could have gone right to the cabstands.

"Any cabs waiting will be snapped up this time of night." Benedict looked up from his phone as we walked. "It's either a call-for-hire or my intern, and I don't want to owe my intern that big a favor." He scanned the people ahead of us. "I should have called him before we took off."

I linked my arm in his, head dropping to thump against his shoulder as we walked step for step together. "You want to grab a cab while I wait for my stick?"

"Could do."

There was a small knot of people at the escalator to baggage claim, and I loosened my grip on his arm so he could go first. I filed in behind, the need to talk to him growing. My meeting with the marshal was right after the guild meeting, and it wasn't so much the lack of sleep I was worried about as Benedict and me getting our story straight. If the mage courts wanted my statement, they'd want Benedict's, too.

Benedict, though, didn't seem concerned, his back to the short wall of the escalator, fiddling with his phone as we went down. So it was only me who saw the curly-haired, somewhat short woman in a cap and suit standing at the bottom of the stair, one hand holding what looked like my fly-fishing case, the other a tablet glowing with the words **Grady and Strom**.

Smiling, I nudged Benedict's elbow.

Benedict looked up, made a pleased grunt, and closed out his phone. "Cool. Ryan, I owe you big."

The woman's round face beamed in a friendly smile as she noticed us and Benedict's obvious pleasure. "She's got my checked baggage," I mused, not sure I appreciated that or not.

"Ms. Grady?" the woman said in a high voice as we got off the escalator, and when I nodded, she tucked the tablet in an oversize pocket inside her jacket. "I'm Beth from We Drive. Let me take that, ma'am."

She was reaching for my roller bag and I let it go, more concerned about my stick tucked under her arm. "Did Ryan arrange this?" I asked as she somehow managed Benedict's bag, too.

"I get the call, I show up." She glanced at the carousel. "Do you have any more checked luggage? This came out first thing. Matched the info I had."

From my shirt pocket, Pluck fizzed for me to not look for moon shadows in the sunlight, and I reached for my stick case before she hit it on something. "No, this is it."

"Great! I'm right out front." Beth turned, her pace fast in her black, no-nonsense shoes as she headed for the big glass doors, confident we would follow. Both roller bags trundled along behind her like obedient puppies until she dragged mine right over a haze of dross. I winced as the glittering distortion spun around on the wheel until the energy broke and sent the roller bag crashing into Benedict's.

"Mundane," Benedict whispered as the small, now-flustered woman righted my bag and continued on. "You're moving up, Petra," he added as the wide doors opened and the welcoming, warm night air whooshed in. "I love seeing you get the credit you deserve."

"Your name was on that tablet, too," I said, and he gave me a sideways hug. "Ryan is more interested in knowing when I get in than anything else. That, and he knew we didn't have a ride home."

"Doesn't matter." He grinned, arm in mine as if we were walking into prom.

And damn me if his arm didn't feel nice there, even if Pluck bubbled sourly and dropped deeper into our shared thoughts.

Beth stopped at a black sedan parked illegally in the white zone, and Benedict and I scuffed to a halt as she popped the trunk. "Wow," I said. "They let you do that?"

The woman's gaze followed mine to the airport police ignoring us. "They do after midnight. I've got these. Get yourself settled. There's water and food bars."

Benedict lurched to get my door, his expression still soft with pride for me. "You deserve the full experience," he said as he opened it with a flourish. It made me feel special, and I grinned as I got in, carefully putting my stick in its fishing rod caddy in the back window.

As Beth had said, there was water and a wooden box with food bars. It was too late to eat, though, and I settled into the cushy seat wondering if anything had ever felt so nice. Smiling, I checked my phone, then shot Ryan a texted **thank you for the car**.

Benedict's door opened and he sighed as he got in, immediately cracking a bottle and taking a large gulp. "You want a sip?" he asked, and I shook my head.

Beth slid in behind the wheel, her head down over her tablet as she brought up her GPS. "Two drop-offs, yes?" she said as she swiped through a menu. "Ms. Grady, you're out past the commons, and Professor Strom, you're across town from that."

"That sounds right." Benedict slumped in the seat, eyes closing.

That is, until I took his hand in mine. "You can stay with me tonight if you want," I said, and his eyebrows went high in question. "You'll get to bed a good half hour earlier. I've got that meeting in the morning, though."

He leaned across the console, our fingers still entwined. "Go to bed, yes. Asleep, no," he whispered, and I smiled as Pluck fizzed sourly. "Thanks," he said, louder this time. "I'd appreciate that." He leaned forward, clearly talking to the woman. "My car is actually at Petra's apartment. Dropping me there would save me some time in the morning."

Beth's eyes met mine in the rearview mirror. "I usually don't do this, but it was your idea, ma'am."

Ma'am. She was calling me ma'am. There was no way she was younger than me. But she wasn't moving, and I nodded that that was what I wanted to do.

"Then the commons it is," Beth said softly as she put the car in drive.

The sedan's suspension was like heaven, and I hardly noticed the speed bumps as we drove out from under the airport lights and into the darkness. Benedict hadn't let go of my hand, and he closed his eyes again, clearly tired. "Any chance you can get that meeting shifted a couple of hours?" he asked. "I'd like to drive you in so I can eavesdrop."

"On my solo meeting?" I said, and he nodded. "I doubt it. I was going to bike in, but you can meet me there if you want. Unless you want to listen in on the group meeting, too."

"Never mind," he said with a sigh, and I stifled a smile. Despite his leggy physique, he was not a cyclist. I'd already checked the weather forecast for tomorrow. Arizona winter mornings were perfect cycling weather, and I was eager for a little pedaling.

Beth cleared her throat, and my eyes met hers in the mirror. "You mind if I listen to my music?" she said as she worked her earbuds into place.

"Please," I said, and she put her attention on the road, alternating between it and her tablet stuck to the dash.

My grip in Benedict's tightened. We hadn't been able to talk on the plane, and tomorrow morning would probably be too busy. Benedict was *not* a morning person. "Benny?" I gave his hand a tight squeeze.

Immediately he opened his eyes, his brow furrowed in question when he saw my worry. Smiling, he brought my knuckles to his lips. "It's going to be okay," he said, gaze flicking to the driver. "Cameron is meeting with everyone, not just you. I'm sure the courts simply want to get the facts firsthand so they can dot their i's and cross their t's."

Probably, but it was the private meeting afterward that had me worried. Not to mention if they were talking to me, they'd eventually talk to him, and I flicked a glance up at the driver. "I'm, ah, I'm going to take the blame for the inert-dross field under the auditorium."

Benedict's frown deepened. "I am the one who made it," he whispered.

"You turned the escaped dross inert to save me," I countered. "I'll take the blame."

"No. I turned it inert to save Pluck. A shadow. It will mean more coming from me." He shifted, letting go of my hand to flip the console up from between us, and slid over. Up front, Beth didn't seem to care, fixing her gaze on the dark road when she realized we were shoulder to shoulder, our heads together like scheming preteens.

Or lovesick teenagers, I mused, and Pluck fizzed at my memories sifting through both our thoughts. "Save him, save me," I said, confident that Beth wasn't listening. "It's the same thing. No, I want you out of it. I'm telling the marshal that I fixed it inert to draw in the desert shadows."

"How?" Benedict eyed me sternly. I was sure it worked on his students, but I just stared back. "Ten years' worth of dross in an unstable field? Through twenty feet of rubble? All at once? Petra, you're good, but you're not that good. It needs a spell, and you can't do it."

"She doesn't know that," I countered. "You seriously want to tell her you used dross to power the spell? The feral shadow that conjured nearly killed us all."

"I'll tell her I had a couple of hidden lodestones." He took a sip of water—as if that was it and that was all there would ever be. "My pride broke the vault. I'm taking the blame."

My hand felt cold without his in it, and I made a point to take his again. "No," I said lightly. "One of us needs to walk away from this with their reputation intact, and I'm used to having people look at me like I'm a pariah."

Pluck's thoughts bubbled to the surface, his mood sour. *Good, because that's not going to change.*

"Petra . . ." Benedict complained, and I shook my head.

"I made it," I insisted. "If you say otherwise, I'll say you're trying to cover for me."

A smile quirked the corners of his lips. "Which is why I'm going to tell the marshal the truth when she asks. It will be your word against mine, and as you say, I'm the respectable one." Eyes fixed to mine, he brought my knuckles to his lips again. "We are in this together, Petra. All three of us."

Pluck bubbled and fizzed sourly, but I appreciated the sentiment and I scooted closer. "I'm not worried about that half as much as what happens if the university blames the shadows for someone else's shoddy workmanship," I said, quickly adding, "I can't believe the vault cracked. That just doesn't happen. I mean, that's the point to it."

Benedict's forming protest faltered, and I snuggled in under his arm. "If they keep blaming the shadows, someone is going to get hurt," I said softly. "I doubt it's going to be an eon-old, living energy source who uses dark matter to change the laws of the universe."

I felt him sigh, his entire body moving against mine. "You think they will hurt someone?" he asked, his voice rumbling through me.

I glanced at the driver, her little cap and curly red hair in bright relief as a car passed us. She wasn't listening, fiddling with her phone and music list. "No. They have too much to lose," I said. "They won't hurt anyone unless threatened with being put in a bottle and burned to death."

But to magic users, a human life outweighed a shadow's existence every time, and I bit my lower lip in worry. It wasn't fair, and it wasn't right, but it was what happened.

Pluck's dissatisfaction twined about mine, darkening my mood. He wasn't sharing something, but I could guess. *We're going to change that,* I thought as a hint of his regret drifted through us. *But it has to be done through human laws and beliefs, not aggression.*

Agreed, he thought, a new sliver of doubt coloring him. *But I understand this only because I have seen the depths humans will go to when afraid. The shadows who have taken up residence in the city have not. They will cleave to the tools of violence because that's what saved us before.*

Cold cramped my fingers, made my leg ache. *You don't look saved yet to me.*

Oblivious to our shared thoughts, Benedict pulled me closer. "As long as the marshal thinks you are controlling them, you can salvage the situation."

"Sure," I said dryly. "Until some stupid mage tries to put one in a bottle and it lashes out. Then it's my ass in court if I say I'm controlling them. Which I'm not. They make their own decisions based on the cruelty of centuries-dead mages. Shadows don't die easily, but they understand death."

A whisper of Pluck's panic twined through my thoughts as he stifled a memory.

Benedict sighed, his worry obvious in the glow of the bridge lights as we passed into St. Unoc. "Three additional months until a functioning vault. Everyone wants someone to blame, and you and Pluck are convenient. The mages are angry with you, the sweepers, and the shadows. Not necessarily in that order." He winced, his gaze on St. Unoc's low skyline. "Can you talk to them? The shadows, I mean? Tell them to at least lie low until the vault is repaired?"

I pulled my hand from his under the excuse of rubbing my chin. "I can try. Maybe if those shadow escape valves were actually going in, they might be more amenable."

"What about Pluck?"

Alarm brought me up cold. "What about him?"

Benedict pulled his arm from behind my shoulders. "Can he talk to the resident shadows?"

I have what they want, Pluck fizzed through my thoughts. *They won't listen to me.*

Agreeing, I slumped into the cushions. "They won't listen to him. They're jealous."

To put it mildly, Pluck thought sourly.

"Fine, I'll talk to them," I added. "Ask them to be patient. But I don't want the marshal knowing I have an in with them." I tilted my head to look at Benedict. "Okay? Tell her I can talk to Pluck, but I can't talk to any other shadow. If she knows I actually can, she'll never believe I'm not telling them all what to do." Shadow spit. Everyone on campus called me queen of the shadows when the truth was, most shadows thought I was an ignorant yeth.

"She won't hear it from me." Benedict took my hand in his again, and we were silent as Beth wove through the night-emptied streets, brightening and dimming like artificial days and nights.

It's an angry loop, Pluck mused darkly. *If society wants something, the natural order always suffers. A bird species is eradicated because it is deemed a pest when it disrupts human sensibilities. The insects they once ate multiply and destroy the wheat that fed the people. The people put down chemicals that kill everything, not just the insects but the butterflies and fireflies and bees that pollinate the fruit trees. People starve. Just leave the birds who eat the insects alone. Whatever damage or disruption they are creating is nothing compared to a human using poison to make the world easy for themselves alone.*

Pluck subsided into a dark fizzing, leaving me alone in my uneasy thoughts. "Benny, if the university reneges on their agreement to put in shadow release valves, I don't know what they will do," I said softly. "Every single one of them has endured the horror of watching their weavers murdered, only to be threatened with being burned alive in a vault of active dross. Now they have a real chance to find balance again." I looked up at him, wishing I could make him understand and knowing he never would. Not really. "They call me an ignorant yeth, but *I'm* their foothold, and as long as I'm alive, they have a hope that they will find weavers."

"Mmmm." Benedict tugged me closer again. "Still, you can understand the university's frustration," he said, making me wonder if someone from the board had talked to him. "You and Pluck are one weaver pair. How many pairs will it take to process the dross from just one city?"

"More than we will have in my lifetime," I admitted. "The shadows know it. That's why they agreed to allow vaults. Can't we start freezing it with your new procedure despite the risks? Stack it up on a shelf somewhere?"

Benedict winced. "I doubt it. The university knows shadows can make it explode."

"Then mages need to stop making it," I said shortly.

I sat up and began to gather my things. We were on my street. It was darker than most because Pluck had blown out the streetlights and there was no one left to complain.

Beth took her earbuds out. "Which building are you in?"

"Here is fine," I said, scooting to the front of the seat.

"The dark one?" she said, voice incredulous. "I thought it was abandoned."

"It's not," I muttered, not sure I liked that everyone in the small complex but Lev had moved out when it became public knowledge I wrangled shadows for a living.

The car halted at the curb, and Beth practically flung it into park before reaching for her door. "Can I help you get your bags inside?"

"No, thanks," Benedict said cheerfully. "We've got it from here."

And as I got out of the car, I truly hoped we did.

5

THE HUM OF TIRES ON PAVEMENT WAS PLEASANTLY FAMILIAR, RUMBLING through my bike and into me to make the chill, dry air feel even colder. My smile widened with the memory of trying to wake Benedict this morning, giving up after he hit the snooze button one too many times. Chances were good that the sudden silence I'd left my apartment in would wake him and he'd beat me to the sweepers' morning meeting. I was taking the bike path, and his go-faster sports car *was* parked at my curb.

But for now, I could enjoy the quiet with most of the a.m. commute several streets away. November was perfect weather in St. Unoc to be on two wheels, and with Pluck loping along beside me and therefore not in my mind, the low sun didn't bother me. Much.

The early hour meant lots of shadows for Pluck, and he had no trouble keeping up as he raced alongside me like, well, a shadow. And whereas I couldn't feel his joy unless he was touching me, I could see it. I'd never dared to ride alongside his namesake like this. The big black lab Pluck had patterned himself on was too gregarious to risk him cutting in front of me or going after a squirrel and yanking me off my bike.

Shadow Pluck, though . . . I thought as he kept pace beside me, his misty feet never really touching the ground. Streamers of gray billowed from him like strands of knotted hair when the sun hit him, reducing his mass as it flashed between the buildings. Obviously he could be in the light, but it left him weak even when he was in a more complex form and had bothered to make "skin." Dark matter couldn't exist within direct light, but Pluck could make a mostly impervious layer. Mostly—which was why I wanted a new chunk of moldavite for him to take refuge in.

As luck would have it, the rock and gem show was in Tucson this month. I was willing to bet I could get Benedict to come out with me, pick up a few nice pieces of the rare glass for Pluck to tune to replace the one Fawn had broken. If I could get Ryan to pay for it, even better. That the tuned crystal could elevate a sweeper to Spinner status was probably half the reason ancient mages had slandered shadows and weavers to begin with. Though fewer in number, Spinners were just as powerful as mages. More, really, as they could safely handle dross without it breaking on them.

Coasting, I slowed as the light changed to red at the intersection, angling to the curb and using it to keep myself upright. My long-stick shifted on my back, and I caught it before it slipped off. I hadn't bothered to put the single stick in a caddy, instead opting to tie my old long-cord to either end and use that to sling it over my shoulder.

Pluck hung in my shadow, fidgeting. "Sun too high?" I asked, and he flicked an ear to send a drift of gray splatting against the pavement, where it dissolved in a spot of light. The cool air was beginning to warm. It might hit seventy today. Not bad for November, and I put on my sunglasses, shoulders easing in the relief.

Not yet, fizzed and bubbled up through me when a strand of icy gray twined about my ankle. Like an especially obedient dog, he sat at my heel, ears swiveling when a truck eased to a halt behind us. *South Main will have less dross.*

"More sun, though," I whispered aloud.

Palo Verde it is.

The light changed, and I pushed off and into motion. The truck stuck tight behind me, making me nervous as it hung too close, breathing exhaust and engine noise. Twenty feet up, a glittering drift of dross lay in the gutter like a heat distortion. I couldn't risk swerving out of the way with the truck this close. I could touch dross with impunity, but my bike couldn't, and if I hit it, it would likely pop my tire or bust my chain or work its way into my brake lines and soften them up. Pluck saw it, of course, and the shadow dog shifted up onto the sidewalk.

I couldn't bunny-hop sideways, so I inhaled to make a field, mentally flinging the class-two energy field out to wrap itself around the dross and turn it inert an instant before I biked through it.

It worked, and inert dross splashed to either side of my bike like rainwater, glittering drops of heat waves scattering. Black specks glistened on Pluck before he shook himself and ribbons of dark matter splattered harmlessly against the ornamental rocks and cacti. Someone else could pick it up, and until then, the now-inert dross wouldn't break anything.

Finally the truck passed me. Relieved, I lifted my hand in a wave only to grimace when someone shouted, "Filthy dross-eater!" out the window, and hit the accelerator to leave me in a cloud of black smoke.

It wasn't anything that hadn't happened before, though "filthy dross-eater" was not only new but risky, and I held my breath until I biked out of it, shoulders hunched as anger fought with frustration. The toxic smoke was legally considered an assault and they could be fined for it. Not that anyone ever was. Which was why they had done it.

You okay?

Fine, I thought as a tendril tightened around my ankle. *I'm going to cut through the quad,* I added as I saw the truck waiting at the next light.

Pluck's grip on me unwound in a surge of tingles and he loped into the park as if chasing a squirrel. I coasted after him, appreciating the open space under the trees. Things had changed in the last five months, and not entirely in a good way. I'd once been able to bike through campus and the surrounding university town in relative anonymity. Or at least, if I was recognized, it was as one of the university's best sweepers. Not so anymore. Everyone not a mundane knew me, with or without my usual stick caddy, though now that I thought about it, it might be Pluck.

Being ignored or looked down on wasn't new. I'd grown up under the assumption I was a sweeper, the unspoken second-class citizens in mage society. Having become a weaver, I'd found even my sweeper peers treating me with anything from a new wariness to a frightened distance. The elitist mages, though, were by far the worst, and their usual disdain had been creeping closer to outright hatred as city dross levels rose.

Wheels ticking, I coasted to the opposite end of the quad and the wide gate that opened up to a busy intersection. The university lay to my right, St. Unoc's limited industry sector to the left, and the desert by way of a city park in front of me. I wished I could just push forward and take the path out into the desert. Ride. Forget everything. But not only was I wearing black jeans instead of a spandex cycling kit, my water bottle cages were empty and I had that mandatory meeting with the marshal.

Which I'm almost late for, I mused as I swung onto the quad's walking path—only to slow in surprise. Put simply, the quad was a mess. Oh, the watered turf was green and trim, and the colored gravel raked. Lacing through it, though, was enough dross to fill a water tote, the glittering heat distortions puddling in the low places and clinging to the spines of cacti.

Pluck was slinking back to me, ears flat as he dodged the burning haze. I'd never seen it this bad apart from a postgraduation cleanup, and I slowed to a halt. "Was there a protest?" I whispered. Everyone was supposed to try to keep dross levels low until we had a functioning vault, but clearly a significant part of *everyone* thought they were exempt. It was a good bet that with the cost of dross disposal rising, people were dumping it en masse.

Pluck trotted to my heel, his whiplike tail low. "Is it like this all the way to the gate?" I asked, and the dog sighed, huffing out stardust as he sat on his haunches, looking so much like his namesake that it made my heart ache.

The truck is gone. Perhaps the road is a better choice, he thought, and I stood, bike under me as I did a shuffle-hop to turn myself a hundred and eighty degrees.

And then I stopped, staring at the young woman in jeans and blue hoodie standing ten feet behind me. Her eyes flicked from me to Pluck with a knowing fear.

"I thought I could do this," she said as she retreated a step. "I can't. I . . . I have to go."

What the shadow spit . . . I thought, my breath catching when she spun around and walked right through a puddle of dross—and it went inert.

Pluck dissolved in a sparking of surprise. His grip on my ankle went bone-numbing cold. *She fixed it inert,* he thought as the latent energy rolling from her feet hazed brighter, then dulled. *Petra, she's a weaver! She's a weaver!* bubbled up through me.

I froze as she walked away, a hundred thoughts falling through me: Pluck's elation, my hope . . . and then the sudden realization in both of us that she was almost to the road and we had no idea who she was.

"Hey!" I shouted, and she quickened her pace.

Pluck's cohesion utterly dissolved. As a serpent, he wove shadow to shadow, chasing her. "Pluck? Don't scare her!" I called, remembering her fear, my body swaying as I stomped on the pedals. She was heading for the viaduct converted to an under-the-road bike path. It would likely be full of dross. Grimacing, I angled onto the grass to try to cut her off.

Pluck got to her first, and she shrieked, darting past him and into the tunnel.

"Hey! Wait!" I called. "I have to talk to you!" I quickened my pace. The handlebars vibrated, hard to hold until I reached the sidewalk and coasted down the ramp to the tunnel.

It was pitch-black to my sun-blinded eyes, and I skidded to a halt. Her silhouette stood dead center, me at one end, a huge black dog at the other. It was too dark to see the dross without Pluck in my mind, but it was there. I could almost smell it. Pulse pounding, I swung a leg over my bike and got off to look like less of a threat.

"I haven't done anything! Leave me alone!"

Her high voice trembled. I took my sunglasses off and stuffed them in a pocket. One hand up in placation, I propped my bike against the wall, then unslung my dross-cored stick and set it aside as a show of goodwill. My eyes had finally adjusted, and it was obvious she was scared, her arms wrapped around her middle as she looked from me to Pluck and back again. "I know what he is. Keep him away from me! I mean it!"

Pluck's ears drooped and he sat down in the opening.

I didn't dare move any closer, either. "I'm Petra. That's Pluck. He won't hurt you." We had found one, or she had found us, and now we were scaring her. She was terrified.

"He's shadow," she whispered. "He's *your* shadow. Get out of my way. This was a mistake."

Hands raised for her patience, I tried to relax, remembering how scared I'd been when Pluck had been trailing me, the shadow desperate for connection. "I won't stop you. You can go."

Pluck whined, his not-there feet hazing. Clearly he disagreed.

"But you came to me. Maybe we can help you?" I added, and she glanced from me to Pluck. "What's your name?"

"Marty."

Her voice broke, and she jumped when Pluck flopped to the bike path as if harmless. I doubted she was buying into it, but at least she wasn't pressed against the wall anymore.

Excitement tingled down to my toes. "And you're a weaver?" I said, and tension pulled her shoulders to her ears. "Wait, this is good! Marty, I've been looking for you."

"I'm not a weaver." It was a bare breath of an answer. "I'm not!" she said, louder. "Please . . . can you make him go away?"

She wasn't looking at Pluck as she said it, and suddenly I got it. A shadow was following her. She was trailing shadow, and neither she nor the shadow knew what to do.

I knew that fear, and yet it was elation that suffused me. "Oh, Marty . . ." I took a step forward, and she bolted for the sunlight behind me. "No! Wait!" I made a grab for her, missing.

The woman shrieked, shoving me into the curved wall. I hit with a thump, gasping when Pluck billowed up from the sandy floor beside me. "Pluck, don't scare her!"

"Can you get rid of him!" Marty backed up, her gaze riveted to Pluck. "Yes or no! I can't live like this!"

"Marty, it's going to be okay," I promised. Until an icy froth raked my mind and Pluck's fear twined about my own. *What* . . . I thought, squinting as every haze of dross burst into a threatening glare through Pluck's eyes. The tunnel was nearly as bright as day, glints of latent energy clinging to the floor and ceiling like lava.

Stay behind me, Pluck fizzed, suddenly angry. Shifting form, he wrapped about my arm as a snake, his tight coils almost deadening my arm. Green eyes glittered, and I looked behind me, my breath catching when I realized we weren't alone.

It was a man, tall, kind of goth-looking in black pants and matching shirt. Thin dark hair hung to his shoulders, and he had a dusky complexion. He didn't take off his sunglasses, steps soundless as he moved forward until the darkness of the tunnel enveloped him.

"Kahu, you have done yourself well," he said, his low voice

seeming to insert itself into the folds of my brain. "Bestowing the long ache to you will be a pleasure. Again."

What the hell? And then I jerked, a hand going to my head when Pluck's frigid thought slammed into me, his usual sophistication gone.

It's Thoth! Pluck fizzed and popped.

You know him? I stared as the man took off his glasses to show green eyes glinting with an inner light. Pluck had those same eyes, but I didn't understand until Thoth shook his hand and the glasses he held simply . . . evaporated. *He's a shadow?*

My arm was frozen solid under Pluck's coils, aching as he hooded into a snake and hissed. His anger was heady, but I was still trying to figure this out. The shadow trailing Marty looked like a person? I mean, I'd seen Pluck take on the image of Lev and some poor woman murdered in the 1800s, but it had been in a dream. Shadow spit . . . this Thoth must be really powerful!

"Make him go away," Marty whispered, her voice ragged as she scuffed two steps behind me. "I just want to go home. Please, can you make him go away?!"

The shadow man's lip twitched as if in annoyance, and then he took a step forward, his feet hazy with dark matter. "Kahu, you know nothing ever changes." Thoth misted, dark ribbons of energy brushing my awareness. "Leave. Save yourself. I have no wish to hurt you."

"Hey, ah . . ." I said, raising my arm for his attention—the one Pluck wasn't wrapped around. "I'm Petra, and you apparently know Pluck. This is all a misunder—"

No! Pluck sparked through my mind as Thoth evaporated. Cold lanced through my brain, alien and unfamiliar. Gasping, I fell to my knees. It wasn't Pluck. As if from a distance, I could feel Pluck's panic, billowing up around me as Thoth burrowed deeper into my mind with a single focus.

Fine, the hard way, I thought, barely able to breathe as I stared at my hands clenched against the cold, hard-packed sand floor of the tunnel. It hadn't been that long ago that I had done this with Pluck. Shaking, I dropped my defenses.

I jerked, ice coating my lungs as Thoth cackled confidently and dove deeper. I let him, throwing my memories at him in a torrential cascade to distract him as I inhaled and made a field about my mind. Exhaling, I made it impenetrable. *Who's the yeth?* I thought, snaring him as easily as an errant drift of dross.

Not helpless . . . Thoth's incredulity scraped like stones against the field imprisoning him in my mind, sparking until I twisted the field smaller. I had him.

At least, I thought I had him. A faint trickle of his cold, alien thought was probing my field as if it was a maze to be solved.

This is why you fail, the shadow mocked, its presence growing spiky and oily in my mind. *This is why you will always fail.*

And with that, my field broke from the inside with a soul-shattering ping. Winter coated my teeth and cracked my lips. A black swirl spun in my brain as the cold raced through my mind and was gone.

Shaken, I got to my feet, hand on the tunnel wall as Thoth rose up before me in a malevolent cloud. He wasn't in my mind anymore, but I didn't think this was over.

My stick, I thought as I backpedaled, unable to look from Pluck weaving a dangerous threat between me and Thoth. Oily coils of black streaked with green wound about themselves until he filled the tunnel—and then Pluck attacked, his presence sparkling with dark matter.

"Pluck!" I reached out when they met in a pop of conflicting energies, twining into one form as they thrashed. Great thumps, felt more than heard, echoed against the walls, and a cold green light burst from them when they crashed into the lingering dross, burning them both alike.

"Stop!" I shouted, and dark matter scattered like dust from a shaken rug.

Horrified, I stood before them, cord-draped stick in hand, unable to do a single damn thing. "Marty, tell your shadow to relax!" I cried. "We're trying to help you!"

Marty stumbled out of the tunnel and into the light, her eyes wide in fear. "He's not my shadow . . . I can't . . ." she whispered, and when she tripped over my bike, she grabbed it and ran.

Pluck . . . I could not follow.

Dark matter hazed the air, and a high-pitched squeal echoed in the tight confines of the tunnel as the two shadows coiled and twisted about each other. Frantic, I danced away when the coiled sparks of gray and black crashed into the wall and agony fizzed through me. The larger was forcing the smaller into the dross, burning him. "Pluck, break!" I demanded desperately. I had to stop them, and exhaling, I made a field, nebulous as I sent it out, then bettered it to a class five when I drew it in, harnessing the dark matter they were throwing off.

They had twined into a black, sparkling lump. I couldn't see where one ended and the other began, and I reached out as I brought the ringing in my ears in line with the ringing of the universe. "Get off my shadow!" I said, blasting them both.

The twined ball rolled into the sun and split in two. "Pluck!" I lurched forward, dropping my stick when one darted away, the flash of hazy nothing gone in an instant. Shadows could kill one another by absorption. It was one of the reasons they sought out a weaver for protection. Was it Pluck before me, or Thoth? "Pluck!"

I jerked as an icy thread wrapped around my ankle, relaxing when a familiar thought foamed through my mind feeling somehow warmer than usual. *I endure.*

His relief twined through mine, washing the last ugly feel of Thoth from me. I sank to my knees to put Pluck in my shade, my hands tingling when I tried to gather him up. I had no amulet for him, and the loss hurt.

"Pocket. Now," I demanded, and he pulled himself together, a thin snakelike form cocking his head at me. "Now!" I said louder. "Marty is scared out of her mind. We have to find her before Thoth does."

She will find you. Pluck curved around my wrist, and I resigned myself to the frozen feel of him. *Thoth is not her shadow. He followed her here, but he is not her shadow. Thoth would sunder himself in the light and die before taking a weaver.*

It sounded a little dramatic, but I had just shoved the angry shadow from my mind. I stood, patting my pockets to find my phone to call Ryan. The joy of finding another weaver lay heavy, soured by Thoth. But we *had* found one. She was scared, but that she'd known enough to seek me out boded well. Pluck was right. She'd find me again.

Phone in hand, I stood inside the dross-laced tunnel and gazed out at the sunlit quad as my thoughts slowed. "You know him. He called you Kahu."

The snake tightened his grip on my wrist in a sparkling of gold and green. *Kahu is dead.*

Kahu is dead? I jumped, startled when the phone in my hand rang.

It was Ryan, and I hesitated all of three rings before I answered it. *Cheese and crackers, she stole my bike.* "Ryan, hey," I said when I hit the icon. "You'll never guess what happened."

Thoth followed a weaver to us. Pluck's head hooded as he gazed out at the sun. *Beat the dark matter out of me. Telling Ryan is a bad idea.*

"Where the blue blazes are you?" Ryan said, voice hushed but intent. Behind him, I could hear a soft murmur of conversation. "The meeting is almost over and you're not here."

Oh, yeah . . . "Um, I found a weaver," I gushed, my gaze lifting over the trees to find the roof of the Surran building. "Here on campus. She stole my bike." *At least she didn't steal my stick,* I thought, seeing it in a patch of sun. "Ryan, she's scared and trailing some really angry shadow, but she's here!"

"A—A weaver?" he stammered, and I picked up my stick, surprised when Pluck coiled about the top third like a decoration. His bone-aching cold left my hand and I shook it in relief.

"Her name is Marty, and, uh, we might have a problem." Still twined about my stick, Pluck narrowed his eyes in warning, but Ryan was my boss. "Um, I really need to talk to you."

"Petra, this is fantastic!"

Pluck shed sparkles like stardust in warning. The tip of his tail was quivering, and I smiled as I tried to touch him, my fingers going ice-cold when they fell right through to the wood underneath. He only looked solid. "Yes and no. I need to find her. She's trailing some mean shadow. I'm going to have to meet the marshal later."

"No!" he blurted, then spoke again, softer. "Petra, it was all I could do to keep the marshal from coming to pick you up this morning. Come in. Tell everyone what happened. What she looks like. I can send everyone out in their usual dross grid patterns to find her." He hesitated. "Did you get her last name? Maybe her family has history here."

"No, sorry." But I was beginning to relax. A sweeper-run search would be extremely thorough and discreet, seeing as the grid patterns to pick up dross were second nature to everyone in the guild. She had my bike, but unless she'd upgraded her theft to a vehicle, she was likely still in St. Unoc.

"Fine. I'll be right there," I said, and both he and Pluck sighed in relief. "But my interview with the marshal will have to wait. I have to find Marty. She's scared to death." My elbow hurt, and my entire side ached. "I can't believe she stole my bike."

"Petra . . ." he started.

"Five minutes," I said as I ended the call and tucked my phone away. My elbow was tingling, and I frowned, twisting it backward to see the haze of dross clinging to it. Grimacing, I pulled the energy off and flung it to the wall, where it began to slowly ooze down. Pluck shuddered at the burning glow, but it was little more than an annoyance to me and I had better things to do than clean out a tunnel.

Head down, I stomped to the light.

You were smart to not tell Ryan that Thoth tried to kill us, Pluck fizzed. *Thoth is dangerous, and it's unlikely that the shadows at the auditorium will provide assistance. We will settle this quietly. Without Ryan's help.*

He was overreacting, and I overlaid a feeling of uncertainty through Pluck's sour anger echoing in my mind. "We could have handled that better, sure, but Thoth won't—"

Do not delude yourself. Others have, and they died for it. Alerting mages that a murderous, disruptive shadow exists might trigger them into killing all shadows on sight. He's here to disrupt, and he's very good at it.

I went silent at the remembered feel of Thoth in my mind. Pushing him out hadn't been that hard. Weavers, even untrained, could protect themselves from shadows. Pluck was the one in real danger, and my hold on my staff tightened as I started across the quad toward the Surran building. I understood why he wanted to keep this quiet, but Ryan had helped me when my dad had died, trusted me when no one else had. Torn, I inched my grip up until Pluck coated my entire hand. "Pluck," I started, faltering when the shadow's conflicted emotions buzzed through mine like fog.

Thoth used her to find you, he fizzed. *She's inexperienced. No threat. But you are.*

There it was again, and Pluck's worried indecision sparked through me. *I'm a threat?*

He would see the balance fail, Pluck fizzed, anger and embarrassment twining in equal parts through his thoughts. *You are a weaver, skilled with hosting shadows within your mind. You can catch him. Stop him. He knows it. You are a threat.*

"He wants the balance to fail?" I said aloud. "Why?"

Pluck's worry swamped my confusion, and I squinted when I

found a patch of sun, not surprised when the shadow shrank to the size of a small stone and hid in my pocket from the damaging rays. "I thought all a shadow wanted was a weaver."

Not Thoth. He's why the mages were able to destroy the balance the first time, setting mage against weaver when he realized he can't best a weaver's skills. I won't let him do it again.

My reach for my sunglasses faltered, and then I snapped them out and put them on, relief filling both Pluck and me as everything took on a dusky haze. "You sure he's not just trying to get Marty's attention? I mean, you were really out of practice." I tried to smile. "Scared the crap out of me."

Very sure, Pluck fizzed. *He's never found a weaver he can join with, which is the core of why he strives against us. It might have begun as jealousy, but it's long since become hate. We are willing slaves, according to him, tricked into servitude. He will go to all lengths to free us from our delusions. When we refuse, he removes the one thing he can. Our weavers.*

"But that's not how it works," I said as I crossed the dross-coated park, my need to talk to Ryan redoubling. "Are you sure Marty isn't his weaver?"

The spot of cold in my pocket seemed to quiver and Pluck's regret twined through my confusion, the sharp ping of his decision to tell me something flashing like a bright spark within our shared thoughts. *Marty is not his weaver. A shadow invariably chooses someone who thinks as they do. It's necessary to find an accord. Thoth has lost the ability to choose through his own hubris.*

You chose me? I thought, quashing a rising surprise. I'd thought I was in the wrong place at the wrong time.

I chose, Pluck fizzed. *Though I will admit I thought I'd made a serious mistake when you bottled me,* he mused, and I cringed. *Hence you and I are both inventive, bold to the point of foolhardiness, and trusting within a small circle of friends. Thoth is charming, confident, extremely manipulative, and possessing a great desire to see the opportunity that destruction brings so as to further himself. Not only is Marty utterly devoid of those traits, Thoth damaged himself while trying to forge a connection long ago. He can bind with no weaver.*

"Huh," I said, remembering her fear. Marty wasn't charming, she wasn't confident, and she was clearly not aggressively seeking advancement.

Surran Hall was one block down, and I turned to the sun, my hand hiding his pocket from the worst of it. "He, ah, called you Kahu. Is that your real name?"

Not anymore.

"I mean, if you like, I can—"

Don't, he interrupted. *Kahu died in the long ache. I am Pluck.*

There it was again: the long ache. "Pluck—" I started, words faltering as his fear flickered through both of us, old, bone-deep, and laced with guilt.

It's too bright out here, and that's a conversation for the dark.

I took a breath to protest, then decided to let it be. Not dark enough? It was clearly an excuse. I could tell from his closed fizzing that it would never be dark enough for that conversation.

Not even on a night with no moon.

6

I WAITED IMPATIENTLY AT THE CURB FOR THE LIGHT TO CHANGE, STAFF IN HAND and fidgeting with the hem of my shirt, now sporting sand from the tunnel. My jeans, too, were scuffed with dirt. My colleagues would understand, especially after I told them what had happened, but I wasn't going to make a good impression on the marshal.

Finally the light clicked over and I stepped out into the street, ignoring the bus inching forward, bullying me into a faster pace so it could turn right.

I missed my bike, and I obstinately took my time, staff smacking the pavement and shoulders hunched as the indulgent diesel labored away in a push of noise and foul fumes. I'd likely catch the last ten minutes of the meeting. Bad luck or good? Time would tell.

"I swear, if I find my bike in a pawnshop . . ." I muttered, and a flash of cold, sour mirth froze my thigh where Pluck sulked in my pocket. Engine revving, the bus continued down the street, past the new memorial garden where the auditorium had once stood. The corner had once been a major bus stop. Now, not so much. Maybe after they finished reconstruction and classes resumed in Surran Hall.

But as I looked over the quiet crossroads, I doubted anyone would want to hold classes here again. One corner of the Surran building was utterly gone. The basement that had housed the loom and given the university's sweepers a place to relax and drop their dross hauls had been filled in, and a new layer of colored gravel made a depressing reminder.

Calling the industrial hood that shunted dross into a glass-lined vault "the loom" was a tradition going back to when sweepers used dross-cored brooms to collect the waste and Spinners knotted it into cords of silk. Once knotted, dross was unable to break into bad luck. Weaving it into cloth made it even more secure. No one wove knotted dross cords to negate bad luck anymore, but Darrell, my old mentor, had turned it into an art before she had died.

On the plus side, with no classes here, Ryan had moved the sweepers' daily brief out of the attic to the first floor, a boon seeing as the elevator had been lost with the loom. A few bikes were propped in the rack at the base of the stairs and a couple of cars were at the curb, but otherwise, the street was quiet apart from the mockingbird pretending to be a cactus wren.

I took the wide, shallow steps fast. Pluck had hardly thought a word the entire short trip; his unusual closeted emotions raised my concern that Thoth had hurt him. The almost subliminal tingle of the immense inert-dross field across the road seemed to press against my right side. It was akin to the feel of a distant fire, and I stifled a shudder when I pulled the door open and went in. Benedict had fixed almost the entire field under the damaged auditorium inert to save Pluck—to save me. It was as much the inert-dross field as the promise of weavers that had lured the desert shadows into taking up residence.

I wasn't surprised that the university wanted to blame Pluck and me for cracking the new vault. None of St. Unoc's newest shadow residents wanted it, but they knew that a vault was necessary until a balance could be created. For that, we needed weavers. Lots of them.

Finding Marty was a relief, but I wasn't sure how much weight that would hold with the university board. One weaver to several thousand mages wasn't doing it. Two to several thousand wouldn't do it, either.

It is a start, I thought as I tucked my sunglasses away and followed the muted sound of Ryan's voice to one of the larger classrooms. The building-long lobby was empty, and I smiled as I lifted my gaze to the new monument/shrine safely behind glass. That Darrell's wooden loom had been lovingly placed among the sweeper treasures was bittersweet. It was still strung with her last project—the knotted dross weft and weave forever unfinished. I missed her steadying presence. Ryan, too, apparently, as it had been his idea to memorialize her.

It had been hundreds of years since a sweeper had used a literal broom and a Spinner had actually spun dross into inert mass unable to break. Now we had wands to move dross around and glass jars to hold it. Thanks to Benedict's process, dross handling would likely change to creating inert spiny nuggets of dross that could be dumped in a hole and forgotten, playing the odds that it wouldn't revert on its own. But was it progress? I didn't know anymore.

". . . Marshal Owens," Ryan was saying, and I stopped thumping my staff on the old marble floor, not wanting to be noticed as I neared the door. "Please extend her your full courtesy concerning the events of last summer."

"I thought we already went through this?" a low voice said.

"And the courts appreciate that," Ryan said, his jovial tone holding a hint of rebuke. "Most of her questions will center around the recent events with the cracked vault and your interactions with the shadows who have taken up residence under the auditorium. If you've seen any . . . If you've noticed any inert-dross nuggets missing . . . That sort of thing."

A soft murmur rose. The sweepers' guild was tight-knit, but I wasn't a sweeper anymore.

Jessica and Kyle still like you, fizzed coldly through my brain, and I sighed as I settled in the open doorway, staff tucked in the crook of my arm. Ryan was behind the podium, and I scanned the brightly lit room in concern. I didn't recognize a lot of the new sweepers. Clearly the university had needed to bring in more help.

"You want to come out?" I whispered as I touched the pocket where Pluck sulked. It was more than wanting him to be recognized. Everyone in the room, me included, had been taught that shadow was an unthinking energy that addled your brain. Showing that it was a lie started by mages to keep sweepers and Spinners at the bottom of the social heap seemed prudent. "How are you feeling?"

Good enough, iced through me, and I stifled a shiver as a cold wash wound around me when he spiraled to the floor. A shimmer of black and green coalesced into a sleek dog, his feet and tail misting with a smoky dark matter. My fingers played with the haze spiking his head, and his relief that the room was clean of dross was obvious.

It must be hard, I mused, to live among people who not only blindly create a tactile poison but then leave it lying around. It was like living in a field of jellyfish. Sure, dross gave me a jolt when I picked it up, but it didn't disintegrate my very substance. *I'm sorry, Pluck.* He was here because I was here. How selfish was I being, forcing him to stay where he was in constant danger?

It's not like that, he fizzed, and I flushed, embarrassed he'd caught my thought.

"Ah, good," Ryan said loudly, his relief obvious as he saw us. "I think we can leave it at that. If you have any concerns, I will be at the records building. Marshal, if you don't have anything to add, Petra and Pluck have some long-awaited news."

Pluck huffed, amused at my flash of adrenaline. Still, more eyes searching for Marty were better than fewer, and we headed for the front, Pluck's feet misty and shedding dark matter. I smirked at the muffled oath as we passed, deciding it had been one of the new students.

I was almost to the podium before I noticed the small woman in the first row, clearly not a sweeper as she was in a trendy black dress suit. She wasn't wearing that snazzy driver's hat now, but her curly red hair and round face were unmistakable.

Oh, Pluck thought, his embarrassment twining about my anger. Marshal Cameron Owens was my driver? *That's unfortunate.*

Grinning, she made a frivolous wave, and my gaze shot to Ryan in accusation.

"Was it your idea, or hers?" I said, and he hesitated, clearly trying to figure out what I was upset about. Behind him, the sweepers began to talk among themselves, oblivious to the ire tightening my gut.

She's good. You and Benedict told her everything she wanted to know and how you were going to lie to her.

The short woman stood, showing not a flicker of remorse. "Were you in on it?" I asked Ryan, my voice tight as I unslung my stick and thumped the butt of it on the floor between us.

"In on what?" The older man extended his hand to Pluck as if he were a dog, his expression blanking when the shadow unexpectedly lifted his nose and it passed right through his fingers. "You, ah, look like someone who found a car in their designated parking space." Ryan hid his hand in a pocket. "And I know you don't have one."

The people in the front row had become silent as they realized something was wrong. Cameron sashayed closer, smug almost. "I think she's mad at me," she said brightly. *Earbuds, my ass.* "Ms. Grady." She stuck out her hand. "It's good to see you this morning."

I didn't let go of my long-stick, didn't take her hand. "Marshal," I said flatly, and her arm dropped.

"Cameron, please." Her smile never dimmed. Damn me to hell, she had dimples. "This isn't an official inquiry. Just a friendly visit. No need to be so formal."

"I'd rather keep it formal," I said, and Pluck huffed. The woman stiffened at his soft exhalation. It was slight, and I almost didn't catch it, and I glanced at the shadow when my ankle went numb with cold. She was afraid of him. Why not? Everyone else was.

She was damn good at hiding it, though.

Ryan shifted uneasily from foot to foot, his bad hip clearly bothering him. "What am I missing here?"

I took a breath. Let it out. Found a fake smile. "The marshal picked Benedict and me up at the airport pretending to be a driver." The need to call and warn Benedict was a quick flash.

Ryan's eyes widened. "Oh. Your text about the car. I saw that this morning. I thought you were being sarcastic." Expression shifting, he looked the unrepentant woman up and down. "Marshal, I agreed to help organize your inquiries. I did not agree to—"

"I'm looking forward to talking to you after the meeting, Ms. Grady," she interrupted, a hint of the hard reality of her position showing. "And Pluck," she added, her gaze flicking down. "I'd like your presence when I go out this afternoon to talk to the memorial shadows about their interference with the new vault construction."

Because going out there without me might end up with her comatose or addlebrained. My eyebrows rose, a sensation of contrariness tightening the corners of my eyes. Thanks to her overhearing us last night, I could not beg off under the excuse that I couldn't talk to them. But as I took a breath to tell her the memorial shadows had overwhelmingly agreed to suffer a vault within the city limits, it suddenly struck me.

Maybe it had been Thoth.

My gaze dropped to Pluck. The shadow's thoughts were carefully hidden, but his ears were down. He'd suspected it from the start. Cheese and crackers. No wonder he didn't want me telling Ryan about the shadow.

"Sure," I said sourly, not knowing what else to do. "You mind if I take care of this first?"

Her smile widened to encompass her teeth. "Please. I have a few emails to answer." She reached for her phone. "I'll be in the back."

"Great. Five minutes." I couldn't get my teeth to unclench.

Motions sharp, I propped my stick against the nearby podium, long-cord and all. It was obvious that our tense conversation had been noticed, and I felt as if I were in a spotlight.

Pluck flopped to the floor beside me like a bored service dog, little rills of shadow poofing up to evaporate as they interacted with reality. Bracing myself, I put a foot in him so we could talk, not surprised my entire leg went numb with cold. *If you knew Thoth was interfering with the vault construction, you could have mentioned it,* I thought. *I can't send the sweepers' guild out to find Marty. If Thoth is with her, he will rip them apart. Weavers can fend off a shadow attack, but sweepers can't.*

Did I not say we should do this alone? Pluck evaporated, shifting six inches to the left before coalescing again. Only a thin tendril of himself remained wrapped around my ankle. *Thoth will not be with her. He used her to find you. He doesn't need her anymore.*

I glanced at Ryan, unwilling to keep him in the dark. He was my mentor and confidant. I knew he wouldn't set the university on a shadow hunt, and yet . . .

"She really pretended to be a driver?" Ryan frowned at Cameron now leaning against the wall beside the door, her head down over her phone. She wasn't there for privacy. She was there so I wouldn't sneak out.

"Yep." I took a steadying breath. "Hey, um, would you text Benedict for me and tell him the marshal drove us home?"

Ryan's hand touched his pocket where his phone lay. "Oh, God. I'm sorry," he said, and then his expression shifted. "They're going to be excited you found a weaver," he added. But my joy was gone as Ryan tapped the podium for attention.

"Ah, sorry about that. Thanks for waiting. Petra?" Ryan gestured to me as he stepped away.

They'd all seen the tension between me and the marshal, and the silence was telling as I looked out over the familiar faces. "Um, as usual, I've got good news and bad," I said. Thoth had broken the vault. I had no proof other than Pluck's past with him, but it could be no other.

Three rows back, Kyle elbowed Jessica. "Petra, there can be nothing worse than what you pulled us out of last summer."

A smile, real this time, flashed over me. I appreciated the vote of confidence, but Cameron let it roll without notice, clearly knowing it was for her benefit. "Ah, Benedict Strom and I have obviously returned from Chicago," I said, not sure how I wanted to handle the Marty situation. "We did not find a weaver in the local school system, but we did find a separatist cell."

Terry and Webber looked up, until now totally uninterested in what I had to say.

"Pluck and I were instrumental in catching one of them, and my militia contact is handling the rest," I continued as more faces lifted from phones to me. "I don't expect any unwanted repercussions. That's the bad news." I took a breath. In actuality it was the good news, but no need to point that out. "Good news is that this morning, Pluck and I ran into a woman we believe to be a weaver."

"That's fantastic!" Jessica exclaimed, and Kyle whistled as the room filled with noise.

"Wait!" I protested, having to talk over them. "The bad news is I need your help. Her name is Marty, and she's, ah, trailing unbound shadow."

Not really a lie, but really not the truth.

Immediately the room quieted, and I winced. "We handled it badly," I said, truthfully enough. "She took off on my bike, and we have to find her." The need to warn them that Thoth was a homicidal anarchist flickered, quashed by Pluck, probably. It was hard to know when our thoughts were intertwined so tightly.

But my words had been understood, and my tension eased as worried frowns peppered the audience. Every one of them had been taught that shadows were dangerous. Even a slight warning went a long way. They wouldn't let their guard down.

Ryan looked pained as he put his phone in a pocket. "I'm open to suggestions, but seeing as we have a university full of dross and a need to tidy it, I'd like to scaffold a search for Marty atop a campus-wide dross purge."

You flirt with disaster saying even that much, Pluck fizzed, and my grip on the podium tightened. I would not send my friends out unwarned.

"And put it where?" Terry complained loudly, a chorus of agreements joining him. "We got nothing. The new vault was supposed to open next week."

Hand in the air, Ryan took control of the meeting, but then again, that was his job. "This is an *excuse*, not a real purge," the older Spinner said, and the complaints eased. "Maybe if they sit in their filth for a while, the mages will stop making it." He glanced at Marshal Owens, the only mage in the building. "But I doubt it. As Grady said, your focus is Marty. We are not—I repeat, *not*—resuming regular dross runs until we have somewhere to put it. Do not pick up anything that's already in a bottle, within a building, or otherwise contained, such as in a rill or under an overpass."

People were complaining, but it was only the usual gripes and none of it was aimed at me. "If you've never been on a purge, pair up with your mentors," he was saying loudly as those closest to the hall stood to grab a doughnut on the way out. "Oh, and if you have the bus or train depot in your territory, hit that first. I'll have vans with empties in the usual places within an hour." Worry furrowed his brow. "Though I do not know what I'm going to do with them."

"Petra, what does she look like?" Jessica said, and those moving to the door turned.

"Early twenties," I said. "About my height, slim build, straight dark hair to her shoulders. She's in jeans and a blue hoodie. And, um, she probably has my bike." I flushed when someone gasped. "I'd appreciate it if you'd give me a call if you see it. It's a modified track bike, Pinarello Prince, WSD with a one-by-twelve drive train and disk brakes." It also had cost me a couple thousand dollars. Replacing it would be hard.

"A pin-a-what?" someone whispered loudly, and Ryan chuckled.

"It's a ladies' red bike," he said.

"With *three* bottle cages," someone from the back added.

"And a bell!" came a high voice. *"Jing-a-jing!"*

They were laughing, but it wasn't *at* me, and I smiled at the unexpected good feeling. Clearly they were still afraid of Pluck, but knowing they could still needle me was helping. "Oh, and I can't stress this enough," I said even as Pluck fizzed a warning. "Do not engage with Marty unless she's in danger. She's probably trailing shadow, and it might react badly if Marty feels threatened. She knows she's a weaver, but she's frightened. Just call it in. Pluck and I will handle it." I shifted uneasily, scanning the faces for a sympathetic expression and finding only a vague unease. It was the most I dared do. They were scared enough already of shadows.

At least, until Terry crossed his arms over his chest and sneered at me. "Can you blame her?" the old sweeper said, and Ryan frowned. Cameron, though . . . I could almost see her mark him to talk to later, eager to dig up what garbage she could get from him about me—true or not.

"I, ah, guess that's it," I said as I met Ryan's gaze. "Thanks, guys. This means a lot to Pluck and me. The more weavers we have on campus, the less dross we will need to pick up."

But that didn't sit well with them, either, and after a moment, everyone moved, the sound of sliding chairs and loud conversations familiar even if I never came to the morning meetings anymore. I exhaled and stepped from the podium, my fingers finding Pluck when he sat up.

Maybe you should have gone with the "more weavers, the more Spinner stones will be produced to elevate them" idea, Pluck fizzed.

"And leave them worried about job security?" I whispered. It was hard not to feel melancholy while watching their camaraderie. I'd lost that when I gained Pluck. I had no regrets. I'd find it again.

Wouldn't I? I mused, my gaze going to the trio walking out, the sound of Jimmy Tross rising high over their conversation.

"You have a good feel for this," Ryan said, and I spun. "If Marshal Owens doesn't put you in jail, have you given any thought to taking over the morning meeting?"

I couldn't tell if he was joking, and I looked at the marshal, her curly mop of hair hiding her face as she worked her phone. "I do not want your job," I said. "Your job sucks."

Mood good, he chuckled, arms over his chest as we waited for everyone to leave. "That's too bad," he said lightly. "I like the idea of retiring. And seeing you and Pluck together eased some of their fears, especially the freshmen. They walked out of here with a lighter mind than when you walked in." Sighing, he reached a hand out for Pluck. "Good to see you, sir. I appreciate your discretion appearing as a friendly dog."

Pluck huffed, rose, stretched, and went to bump his head under Ryan's offered hand. A wash of gratitude flooded me at Ryan's easy manner. Maybe he was right. Maybe I had been keeping myself at a distance. But that didn't mean that I was going to take over herding the university's sweepers' guild.

"Cold." Ryan pulled his hand from Pluck and tried to massage the warmth back into it. "You look good, Petra. Different. I almost didn't recognize you in the doorway."

The need to find Thoth made me fidget. "Because I have one long stick instead of three normal-size ones?" I said as I slung it over my shoulder.

"No." He beamed at me as if proud. "You're wearing head-to-toe black. I usually see you in bright spandex."

"Oh." I glanced at my dark pants and shirt: large pockets for angsty shadows, dark colors so Pluck wouldn't show up so clearly when he perched on my shoulder. What I needed, though, was a big, floppy hat. The sun hurt both of us when Pluck was touching me. Sunglasses didn't cut it anymore. "Ah, it's for Pluck," I added. "Which reminds me. Any chance the university can fund a shopping trip out to the rock and gem show?"

Ryan's gaze jerked back from the last of the sweepers leaving. "You broke another one?"

A fizzing annoyance twined through my embarrassment. *Tell him I will replace it if given access to raw crystal. I will tune as many as he wants—provided I retain the best.*

My lips quirked at Ryan's obvious distress. "Pluck will tune as many stones as the university wants. He gets a tuner's fee, though. One crystal of his liking. For free."

Ryan's cheeks puffed out in relief. "The board has been bitching at me about when Pluck would be outgrowing his lodestone. They're anxious for the two of you to turn a profit. A Spinner stone or two would do it. I'll get the paperwork through. Buy as much moldavite as you want." He hesitated. "Ah, three to five pieces."

The shadow dog flicked an ear, dark matter evaporating in a silver smoke.

Ryan jostled my shoulder, nodding to the door. "Marty, huh? You scared her? Bad luck. I'm sure you both will get better at this."

Careful, fizzed through me like a cold fire, and I put a hand on Pluck's head. Well, I tried. It was more like putting a hand *in* his head. "I got excited," I said, truthfully enough.

Ryan followed me, one step behind. "We'll find her. Calm her down. Get the two of them together safely."

Worry was a cold zing, my pace faltering. "You'll tell me the instant someone sees her, right?" I said. "Pluck thinks the shadow who followed her here is not a good match and it might react badly. We've come a long way in convincing everyone that shadows can be safe, but some aren't, and I don't want anyone hurt."

Ryan ran a hand over his chin, eyeing me in speculation. "What aren't you telling me?"

Sometimes I really hated that he knew me so well, and I forced myself to smile when Pluck's warning hit my heart like an icicle. "Nothing," I lied, head down as I pushed into motion again. "I don't want to screw this up. People do stupid things when they're scared, and being a weaver isn't an easy thing to come to grips with." I stifled a shudder when the memory of my own confusion and selfish fears flooded me. I didn't want Pluck to sense them, but he did.

Sorry, frosted up through me, his green eyes holding a hint of guilt.

I'm not, I thought, fingers prickling as they touched his essence. He was bone-aching cold if I let him past my surface thoughts, but his soul was warmer than the sun.

Ryan glanced at Pluck. "Well, I'm glad you're back. We've got to get you out more. You and Pluck. You used to be on the streets all the time. People knew you by sight."

"They still do," I said, remembering being gassed by a truck that morning.

"We need to show you and Pluck doing something good for the university," Ryan continued, pace slowing as we neared Cameron. "Something that will foster a sense of trust. Finding whoever cracked the vault will do that."

Cameron tucked her phone away in a pocket. "Which is why I want to talk to the shadows at the memorial," she said, butting seamlessly into Ryan's and my conversation.

"It wasn't them," I said bluntly. "They agreed that it needed to be built. Not that I would blame them if they *had* done it, seeing as somehow the new vault has neglected to be fitted with a shadow release valve. Why is that, Marshal?"

The short woman eyed me up and down. "Because if a shadow can get out, it can get in," she said. "No escape valves until we know who broke the vault."

My eye twitched, but I didn't need Pluck's heady warning to keep my mouth shut about Thoth. He was right. We'd handle this ourselves. Anything else was too risky.

And yet I couldn't let that go. "Have you ever been on fire, Marshal?"

"Whoa, whoa, whoa." Ryan raised his hand. "Marshal, Grady was simply pointing out that active dross burns shadows the way fire burns us. She was not threatening you with being burned." He glared at me. "Right?"

Cameron's smile never dimmed. "I understood her question. That's why she's still standing and my knee isn't in her spine while I cuff her."

My eyebrows rose, and I shifted my stick more firmly onto my back. *You want me to kill her?* iced through me, and my lip twitched.

"Marshal Owens," I started, and the short woman shook her head to cut off my words.

"Cameron, please."

As if. "Marshal, I would love to spend the day answering stupid questions, but I need to find Marty."

"No problem." She shrugged out of her coat and draped it over her arm. "I'll come with you. I suggest we start at the memorial garden."

Pluck flicked an ear, his dry amusement fizzing up through my annoyance, coloring it. "Great. I need to tell the shadows about Marty anyway. You can ask them which one of them sabotaged the new vault. I'm sure you can fit your size-ten shoe between your teeth just fine."

"Lots of practice," Cameron said brightly. "I do it all the time. I'll take you wherever you want after that. Your personal for-hire. Seemed to work fine last night."

That I could not get a rise out of her was starting to bug me. Still, I wasn't going to start another shadow war by telling her who *had* busted the vault. We'd play it out if only to give Pluck and me the time to find Thoth.

"Well . . ." Ryan looked between us nervously. "If you two have this, I'll be in my office, coordinating the search for Marty. The gardens aren't on anyone's dross-cleaning grid. It's not a bad place to start." He hesitated, bumping into my shoulder. "The marshal has a car," he coaxed.

"I've seen it," I muttered, and the small woman hid a smirk.

Accept her services, Pluck bubbled through my thoughts. *It will make the search for Thoth faster. Unless you want Benny to drive you around?*

God, no, I thought, not wishing to put him in any danger, and Pluck stood, stretched, and then spiraled into a haze that vanished into my pocket. I couldn't get a new piece of moldavite soon enough. He was far too wispy for my liking, and some time spent in the dark surrounded by inert dross would do him some good.

Cameron froze as the shadow evaporated, but Ryan took it in stride, his thoughts already somewhere else as he patted his pockets with an absent-minded, "Good, good, good. We'll find Marty before the end of the day if she hasn't left St. Unoc." Beaming, he turned to Cameron. "Thank you for driving Petra around, Marshal. I'm sure she and Pluck will answer any questions you have."

Not likely, Pluck fizzed as Ryan touched my shoulder in farewell and left the room.

Breath held, I looked at Cameron. Today had not started well. I had a feeling it was only going to get worse. "After you, Marshal," I said, and the woman strode forward as if uncaring if I followed or not.

Funny. I felt the same way.

7

CAMERON'S CAR WAS ACROSS THE STREET IN THE AUDITORIUM'S OLD PARKING lot. Assuming she was a driver and getting in the car with her had been an honest mistake, but I still felt dumb, and I had to work to keep my disgust from showing.

My long-stick thumped across my back as we wove between the construction equipment and a shuttered food truck. The major repairs to the building had been completed last month, leaving a considerable amount of dross glinting in the shadowed places. The typically easy-to-miss heat distortion shone like miniature suns since Pluck was in my pocket, his touch raising my sensitivity to his level. The area was still fenced off, and I pointed out the gate to Cameron.

The marshal immediately took the lead, bootheels clicking as we went through the chain-link gate and into the block-wide construction zone. The auditorium was silent in the warming sun, better now that the scaffolding was gone. It was just four two-story walls buttressed by a few empty classrooms and a pair of remodeled restrooms . . . and would likely never be anything more. Shadows now lingered in the damaged belowground areas where the inert dross lay, and it was doubtful that classes would ever be held here again. The auditorium would remain an open-air garden memorial to all who had been lost.

You could teach weaver studies here, twined through my thoughts, a hint of optimistic anticipation lacing the frosty pinpricks . . . and for the first time, Pluck's words kindled a faint hope. Once we had Thoth in hand, Marty would find a shadow. This was who she was, after all.

"Your shadow is in your pocket? How come?"

Cameron's voice shocked through me, and I started. "Ah . . . the sun damages him. Saps his strength. He usually takes refuge in a lodestone, but a separatist mage busted it in Chicago."

"Like a bad sunburn?"

I eyed her, not sure where the curiosity was coming from . . . or going to. "Not exactly. He's basically organized sentient energy. He can form a skin of sorts to block most of the sun's energy, but it's easier to shrink down and stay in the shade."

"Huh."

Steps in unison, we took the low, wide stairs up to what had once been the main door. The multiple glass panes were gone, replaced with more chain link and a smaller gate. It was cooler out of the sun. She was going to want to come down with me. I knew it. "How much do you know about shadows?" I asked.

Cameron's questioning face looked too cute with those curls of hers. "As much as anyone, I suppose."

"So, nothing," I said, and ire flashed across her. "I mean, nothing current."

The short woman stopped before the padlocked gate, her gaze roving over the sunlit garden growing warm in the early sun. "I try to be pleasant. I don't have to be."

I flipped the lock, then unslung my long-stick to find a drift of dross. Pluck could turn it to dark matter for me and skip the amulet portion of our magic trick. "You use your smile to disarm, which I think is worse than letting people see how smart you are. I've got two rules before I take you down there."

Cameron eyed me, the play utterly gone. "You are not in charge, Ms. Grady."

"Three rules," I amended. My dad's old staff was akin to cool water in my fingers. The red wood was polished to a shine, and the esoteric glyphs he'd etched into it for show had been rubbed with black. Silver shod the heels, and the core held enough dross to attract nearly any dross spill. The drift by the gate did not pose a problem. "One, I do the talking, not you."

"So you're dropping the lie that you can't communicate with them."

I glanced at the wishing well. At night, shadow-animated rezes were known to gather around it, but now, in the sun, it was empty. "If they want to talk to me. Two, no trying to catch a shadow. I don't care what you hear or what you think is going on. You try to put one in a bottle and I will take you apart before they decide to kill you."

Her gaze followed mine to the well, the woman clearly not impressed. "And three?"

Dross clung to the bottom of the chain-link gate like a plastic bag, and I used the butt of the staff to collect it. "You might be in charge up here. I'm definitely in charge down there." I spun the stick to collect the dross, pulling it free and feeling it burn until it became inert.

Eyebrows high, she smirked. "Here's my list. One, you will summon a memorial shadow for me to question or I will subpoena you and stuff you in my car and drive you to DC myself."

I'd like to see her try, fizzed in my thoughts, but I wasn't sure how much of the sentiment was mine and how much was Pluck's.

"Two, I will catch and contain any shadow I please."

This time, I knew the dry chuckle was Pluck's as cold shivered through me. Only a weaver or sweeper could catch a shadow, and even then, there was a chance the shadow might fight, leaving you comatose.

Cameron flicked the lock with a flippant carelessness. "And three, I am in charge, Petra Grady, whether we are in the sun or not. Do you have a key for this or is this a stall tactic?"

Pluck swirled from my pocket with no warning, coating my fingers in frosty pinpricks and accepting the cooled dross before pooling upon the ground to manifest as a sleek dog.

Ashen, Cameron rocked back, silent as Pluck walked through the bars, thin tail waving when streamers of himself pulled free to evaporate in the warm day.

"Hey! Wait up," I called as I twined my fingers amid the sparkling vapor of nothing he'd left behind. Dark matter tingled as I made a field around it. The coldness of space had once been painful but now only spoke of power. Quick from practice, I wound my mind through it to find the chiming of the universe within. A second chime echoed in me. It was everything, it was all, and by bringing my echo in line with the universe's, it was mine.

Hazed like a ball of heat within the confines of my field, the energy swirled with hidden glints as I organized it and dropped it into the lock. A soft tweak to bring everything out of alignment . . . and the energy expanded to break the lock with a sharp *ping*.

"A point to you, Grady." Cameron drew the chain from the gate with a rattle, leaving it to hang as we went in together. Her boots clicked a steady pace on the newly set pavers . . . until she unconsciously slowed to take it all in.

The garden was surprisingly dross-free for a public space—but it *had* been locked. My shoulders dropped at the sound of insects and the soft chatter of a fountain. The memorial park had begun as a spontaneous citizen effort when the hastily erected chain-link fence around the sunken stage had become covered in notes, plastic flowers, and a few cacti in pots. Most of the dross lingering underground was inactive—but enough hidden pockets of bad luck remained to make rebuilding dangerous.

So the university had followed popular sentiment and turned it into a memorial. The surface debris had been carted away and a false floor had been erected over the pit, now called the grotto, to hide the mix of active and inactive dross under a shell of concrete and stone. The upper bowl of the auditorium had been kept intact, but it was now landscaped with tiered gardens and benches, most of them having shade structures holding colorful bougainvillea vines. The new floor was even with the street level, tiled in a mosaic of stone that, if you looked closely, was a sweeper emblem, with its three crossed sticks and five-pointed asterisk in the middle. It made a bold statement that had the silence censors wringing their hands.

A fountain masked the street noise, but the dry wishing well was the garden's focal point. The walled hole set above the hidden stage was an easy way for the memorial shadows to access the enormous inert-dross dump far below. At noon, the sun dove deep to touch the original stage—a beacon for the dead should they feel the need to rise.

And occasionally they did. Or, rather, their memory did, animated by a shadow drawn to the residual imprint left when death comes fast and unexpected. The mix of human memory and living shadow was cruelty upon cruelty, for though a rez mindlessly repeated the last thoughts and actions of the dead, when animated by shadow it took on a sense of life that was neither human nor shadow but painfully both.

It was uncomfortable to say the least, but those who had lost people in the collapse often came at dusk hoping to see a memory of their loved ones sitting in a quiet corner. *Which is probably why the university put a lock on the gate,* I thought.

"Nice park," the woman said, the hand held to shield her eyes falling when she noticed Pluck sitting next to me in the shade of a cactus. He looked sleek and powerful, wisps of himself drifting about his feet and ears.

We need to go down, he thought as a curl of ice cramped my ankle. *The marshal should stay at the well. She can shout her questions from there.*

"You don't want her down there?" I said aloud, and anger creased Cameron's youthful face.

The icy grip on my ankle tightened. *She's a mage. Our memories are stronger than her need to understand. Her presence will cause unneeded pain.*

I glanced at Cameron, the woman clearly working up a protest. *Benedict is a mage. Does he pain you?*

Pluck's grip around my ankle eased, but the strength of his thoughts did not. *My scars are thick, but the shadows here are raw. Benedict is . . . tolerable because he cares for you.*

It was the nicest thing he could have said about the man, and I turned to face the marshal. "Ah, you need to stay up here. I'll tell you what they say."

"Try again," she said, hands going to her hips.

Pluck lifted his lip to show a glimmer of tooth. *Tell her she's being an insensitive yeth.*

"I don't think she cares," I said, and then louder, "Fine. Do what you want. Remember my three rules. If you break one and get hurt, I'm not responsible. I don't control them."

It was something she wanted both to be true and to prove was false. Contradictory, but she would hate me either way. Her eyes narrowed. "Your three rules. For now."

It was the best I'd get. "Well, Pluck?"

I will warn them. A shiver pulled through me as his tendril slipped from my ankle. Whiplike tail swishing saucily, Pluck trotted down a gravel path to the little cinder-block hut tucked behind a wooden fence so new it was still unbleached from the sun. It was the old emergency stair, landscaped to be unnoticed, and Pluck evaporated into a sparkling haze before slipping under the metal door and into the stairwell beyond it.

"Give me a second," I said as I stopped before the fire door. Cameron pressed close as I woke up the inset panel and the high-tech screen lit. I hadn't been to the grotto since Benedict had fixed ten years of dross inert, but anyone assigned to the loom should have twenty-four/seven access.

"Petra Grady," I said when the light changed to green. "Weaver third-class," I added, glancing sidelong at Cameron. With a thunk, the door unlocked.

Third-class, I mused as I pulled it open. As if there were any second- and first-class weavers. First-class traditionally taught, though, and I was *not* doing that.

"You have access?" Cameron asked, and I hesitated, waiting for her to go first.

"For almost ten years. I've worked for the university since I was eighteen," I said, my pride obvious. "Before I was a weaver, I was one of their best sweepers. They left me in the system because they still call me to handle the hard stuff. After you."

She hesitated as the automatic lights flickered on to show a stark stairway leading down. "That's how you broke the lock on the gate? Magic? How? You don't have a lodestone."

"It was weaver magic, and as long as they have their shadows, weavers don't need a lodestone." My neck felt empty, and I touched my upper chest where my amulet would be. "You want me to go first?" I added, and she went inside. For an instant, I toyed with the idea of walking away. But no. I'd be blamed for whatever happened, and something would. She was a mage walking into a shadows' warren.

"At least it's daylight," I whispered as I pulled the door shut behind me. I couldn't see Pluck, but he was probably at the bottom, waiting.

"I'm not afraid of the dark," Cameron said, having heard me.

An icy mirth bubbled up in my thoughts, and I jumped when a comforting cold dropped from the ceiling, coating my shoulders. *You are the dark, and she is afraid of you.*

The handrail was grimy from a thousand desperate hands, and I wouldn't touch it. *Pluck, how bad an idea is this?* I asked, and he slithered to the stairs, my side going numb in cold.

Right. I'll find them, he thought, then streaked past Cameron.

The woman jerked, a small noise escaping her.

"Sorry," I said, and she started moving again, her boots tapping out a new anger. "He's telling them you're coming. They don't like mages."

Two stories down was the original floor of the auditorium. This was where the memorial shadows would be sipping on twenty years' worth of collected dross, turned inert by Benedict to save Pluck from burning to death while protecting me from my old roommate. *And still the shadows don't trust him?* I wondered when we reached the fire door at the end and went through.

The sunlight spilling in from the well made a surprisingly bright beam on the original oak-floor stage, a good thirty feet below the new ceiling. The rows of dusty chairs remained, looking eerie as they rose right up to the new ceiling, and though Pluck was correct that the university could probably hold a class here, it would be far too uncomfortable.

"They left it like this?" Cameron said as she squinted into the shadows. "Kind of foolish to put your city's dross dump under an auditorium to begin with."

"Kind of foolish to allow an untested material into your dross dump," I countered.

Cameron frowned. "No one knew it could revert."

I couldn't stop my laugh. "That's not true. I warned them. Repeatedly. Ask Ryan if you think I'm exaggerating." Her eyes narrowed in suspicion, and I added, "Are you really going to stand with your feet amid the fallout and tell me I am misremembering what I lived through?"

Doubt creased her forehead, and in the new quiet, a whisper of a voice hissed against the dusty walls, the words unclear even as a regular cadence became more obvious. *Good, someone's here.*

"Do you hear that?" Cameron spun to the stage, where a hazy nothing sat slumped against the podium. "My God, is that . . ."

"A shadow? Not yet," I said as heartache tightened my chest. It was a rez, and I squinted to pick out the ratty throw over a professional skirt, her legs outstretched and a hand held to a length of beaded hair. A mundane would call it a ghost, and they would be right. The energy from a sudden death had made a circuit of energy that dross could activate, in essence creating a ghost reliving the last moments of a person's life.

"Go," the rez whispered, and the haze of a face became more certain, as if the energy trapped in a circular pattern knew we were here. "I'm sorry. Tell everyone I'm sorry."

The rez was my old boss, Darrell, and my heartache deepened. I had washed the grit from her eyes. I had held her hand as she told me how the loom and vault had been destroyed. She had been dying—and still she held back shadow to try to save me.

"Go," the rez said again, its voice gaining clarity. "I'm sorry. Tell everyone I'm sorry."

Hands on her hips, Cameron inched closer to the stage. "That's a rez," she said, anger tightening the corners of her eyes. "You seriously thought I'd believe that's a shadow?"

"Marshal, you are a piece of work." Frowning, I stayed where I was in the orchestra pit. "Did I not just say it wasn't a shadow yet? Not everyone lies to you."

"Most people do," she said softly.

Which might be why she used that act of friendly good cop, I mused. "You're right that that's a rez," I said. "But a shadow has been using it. Moved it here."

Cameron laughed bitterly. "More lies. Rezes can't move."

I flipped a cushion down in the first row, surprised to find the fabric clean where it had been touching the back of the chair. "Right again," I said as I sat in it and propped my stick against the chair beside me. On the stage, the rez continued to beg me to go. Maybe Darrell was right. "Yet there it is."

"Then how did it get here?"

Finally, a good question. "A shadow animated it. Brought it here. Dropped it when done," I said, and her eyebrows went high in question. "Shadows are able to use a rez to communicate. Even I wouldn't let a strange shadow into my mind."

I swear, Cameron Owens, if you arrest me because I can't produce shadows . . . I thought, my attention going to the darker places of the grotto. "Where is everyone?" I whispered. Sure, the sun was pouring through the hole in the ceiling, but someone should be about.

Gone, iced through me, and I jumped when Pluck's suspicion, worry, and annoyance suddenly twined about my own. *Only Aasta remains.*

"Gone where?" I asked, and Cameron scowled as if I were making up the entire conversation.

"I'm sorry. Tell everyone I'm sorry," the memory of Darrell whispered, and then a chill dropped through me when the rez turned and looked straight at me. "They have fled the eater," she added, the cadence and faint accent both familiar and wrong.

"Darrell," I blurted, finding my feet in a splurge of motion.

Aasta, Pluck corrected, and I warmed in embarrassment.

"My God," Cameron whispered, and the shadow animating Darrell made the apparition frown. "I don't believe it."

Takes practice, fizzed through me, Pluck's embarrassment a quick flash. *But it's easier than creating a fully solid form who can talk. Be careful. Aasta is viciously protective of those she takes into her circle. You are not within it.*

Great, I mused. "Yeah, not many people know it's possible," I said to Cameron. Nervous, I moved closer to the stage. The hazy form slumped against the podium wasn't my former mentor and boss; it was a desert shadow pulling the memory of Darrell on like a sweater. It hurt to see her with her beaded hair and brown skin wrinkled by time—bittersweet.

The apparition even had some of Darrell's memories, especially those concerning me. But it wasn't Darrell. It was a shadow, one so desperate for a human connection that it had wrapped itself in a dead memory. The old Black woman would probably find it amusing, not horrifying as most people did.

"Weaver Grady." Aasta nodded at me, Darrell's beads clinking as she slid her cold gaze to Cameron. "Is the mage an offering or a mistake?"

Offering? I wondered, stiffening when an image of Cameron lying on the filthy carpet, shaking in a seizure, flashed through me via Pluck. "A mistake!" I blurted, and Cameron frowned at my obvious panic. "She's a mistake."

"I'm not a mistake!" Cameron predictably argued, then stifled a gasp when the apparition hazed, solidifying again a few feet closer, green glittering eyes fixed on her with malevolence.

"You are a mistake, or you are mad." The shadow animating Darrell eyed Pluck. "But perhaps we are all mad and it's time to stop pretending."

It was an odd thing to say, and my brow furrowed. "Cameron is here to ascertain that the shadows taking refuge in the grotto aren't responsible for cracking the new vault." Annoyed and a little worried, I turned my frown to Cameron. "You agreed to not say anything," I added. "Shut up or I'll let her drive you insane."

I wouldn't, obviously, but it gave them both pause as I called their respective bluffs. Aasta had halted Darrell's image at the edge of the stage's drop-off. It felt too close to me, but I didn't want to retreat and look nervous, even if I was. "Those who lie fear the most to be lied to," the shadow said, and Cameron flushed.

"Tell her you didn't damage the vault and we will leave," I muttered, and Aasta scoffed.

Head bowed, she laboriously worked her way down to sit with her feet dangling over the edge. The shadow was drawing heavily upon Darrell's memory, and it hurt. "You already know who broke the vault. The same who broke us."

Broke us? I thought, and Pluck's thoughts fizzed nervously. She knew about Thoth and Marty? How? Maybe that was where the other memorial shadows were—looking for her.

"This means nothing," Cameron said under her breath. "She'll say anything to exonerate herself and the rest of them. The only faction to benefit from no vaults are shadows. End of investigation."

Aasta waved Darrell's hand flippantly, as if swatting flies. "Shadows do not benefit from dross in the streets. It's why we agreed to constructing a storage vault. One with a shadow release valve. Balance takes time to find, and no one wants to wallow in filth for a thousand years until we do." Darrell's eyes glittered green as they met mine, and Pluck hazed, his guilt and anger drifting through me. "Did the new vault have such a shadow release valve?"

Cameron cleared her throat. "Until we find out who damaged the vault, the modifications to existing containment systems are on hold. And seeing as no mage in their right mind would damage it—"

"It was not us!" Aasta shouted, her raspy voice coming back hard from the low ceiling as she swung her legs up onto the stage and worked herself up onto her knees. "You, Grady's Mistake, are a fool yeth! Looking for a reason to destroy the thing that can pull you from the brink because it is easy."

"I am not a mistake. I represent—"

"Nothing I care about." Darrell's image stood, her beaded hem shaking as she extended her arm. "Perhaps I should show you the truth of my innocence, mad though it will leave you. Take my hand and die from the truth, Grady's Mistake."

"Enough!" I exclaimed, and Cameron spun to me, her expression a worrisome mix of anger and fear. No one but a weaver could survive a shadow in their mind, and Cameron knew it. "You are *both* acting like fool yeths!"

"You smell of Thoth, and you *dare* come down here and accuse us of destroying the chance of finding the balance?" Aasta said, finding Darrell's temper and patterning her own voice upon it. "You look for a malefactor. You have seen him. He is before you."

My breath caught. Beside me, Pluck hazed to a puddle of black, a single tendril coiled about my ankle. Damn it, I had wanted to keep this quiet. Or at least from the university.

"Ah, who is Thoth?" Cameron asked, voice honey-sweet, and I warmed with embarrassment and anger. The embarrassment was me, the anger Pluck.

Tell Aasta that admitting one of us is a homicidal malefactor will not help us, Pluck practically whined in my mind.

I took a breath, catching it when Aasta slid from the stage to the orchestra pit. As one, Cameron and I started a slow retreat. "Thoth is an abomination." Aasta twitched Darrell's beaded skirt, channeling my mentor right down to the furrow of her brow. "His goal is to pit mage against weaver and shadow. He ruined himself trying to find a weaver, and so now he deems us deluded for doing so and strives to save us from ourselves. He can't kill our weavers, so he convinces others to do it for him." Aasta's lips twitched. "There will be no more weaver/shadow pairs. None of us will risk it. It's over before it is begun."

"Wait. Thoth is a shadow?" Cameron's eyes widened. "The one who followed Marty here?"

Shadow spit, Aasta was laying it all out there, and I scrambled for an answer that wouldn't start a campus-wide shadow hunt.

"You stink of him, Kahu." Aasta paced forward, and I continued to back up, careful to keep Cameron behind me. "Find a form that can speak," she demanded, and Pluck hazed to a fine, glowing mist. "I want to hear from your lips how you managed to stay alive when he found you."

Alive? "Whoa, whoa, whoa." I put out a hand to stop Aasta when my calves hit the dusty chairs. My stick tipped over, hitting the filthy carpet with a dull thunk. Never taking my eyes from her, I felt around until I found it and picked it up. "We need to slow down."

Pluck's ears went flat. *Tell her to shut up,* fizzed through me, the icy bubbles of his thought giving me a headache.

Cameron's lips parted in understanding. "If Thoth wants all weavers dead, why protect him?"

Aasta was glaring at me in disgust, dark matter hazing over the image of my mentor like a poisonous fog. "No one is protecting Thoth." Darrell's beaded hair clinked to sound like dry bones as she turned her cold gaze to Pluck. "Take a speaking form and explain how you survived him. I know you can manage it, Kahu!"

Ears flat, Pluck paced a circle around me, wisps of himself pulling free until I was surrounded by him. His thoughts frothed in mine too fast to be realized, but I could feel his regret, and my fingertips dabbling in his haze became blue from cold. *Distract her. Remind her Marty is unbound,* he fizzed. *Tell her the girl needs protection.*

"Marty is still unbound. She's vulnerable," I blurted, and Aasta made my mentor's eyes wide in an agonizing hope.

"You don't think I know that?" Aasta rasped. "No one dares to contact her lest Thoth deem her a threat. If she is tuned, he will kill her."

Tuned? I thought, nodding. She meant bonded, and though the usage was new, the idea was not. It sort of made sense, seeing as shadows tuned moldavite to better hold energy. Perhaps it was the same with minds.

Cameron's brow furrowed in frustration that no one was answering her. "You're telling me this Thoth cracked the vault?"

Pluck wound his way up my dad's long-stick, chilling my grip until he perched at the top like a snake. The truth was out, and Pluck reluctantly bobbed his hooded head.

"Probably?" I said, wincing at Cameron's elation. "Yes, he followed Marty here. He didn't admit to the sabotage, but he does have a history of setting mage against weaver." I took a slow breath. "Blaming the memorial shadows for the destruction would do it."

"And you're protecting him." Cameron's jaw clenched. "Because he's a shadow."

"No, I'm protecting everyone else," I said as Pluck's frustrated anger simmered in me. "What do you think will happen if it gets out that a shadow cracked the new vault?"

Cameron glanced at Aasta. The shadow had gone silent, head bowed in a nameless grief. "It will be caught and dealt with."

My gut hurt, and I shook my head. Pluck had been right. No wonder the shadows were hiding. "Who will catch him? Mages? Not likely. It will be up to the sweepers, and even then it's dangerous. One touch could leave them comatose or worse. But knowing how pig-headed mages are, you will insist on trying, getting yourselves hurt and whipping up anti-shadow sentiment until a bounty is placed on all of them. The memorial shadows are not to blame, so back off and let Pluck and me take care of it."

Cameron reached for her lodestone, a faint glow peeping between her fingers. "And in the meantime, he destroys every vault in St. Unoc?"

"He doesn't care about vaults," Aasta muttered. "Cracking them is the fastest way to set mage against weaver and shadow. He's trying to prevent the balance."

Frustrated, I thumped the butt of my staff onto the musty carpet. Jolted, Pluck phased solid for an instant, his green eyes thick with annoyance. *Sorry.* "Marshal, why do you think Aasta is the only shadow here? They're gone. Hiding because they've seen this before. Aasta is the only one brave enough to risk being put in a bottle."

Aasta jerked, pain crossing my mentor's face until a curtain of beaded hair hid it.

She's here because of her guilt-driven death wish, Pluck fizzed angrily. *Fear rules her, and because of it, she lost everything.*

But they had *all* lost everything, and dread flickered within Aasta's green eyes. "You think you can snare Thoth alone, weaver Petra Grady? Perhaps, but keeping his foul plan from the mages will require you to take the blame of his actions on yourself. Thoth is not called 'the mind eater' for nothing."

The memory of Pluck and Thoth twined in a self-destructive

tangle flashed through me. If I hadn't been there to break them apart . . .

Aasta's half-lidded gaze came to mine, the beads in Darrell's hair clinking. "Thoth will destroy you through your own desire for change," she intoned, and I couldn't tell if she was angry, selfish, or jealous. "As he destroys all things. We gathered here in the hope of finding weavers; Thoth will never leave until we abandon it." Aasta twisted Darrell's lips into a sour expression. "That's why they have fled. Marty is untuned, but no one will risk the heartache of her dying to defend the one who bonds with her."

Pluck made a doggy huff. *Remind her we are wise to him now.* It was a hard, icy statement, and I winced when a soft headache started. *Thoth will have no sway with me. I know his every trick, have felt his every burn. When we meet again, it will not be me who suffers.*

But Pluck was my responsibility, just as much as I was his, and I couldn't help but feel this was a mistake.

Sensing it, Pluck bristled, spikes of cold stabbing into my hand. *If I wasn't able to withstand him, why did he flee? Aasta is right about only one thing. He followed Marty here to find you. Through his own failings, Thoth has acquired the ability to possess both magic user and mundane without destroying their minds, but an experienced weaver has the field strength to keep him out of their thoughts, and he knows it.*

I am a threat? I thought as Pluck's thoughts became gritty in mine, ruinous.

All we have to do is lure him to a place of our choosing and snare him. Cameron knows the truth. She won't let you take the blame.

That a shadow could enter someone's mind and possess them without leaving them comatose or clinically insane didn't seem like an improvement. *Lure him with what? Me? The only other thing he might want is another vault,* I thought, then jerked when a new idea surfaced. There was a small vault under the records building. No one knew about it apart from the older sweepers and Spinners. If we made it public knowledge, Thoth might try to break it. Prepared, we could catch him. Stuff him into it maybe, like a big bottle. Add a shot at me to the mix, and it would be irresistible.

I have to talk to Ryan, I thought as I reached for my phone, and Pluck's anger vanished as my plan spilled into his mind as if it were his own. His doubt filled me . . . and then a tiny sliver of hope. Mine? Pluck's? It didn't matter. We both felt it.

"Marshal, you have your answer. It wasn't them. I have to go."

The woman jerked from me as I reached for her elbow. "I'm not done."

"*They* didn't do it," I said, pointing my chin at Aasta staring at us with wide, questioning eyes, and Pluck evaporated into nothing, his chill presence winding into a sparking haze that dove for my pocket. The time in the dark had done him good. "And I think I have a way to catch Thoth without turning this into a shadow massacre."

Suspicious, the marshal rubbed her hand, hiding her lodestone ring. "How?"

Wanting to talk to Ryan first, I glanced at the stairway, and Cameron's eyes narrowed in suspicion. *Whatever.* "Aasta, thank you for forgiving my mistake."

The shadow-rez waved me off, the swatting-at-flies motion reminding me so much of Darrell that it hurt. "Goodbye, weaver Petra Grady and Petra Grady's mistake," she intoned, even as her outline hazed.

Cameron lifted her chin. "My name is Marshal Cameron Owens."

Aasta's knotted throw misted at the edges. "Survive Thoth, and perhaps you will deserve a name, mage. But I think he will eat your thoughts, too. You know too much."

Cameron took a breath to protest, but the shadow within Darrell's rez seemed to spill out into nothing. As if a switch had been thrown, the rez was empty. Soulless eyes filming up as the ghost began to silently weep, a great gash in her forehead trickling blood into her eyes. The shadow was gone, and the rez was now just a rez. "Go," the rez moaned, slumping against the wall of the stage. "I'm sorry. Tell everyone I'm sorry."

I started for the stairs, the butt of my staff thumping. Behind me, Darrell's rez lost all definition and vanished. After a moment, Cameron began to follow. "You want to fix the vault and catch Thoth when he comes to break it again?" she guessed. "I can't get that past my people. We need that vault working, not as a million-dollar shadow prison."

Damn, the woman was smart, and I winced at the harsh squeak as I pulled the stairwell door open. "Agreed. Good thing I have a smaller one available right this moment."

The marshal was fast behind me, and I jumped when the door slammed loud after her. "The university has an unregistered vault? Seriously?"

"It's not unregistered. It's too small to be of any use. It's likely no one remembers it's there." The stairway was ugly with a remembered panic of fleeing survivors, and I kept my gaze on the top, eager to be out of it. "I just hope it's empty. Thoth might not risk breaking one that's full."

She was silent for all of three steps. "You don't have *any* control over them, do you."

Maybe now she would believe me, and I pushed open the door, wincing as the light from the low sun poured in. "No more than anyone has over the night."

8

THE LOW SUN MADE BRIGHT STROBE-LIKE FLASHES BETWEEN THE BUILDINGS, irritating as Cameron drove me across campus to the records building. I had no proof, but it seemed that I'd become more sensitive to the light since Pluck's thoughts in mine had become second nature. It was a small price to pay.

Cameron was silent, her hands alternately clenching on the wheel and relaxing in her private musings. That shadows could be reasoned with was not going down well, seeing as we'd been exterminating them for thousands of years. It was always easier to compound an error with more wrong than admit one had been made and make reparations.

"Go right here," I said, and she glanced at her phone on the dash when it hummed, then turned it over to hide who it was. Most days it didn't matter that I didn't have a car, but I was kind of stuck without my bike. Maybe I should be nice. "You, ah, did good under the memorial," I added, and surprise flooded her expression.

"I did, huh?"

It was more than a little sarcastic, and I smiled. "Yep. Very refreshing. You can't imagine how tiring it gets. Everyone afraid what might happen if you touch shadow. Leave you clinically insane." I pitched my voice in a tired falsetto. "Oh, no-o-o-o . . ."

Cameron's grip on the wheel relaxed. "Shadows don't generally attack unless provoked."

True, but it was relying on "generally" that got people in trouble, and a mage going into a shadow grotto was the definition of provocation. "Good thing you didn't annoy her," I said faintly. Cameron seemed sincere, but I had believed that Lev was mooning after my roommate for two years, not spying on her. I was a terrible judge of character. "It's a left at the next intersection."

Cameron flicked on her turn signal and rolled through the stop. "How long on this?"

"About a mile?" I wasn't surprised she didn't know where the records building was. It was a piece of forgotten history that might not have ever been recorded.

Again she was silent, and I put a protective hand over Pluck's pocket, glad he had been able to spend some time in the dark. I'd always felt he lingered too close to the light because of me. His faint fizz of assurance twined through my lingering concern, and my shoulders lost their tension. "See that little adobe house after the miniature golf course? That's it."

"Got it."

She slowed, brow furrowing at the tiny drive before committing herself. It had obviously been a home before the area had been rezoned light commercial, and the generously named "parking lot" could hold only three vehicles. It was tight, especially with the empty pallets and bottles taking up one spot. The low-slung building was St. Unoc's original loom, relegated to paper storage when the university expanded and a larger vault was needed. The basement-size vault was too small to be of any use, but the building itself had been the logical place to move both Ryan's and Akeem's offices after the original loom was destroyed.

"You want me to help sell your idea to Ryan? Risking a functioning vault is tricky."

My reach for the car door hesitated. "Ah, no, but thank you. I think he'll go for it. I'll call you when I get a confirmation."

Phone in hand, she brought up her GPS and dropped a pin. "Don't bother. I'll call you. I have to talk to my people. They're going to want to know why I'm not bringing you in." Her head came up, eyes wide and innocent. "You can get home from here okay?"

Yeah, I wouldn't want to wait around and play taxi, either. "I'm good." I got out, my long-stick knocking the console as I wrestled with it. "Thanks for the ride." But she didn't move when I slammed the door shut, and I peered in through the open window. "Thanks for not carting me off to marshal jail?" I added, wondering why she hadn't left, and a smile quirked her lips.

"You got Pluck, right?" she asked, and when I touched my pocket, she added, "Don't leave St. Unoc."

Yup. Hedging her bets. I patted the sill of the open window and took a step back. "Perish the thought." A little miffed, I started for the bougainvillea-draped archway that led to the front door as she put the car in reverse and drove away. My soft-soled shoes were silent on the sun-bleached cobbles, and a lizard skittered in the gravel, almost unheard over the nearby traffic.

Pluck swirled out of my pocket when I found the shady path to the front door, little wisps of dark matter rolling from him as he took on his dog form. "You look a little thin," I said, fingers numb with cold. "You sure you want to be out?"

He flicked an ear and a splat of energy hissed against the cool gravel. *I've been reflecting on Ryan's theory that shadows need to be visible to be accepted.*

"I don't think there will be anyone here who hasn't met you," I said.

Pluck huffed, his nose rising to point out something behind me. *Even so . . .*

I slowed, shoes scuffing as I saw my bike propped against the two-foot wall. "Someone found it!"

Not exactly.

Pluck's thought iced through mine in excitement, and I followed his ear-pricked gaze to Marty standing in the drive between the pallets and empty dross bottles, her hands in her pockets and her hood pulled over her head. She looked ready to run, and I knew in an instant no one had found her and brought her here. She was here on her own. *How did she know where I'd be?* I wondered, and then, *Did Thoth follow her?*

No. Pluck's thought bubbled through mine, laced with worry. *She's alone.*

"I, ah, didn't mean to steal your bike," Marty said, voice soft.

Pluck's feet hazed in anxiety as my gaze darted from Cameron's distant taillights to Marty. I didn't want to scare her off again, so I didn't move. "Thanks for returning it."

"I'm not a thief." Her gaze lifted to the street. "I have to go."

Shadow spit, she was leaving, head down and pace fast. Pluck sank into himself, weaving through the cacti as a snake to cut her off. Seeing him billow up before her, she jerked to a halt.

"Pluck, let her go," I said when he rose up almost as tall as she was, his hood spread in threat. "Pluck!" I said louder when anger tightened her expression, and he hesitated. "Let her go, but you and I both know she will be fighting this her entire life if she runs." I paused to let her think about that. "Marty, let me help you. Can we talk? I'll get you to the bus stop if you want, afterward. I promise." Which wasn't exactly a lie, but it wasn't the truth, either. She was a weaver. This was where she belonged. The trick would be to show her that.

She bit her bottom lip, gaze flicking to Pluck. "Can you get rid of that shadow following me?"

I shrugged, willing to say anything to get her to come inside. "That's the goal. It would help if you came in." I gestured at the door. "Tell us what you know?"

She took a deep breath, then nodded. Pluck immediately collapsed, and Marty stared at the silky black puddle for a moment before picking her way through the gravel front yard to join me. She glanced back once to see if he was following—which he was, the shadow hitting every possible dark spot.

This is risky. If Thoth thinks she will become a weaver, he might hurt her, Pluck fizzed when he reached me and coalesced into a dog.

Only if we can't catch him, I thought. *She's safer with us than alone.*

"Thank you," I said softly to Marty, and she gave me a thin, nervous smile. A good three feet between us, we headed for the unassuming front door with its potted cacti and flowering kalanchoes. She was a weaver. There was no escaping it. No going home. "I'm glad to see you. I've got the entire sweepers' guild out looking for you."

"Yeah?"

Nodding, I opened the door and gestured for her to go into the small foyer done in tile and bright colors. The traffic noise vanished when I shut the heavy door behind us, replaced by the whir of a fan and the faint sound of Jimmy Tross, the singer wailing persuasively from the front room to our left. The large, low-ceilinged room was open to the hall through a huge archway, a comfortable mix of living room and game area to give sweepers somewhere to talk to Ryan or decompress after a hard day. It was a far cry from the expansive and modern break room, offices, and adjoining lockers we had lost with the loom, but it worked.

The cool floor was tiled in shades of red, brown, orange, and purple, a loving rendition of the desert. I propped my long-stick in one of the cubbies built against the long hallway wall with a feeling of belonging. I wouldn't need it here; the place was spotless, and I could feel Pluck's thoughts ease into a fizzy hum of wary speculation.

To the other side of the foyer was the kitchen, still used as such, but the back two rooms that had once been stacked to the ceiling with boxes had been turned into offices. The paperwork was now in the attic, left to slowly yellow in summer's heat.

"Not what I expected," she said, eyes roving over the homey space. "It's nice."

Ears slapping, Pluck trotted past me, a ribbon of dark matter stretching between us. *I'm going to check the vault. See if it's empty.* He pulled from me with a twang of unsatisfaction, and Marty shifted to stay out of his way, the woman clearly uneasy.

"You need to meet Ryan. He's got his office here," I said, hearing a faint conversation, and she followed me down the hall, her eyes darting over the narrow space made even tighter by the empty glass bottles lining it.

"Where did Pluck go?" she whispered.

"No idea," I lied, pleased she'd used his name. It was a start. "He'll show up when he wants." My pace slowed as the voices became louder. The small room might have been a den once, the outside wall holding a sliding glass door that opened onto a sun-damaged, walled yard, complete with the obligatory fruit tree in the corner.

"He's not with you all the time?"

"Most times, but not always." The knot in my gut eased when she seemed to lose some of her worry. Maybe just showing her it was okay would be enough to convince her to stay. I'd been absolutely terrified of Pluck, but there'd been no one to show me otherwise.

"The easiest thing would be to turn the stuff inert and toss it down the wishing well," an unfamiliar, feminine voice said, and I put a hand on Marty's arm, pulling us both to a halt.

"Store it on top of the existing dross dump?" Ryan's laugh sounded tired. "Dana, you were in here not three days ago complaining that the area isn't stabilized. If you dig down twenty feet you're likely to find active dross. That's why they designated it a park."

"We aren't going twenty feet," the woman—Dana, apparently—said persuasively. "We're filling an existing open space with an inert material. Like dirt."

"Dirt?" a third person chimed in, the richly textured voice holding incredulity, and I grimaced. It was Akeem. The flamboyant

Spinner had been out of town when the original vault blew, and I wasn't sure if he trusted me—now that I was something different.

"There's tons of room down there," the woman said confidently. "It will take at least three months to repair the crack and open the new vault."

"No." Ryan cleared his throat nervously. "The shadows in residence will not approve, and I won't stress our relations any further. They are the future."

"They are the past," Dana muttered.

I'd heard enough, and I pushed forward. "Knock, knock," I said brightly as I tapped the doorframe, and everyone turned, their expressions still holding their last thought. "Hey, Marty found me. She has some questions before she decides if she wants to stay."

Ryan bolted to his feet, clearly elated as he gestured for us to enter. "That's wonderful! Marty, come in. Come in!" he said, and I practically pushed Marty into the room as the well-dressed woman crowding Ryan's desk straightened, her lodestone jewelry clinking. "I can't tell you how pleased I am," the older Spinner added as he leaned over his desk to shake Marty's hand enthusiastically until he realized he was overdoing it and let go. "Trailing shadow, eh? Not surprised. Petra ran halfway across the desert trying to lose Pluck until they figured it out." He took a breath, flushing. Dana and Akeem were staring at him as if he was fanboying over her. But he kind of was.

"Um, this is Akeem," Ryan said as he glanced at the slim man in his early thirties now standing up from one of the two chairs before the desk. He was clean-shaven with tightly curling hair, looking sharp in a vest that matched his psychedelic plastic-framed glasses. To say that Akeem took pride in being different was an understatement, as evidenced by his purple socks. "He's one of the loom's Spinners," Ryan continued when Marty extended her hand.

"Hi," she said softly, and Akeem grinned at her shyness.

"Marty, eh?" he said. "You are as welcome as ice cream at a birthday party."

Ryan cleared his throat as the young woman flushed. "And the woman to my right is Dana. She hired in to the university board last week. Airologist. We were lucky to get her."

"Nice to meet you," Marty said as Dana shifted to make room for us. She was a hundred percent business in her turquoise suit-dress, short-styled brown hair, and middle-age confidence. I'd never met her before, but the glass lodestone glinting on her bauble bracelet said she was a mage if the "airologist" tag wasn't enough. Her pale complexion said she hadn't been here long.

"Petra, I don't think you've met Ms. Dana Vean, either," Ryan said, and I extended my hand.

"Hi. Welcome to the university," I said, and she took it without hesitation, meeting it with a firm grip. That alone gave her good marks in my book, and I decided to cut her some slack—even if she was probably here to make my life difficult. "Nice to meet you."

"Glad to meet you, Petra. I've heard good things."

Ryan remained standing, clearly uneasy. "Where's Pluck?" he asked, his eyes where my amulet would have been.

"Not sure. He might be downstairs checking the vault," I said. "Which brings me to why I'm here. Ah, other than to give Marty a chance to see what we're all about. Marshal Owens and I have an idea I need your permission to implement." I glanced at Marty. There weren't enough chairs for everyone, and no one was sitting. It was getting uncomfortable. "Should we come back?"

Marty's gaze dropped from the three reddish sticks reverently racked behind Ryan's desk. They were twins to the one I'd left by the door, but I didn't mind that Ryan had them. He had loved my dad, too. "Ah . . . I'm only here to find out how to get a shadow to stop following me. I'm not staying. But you look busy, so . . ."

Ryan's smile faltered. He knew that since she was a weaver there was no going home, not without a shadow protecting her from the separatist mages. She couldn't change who she was.

"No, this is fine," Ryan said with a forced cheerfulness. "Akeem and Dana were heading out," he added pointedly. "I'm always available and we are *very* glad you're here."

Dana cleared her throat, settling before the desk all the more firmly. "Ryan, I have several pule-tons of dross I need to find a home for. I'm not leaving until we have agreed where to put it. Turning it inert and storing it in the grotto hurts no one." Her gaze came to mine. "Unless the shadows will explode it again?"

"What happened at the auditorium was an anomaly," I said as Marty fidgeted. "Pluck did it to save his life. There's no reason for a shadow to do it again unless the university resumes its practice of killing them."

Dana beamed as if having scored a point. "Then dumping it into the memorial garden won't be a problem."

Akeem eyed Dana over his purple-rimmed glasses. "Stop twisting her words, Dana. That's not what she said."

A shudder rippled through me when Pluck wrapped a tendril about my ankle, and the small drift of dross that had found its way inside the walled garden burst into a sunlike brilliance. He was back, and I breathed a little easier.

Good luck, Thoth is not on-site. Bad luck, I couldn't ascertain the vault's status, fizzed through me. *Can you ask Ryan if it's empty? Thoth will avoid destroying a full one lest he get caught in the dross release.*

Soon as I can edge a word in, I thought, and Pluck settled into a cold impatience.

"Dana, I hear your concerns." Ryan's smile was beginning to look forced, the man clearly wanting to get them out of his office. "We're all under a lot of pressure to resume normal dross collection, but until you find the mages willing to turn it inactive, we have nowhere to put it. You get mages on board, and we could put it in, say, the old high school gym?" He slumped. "I agree shipping the active dross out of state is prohibitively expensive."

Akeem fiddled with his glasses. "You'd need somewhere hidden to process it all. The gym has zero safeguards."

Perhaps mages could go out with the sweepers? Turn it inert at the site of pickup?

I made a small noise of agreement, then realized everyone was looking at me. "Ah, Pluck suggests pairing mages with sweepers. Turn the dross inert at pickup. No clearinghouse needed."

"Send mages out with sweepers?" Dana's lips parted to show her affront.

"Sweepers and mages working together? That's a great idea," Akeem said sarcastically.

"I can't put a fleet of high-end mages under the loom's directive," Dana argued. "I agree it would streamline the effort, but no mage will stomach going out into the field like a sweeper. We can implement new safeguards at the gym. Do it there."

"Perish the thought of anyone knowing a mage is taking responsibility for their own waste," Akeem scoffed.

"Enough!" Ryan exclaimed, and Marty flinched. "Dana, Pluck's idea has merit. We can at least ask if there are any volunteers to go out on sweeper runs. Bring in pizza or tacos or something. If no one steps up, go with the original idea of taking dross to the gym."

"Your department is buying." Dana settled herself into a chair. "Marty, how long have you been on campus?"

"Do you have a bathroom here I could use?" the woman blurted, and Ryan choked back his next words.

"Um, sure." Ryan gestured to the hall, his train of thought clearly lost. "You passed it on the way in. Second door on the left."

"Thank you." Head down, Marty practically ran into the hall. Torn, I rocked from foot to foot. Yeah, she had been fidgeting for a while, but I didn't want her to continue out the front door when she was done.

"Akeem, follow her," I whispered, and the tall man eyed me, clearly annoyed.

"I think she can handle that on her own."

"Is there a problem?" Ryan asked, suddenly concerned.

"She's a flight risk," I said to Ryan, then turned to Akeem. "And I need to talk to Ryan. Stall her when she comes out. Show her the long-sticks or trap ties. I need five minutes."

"Dana can show her the trap ties," Akeem protested. "Don't ask me to be the creepy professor."

"Please, Akeem," I whispered. "I don't want to scare her."

Dana smirked, her long fingers laced. "Go on. I'll fill you in over lunch."

"Fine." Adjusting his glasses, Akeem ambled out of the office. "Five minutes."

Ryan dropped into his desk chair, his exhale loud. "Petra, I am too tired for the cloak-and-dagger. What don't you want Marty to know?" He went ashen. "Where's the marshal? Did the memorial shadows . . . She's not . . ." His eyes went wide.

"She's fine," I muttered, appreciating the cold air beginning to drift out of the vents. I tugged the second chair a few inches from Dana and sat down, not surprised when Pluck curled up under it, a thin trace of himself around my ankle so he could kibitz at will. "She dropped me off here, actually," I added. "I didn't know Marty was in the parking lot until Cameron drove away. Ah, I should have told you this before, but I didn't want the entire campus to know. Pluck and I have a good idea of who cracked the new vault."

Ryan's gaze shot to the hallway, his expression blanking. "The shadow trailing Marty . . ."

"None of this is Marty's fault," I blurted, embarrassed that I hadn't told him earlier, and Pluck fizzed sourly. "He's not her shadow. His name is Thoth, and he might have followed her here, but he's acting on his own. Pluck says he has a history of wanting to see the balance fail." The image of Thoth's thin, gaunt form flickered in my mind. He had looked like a person. I hadn't known the difference until he had evaporated.

Dana leaned to look down the hall to where Akeem waited in the front room. "Thoth? What are the chances that they are bonded?"

A snowball's chance in the middle of the sun, fizzed through me, and I shook my head. "They're not compatible. Cameron agreed to keep it quiet so every mage and sweeper with a grudge and a class-five field doesn't get themselves killed trying to bring him in, but I think her silence is contingent on Pluck and me actually catching him."

Ryan smiled. "She lets you call her Cameron? I was read the riot act."

"Um, she asked me to." I hesitated, unable to place when I'd begun to trust her enough to think of her by her first name and not her job title.

Ryan's smile slowly faded. "I can't believe you convinced the marshal it wasn't one of the memorial shadows. The courts want it to be them. The university wants it to be them. The truth doesn't matter. All they want is a quick resolution and the world to return to the way it was."

That's how the balance fails, I thought. Thoth didn't have to do a thing more.

Ryan smacked a yellow tablet onto his desk and clicked a pen open. "What do you need from me?" The pen wasn't working, and he began to make little circles to coax out some ink.

Ask if the vault is empty or full, iced through me.

"Ah, is the vault here empty?" I asked. "If we can lure him in, we can trap him. Thoth might not show if the vault is full, and Pluck can't get in to tell."

Ryan looked up from his inkless scribbles. "Here? You want to use the vault downstairs to lure him in?" He put the pen down, wincing when Dana pointedly cleared her throat.

"Why are we fixing dross inert and storing it on a shelf if you have a vault?" she asked.

"Because it's small and glitchy," Ryan said, but my reasoning in asking Dana to stay was obvious now. Ryan would need the board's approval to risk it, old or not.

Dana predictably shook her head. "No. I can't justify risking a functioning vault."

"'Functioning' is a generous term." Giving up on the pen, Ryan threw it in the trash. "Besides, Henry mans it. Only a sweeper or Spinner can open it. No access, no risk."

"And who is Henry?" Dana asked, and I chuckled.

"It's what we call the loom's security," I said. "He's not AI, but everyone talks to him as if he were. Voice-recognition locks. You state your name and your status, and he opens the door. It's the only tech attached to the original vault."

"Hence us not using it. Giving the loom computer a name was Darrell's idea." Ryan's tone was soft in regret, and then his focus sharpened. "If Pluck can't get in there, Thoth can't, either." He turned to Dana. "We need to catch Thoth. The risk is minimal. Can you get the board to agree?"

I thought about what Pluck had said about Thoth being able to possess someone. The risk didn't sound minimal to me, but I said nothing, even when Dana slowly nodded her head. "I can do that."

My breath came out in a slow exhale. "Catching Thoth would exonerate the memorial shadows," I said. "Thank you."

Petra, is the vault full or empty? Pluck fizzed impatiently.

It doesn't matter, I thought. *As long as we say it's empty, he'll come.*

Ryan ran a hand over his bristly chin in thought. "Petra, perhaps you and Pluck should distance yourself. With Marshal Owens handling it, we can drop this entirely onto the militia—"

"No," I interrupted, Pluck's agreement sliding through me. "For better or worse, I'm part of the lure. As the only working weaver/shadow pair, Pluck and I are his greatest threat. There's no one more qualified than Pluck and me to catch shadow. You get the word out. Pluck and I guard the vault. Catch him. He won't show unless I'm here. It's me or no one."

Ryan looked at Dana, sighing when the woman gestured her ambivalence. It was his call. "Okay, but we need to organize this better," he said when Marty's voice sounded in the hall, quickly joined by Akeem's. Our five minutes were done. "Dana, since finding vault space is on your to-do list, why don't you be the one to get the word out that we have a temporary vault here accepting active dross?"

Cold cramped my ankle in a sudden unease, but I was already ahead of Pluck. "Thank you," I said softly. "Can you put it off until I get a new lodestone?"

Grimacing, Dana nodded. I wasn't sure if she was unhappy about the delay or the cost of a new stone.

Sighing, Ryan leaned back in his chair, eyes going to the sun-drenched yard. "I could use a day as well. We've been finding jars of dross on the steps of the Surran building like boxes of lost kittens. Telling the campus we have a vault will invite them to abandon them here instead. We can fix everything inert and move it to the gym, I suppose."

Ryan's gaze went to the door, and I shifted to see Akeem and Marty standing there, the former with a wide smile, Marty with a shy one. "Hey, Marty has a great feel for dross," the tall man said. "You know those knotted cords we salvaged from the loom? She just matched three to their stick sets."

Marty's shoulders were high about her ears. "I worked in a secondhand shop for a while. A stick set is worth five times more with a proper cord. You wouldn't believe the cords we'd get."

"I just might," Ryan said, his eyes holding a hint of worry.

Akeem leaned against the doorframe. "So, when is Marty's skills test? We need to get her before the militia does."

Marty's smile vanished. "Ah, I'm only here to see if you could make that shadow go away," she said, her gaze wary as it found me. "You said you could get rid of the shadow. I thought that's what weavers did. If you can't do that, I'm leaving."

Shadow spit. If she walked out now, the separatists would find and kill her. "Herm might know," I said, snatching at straws, and Ryan snapped his fingers, his relief obvious.

"Herm?" Dana said. "Herm Ivaros? He's a Spinner. What does he know about shadow?"

"More than I do," I said, and Pluck fizzed sourly in disagreement.

"Herm helped Petra figure everything out." Ryan gave me a fond look. "But he's not on campus. It will take me a few days to track him down. Let me get you a room at University Arms."

Again he reached for his tablet, even as Marty paled. "I've heard of him. I thought he was a dross . . . eater . . ."

Ryan winced, but I was used to the slur and let it roll off. "No such luck," I said. "He took the credit for my dad's weaver skills to keep the separatists from coming after me. Gave me a few somewhat normal years."

But Marty still looked ill and my pulse quickened. *Keeping her close would be prudent,* Pluck fizzed. *We have time before Thoth's trap is set.*

My gut cramped. "Um, Ryan, how about Marty stays with me?" I said, and Ryan's reach for his phone hesitated. "I have a spare room. You can get some rest. Chill out. Pluck and I are going out to Tucson tomorrow to the rock and gem show to get a new piece of moldavite. You'd love it. Herm might be a while. He's kind of flaky."

Pluck's appreciation bubbled. *A stone I tuned myself would be much appreciated.*

"I go every year," Akeem said. "It's amazing. Like touring the world in a day."

"Sounds messy." Dana stood, and Akeem retreated into the hall when she made an ushering motion. "Ryan, I'm heading out. Text me when Petra has her new lodestone. I'll talk with the board, but I don't see any complications in Petra's plan."

"Petra, hang on," Ryan said absently. "Let me give you the university's credit card for Pluck's new lodestone."

"Ahhh." Dana jerked to a halt, and Akeem chuckled.

"Give it up, Dana," he said, giving both me and Marty a wave before pulling Dana into the hall. "If the university doesn't buy it,

Pluck and Petra can sell it online when he outgrows it. Marty, it's been a pleasure. I hope you decide to stay."

"It was nice meeting you," she said, but it sounded superficial, and her brow was furrowed. She looked worried, but that seemed to be her resting state.

Dana leaned to look at Pluck under my chair. "How long does that take? To outgrow it?"

"Depends," I said as Ryan handed me a credit card with the university logo on the front.

"Marty, if you see a moldavite crystal you like, it's on us." Ryan waved a hand at Dana to be quiet. "Whether you stay or not. No commitment. You're a weaver. You need one."

"Ahhh . . ." Dana started, clearly worried about the cost, and Akeem tugged her another step down the hall.

"Come on, Dana. You owe me lunch," the man said, adding a cheerful "See you around, Petra. Don't take any bad shadow buttons, Pluck."

What is he talking about? Pluck grumbled, clearly pleased that he'd been included.

Marty, though, was staring at Ryan in near panic. "I don't need a lodestone. I'm not taking a shadow."

As if she has a choice? Pluck fizzed, and I sourly agreed. Pluck had been insistent.

"That's fine," Ryan said. "But if there's a shadow trailing you, it might go into the stone if stressed. Herm might know a way to keep it there. Tell you what. Until you can pick one up, you can wear mine."

My lips parted as the older man took the amulet from around his neck, exhaling shakily as he extended it. Marty reluctantly took it, and Pluck fizzed in surprise. Ryan was giving her the loan of his amulet? He wouldn't be able to do any magic without it.

Seeing me staring, he shrugged. Then I got it. With it, she could do magic. It was an incredibly powerful motivator to stay. Sure enough, she stood a little straighter after she laced it over her head, but it felt manipulative. Herm had done the same thing to me.

"Um, I'll see if Benedict can take us out to the show tomorrow before his class," I said as I tucked the card into my pocket. "I don't like Pluck not having somewhere to go."

"Sounds sensible." Ryan blew out his breath in anticipation of getting the stone back, but I could see his stress in the pinch of his eyes. Spinner stones were rare. The one he'd just given her probably dated from the early 1300s. That was how much Marty staying meant to him. "I'll call the marshal. Let her know we're good here. Marty, since you're going to be with us for a few days, are you sure you don't want to take a skills test?"

The woman dropped the amulet, her fear returning as it thumped against her chest.

"Shadow spit, Ryan," I said as I stood. She'd had enough, and if I was hungry, she was probably starved. "You're as bad as Lev. Marty, how about some lunch?" I touched my pocket with Ryan's charge card. "The university's buying."

"Um, sure." She fidgeted, clearly uneasy. "I haven't had anything to eat today except a vending machine doughnut."

"Great. We can stop and get some toiletries, too," I added.

"Also on the university," Ryan blurted. The man stood behind his desk, a worried pinch to his brow. "Petra . . ." he added, and I exhaled in exasperation, halting with one hand on the doorframe. "If you get the chance, will you do an informal skills test?"

"Ryan," I complained when Marty stopped as well, a wary slant to her eyes.

"Field strength. Volume," he persisted. "Put on paper that Marty is shifting active dross inert. That's all." He came out from behind the desk. "Marty, I want to offer you a full ride."

The woman took a breath. I thought he'd gone too far, but then her expression unexpectedly softened. "Like a student?" she asked, and Ryan nodded, the pinch of his eyes easing when her shoulders dropped.

"Four years with a small allowance and option to continue as far as you want. I just need something on paper to get the ball rolling. Grady can do it," he gushed when Marty hesitated. "Tonight, when you're rested and relaxed. Or tomorrow. Whenever."

"Ah, Benedict has been the one signing the skills tests. I'm not a teacher," I started, and Pluck fizzed and bubbled at the edges of my awareness.

"Semantics," Ryan said brightly. "I simply need a name on the paper as her tester, and you *are* a weaver." He beamed at Marty. "No pressure. It's only in case you're interested."

Marty looked at me, and I shrugged. "We could give you some guidance on what is going on if nothing else," I encouraged. "Sounds like you need a place to be for a while. You could do a lot worse than St. Unoc."

Ryan laughed, the honest sound of it turning Marty's smile real. "Great. Petra, you've got the forms in your phone already, yes? Just add a box for weaver and check it."

"Will do." I followed Marty into the hall, thinking finding weavers might be a lucrative career choice if I could attach a finder's fee. "Marty, you like In-N-Out Burger?"

"Love it," the young woman said, and I gave Ryan a look to stay in his office and not follow us to the door.

"Thank you," he said soundlessly, and I waved my goodbye. Marty was destined to be one of us, but I wasn't going to push it. Flies and vinegar, and all.

9

MY FOOTFALLS WERE NEARLY SILENT ON THE STAIRS DESPITE MY ENTIRE RIGHT leg being numb with cold. Pluck hung so tight I was almost walking inside him. I couldn't tell if he was worried about Thoth or simply trying to give Marty space. The young woman was to my other side, silent as she took in the building's elaborately tiled floor as I led the way to my apartment. The corridor was dusty, but not a hint of dross marred it, and I could tell Marty noticed.

"Is that your Hummer in the lot?" Marty asked as we reached the second-floor landing.

"It's Lev's. He's across the hall."

The plastic bag with her new toiletries rattled. "Everyone else working?" Marty pressed against the wall as Pluck ghosted past us, dissolving to a ribbon of black to slip into our apartment. He was shedding wisps of energy even in this dim light, and I didn't like it. "There aren't any other cars out there."

"Oh." I propped my long-stick against the wall to fumble for my key. The door squeaked open after I unlocked it, and I squinted at the last sliver of light coming in through the balcony. "No." I moved my stick to the other side of the wall and went in, leaving Marty to close the door. "Lev and I are the only two in the building at the moment," I added, embarrassed.

Marty pushed the door shut, then scuffed to a halt between the modern, open-concept kitchen and living room as I went to shut the blinds on the sliding glass doors. Immediately it felt cooler, and my shoulders eased. "There are a lot of mailboxes in the hall . . ." she prompted.

"Yep." I glanced over the quiet corner apartment, not surprised Pluck was hiding. He could tolerate the sun when he bothered to make a skin, but he didn't enjoy it. He was either sulking under my bed or, more likely, under the couch. "No one wants to live next to a shadow."

I set the bags on the low coffee table, then went to do a quick visual inspection of the bathroom. *Clean enough.* Marty was peeking past the blinds at the town houses across the street, and I took a moment to shoot off a text to Herm before I forgot.

Found a weaver. The shadow following her busted the new vault. Could use your help before Lev and Benny complicate it. Done, I shoved my phone in a back pocket.

"Ah, you want something to drink?" I said, wincing when I looked into the empty fridge. "I really need a coffee, but I've got fizzy water or a beer if you'd rather."

"After this morning I could use a beer, but I'd better stick to coffee."

"Coffee it is."

The sudden knock on the door pulled my attention up as Lev's voice came faintly from behind it. "Hey, Grady! You got a sec?"

"She's not military fodder," I whispered as I went to the door. Ryan had probably called him. Still, I found myself glad to see him as I opened the door. He was a good guy. "Hi, Lev. What you need?"

Lev came in, the lean man confidently shutting the door with his foot. "Oh, hey," he said when he saw Marty. "I didn't know you had company."

It was an outright lie, and I eyed him as Marty smiled uncertainly. His narrow face still held a morning stubble and his long, dark hair was in disarray. 'Course, it was always in disarray, and I stifled the urge to smooth it. His faded jeans and soft pullover shirt made him appear harmless, but his sharp blue eyes took in everything, and his easy self-assurance said military even if his casual dress and stubbly chin didn't. His earring lodestone was the only shine to him, but he counted on people misjudging him.

Which is why I'm not kicking him out, I thought. If he was here, he was here, and his opinion on Marty would be helpful. Not her skill level—which I could measure for myself—but what he thought about her.

"I'm Lev," he said as he went to Marty, hand extended.

"Marty," she answered as she took it, clearly immune to his charms.

"She's staying with me until Herm shows up," I added. "What can I do for you, Lev?"

"You're the new weaver!" Lev beamed, his guile absolute and convincing as he came deeper into the room. "The entire campus is talking about you. Smart of you to find Petra. There are too many people who don't understand what you represent, and Petra knows what she's doing. She'll get you situated in no time."

"Ah, we're still working on that," I said quickly. "Marty is keeping her options open."

"Oh." Lev eyed her unease and gave her a wink. "Got it."

"Nice to meet you," she said, clearly distracted. "Petra says you're across the hall?"

"Yep." An easy expression found him as he plunked his ass into a chair with his back to the gas fireplace where he could see both the door to the hall and the balcony's sliders. "Petra, I will take your recycling to the curb next week for a cup of that coffee. I had an extremely late night."

Coffee? He'd been listening at the door. Sighing, I went to check the pot, glad I'd cleaned it before I left. "Deal," I said as Marty dropped her bag of toiletries beside the chair directly opposite Lev and gingerly sat down.

"Hey, Pluck." Lev perked up as the shadow oozed out from under the chair, startling Marty as he hazed into a dog and trotted into the kitchen. "How's it holding together, old man?"

Pace steady, Pluck flicked an ear to send a splat of dark matter to hiss against the floor beside Lev's foot. An oily film drifted up from it . . . and then it was gone. Sure, he couldn't talk as a dog, but he usually got his point across.

"Guess it's holding together okay," Lev said, unfazed.

"Ryan sent him," I whispered, annoyed as an icy tendril coiled about my ankle. *I shouldn't have told him we were a target. This wasn't a mistake, was it? Asking her to stay with us?*

A calculated risk, Pluck fizzed. *Thoth strove to destroy weavers because only weavers are immune to his possession. Ryan was wise to alert your support.*

Lev isn't my support, I grumbled, but concern laced Pluck's thoughts. A drift of dross had come in with Lev. I'd hardly noticed the little heat shimmer before, but with Pluck's grip on my ankle, it glowed like a living sunbeam, hot enough to burn.

"So, Marty-of-many-options. What do you want to do if university life isn't a good fit?" Lev asked.

"Lev, put your militia pamphlet back in your pocket," I said over the chatter of water as I filled the coffeepot. "She's staying with me until we talk to Herm."

"Just asking questions." His eyes closed as if tired. "No harm in asking questions."

Marty's brow furrowed in worry. "You're in the militia?"

Lev opened his eyes and sat up. "Lev Evander, Master Ranger, at your service, ma'am," he said. "But I don't bother with the 'Master Ranger' part unless I'm wearing a hat and am in the field."

I filled the filter with grounds and set it back in the coffeemaker. "He's my babysitter when I leave St. Unoc."

Marty stared at me, horrified. "You need a guard?"

Yes, Pluck fizzed, his cold amusement obvious as he drifted about my ankles like a cat wanting his supper.

"Oh, if only it were that simple," Lev said. "I'm her babysitter while she's on campus, too. If not for Pluck, I'd be tailing her twenty-four/seven to make sure those nasty separatist mages keep their ugly spells off her."

I scowled at him as Marty lost her smile. *Way to go, Lev.* "Don't listen to him," I said, arms over my middle as I leaned against the counter. "He's a spy, not a guard. A weaver protects his or her shadow, and their shadow protects them. End of story."

"True, so don't tell my superiors, okay?" Lev leaned to look into the kitchen as if waiting for coffee. "He thinks I'm driving away separatist mages twice a week. Keeps me out of the barracks. Petra needs me like a hole in the head. So, Marty." Lev eased deeper into his chair. "Everyone at St. Unoc is from somewhere else. Where are you from?"

I would have told him to stop, but I was interested, too.

"Everywhere." Marty shrugged. "We moved a lot when I was growing up because my mom is a visiting nurse. Mage, specializing in clearing plaque from circulatory systems with a combination heat and gravity spell."

"Damn." Lev blinked, impressed. "That's a heavy hitter."

Marty nodded. "My dad could do his job anywhere. He was a sweeper, though he didn't use it much. Or so my aunt says."

Could, I mused silently. Was he retired, out of the picture, or dead? Interesting that her parents were not both mage or sweeper, but one of each. Not unusual, but telling, maybe.

"My mom doesn't talk about him much," she continued, but the way her gaze wandered over my bookshelf made me think he was dead. "I guess that's why I'm not very good at fields. A little of everything, and not enough of anything." She laughed, but it sounded tired.

The coffee was beginning to brew, and I went to get the mugs. "Not everyone uses their magic skills in their everyday work." I took three, shoving the white one with my name on it in silver foil to the side. Someone had found it in the rubble at the Surran building and given it to me. I hadn't been able to bring myself to use it.

"I can't imagine doing my job without magic," Lev said, grilling her softly. "What do you do when you're not avoiding rogue shadows?"

Marty shrugged. "I've been working as a mechanic in Florida for about a year lifting dross out from under the carriage, wiring, et cetera. It gives me a chance to work on my fields." Her gaze flicked to me. "I had to quit when—that shadow showed up."

"A mechanic! Very cool." Lev nodded encouragingly. "Your fields can't be that bad. Let's see 'em."

The last mug hit the tray with a warning clatter. "Lev, give her a break."

I want to see them, too, fizzed coldly through me, and I started, having forgotten Pluck was there. *The worse her fields, the safer she is, and she didn't do a thing at the viaduct.*

True. I set the coffeepot next to the mugs. "But it would give me something to put on that entrance exam . . ." I prompted.

"Won't it bring in that shadow?" Marty said, clearly concerned. "That's why I had to quit my job. Every time I made a field, it showed up."

"Were you fixing dross inert?" I said, and she bobbed her head. "That's what brought him in, not the field itself." Still, she looked uneasy, and I frowned at the haze of dross clinging to Lev's ratty slipper. "That's how I caught Pluck," I added, shifting all my weight to my left leg when Pluck froze my right in protest. "I gave him some inert dross and he popped right into a lodestone."

Lev's eyebrows rose. "I seem to remember it a little differently."

Yeah, it was a lot different, but I wanted to see what Marty could do.

"You sure?" Marty glanced at Pluck puddled about my feet.

"Absolutely." I went to set the tray on the low table, stifling a shudder when Pluck's grip on my leg stretched and snapped. "Shadow spit, Lev. I am not your cleaning service." Taking the heat distortion from his foot, I balled it up and tossed it to the trap by the door. The coffee smelled wonderful, but I ignored it, clearly waiting.

Marty sat straighter. Palms pressed, she inhaled, pulling them apart to make a slight distortion between them.

I kept my neutral smile in place. It was a field, but it was thin and patchy, hardly holding together. *Maybe she's better with a wand . . .*

Her skill level is like minus two, Pluck fizzed and bubbled, a thin trace of satisfaction coloring his thoughts. *No wonder she hasn't attracted a shadow yet. She's a yeth.*

Marty squinted, her face showing the strain as she shifted her field a little denser before letting it go. *You thought I was a yeth, too,* I reminded him.

Yes, but you came with skills. Marty has none. Thoth wouldn't be interested in her, even if he could mesh his psyche to hers. There was a flush of worry, and the shadow pulled from me to hide under the couch again.

Marty was staring expectantly, and I found my train of thought. "Ah, not bad," I said, and exhaled in relief. It was obvious, though, that she knew she was behind the curve.

"I'm working on them," she said softly, startling at the sharp rap on the door.

"Hey, Petra? You home?"

Benny, I thought in a mix of relief, worry, and delight, glad Pluck was under the couch. He didn't like Benedict and I needed a hug without the shadow's sour commentary.

"That coffee smells good." Lev unfolded himself to reach it as Marty collapsed her field.

I crossed the room with a definite bounce in my step, not caring if Ryan had sent him to check on me. Pleased, I opened the door with a flourish. "Hi, Benny."

My shoulders eased at his smile, and I sighed when he lifted the bakery box in his hand high so as to put an arm around me and give me a hug. "How are you doing? Is Pluck okay?"

Yep, Ryan had talked to him, and I gave him a kiss, whispering, "Fine. We spent some time in the grotto and he's recovered. I thought you had class today."

Benedict's gaze flicked over my shoulder. "Ryan called. Said you thought a murderous shadow might be tailing the new weaver."

I took a breath to protest, and he pulled me closer. "I heard about your trap at the records building. Until he's caught, there's a chance Thoth will show here. It's me or Lev. Your choice."

Choice? Not really, and I nodded as I pulled my arms from him. "So, no class?"

"Thanksgiving break starts this week." Benedict came in and set the box on the eat-at counter. The scent of his cologne hit me when he took off his jacket, and I breathed it in, enjoying it.

"Is that coffee?" Benedict said, his smile genuine as he nodded at Lev. "Perfect. I brought Danishes. They're left over from my meeting this morning, but still good."

"Ooh, cherry," Lev said when he flipped the lid open and helped himself.

"Marty?" I asked, and she shook her head. After that megaburger, I wasn't hungry, either, and I tugged at Benedict's elbow. "Benedict, this is Marty. Marty, this is Benedict Strom. He's a professor of mage studies."

"Boyfriend," Lev coughed, as if the kiss hadn't made it obvious.

"Junior professor," Benedict admitted as he gave her a charming, goofy wave. "But you can call me Benedict. It's great to meet you. Petra's been looking for you—or someone like you, rather—for months. You have no idea."

Marty stood, leaning over the coffee table to briefly take his hand. "Marty Mayson," she said, her gaze shifting nervously as she sat down again. And just like that, I finally had a last name. "It's nice to meet you," she added, but again, it was by rote, sounding even more tired.

"Coffee and Danish . . . this day is shaping up." Lev settled himself, hands full. "You sure you don't want to get in on this, Marty?"

"Just coffee," she said, and I went to get another mug. Pluck was glowering at me from under the couch, his green eyes snapping sparks. With both Lev and Benedict here, it was starting to feel a little oppressive. And yet I was glad when Benedict followed me into the kitchen, the large man pushing a little too close as he got a couple of plates for his pastries.

"Are you sure her being here is a good idea?" he said, his voice low so Marty, now talking to Lev, wouldn't likely hear. "What if that shadow shows up?"

I glanced at Marty, worried. "Then I catch him. You tell me who on campus is better suited for this than Pluck and me. The only reason I'm not at the records building tonight is because I want to get Pluck a new stone first."

"Fine. I'm staying the night even if I'm on the couch." Fake smile in place, he headed into the living room, plates and box of Danish in hand.

"Where's Pluck?" Benedict asked, and when Lev pointed to the evil green glare coming from under the couch, Benedict sat down right over him. "Hey, Pluck."

I took the corner of the couch, my feet tucked under me so Pluck couldn't freeze my ankles. If he wanted to be a part of the conversation, he'd have to put in an appearance.

"Ryan said you might need a ride out to the rock and gem show." Benedict set a pastry on a plate. "Count me in."

Must he sit over me? fizzed through me, and I jumped. Pluck had snaked a tendril up through the cracks of the couch, and I put my feet on the floor, not surprised when he coiled about my ankles.

"And, Marty," Benedict continued, turning to her, "I'm sure you'd rather have a stone you picked out yourself instead of Ryan's."

A flash of fear crossed Marty. "I just want that shadow to stop following me. I've never been good at school. I'd be wasting everyone's time."

She was getting agitated, and I put up a hand, asking for patience. "Marty, everyone learns differently. There's a place for you here even if you decide against taking classes. I know this is scary, but shadows are what we make them. Pluck was an ugly, pus-dripping fiend when I first met him because that's what I saw. Now he's . . ."

A dog, Pluck fizzed.

Hurt, I leaned to look under the couch. "I told you before, if you want to be something else, be something else. You said this was what you enjoyed being. Pluck . . ."

Pluck slithered away, little rills of dark matter spilling from him as he snaked through a sunbeam. Green eyes virulent, he curled into a ball on the floor in the kitchen and glowered.

"Pluck . . ." I started to stand, then caught myself. Marty was staring at me as if I'd gone crazy. But then again, she could only hear half the conversation. Lev and Benedict were used to it, but Marty? Flustered, I hid behind a gulp of coffee, almost choking on it.

Benedict scrubbed a hand over his face. "Ah, so tomorrow morning? Whether you stay or not, you should have your own chunk of moldavite, Marty."

"Sure."

It was a listless response, and I winced, feeling the conversation lag.

"So, Petra." Benedict shifted his Danish to his other hand so he could lick his fingers. "Dana is fit to sever heads. Did you really suggest that mages go out with the sweepers to fix dross into nuggets?"

"Seriously?" Lev said, and I cringed, nervous at what he might think.

"Ah, yeah. It was Pluck's idea. I think it's a good one."

Benedict slurped his coffee. "Good or not, it's already causing a lot of discussion."

Discussion, he said, but what I heard was anger. "How much—discussion?"

"Well . . ." Benedict turned his Danish, eating the gooey side before it dripped onto his jeans. "The sweepers don't want to take the mages out with them because they think they will eventually lose their jobs, seeing as once the dross is inert, mages can handle it safely. The mages feel insulted to have been asked to do this in the first place."

I wasn't surprised. "Sweepers are not trashmen," I said, not caring that Marty was getting a look at the boulder-size chip on my shoulder. "None of this would be necessary if the mages handled their own waste."

"I'm not arguing, just relating the mood." Done with his Danish, Benedict eased back with his coffee.

"So make a class," Lev offered. "This is a university, isn't it? Freshmen have to take a dross-handling class already. Extend it to them partnering with a sweeper for a year."

"Oh, if only it was that easy." I dangled my hand to find Pluck, forgetting he had put himself in the kitchen. "Most freshmen don't have the skill to fix dross into inert nuggets."

Marty's eyes were wide, and I forced myself to smile. "Don't worry about it," I said. "It's nothing you have to be concerned over."

Benedict heaved a sigh, his entire body moving. "The most skilled mages—the ones capable of making this work—are understandably reluctant."

I extended my foot across the space between us and pushed on his knee. "Then maybe you and I should work together as a sweeper/mage pair for a semester. Show them how it's done."

That's the balance, Pluck fizzed, my ankle cramping. He was back.

"But my work," Benedict said, and my smile faltered. "I mean, I'd love to, and it needs to be done, but I'm teaching. We can find someone—"

"Forget it," I interrupted. Jaw tight, I stood. "Anyone want more coffee?"

Shadow spit. I knew he didn't think of me like a trashman, and yet . . . there it was.

"Petra, I'm not saying it's beneath me. I'm busy," Benedict said, and I flipped the top to the coffeemaker up, grabbed the grounds, and threw them out.

Groaning, Lev got to his feet and swallowed the last of his coffee. "Look at the time. I have to go. Three is fun, but four is too much work. Yell if you need me. Marty, it was good to meet you."

The young woman looked at him from over her mug. "Bye."

"Thanks, Lev," I said as he set his mug in the sink, touching my arm before nodding to Benedict. Shoulders tense, he slipped out and shut the door behind him.

"Petra . . ." Benedict tried again, and Marty stood.

"Hey, uh, you mind if I take a shower?" she said, her plastic bag of toiletries rattling as she picked it up. "It took me two days on a bus to get here and I can hardly stand myself."

"Oh, my gosh, go." I knew my expression must have looked sick, and Pluck's eyes glinted green from under the couch, his told-you-so attitude obvious. This kind of sucked.

"I'll take my coffee," she said, head down as she walked to the bathroom.

"She seems nice," Benedict said when the door shut with a soft click, and Pluck's eyes under the couch seemed to vanish. "New weaver. Exciting stuff."

The shower was already running, and I leaned back against a counter, ankles crossed. "You shouldn't miss class. I doubt Thoth will show and Lev is down the hall."

"Petra, I'm sorry," he said as he stood, his hands hanging at his sides. "I didn't realize how it sounded until it was out of my mouth. I think it's a great idea that you and I show everyone that being paired up with a sweeper is not a demotion. I can—"

"Stop," I said, cutting him off. My head was bowed, and I pressed my fingertips into my temple. "It's okay. I'm not mad, and I'm sorry I took it the wrong way. But do you see the hill we're facing? The rock we are trying to roll up it? Asking a professional to put everything they worked their ass off to attain on hold to turn dross into nuggets?" My shoulders slumped. "You thought my image was bad now . . ."

"Petra, I am so sorry." Benedict brought his plate and empty mug to the counter.

I thumped my head into his chest and his arms encircled me. "Forget it. I'm the one with the thin skin, not you." My shoulders dropped as he pulled me close, and for a moment, I listened to his heart beat as I reassured myself that I was here, and he was here, and we were both okay. Better than okay.

"I can stay the night, right?" he asked, and when I nodded, he rocked into motion. "Great. You mind if I use your balcony to call Dana? I have a few ideas to sweeten the pot. If we add some sort of tenure incentive, a mage or two might surprise us."

"Sure." *Tenure? He thinks it's going to take tenure?* Moody, I gestured to the wide glass doors, and he gave me a final kiss before stepping away and somehow leaving me feeling warm and content. There was a flush of noise as the slider opened, and then it was quiet.

Thoughts heavy, I returned to the couch. Marty had been reaching for her phone when she'd gone into the bathroom, and I wondered who she was calling. Her mom? *That must be nice . . .*

"Pluck?" I sat down, and little rills of dark matter curled up around me, the shadow coalescing on the couch to sit as his namesake had done so many times before. I glanced at the closed bathroom door, glad the shower hid my words. "We're not making a mistake, are we? Trying to convince her to stay?"

It's hard to know what is in her past.

His mood had gone introspective, and my fingers tracing behind his ears halted. "There's something more here than you're telling me,"

I guessed, and his indecision twined through me, sharp and sour. "What happened between you and Thoth?"

Again his fear flickered through both of us. *I don't want to talk about it.*

"Pluck . . ." I whispered. He didn't answer, and my concern deepened. Worse, when I tried to lift his head, his face flowed right through my fingers. *Pluck, if you don't want to talk about it, okay, but what is Thoth's problem? Why is he trying to break the balance before we can find it?*

Pluck seemed to shudder. *Thoth is why we never took new weavers after the mages killed our bonded. He's hate made real, pain given voice. But it was not always so. Of all of us, he was the most desperate to not be alone. Of all of us, he searched the hardest, and it's believed that in his efforts to find a weaver to join with, he identified and destroyed the parts of his mind that prevented an easy melding into another's consciousness, be they magic or mundane.*

And being able to enter another's mind safely is a problem how? I asked.

Pluck's thoughts gave me the impression of a shrug. *That's what he thought, too. But it's believed that the multiple impressions from the many minds he searched adhered to his own in a slurry of chaos. To a person, those he tried to connect with were frightened, savage in their attempts to regain control, and so that's what the damage to his psyche was filled in with. Not only did it ruin his chance to find a compatible weaver, it left him believing that we're coerced, blinded slaves and that the only way to free us is to destroy those we take as our own. Failing that, he will destroy us. He's the reason shadows are reviled and killed on sight. He is the one who taught us to kill, then gave us a reason to, false though it is. He believes you use us. That we're stronger without you,* he fizzed, his thoughts hardly there. *He is wrong.*

And yet just today I had used Pluck's energy to break that lock, giving him what in return? I'd always felt that our relationship was uneven, and I glanced through the skewed blinds to where Benedict talked urgently on his phone, squinting in the bright light.

Petra, he's wrong, Pluck said again, his thoughts firm with conviction. *What I gain is far more than I give you. I was existing under a rez when I found you, starving for a real connection, the ability to walk under the stars without fear. I'm a part of the world again. You have no idea the gift that is. That you gave me.*

"As a dog?" I whispered, and his thoughts in mine simmered. "You aren't a pet."

I don't mind looking like a dog. It gets me places and no one expects anything of me.

"Oh, Pluck," I whispered as I fondled his pointy ears, the cold like ice against my fingertips. "You could talk to more people if you took on a more complex form. If you want—"

Pluck lifted his nose, pulling from me. *No,* he said firmly, green eyes glinting in what might be anger. *I chose to be what I am because it's comfortable for you as well as me.* His head drooped. *Unless you are embarrassed and wish me to be more.*

Stop. I took his head in my hands, making him look at me. "Never," I said aloud, and his eyes sort of vanished. "You are you," I insisted, thumbs rubbing his jowls until his eyes re-formed. "And I'm not comparing you to anyone else. But if there is ever a time you want to be more, I will support that."

He huffed, his eyes a molten green as his head melted through my hands and he re-formed it upon my knee.

I am content. That's all that's important. That, and keeping you safe.

Smiling, I put a hand atop his head, needing only the barest lift to keep it from falling through. *That's all that's important,* he had said, but that wasn't all that mattered.

10

TUCSON'S ROCK AND GEM SHOW RAN FOR THE BETTER PART OF SIX WEEKS AND involved the entire city, from mini venues in hotel parking lots to sprawling mazes at the fairgrounds. The vendors came from every corner of the world, their wares ranging from dirt-encrusted raw stone to polished gems set in precious metals, and everything in between. Though the show had once been limited to rocks, fossils, and gems, you could now find exotic fabrics, carved wood . . . everything. As Akeem had said, it was like browsing the bazaars of countries I'd never be able to visit.

I'd been before, obviously, though never to find moldavite, and Benedict and I had decided to focus on one of the larger sites with good parking and a few covered buildings. It wasn't the weekend, but the foot traffic was heavy all the same, and my hand was cradled lightly in Benedict's as we strolled under the faultless blue November sky. Marty hung close, walking a little apart but clearly interested as we inched along looking for a nondescript but costly green glass among the unfinished gems and crystals.

The sun was low, and apart from the occasional beam making it past the tents and people, Pluck could have walked beside me with impunity if we had been on campus, where a ghostly demon dog wouldn't have been noticed—or at least questioned.

That is, if not for the disgusting amount of dross rolling like tumbleweeds between the tents. Needless to say he was safely ensconced in my pocket to avoid the questions that would require an ether mage to erase.

My fingers went cold as they brushed my pocket, and I wondered, not for the first time, what it would be like if mages and sweepers could freely be themselves anywhere. Marty had grown up being taught to hide her skills to the point where she couldn't do anything of note. I had been, in hindsight, fortunate that my dad had embraced his skills . . . and mine.

Being different is a path to destruction, fizzed coldly up through my mind, and I made a fist of my fingers. *Disparities are not celebrated, they are feared.*

"I don't want to believe that," I whispered, his opinion bubbling in my mind.

"Believe what?" Benedict asked, and I forced Pluck's dreary thoughts from mine.

"Nothing." I swung our hands, determined to not ruin the day. It was wonderful being out like this shopping, even if the low sun was almost . . . painful. "Let's take a closer look at that stand," I said as I saw a colorful banner and clearly Slavic name. "He's got a lot of stuff mounted in silver, but he's got raw crystal, too."

"And that's what you want," Benedict said, making sure Marty was still with us as we angled toward the stand. She'd been texting all the way out here, getting more and more agitated with each send, but now she was ignoring the incoming pings, her phone in a back pocket. Clearly eager for a distraction, she studied the multiple display cabinets.

My hand cramped with a sudden cold, and I wasn't surprised at the tiny, thin snake of dark matter wrapped around my wrist. *It doesn't matter if it's cut, polished, or raw. Moldavite is moldavite.*

I wasn't sure if asking the vendor if he had any moldavite would get the price jacked up or not, so I strolled down the row of dusty boxes, looking at rose quartzes here, pyrites there. Moldavite was rare, and I doubted the man would have it front and center.

I'm not sensing anything, I thought, and Pluck sourly agreed.

"Petra?" Benedict's cheerful voice brought my head up to find him with the shop owner standing expectantly before him. "He's got some."

Grinning, I looped my arm—the one without Pluck—in Marty's and came closer. "Cool."

"They aren't pretty, so I keep them in back," the man said, waiting until his daughter, presumably, put her breakfast down and came forward to watch the stand before he set a tray of light green unworked stones before us. Most were little shards, but there were about four the size of my thumbnail and one as big as my thumb—all five wrapped in wire and ready to wear.

"These are nice." I reached for the largest, feeling a faint hum pushing against me.

"My cousin lives in the Czech Republic. He gets them from the farmers right from their fields. They're made from a meteor strike, where they fell to earth and cooled. Some people think they give off vibrations to cause tumultuous but needed change, so be careful if you wear it. You might get more than you want."

My fingers curved into a fist to avoid touching it. "Is that so." I eyed the man, wondering if he knew what they were really good for or if it was just sales patter.

Benedict leaned in, clearly pleased. "Do you see anything you want?"

Me, no, but Pluck was clearly excited, bubbling and fizzing as I studied the smallest of the wire-wrapped nuggets. It was rough, full of furrows and imperfections, but this was the one he clearly liked, and I pointed. "May I?"

The man nodded and I picked it up, feeling Marty's attention sharpen as I took a slow breath. The arctic nothing of the glass zinged uncomfortably across my thoughts. It had potential, but it wasn't ringing true with the universe. It needed a shadow to realign it before it could store dark matter and become . . . perfect.

"Feel that?" I handed it to Marty. "That's moldavite."

She jumped, her hands spasming open. Adrenaline pulsed as it slipped from her and my hand flashed out to catch it.

"Oh, my God. I'm so sorry," she gushed, face red, and I put the piece back on the tray.

"We'll take that one," I said, grinning at her. "Why don't you pick out a piece?"

"Um, aren't they kind of expensive?"

"Not for what you're getting," I said, pleased she'd felt something. She was a weaver. We just had to get her to admit it, become comfortable with her new skin.

Benedict pushed some of the smaller shards around with his finger, clearly sensing nothing. "You got anything bigger?" he asked, and the man behind the makeshift counter set the tray behind him before finding a second.

Relax, we'll get the small one, I thought as Pluck fizzed and bubbled through me, but it didn't make any difference, and he swirled, stabbing my wrist with impatience. *Marty needs to pick out a lodestone,* I reminded him, and he finally settled into a sulk.

"What looks good?" I prompted Marty as she looked over the larger unwrapped stones, her brow furrowed; she was clearly afraid to pick them up. There were no shards in this tray, and Pluck hummed in impatience as she touched one, then another. But her gaze, I couldn't help but notice, kept returning to an almost square one to the side.

"This one," Marty said, tapping a brownish-green crystal that looked about the same size as the one Pluck had chosen.

"Great, can you add that to my pile?" I said. "And that square one, too. Just because I like it. It's got a great shape."

A surge of worry flashed through me, but it wasn't my emotion. *She doesn't need a stone that big,* Pluck protested, but I was reaching for my wallet.

It's the one she likes, I thought. Not even Ryan would squeal, especially when it might eventually come back to the university primed for a Spinner.

The vendor set the two unwrapped stones next to Pluck's, carefully taking the price off the bottom of each. "You're a lapidarist, then?"

"Not really. I just wrap them in wire the way you have and let them be what they are. They are really nice pieces. I'm glad we found you."

Smiling, the man bobbed his head, his thin brown fingers expertly wrapping each crystal in black paper before putting them in a surprisingly posh black bag with his name on it.

Marty edged away, her brow pinched and her phone in her hand. "Hey, ah, I'll be over there," she said, pointing across the walkway to a quiet storefront. "I need to answer this."

"Okay." I turned to the vendor. "You take cards, right?"

"Sure." Sighing, the man got his phone out, head down as he brought up his pay app.

Benedict bumped my shoulder, his eyes on Marty. "Is three enough?"

"We can come back next year." I handed Ryan's card over, anxious to have that little black bag in my hands. The memory of Thoth flitted through me, and I stifled a shudder.

"My card is in there," the man said, his smile so wide I wondered if he knew who I was. "Call me direct next time, and I can mail anything to you. No need to wait a year."

"Thank you. I might just do that." Pluck fizzed and bubbled, and Benedict took the bag seeing as Pluck was still wrapped around my wrist.

"You want to grab a coffee for the ride home?" Benedict asked as we left the vendor, and a feeling of rightness suffused me. Whatever happened in the future—today, this very hour, was good.

"That's actually not a bad idea." I lifted my gaze to the far side of the walkway to ask Marty if that might be something she'd like . . . only to find a new worry. "Where did she go?"

Benedict stiffened, his hand slipping from mine as he looked both ways, his height making it easy for him. "She was right here."

I looked one way, then the other. "Pluck?"

On it, he thought, and I shivered when he spiraled to my fingertips and hazed to the ground, becoming one with the shadows as he vanished under the shelves and tables.

My first thought was that she'd run, but I'd seen her eyes alight when she touched the moldavite. More telling were those texts and the stoically ignored calls. "I'll check the bathroom," I said, seeing the low-slung building at the end of the row.

"Good idea. I'll wait for you at the gate." He took off, pace fast as he glanced down every aisle with the agitated worry of a parent looking for a wayward child.

She wasn't running, at least not from us. Still, there was only one easy way in and out of the fairgrounds, and Benedict waiting at the gate was a good idea. Pulse fast, I dodged around the few shoppers between me and the bathrooms, glad there wasn't a line as I entered the stone-block building.

"Marty?" I called before I even got through the switchback entrance. "You in here?"

A loud sniff pulled my attention to the breastfeeding nook. "Yeah. Sorry." Marty stood from the hard-back couch, phone in hand. "I should have told you where I was going."

"No worries. I, ah, just came in here to wash my hands," I said, thinking fast. She looked miserable. "Benedict went ahead to the gate," I added as I faced the sink to give her a moment to collect herself. Clearly something was wrong, and I watched her through the mirror when she stuffed her phone in a pocket.

Her screen saver, I realized, said it all: two smiling faces in snow hats; one was Marty, one was a young man her age with love in his eyes.

Immediately my shoulders eased. Marty hadn't just fallen out of the sky. She had a life, and it was trailing her as much as Thoth was. This, though, I could help with, and I dried my hands with a feeling of sympathy and understanding.

"Sorry," Marty said when our eyes met. "I didn't mean to worry you."

She was heading for the opening, and I jumped to follow. "Hey, Marty . . ."

"Benedict has the moldavite?" she said, overly cheerful.

"Ah, yeah." I squinted in the sudden light even as I appreciated the fresher air. "Marty?"

Her pace was fast and she scanned the light foot traffic. "Gate is this way, right?"

I took a long step to catch up. "Benny thought you might be running away."

Marty made a sad bark of laughter. "I can't go anywhere until you get that shadow to stop following me. And then I'm going home."

Silent, I met her stride for stride, watching her expression crumble.

"I can't go home, can I," she whispered, and I reached out, taking her arm and turning her to me.

"I am so sorry," I said earnestly, feeling awful as her eyes began to swim. "But, Marty, there's no reason he can't come here. I mean, the university wants you so badly that they will move heaven and earth to find job options for him. Good ones with opportunity. Not a handout."

Head shaking, Marty screwed up her face, a hand going to hide her eyes. "I am so tired of the lies," she said. "I just want everything to go back to the way it was." Blinking fast, she looked up at me. "I told him it was a family emergency when I left. That was three days ago. He's taking two weeks off to come out here to be with me. I told him no, and now he thinks I'm lying. The little lies didn't matter, but I can't keep doing this."

"You don't need to," I said, totally getting why she hadn't wanted to tell her boyfriend that she was attracting shadow. "What's his name?"

A fond emotion flickered and vanished. "Victor," she said softly. "I can't bring myself to lie to him anymore, but I really need to stay here and figure this out. I think . . . I think I should break it off."

Her voice had gone up at the end, and I wasn't surprised when she began to cry.

"Oh, Marty." I gave her a quick hug, but it only made things worse. "Marty, if he's taking off work to help you through a family crisis, he's a good man. He will understand." I tried to get her to look at me, failing. "I get that asking the person you love to uproot themselves and move two thousand miles to a new job and friends is hard, but give him the choice." I smiled when her eyes flicked up to mine. "No more lies."

"I can't," she whispered.

"Marty . . ."

"I can't!" she said louder, then leaned closer. "He's not a mage or a sweeper." She blinked fast, brow furrowed as if she was pained. "He's a mundane," she whispered, and I felt my expression go slack. "Even if he came out here, I'd still have to lie to him. How am I going to do that if I'm a weaver?" She gestured helplessly. "I've seen you and Pluck. I can't ask a sentient being to hide. Forever. It's either him or shadow. And I just don't know . . ."

She wiped her eyes again, and I stood there, not knowing what to say, gobsmacked. Her boyfriend was a mundane? No wonder she was upset. It wasn't unheard-of for mages and sweepers to marry mundanes, but she was right. Unlike a mage or a sweeper, she couldn't hide her magic from Victor. Ever.

"There you are!"

Benedict's hail pulled me around, but his cheerful expression faltered as he saw my face. "What happened? Is everything all right?" he asked.

Silent, Marty spun on a heel and headed for the gate.

"No," I said, relieved when Pluck's cold presence wrapped around my ankle and the sunlight suddenly became painful. "I found out why all the texts and phone calls. Marty's boyfriend is a mundane."

"So?"

I linked my arm in his, stifling a shudder as Pluck settled himself in my pocket. His presence fizzed through me, his relief at finding Marty shifting to worry as my thoughts melted into his, carrying her situation. "So you can't hide a shadow like you can a lodestone. It's him or us, and she knows it."

"Oh." His brow furrowed as he gazed at Marty walking a good eight feet ahead of us, the woman's shoulders hunched in heartache. "Ah . . ."

You trust five-year-olds with the silence, Pluck fizzed. *Why not a mundane in love?*

It was a good question, but my phone was humming, and I reached for it seeing as it was Ryan. Maybe he knew a way. True, we trusted children, but they were a part of our world—mundanes were not.

"Hey, Ryan," I said as we followed Marty through the turnstiles and into the parking lot. "We got the moldavite. Um, I need to talk to you about Marty. I found out why she isn't all over your free ride. It might be tricky, but I think we can convince her to stay if we bend a rule."

"Bend a rule?" Benedict said incredulously, and I frowned at him.

"Where are you?" Ryan said, the tension in his voice almost bringing me to a halt.

"Tucson." I gripped my phone tighter even as I scanned the parking lot. "It's kind of a good news, bad news thing about Marty."

His exhale was long. "And Pluck is with you? Please tell me Pluck is with you."

"Of course he's with me," I said, feeling my cold pocket as the shadow fizzed a dull warning. "Ah, why did you want to know where Pluck is?"

"Marshal Owens is in St. Unoc General. We think it was a shadow attack," Ryan said, his gravelly voice rumbling.

"Cameron?" My breath caught and I angled the phone so Benedict could hear. "What happened?"

"We're still piecing that together," Ryan added as Benedict bent close. "Best guess is she went to talk to you at your apartment and was attacked in the hall."

Shadow spit . . . Thoth had come for me and gotten Cameron.

"Is she okay?" Benedict asked, clearly as worried as I was.

"She's stable, but in a coma. Thank God Lev found her." Ryan's voice became hushed. "The courts think Pluck is to blame, but if he is with you, that doesn't fly."

It was Thoth, Pluck fizzed, and I touched my pocket, both relieved and frightened. *He was waiting for us and she got in the way.*

"If Lev hadn't been there . . ." Ryan hesitated. "He said he took on the appearance of a man."

"It was Thoth," I said, distracted. Dumb, dumb, dumb! I should have warned her. Put a note on the door. I was walking around as if I were impervious—and now someone was hurt.

"Shadows can look like a person?" Ryan's surprise was obvious, and I winced. I was starting to think Pluck didn't want to take on a more complex form because he couldn't.

"Ah, it's not making the news yet," Ryan continued. "But the magic community has already put two and two together and gotten shadow attack. I need you here to head off any anti-shadow sentiment. I just thank God that you and Pluck were off campus at the time."

They will blame us regardless. Pluck's thought simmered through me, but I'd been thinking it, too, and I quickened Benedict's and my pace.

"Has anyone warned the memorial shadows?" I said, and Benedict reached for his fob, unlocking his car's doors as we approached.

"No." Ryan hesitated. "I'm sorry, Petra. I never even thought of that. I don't think I could get anyone to go down there now anyway."

Marty got in the back and slammed the door shut, lost in her own misery. "Good," I said. "I'll do it." I bit my lip, not looking forward to the conversation.

"Meet me at the hospital first," Ryan said. "Okay? It's publicly being blamed on a severe allergy."

"Sounds about right. Ryan, we are on our way."

I ended the call, exchanging a worried look with Benedict as I went around the car and got in. Allergy? Magic users would know the truth. Somehow they'd find out that a shadow had attacked a mage—in my apartment building—and put her in a coma.

Accident or intentional? I thought, and Pluck fizzed sourly, unable to hide his worry.

Concerned, I settled into the car's plush seat and tried not to chew on my fingernails. Marty was a knot of misery, but she looked up when Benedict got in, drawn by the chatty man's unusual silence. It was a good bet that the marshal had found Thoth waiting for us and tried to catch him.

Rule number two . . .

11

I WAS LEAVING FAIRGROUND DIRT IN MY WAKE, OBVIOUS ON THE POLISHED WHITE hospital tiles. Flushed, I walked quickly past the main reception desk. Ryan had texted me Cameron's room number and I was anxious to see her. So much so that I'd left Benedict and Marty to park the car and come in alone.

Pluck padded along beside me. The shadow made Benedict's absence feel a little less sharp. Fortunately I was familiar with the hospital from my previous work as a sweeper, and I confidently headed for the secondary, seldom-used bank of elevators around the corner. The shadow currently looked like an especially robust, powerful hairless service dog, one so well trained he didn't need a leash. Hopefully no one would notice his feet weren't touching the ground and the hints of hair about his toes and tail and atop his head were actually a hazy mist.

My tension spiked when we turned the corner and the elevators came into view. "Do you want to take refuge in your new stone?" He hadn't thought a word the entire ride from Tucson to St. Unoc, avoiding the untuned moldavite and worrying me. "It's already wrapped. Just need to put it on a knotted silk string."

Pluck flicked a pricked ear and a ribbon of icy shadow splatted against the wall, melting into a dark haze that evaporated to nothing. *No need,* he thought, the words in my head making my teeth ache. *There's minimal dross here. I'm fine.*

"It's nice, isn't it," I whispered, glad the hallways were clear of dross and people both. Oh, many of the doctors and nurses here excelled in covert magic, but of all the professions, healthcare was the best at cleaning up after themselves.

An orderly looked up from his paperwork as I passed, his first impulse to tell me to take the dog out faltering when he recognized me despite my being in black pants and a black band tee and not my usual spandex bike kit. I hadn't been sweeping in months, but when you find and clear out an illegal dross dump leaking into the hospital servers, they tend to remember you. Or maybe it was Pluck striding at my heel like a sleek dog from hell. The guy looked a little pale.

You used to make dross pickups here, Pluck said with a wolfy chuckle.

"Hospitals have their share of unique issues," I said, and Pluck bumped into my hip to send a wash of cold through me.

He knew you. That, and your satisfaction for a clean floor is very loud.

I scuffed to a halt at the elevators and hit the call button. "Once upon a time."

Pluck sat and waited, his pricked ears flat. *There's a dross pit here. I can feel it.*

"They have one main and a handful of transfer stations." I hit the button again to try to hurry it up. I hadn't checked in at the front desk, and that Pluck wasn't really a dog would cause more problems, not less. "The hospital isn't under university mandates. Ryan tells me they will put in the shadow release valve when they empty the vault again. Few years? Until then, the loom operators will be required to check all bottles for shadow."

Understandable, but rife with opportunities for corruption. Pluck made a doggy huff.

The elevator dinged and I stood aside as a lab-coated someone exited. Mood closed, I got into the elevator and pushed the button for the third floor. The sound of Jimmy Tross was a faint hint, and I sighed, the forced immobility making me agitated as the lyrics echoed in my thoughts.

Can't put it back, black coin ill spent. Ten thousand years, at detriment. Down in the earth, buried deep. Down where the demons sleep. Down where God can't speak. Black coin spent, our soul to keep. Just killing time, as black coin seeps.

"You think he's talking about dross?" I whispered as the mage-born musician wound into the climax, his rough voice faintly shouting "It's killing time!" over and over.

That or oil, sifted coolly through me as Pluck twined a wisp about my ankle.

It wouldn't be the first. Many nursery rhymes were actually messages through the ages, warnings or instructions whispered one generation to the next, and as the silver elevator doors opened and Pluck and I got out, my feet seemed to pound to one of my favorites.

One stick, two sticks, three, four, five. Stand them straight to stay alive. Six sticks, seven, eight, nine, ten. Shadow held, its strength to lend.

Pluck made a little huff. *I'd say that one was about me, as no one ever needs more than three sticks to capture dross, and shadows are evasive.*

"I'm not getting that part about held shadow lending strength," I muttered, then brightened as I saw Lev in the hall.

The young man was sitting against the wall, his feet spread wide, elbows on his knees, head bowed. Dressed in jeans and a plaid coat against the morning's chill, he looked as if he should be at a bowling alley knocking back a few beers, not sitting in a hospital—waiting.

"Excuse me, ma'am," the nurse stationed at the desk said as I passed, and Lev looked up. "You can't take a dog . . . Oh . . ."

I didn't need to look at her to know she'd gone pale. It was in her voice.

Lev stood, his welcoming smile forced. *Maybe I should . . .* the shadow dog started.

Stay by my side? I thought. *Good idea.*

Pluck began to fade. *My presence is not helping.*

I dangled a hand into his icy, prickly not-there self. *You are my friend. You shouldn't have to hide.*

Then why did we get a new lodestone? It would be easier if I hid, he insisted.

"Easy is overrated," I muttered as I gave Lev a hug. His grip was tenuous, and he let go almost immediately, his mind clearly on whatever was behind that door.

Lev glanced at Pluck, the shadow dog's ears pinned to his not-there skull. "Hey, Pluck," he said, his brow furrowed in what might be guilt.

Pluck lifted his muzzle as if to say, "Yo." Mist drifted from him to the floor in a ribbon of sparkles. The nurse was watching, and I dangled my fingers in him to make him look harmless. "We came as soon as we heard," I said. "Benedict is parking the car. I didn't want to bring Marty into this until I knew how bad it was."

She's staring. I'm going to evaporate. Pluck flicked his ear and padded to the nearby bank of chairs, leaving only a thin trace of himself chilling my ankle as he slipped under them.

I frowned at his glowing green eyes. *Get back out here,* I thought. *Let her stare.*

A sulky, icy thought blossomed. *No. It's too hard to maintain a pleasant appearance when everyone sees me as a spit-dripping, decaying fiend.*

"That's probably a good idea," Lev said faintly, oblivious to our private conversation.

I touched his elbow, and his attention sharpened on me. "How is Cameron?"

He took a breath, hesitating. "Stable?" he ventured, that same flicker of guilt marring his usually carefree attitude. "Petra, I am so sorry. I didn't know she was your friend."

"She isn't," I said. "She's a marshal of the courts sent to find out if Pluck and I are responsible for the attacks on the vault construction." That she had been assaulted by a shadow outside my apartment didn't look good. At all.

"Yeah." Lev ducked his head. "I figured that out when I found her ID. Ryan and a woman named Dana are in there with her right now."

Pluck lifted his head, his skull taking on clear definition. "Dana? That's not good," I said.

Lev shifted from foot to foot. "She came in right after Ryan. How come that's not good?"

I lifted a shoulder and let it fall. I trusted Lev, but I didn't want to sound petty. "She's a problem fixer the university brought in, and I tend to be a problem. How about you? Are you okay? Ryan said you were there. Jeez, Lev, you look awful."

"I'm not the one in a coma." Gaze furtive, he glanced at Pluck hiding under the chairs. "I didn't even know she was in the building until I heard a thump. I thought it was you. Went to check. Your door was open."

"She was in my apartment? Ryan said they found her in the hall."

Lev's expression became empty as he fell into "report" mode. "I moved her there. She was in your living room when I found her. I made the mistake of not doing anything," he said, then took a moment to clear his throat, gaze fixed on nothing. "Until he turned into a man, I thought it was Pluck. That he was protecting you." His eyes were haunted, and his iron hold on his emotions was breaking. "I mean, she was *in* your *home*. I didn't know who she was."

I touched his arm in support. "It's okay."

"When she went into convulsions, I knew it couldn't be Pluck." Blinking fast, he focused on the deeper black haze under the chairs. "You wouldn't hurt anyone like that."

I would if they came after Petra . . . fizzed through me as my ankle went cold.

"I'm assuming it was Thoth. He's one tough mother," Lev said as Pluck hazed out from under the chair. "Magic didn't do a damn thing. I had to beat him off with your dad's stick."

I nodded. Not wanting to stand out at the rock and gem show, I'd left it by the door.

Lev looked at his hands, gauging their slight tremor. "I used it to gather the dross from the magic I'd just done on him. Hit him with it. He shrugged off the spell, but the dross he noticed. He fled."

Pluck's worry iced through me. *The only thing Thoth fears is dross.*

"Good luck I was out," I said. "Bad luck that Cameron found him."

Lev shifted from foot to foot, brow furrowed. "Petra, I could have done something sooner, but I thought it was Pluck. She was *in* your apartment. I'd never seen her before."

"This is not on you." I touched his arm again. "She'll be okay." *Please let her be okay . . .*

"I moved her to the hall so you wouldn't be implicated." Clearly distressed, he ran a hand over his chin. "I didn't want the paramedics in your place."

Shadow spit, he had been in combat mode. "Lev." I waited until his eyes met mine. "Thank you for that. Listen to me. This was not your fault." Maybe if I kept saying it, he would believe me. This *wasn't* his fault.

He took a slow breath. Held it. Let it go. "I should have acted sooner." His attention went to the door, a false, stoic calm finding him. "Ryan got the paramedic's version, which is that I heard her fall. Found her comatose in the hallway. Saw a shadow flee. If you want to tell him different, it's up to you."

"Thank you." I gave his arm a quick squeeze. "I, ah, should probably go in."

Tense, he rocked into motion to stay with me. "I'll come with you."

I wasn't surprised, and after checking to make sure Pluck was with us, I knuckle-knocked on the heavy, wide door and went in at a soft hail.

My pace slowed when the short entry opened up into a small private room, and I stifled a shiver at the icy draft of hot pinpricks spiraling about my feet. Pluck didn't rise up to take refuge in his new wire-wrapped stone in my pocket; instead, he hazed about my feet to seek shelter in whatever dark place he could find. Perhaps the glass needed to be tuned first to be comfortable.

Cameron lay like Sleeping Beauty, red curls arrayed against the pillow, her eyes closed, and her face pale. The only thing hooked up to her was an IV and probably a catheter.

Beside her in a chair pushed up to the bed was Dana. The woman's brow was furrowed as she texted someone. Ryan ran a hand over his thinning salt-and-pepper hair as he saw me. Hands extended, he came closer, his limp more obvious with his distress.

"Hi," I said as the older man tugged me into a quick hug. "I got here as soon as I could."

"Petra. I'm glad you're here." Ryan's worry eased but didn't leave his face. "Where are Benedict and Marty?"

"Parking the car. Lev told me what happened. How is she?"

Ryan took his gaze from the hint of green eyes peering out from under a cabinet, and I wondered if Pluck and I had lost every shred of trust gained in the last five months.

"We don't know." Ryan gestured for me to take the second chair. "I'm glad you're here."

An icy ribbon snaked around my ankle. *He's said that twice now,* Pluck thought, and I inched closer to the cabinet so the tendril of himself stretched across the floor wasn't as obvious.

"This is an ugly situation," Ryan said. "It seems certain that it was a shadow assault." His gaze went to Lev. "Thoth, probably, but everyone will assume it was Pluck, since it happened outside your apartment. I don't know how I'm going to keep this quiet."

Yeah. I got that, seeing as Cameron had been investigating me when she had been attacked. Damn it all to hell and back. We'd given Dana all the ammunition she needed to force a review of the university's policies regarding dross and shadows. "Marshal Owens is a bull in a china shop," I said regretfully. "Yesterday she stood in the grotto and antagonized a memorial shadow. Some of this might be her fault."

Dana looked up. "Blaming the victim?"

My face warmed as Pluck's anger fizzed through me. "I do if she jumps the fence and waves a red flag in the face of a frustrated shadow." Okay, I was talking big, but the reality was it had undoubtedly been Thoth—looking for me—and a twinge of guilt rose and fell.

"Even so," Dana said. "We can't allow shadows to attack people with no reprisal."

"Yeah? Then perhaps people should stop threatening to burn them alive," I countered. "Why haven't any shadow release valves gone in? It's been months!"

Ryan shifted uneasily. "Can we keep it down, please? This is not the place to be discussing university business."

Expression sour, Dana turned away. My gaze, too, went to Cameron, peaceful on the outside, who knew what on the inside. "Has anyone tried to go in and find her?" I asked. "Pluck tells me Thoth can possess people without breaking their mind. She might be okay."

Dana's shoulders slumped, her thoughts visibly shifting. "The hospital doesn't have an etherologist on staff with enough skills to tell," she admitted, and Lev ran a hand over his chin in agitation. "It's a shadow attack. That she's still breathing is a miracle."

There was blame in her voice, and my spine stiffened.

Ryan pushed forward, his expression pained. "The hospital has a specialist coming in tomorrow. They offered to fly Marshal Owens out to him, but we have control here."

"One more day won't make a difference," Dana said, and I crossed my arms over my middle in a show of disagreement. "No one survives a shadow within one's mind." She glanced up at me. "Except a weaver."

Up until today, I would have agreed with her, but the need to correct her died when I noticed the faint ribbon of black hazing up behind Cameron, settling just under her ear. It was Pluck. He wasn't touching her, but he was so close that the woman's eye twitched and went still.

"Who is to blame doesn't matter to the common mage," Dana said, oblivious to Pluck. "For the first time in thousands of years, we are openly seeing shadows in the streets. Without a functioning vault containing enough dross to be a threat, shadows feel free to attack the very people who have the power to enforce the traditional method of shadow maintenance."

My attention jerked from Pluck's hazy shape. "Maintenance? Call it what it is. Murder."

Dana huffed as she stood. "Ryan, I'm sorry, but I can't do anything here and I need to prepare a report for the board."

One that I was sure wouldn't put shadows in a sympathetic light. Panic gripped me. I wasn't sure if it was mine or Pluck's. Not that it mattered. "Lev saw *a* shadow," I blurted. "Chances are it was Thoth looking for me. Give me the opportunity to catch him before you set the campus on fire."

I think we can reach her, Pluck thought suddenly, the crystalline surety of it ringing through me like a bell.

Wait. What? I thought, almost oblivious to Lev backing me up, his words fast and succinct as he warned Dana what a potential shadow purge could cost the school.

With my skill and your fields to get me past her natural safeguards, I think we can safely reach Cameron.

"That's an etherologist skill. You can do that?" I said aloud.

"Do what?" Ryan looked up from Lev, his eyebrows high in question.

Pluck gained substance until he was again a dog at my heels, his hazy ears pinned to his not-there skull in a show of reluctance.

Maybe? His thoughts were tinged with worry. *Thoth put her into a dream loop. I can't get into her mind without causing damage, but you can. Once in her dream, we could possibly get her out.*

Breathless, I focused on Ryan. His brow was furrowed with impatience; he clearly knew that he wasn't privy to half the conversation. "Can Pluck help?" he demanded.

"She is still in there," I said, knowing what I was asking. "He thinks together we can wake her up."

Dana's attention snapped to me. "From a shadow attack? Everyone knows only a weaver could survive a shadow within their mind."

Lev chuckled as I squared my shoulders. "Pluck is in my mind right now," I said. "He's not damaging me. Thoth put her into a coma. Pluck thinks we can get her out. What is the problem?"

The woman looked at Ryan, clearly surprised when he didn't agree with her. "Ah . . ." she hedged at his sly smirk. "No. A shadow caused the damage. I'm not going to sit here and let another—"

"Pluck says she's stuck in a dream loop," I interrupted. "If we can get her out, she'll wake up and can tell us who attacked her. I'm not going to let an entire demographic of sentient energy become scapegoats because another demographic doesn't want to learn how to handle their own waste!"

"That's not what's going on here." Dana held her clasp purse before her like a fig leaf. "I cannot allow another shadow—"

"Pluck thinks we can get her out," I insisted. "Dana, I want to try."

"You didn't let me finish." The woman glared at me. "I can't go back and write a report saying that I let another shadow touch her, so I'm going to . . . *leave*."

I froze, my next outburst dying amid a cold fizzing. Behind me, Lev snickered.

"Oh," Ryan said, his own distress melting into a confused realization.

"You're coming with me, Ryan," she added, and the older man lurched to his feet. "I don't want you to lose your job because of your weaver's hubris."

"I'm staying," Lev said. "Make sure no one interferes."

"Fine." Dana gestured for Ryan to go out before her. "Grady, your fields are flexible?"

"No one better," Ryan said from the door.

Dana rocked to a halt, concern pinching her eyes. "I hope you're right about this."

I dangled my fingers in Pluck's icy presence, remembering having fought him, the ice cream headaches I used to get. Either he had gotten better, or I had. "We are."

She blinked slowly as if to gather strength. "If anyone asks, I left before you got here. Succeed or fail, this is on you and Pluck."

A dread anticipation bubbled through me, and seeing it, she lifted her chin and pushed Ryan out, her heels clicking smartly. The door slipped silently shut, and I stifled a shiver.

"I'm not sure if she gave you the rope to pull Cameron out or hang yourself." Lev slid sideways to stand next to me. "Can I help?"

No, Pluck thought, his mood both sour and eager.

"Ah, don't let anyone interfere?" I said, and Lev gave me a mock salute.

"The room is yours," he said boldly, but his confidence faded when he glanced at Cameron. "I, ah. I will be in the hall. Yell if you need me."

I waited until I heard the click of the door latching before I turned to Cameron. It was just her, and me, and Pluck, and a stab of worry came out of nowhere, poking holes in my confidence. "Okay, Pluck." I sat down in the chair that Dana had been in, feeling odd as I took Cameron's cold hand in mine. "Light meditation state?"

Ice cramped my ankle, and I shivered as his presence took a stronger hold in my mind. *Light meditation will work. I'll take you in. I've already mapped out as far as I can safely go.*

I closed my eyes, and the bubbling and fizzing that were Pluck's thoughts grew stronger, more real than Cameron's fingertips in mine. The lack of a need to breathe swelled as Pluck's presence in me flip-flopped—and suddenly I was outside my mind looking in instead of inside it looking out.

I was within Pluck's psyche. It could have been frightening—it had been, once—but I quashed the flash of panic, my mind's first response to fight back as I exhaled into the almost subliminal rise and fall of the universe echoing in him. I studied the richer complexity, both familiar and not, with which he saw the world. I tried to make my thoughts small, limited, focused on the corporeal sensations I was still feeling: the chair leg against my ankle, the grip I had on Cameron, a strand of hair tickling my cheek. I was swimming in Pluck's mind, and I could feel his discomfort fizzing against me.

Steady, I thought, but it wasn't me. It was him. *I'm taking you to the barrier of her mind.*

I felt myself take a breath, and on the exhale, everything vanished. The chair leg, the hair tickling my cheek, even the faint hum of machinery I'd never noticed was gone. A gray haze fuzzed through my mind.

And then, like a silver ribbon, came Pluck's thoughts. *This is the wall Thoth put her behind. She's in there. Listen.*

It wasn't hard with my usual sensations quashed down to nothing, and I opened myself to the universe. My feet, I decided, were wet, and from there came the sound of angry water. Someone was coughing, a ragged, dangerous sound, and grit ground between my fingers.

Feel, Pluck fizzed. It wasn't physical sensations he meant but emotion, and I fastened on a thread of despair welling up in me. It was Cameron's fear and frustration. I focused on it, sifting it through my own mind to seek out the source. Nothing.

Cameron? I thought, feeling myself jump when a flash of terror slapped me.

Cameron, wait! I thought as Pluck's fizzing presence latched on to mine and I pushed through the murk to follow Cameron's frustration. The water gurgled and frothed. The grit between my fingers pricked like a thousand knives. From somewhere came the distinctive stink of wet desert. Until, with a ping that reverberated through my entire soul, sound, touch, smell, and emotion swelled until they blended into a new, alien existence.

I was there.

12

MY MIND HICCUPED AND I GASPED, SHOCKED TO HAVE EYES AGAIN. THEY flashed open, closing immediately as I was floundering, submerged in dirty water. The flood filled my ears with a muted rumble as I struggled to the surface. It was a dream. I was in Cameron's mind, and it was a dream.

Nightmare, I amended when I broke the surface, coughing as I treaded water. "Cameron!" I tossed my head to get the hair from my eyes. I could feel my pulse hammer, and somewhere in the distance, my hand gripped Cameron's. But here . . . Here I had to find her.

"Cameron!" I called again, working hard to keep upright amid the frothing current. I tried to imagine a shore, but one never appeared.

"Petra!" someone shouted, and I choked, blinded by water when I turned. Something bumped into me, black, hard, and shiny. I grasped for it, unable to find purchase until a sun-browned hand reached for me. I grabbed it, body shaking as I coughed out water and stardust. Blinded, I flailed, hitting whoever was hauling me out of the torrent and onto the hood of a black SUV.

She's dreaming of a flooded wash . . . frothed faintly through my mind, and then I blinked, shocked not at the sudden appearance of the ragged edges of desert bracketing the floodwater, or the black

SUV that I was now half lying on, but at the green-eyed man staring at me as if he cared if I lived or died.

Brown hair plastered to his head, clothes soaked from the river: I'd never seen him before—but I knew him.

"Pluck?" I whispered, and his lips parted.

Clearly surprised, he looked down at himself. "Well, that's unfortunate," he said, obviously embarrassed as he wiped the grit from his face. But again, I knew the cadence of his words, the slight twang of sour humor. It was Pluck, and I tried to look at him even as I coughed another spate of water from my lungs.

The car slowly spun, carried down the flooded ravine as trash and dead animals banged into it. Finally I managed to stop coughing. "This is Cameron's mind?"

Pluck sniffed, and my mind went back to the feel of his hand in mine, warm and sure as he pulled me from the water. "It is. Her fear has taken the form of a flood wash."

My eyes flicked over him. "And she sees you as a person?"

He stared at nothing, avoiding me. "Ah, no. This isn't coming from her. Or you," he gushed. "I, ah . . ." His gaze flicked to me. "It's, ah, been a while, but . . ."

"Grady!"

I looked down as a muffled thumping sounded on the window, cutting off Pluck's stammering statement. "Cameron?" I blurted, seeing the small woman hammering on the front window for my attention with her fist, water to her armpits. "Cameron! Put the window down. Get out of the car!"

I yelped as the SUV crashed into something submerged and my hands smacked the top of the roof to keep from falling off. Cameron gasped, her face pale as the car made a dramatic bob and swoop and broke free.

I suddenly realized that Pluck had an iron grip on my arm to keep me safe. "This is a trap," he said, expression grim. "It's as real to Cameron as any dream she can't wake from. You must get her to come out of the car. The river is her fear and she is hiding from it, falsely thinking the car is safety, that her coma protects her. If she leaves the car, the barrier Thoth has put around her mind will fragment and she will wake."

I stared up at him, wondering if it was that easy. "You're sure Thoth did this?"

"Very." His gaze was hard on the muddy river. He looked both terrible and wonderful: unkempt, wet, and bedraggled. It was odd not seeing him misty at the edges.

"I'll try," I whispered. "Don't let go of me."

Never, fizzed in my thoughts, so deep I almost imagined it.

Holding tight to his arm, I leaned over the front of the SUV. "Cameron?" I tapped on the glass, and she looked up at me, her fist red and swollen. "Pluck says if you come out of the car you'll wake up. You're in a coma."

"You don't think I know that?" she shouted, angry and afraid.

I edged out even more until Pluck's grip became almost painful. *Don't go misty on me now . . .* "You have to come out," I begged. "Put down the window!"

"I can't!" she said again, and then, in a fit of anger, she pounded on the dash. "I've gotten onto the roof like six times already. Every time I do, that damn shadow shows up and puts me back here!"

Shadow? Thoth is here? I thought, gaze darting to Pluck.

"Thoth is a fiend!" Cameron shouted through the glass. "He wants you dead. I wouldn't let him possess me so he stuck me here. He's going to tear the university apart to bring you down. And when you're gone, Marty is next."

Marty! Breathless, I turned to Pluck, only to have every last thought vanish from my head.

Behind Pluck stood Thoth, an ugly smile on his long, narrow face. "Look out!" I shouted, and Thoth shoved Pluck, sending him off the roof and into the wash.

"Clever," Thoth snarled as he balanced on the car's roof. "I thought it would take at least a day for you to convince your weaver to carry you in."

"Pluck!" He was drifting away, expression grim as he tossed his hair from his eyes and began to swim after us. *Hang on, Cameron,* I thought, then gathered myself to jump in after Pluck—only to find myself yanked to a jaw-snapping halt.

"Let go of me," I threatened, and Thoth's grip tightened. In my mind, something snagged and caught. A bitter cold seeped up, chilling me. He didn't have hold of just my arm in Cameron's dream, he had my mind.

"I came here," Thoth said, expression tight with anger, "thinking the first weaver of the new age had blown a full vault to announce the beginning of our rebirth. Imagine my excitement. Not only a weaver, but a weaver ready to return us to greatness. Who believes as I do."

I tried to pull from him, failing.

"Imagine my disappointment," the shadow continued bitterly, "when I found it was an accident and you would have shadows burn in the hell of your making. Petra, the yeth."

"You need to let go!" I demanded again, but all the tugging in the world would not free me. The dream was a reflection of reality, and in reality, this shadow had me, trapped in not just Cameron's mind but his.

"You put yourself here," he said, and the icy chill in me deepened. "There's no getting out. And now, no reason to keep the marshal alive. This is so much easier than the first time. But then again, Kahu is blinded by hope. He will curse you for giving that to him in the end."

His fingers gripped harder, and I gasped, pain arcing through me as Thoth flooded me with cold, his mind wrapped about mine, crushing it. Groaning, I exhaled, hands shaking as I made a field around my core and stomped on his instep, shoving him away when he howled.

The pain vanished, and I stared at him as the SUV slowly drifted through the rain-soaked desert. I could feel him trying to find a way back into my mind, and I smacked his reaching hand from me. "No," I said, voice trembling but sure, and his eyes narrowed.

"Kahu didn't teach you that," he muttered, mood bad. "Your fields will have to go first."

His hand flashed out, ironlike fingers gripping my wrist. In my mind, I felt his strength swamp mine . . . and pain found me again. Groaning, I fell to a knee before him atop the roof, my arm stretched between us, trying to breathe as his maggoty thoughts bored their way into mine. With a dull crackle, he crushed my wrist, and I howled, trying to see past the pain.

"You use and you take," the shadow said as he pulled me closer, the agony redoubling until I couldn't see, couldn't breathe. "And for that you will die, Kahu's weaver."

In agony, I tried to pry his fingers off me. In my mind, I attempted to make another field to push him out, but something was wrong, and I felt it dissolve into a tangle of threads, falling apart as large holes grew, unstoppable. "Why are you doing this!" I yelled.

"Let her go!" Cameron shouted, hammering on the window, helpless.

And then the grip on my wrist ripped away in a flash of black shadow.

The pain turned to an unbearable throb and I held my arm close and looked up. It was Pluck. He'd pulled Thoth from me and thrown him in the water. Thoth's hold on my mind was gone along with his grip on my wrist, and I felt tears of relief start when Pluck helped me stand. In Cameron's dream, his arm was about my shoulder. In reality, his mind cradled mine.

"Go!" Cameron looked up at us, her expression twisted. "Get out of here! You heard him. As long as you're alive, he won't kill me. Go!"

Pluck stood beside me, hunched in pain. "She's right," he said raggedly, and I followed his gaze to where Thoth broke the surface and began to swim for us, motions holding a murderous intent. "If he reaches the car, I'm done for. He's stronger than me. Surprise gave us a chance to escape, not strength."

I stood within the shadow of Pluck's protection, my broken wrist held close. In reality, my arm was fine, but whatever happened here was a reflection of the truth and I wondered what I'd wake up to. "I can't," I said as I looked down at Cameron.

"You will make it. I will carry you," Pluck said. "Just hold on."

He was inching us toward the edge, and I resisted. "I can't leave Cameron."

"Get out of here!" The marshal hammered on the roof, the vibrations coming through the soles of my feet. "I'm an etherologist. If I can put him to sleep, I can escape."

What if she can't? I thought, and a grimace pinched Pluck's young face. I'd never seen it before, but it held the same annoyance as an ear flick.

"She'll be fine as long as you are alive." Pluck tugged me to the edge of the roof. "He will kill you if you stay," he said, his grip on my shoulder tightening. "But I will die in front of you first. Is that what you want? Hold on to me."

Torn, I hesitated. "Cameron, I won't leave you here," I started, gasping when he slung his arm around my waist and jumped us both into the water.

"Pluck!" I protested as his field wrapped around my mind, mirroring his arm around my waist as he pushed to the distant shore, foggy with an indistinct reality.

I looked back once to the slowly spinning car. Thoth had regained it, standing atop it to yell at Cameron as she watched us swim away, eyes fixed and holding a harsh hope.

"I'm sorry," Pluck said, his rhythmic kicking moving us closer to the shore, but the closer we got, the more indistinct it became. "This is my fault." *I made a mistake.*

My foot touched bottom and the gray of the shore enveloped us. I took a step toward the land, and the sound and stink of dirty water vanished as if a window had closed. The pain in my wrist was gone. I felt myself jerk as reality reset, and my eyes flashed open.

I was in the hospital, my hand lightly in Cameron's. I held my breath as the woman frowned, and then her expression smoothed to a bland nothing. We'd failed.

"Pluck?" I said, surprised my voice was clear, not raspy with floodwater.

Cameron's hand was hot, and I let it go.

She lives, fizzed through me, Pluck's usual clear thoughts somewhat ragged. *Thoth won't hurt her as long as you exist. He knows you will return for her.*

The image of a slim, soaked man flashed through me, and I quashed it before he could see it in my mind. "Damn right," I said, fingering my wrist. It was fine, but something had broken, and I stared at the room, wondering at the glitter of dross skirting the corners like dust in a sunbeam. It hadn't been there before. Lev must have checked on us. Brought it in. "Thoth is a dick."

In a word. Pluck collapsed into a black puddle, not even an eye showing.

"Lev?" I turned as the door swung open, but it was Benedict, his shoulders hunched in worry, eyes holding a heavy concern for me.

"Hey . . ." he said, gaze going to Cameron unmoving and still on the bed. "Lev brought me up-to-date. He took Marty down to the cafeteria. He said you were going to try to bring Cameron out of her coma." His eyes went to the woman, clearly asleep. "I'm sorry."

I stood, my arms going around him in a needed hug. My eyes closed and I lingered despite Pluck's annoyance fizzing lightly through my thoughts, breathing Benedict in and soaking in his belief in me. "It was Thoth," I said, voice muffled by his shirt, and then I pushed back, my grip easing. "We found her, Benny. Thoth did this to her to get to me. I can't believe I left her there, but as long as I'm alive, he won't hurt her any more than he has."

A drift of dross glinted like a sunbeam in his hair, and I let go to reach for it, thinking it looked especially bright.

Benedict's smile was thin but honest. "Then there's hope. Pluck, you okay?"

The black puddle took on the hint of a dog, flicking an ear to send a splat of dark matter to hit the IV stanchion. The knot in my gut eased at the ofttimes-used show of annoyance. "He's okay," I said, remembering the slim man atop the SUV. "I need to talk to Ryan. Cameron is trapped in a dream state, but we saw Thoth, and he admitted to attacking her." I reached to arrange Benedict's hair, running my fingers through it to catch the dross drift before it could break on him. "Not that anyone will believe what I say," I muttered, then yelped, jerking away when the dross haze burned my fingertips like fire. Shocked, I wildly shook my hand to fling it off, staring at my fingers now a bright red. Dross had always burned, but this? This had been like touching fire.

Benedict stared at me. "You okay?"

"Ahhh," I hedged as the dross drifted to the floor, then I jerked at the odd rasp across my senses, jumping clear when Cameron's bed rail crashed into the lowest setting.

"Petra! Oh, my gosh." Worry creased Benedict's brow as he yanked me clear. "Are you okay? It must not have been fastened securely."

Still under the bed, Pluck sank deeper into himself, almost disappearing. "Um, I'm fine," I said, gingerly rubbing my burned fingertips as I eyed the dross eddying about the floor. It was the same drift I'd pulled from Benedict—but there was less of it. Disbelief swirled about my mind as I remembered the odd rasping sensation, like the cogs of the universe catching—balancing its books. My pulse quickened. "I think that dross just broke on me."

"No way!" Benedict exclaimed.

Brow furrowed, I reached for the small wisp, steeling myself against the unusually hot feel. It prickled along my fingers as it usually did . . . and then, when I touched it, it went hot.

Yelping, I jerked clear, my hand whapping against the rolling bedtable and bruising my knuckles. Shocked, I held my wrist tight to my chest, remembering the feel of Thoth breaking it in Cameron's nightmare. Shadow spit, what if . . .

I am sorry, Petra, fizzed through me, and I jumped yet again, startled at the flush of prickly sensation on my ankle. *I never should have suggested we try to free her. It was a trap, and I led you into it.*

"Petra?" Concern pinched Benedict's voice. But I couldn't look from Pluck as I remembered trying to wall Thoth off from my thoughts that second time . . . and failing. He'd done something, broken something. Weavers couldn't be bested by shadow, but he'd done something to me.

"Um . . ." I waved Benedict's concerned hunch away, the beginnings of horror trickling through me. "Give me a sec," I whispered, then exhaled to make a small, tidy field.

My shoulders slumped in relief when I felt it begin to form, but it didn't last, and panic edged in when the entire thing unraveled into a massive tangle of unusable threads. I could hear the weft of it ringing like a giant bell, the soundless boom of the big bang echoing off the edges of the universe—but the weave that came from me didn't follow, and without that, I wasn't making a field. I was making a long, useless, tangled string.

I can't make a field, I thought in panic as my gaze rose to Benedict's. *I can't make a field and dross is breaking on me.*

"Petra?" Benedict took my elbow and bent close. "What is it?"

I licked my lips, my gaze going to Pluck slouched with his ears pinned. "I can't make a field," I whispered.

13

MY STOMACH WAS ONE BIG KNOT AS I SAT ON THE COUCH AT THE RECORDS building, scrolling through my feed with a nervous agitation, waiting for Herm to get back to me. He was the only one who might know how to fix this. It didn't help that Pluck wasn't talking, having taken the unusual stance of holding himself and his thoughts apart from me. I hadn't told Ryan what had happened other than we'd reached Cameron and failed to free her, scared it might be permanent, and a heavy foreboding had settled into my thoughts like a cold rot.

Benedict and I had found the records building empty but for Nog, not unusual after sunset. In the light of knowing Thoth could break a magic user's ability to make a field, I'd told the old sweeper to go home. I hadn't told Nog why. If it got out that shadow could rob a magic user of their abilities, the thin trust that Pluck and I had started would vanish and vanish hard. How far would mages go to protect their supremacy? Maybe that was how the whole thing got started.

In hindsight I should have told Ryan what had happened, but he would have put a halt to my plan to trap Thoth. Word had gone out that the vault here was accepting dross, and for better or worse, good luck or bad, our trap was set. Until we caught Thoth, I wouldn't let anyone else stand between me and the shadow. I was here for the duration.

Frustrated, I tossed the phone onto the low table before me, accidentally knocking the bowl with the two unwrapped moldavite stones we had bought at the rock and gem show. Pluck had tuned them, and the newly priceless stones deserved better than sitting in tomato-stained Tupperware. I'd laced Pluck's new amulet on a thin red strand of knotted silk and draped it around my neck, and the shadow's presence under the couch swirled into a watchful haze at my very thought of it.

But still, he wouldn't talk to me, and my worry deepened.

Mood bad, I lolled my head back along the top of the couch to stare at the ceiling. Marty was upstairs seeing if it was worth the trouble to try to make one of the attic bedrooms usable, but that had been ten minutes ago. I already knew the room was ceiling-to-floor boxes and figured she was talking to Victor.

Lev had volunteered to pick up Herm at the bus station, which left Benedict clattering about in the tiny kitchen. He cooked when he got nervous, and who was I to interfere with a man who knew what to do with rice, beans, and corn? There was no place to sit in the tiny space and he had kicked me out after I had knocked over the knife caddy thanks to my triggering some dross.

Short story shorter, I'd become a walking OSHA violation. Dross had been breaking on me all afternoon, and I slumped deeper into the cushions, fingering the hole in my shirt I'd gotten getting out of Benedict's car. The chipped nail was from ransacking the junk drawer for a safety pin, which I had needed because the zipper on my jeans had gotten stuck. The worst, though, had to be my stubbed toe gained on the raised tile on the walkway. Ow.

And it wasn't as if there was that much dross around to break on me. Yesterday I would have said the front room of the records building was clean, with no hazy drifts or glowing puddles other than Pluck's eyes under the couch. But now?

I scowled at the glittering dust in the corners and clinging to the sticks in the rack by the door. I wasn't touching Pluck, and yet I was seeing tiny amounts of dross with the clarity of full-bore drifts. The dross dust likely stemmed from the vault breach last summer, oozing from the main plume to contaminate everything in a malaise of bad luck like microplastics showing up in fish tissue. The question remained, however—how was I seeing such minuscule amounts, and why was it breaking on me?

Leaning forward, I pulled the two tuned moldavite stones closer, taking the square piece up and holding it to the light to study the tiny bubbles of ancient air trapped within its green imperfections. As before, the ponderous ringing of the universe in my ears grew worse. I'd first noticed it in the car. *No, in Cameron's nightmare,* I decided, wondering if it was the cause or the result of the damage. I thought it interesting that the untuned glass around my neck didn't elicit such a response. Mood sour, I set it back in the bowl, relieved when the magical tinnitus eased.

"Oh, that will work," Benedict said from the kitchen.

"You sure I can't help?" I called, head lifting to look across the hall.

"No!" he blurted, then leaned to see me, a forced smile on him. "I mean, thanks, but no. I want you to rest. It's got to be like a bruise or something. Herm might know for sure. He knows more about weavers than anyone."

Which was odd, seeing as Herm was a Spinner. He'd been best friends with my dad, though, and my dad had been a weaver. Unsure, I shifted to sit sideways with my feet on the couch so I could see a slice of the kitchen. "I shouldn't have left Cameron there." I dangled one foot down in invitation, but Pluck didn't twine a tendril around my ankle, didn't spiral up to sit under my ear like a little snake. My worry deepened.

"Pluck said she'll be okay, and I believe him." His back to me, Benedict put a pan on the stove to flash cook the peppers and onions he had found in the fridge. "Once we have Thoth, Cameron is free to escape. Everything will return to normal. You included."

His voice was cheerful, but we both knew things seldom ever "returned to normal."

Depressed, I ran my hand over the coffee table to wipe off a haze of energy. My palm warmed in warning, and I hesitated, not knowing what to do with the dross dust. I was starting to think it had been here all the time, never noticed until Thoth had damaged me, increasing my sensitivity. Not only did all dross look brighter, but it felt hotter. The night, too, had gone from a fairyland of glow to a firepit of hell, and Pluck wasn't even touching me. If I concentrated, I could actually see the individual dots of micro dross glowing on my fingertips. It clearly wasn't enough to organize into anything destructive, so I held it there, glittering like diamond dust in my palm. Inhaling, I focused on it to try to make a field and snare it.

As before, the background humming in my ears became louder, but the echo of it in my head was gone. It simply wasn't there to weave through the weft of the universe and make a net—and I gave up and let the massive knot of threads that I'd conjured dissolve. *Threads,* I mused as I tried to shake the dross dust off my hand, failing. "Pluck?"

He didn't answer, and I tapped my toe on the floor in invitation, waiting until my ankle grew cold. The humming rise and fall was the reverberation of the big bang, and if I couldn't marshal my thoughts enough to weave a net with it . . . no field. *Pluck? Can you hear the universe all the time? Not just when you do magic?*

Guarded and depressed, his thoughts slipped into mine. *Yes. I can hear creation singing as easy as you can see the sunlight.*

Ice cramped my ankle, and I left my foot where it was. *I can hear it now, too. All the time, not just when I try to make a field. But I've lost the echo I used to hear in my mind. Is it that echo in me that weaves the weft and makes my fields? Holds it all together? I'm only making tangled threads now. See?* Again I concentrated to make a field, but without the echo within myself to bind it into a cohesive form, it tangled into a useless knot.

Pluck didn't answer, but the tendril of his presence unwound from my ankle and he withdrew. "It's not your fault," I whispered, and I sensed him sink deeper under the couch.

Well, this just sucked dishwater; annoyed, I reached for my phone to see if Herm had texted me. The tingling of dross dust on my fingers burst into a sudden heat as it broke—and my phone slipped from my hand, hitting the table with a dull *thwap* on the way to the floor.

Shadow spit and dross, I swore as my groping hand failed to find it. It had gone under the couch, and I rolled to the floor, dropping to my hands and knees to shove my arm under the couch to find it by feel.

"Got it," I muttered, then started at the new, unexpected flash of heat as a patch of hidden dross found me. I jerked, my shoulder hitting the underside of the table to knock it into a mini quake. Moldavite rattled in the bowl, and I flushed as I worked my way out to sit on the edge of the couch. Elbows on my knees, I cradled my head in my hands and sighed. I had no idea there was so much micro dross. I'd never even noticed it before, much less had it break on me.

Pluck oozed out from under the couch, coalescing into a dog as he slunk into the hallway.

"You okay?" Benedict said, and I sighed.

"Fine." I was a friggin' dross magnet. I wouldn't want me in the kitchen, either. How in the shadow-spit hell was I supposed to catch Thoth when I couldn't make a field? I should have told Ryan, even if he would have nixed our little plan to snag him.

Pluck flopped onto the floor in the hall, one eye on me, the other on Benedict as little curls of dark matter drifted from him, evaporating. *I have to fix this,* fizzed through my mind.

Pluck, it's not your fault, I thought, and his attention arrowed to me. *It could have easily been you that Thoth went after.*

But it wasn't, he thought, and then his wolfy head lifted. *You can hear me?*

My lips parted, and I sat up even straighter. *Uh, yeah. You're not touching me.*

Pluck's eyes narrowed, the black flecks in them sparkling. *That's interesting.*

And then he turned to the front door when someone came in, bringing the sounds of the night.

It's Herm . . . echoed through me—both of us.

"Grady?" Lev called, overlapped by Herm's enthusiastic, "How come you only call me when you're in trouble?"

Pulse fast, I stood and dusted my hands on my jeans, quashing the worry that the older man might see me as an invalid. If there was anyone I could be honest with about my condition, it was him. "I'm always in trouble," I said as I crossed the room, eager for a hug.

"More rice," Benedict muttered as he put another pot on the stove.

Herm's eyes lit up as he saw Pluck in the hall. He bobbed his head in greeting, then looked at me, arms spread wide to take me in. After my dad had died, Herm had paid my tuition—a silent, watchful presence as he kept the separatist mages focused on him and oblivious to me. The older man was gruff, surly, and really smart. He'd probably had lots of friends once, but he'd been living off-grid for a long time, pretending to be a weaver so I could grow up safe. I owed him a lot.

"I am so glad you're here," I said, and then his arthritic, knobby hands pulled me close to send the scent of coffee puffing up between us. He looked as if he'd just come in off the desert in his faded jeans, dusty cowboy boots, and wide-brimmed hat. His red shirt was open at the neck to show a patch of sunburned skin, and his tan was deep despite it being November. Kind, wrinkly eyes smiled at me when he pushed back.

"You look good. I hear the new vault cracked," he said, and I shrugged. "They blaming you and Pluck? Typical. How come Ryan hasn't quashed this?"

"Give me a chance to say hi before I ruin your night." I tugged him into a second, quick hug. I'd missed him. I hadn't known how much until this moment. "You heard about Marty?"

"I knew you'd find more weavers," he said, the pride in his gravelly voice obvious. "You and Pluck," he added, and the hazy shadow pricked his ears.

"She's upstairs talking to her past. Come on in. Sit down." I tugged his elbow. "Benedict has kitchen duty. I have no idea what he's making. He won't tell me."

"That's because it doesn't have a name other than dorm-room rice!" Benedict shouted from the kitchen. "It's everything in the fridge plus hot sauce."

"Sounds good." Herm gave my shoulder a comforting pat as Lev collapsed the Ping-Pong table to make more room. "I could do with something I haven't cooked myself," he added, then hesitated. "Ryan mentioned you wanted to use the old vault to lure the shadow in, but how is this going to work?"

Startled, I looked at Lev as Herm settled himself in one of the firmer chairs around the coffee table. "You didn't tell him?"

Lev flopped into a beanbag chair. "I told him about Thoth. The rest is up to you."

Herm's gaze on me sharpened. "It's more than the university blaming you for the damaged vault?"

Yeah, I wouldn't want to tell Herm bad news, either, and I sat down on the couch across from the older man and tucked my feet under me. Herm's expression settled into a hard waiting, and yet his concern only made me feel better. Or maybe it was Pluck's grateful emotions spilling into mine. Herm had been the first person who had treated Pluck with respect, something more than a deadly monster bent on destruction—though shadow could be that, too.

"Ah . . . I was hoping you might have some insight into, um." I looked at Pluck, and the shadow melted into a hazy black puddle, right there in the hall.

"What happened?" Herm lost every ounce of good humor. "Is this about the marshal?" His gaze shot to what was left of Pluck. "Was she asking too many questions? Please tell me it was an accident."

"No," I blurted as Lev shifted, his flash of guilt quickly hidden. "I mean, that wasn't us, but it is kind of our—my fault."

His sun-worn face creased in worry, Herm leaned across the table. "Petra?"

I took a steadying breath. Pluck had eased himself closer, but he didn't look like much more than a snake. "Um, when we learned Cameron was unconscious, Pluck and I went into her mind to try to get her out. Thoth was there, waiting. That's the shadow who destroyed the vault?" I said, and Herm nodded, glancing at Lev. "He followed Marty here."

"And they are not bound?" Herm chewed on his lower lip. "Lev said they are not a pair."

"Pluck says Thoth can't bond with anyone. That he lost the ability," I said, and Herm's brow furrowed. "It was a side effect of learning how to, ah, enter a mind and possess it without leaving them insane. That's how he put the marshal's mind in a loop—sort of a living nightmare," I said, voice soft. "And he did it to lure me in. Ah . . ." My throat turned into a lump. I couldn't say it. "It was a trap," I said instead. "Cameron was the bait. I can't believe I left her there . . ."

I stopped talking before I started to cry. I was a weaver, damn it. Or at least, I had been.

"Shadows can't harm experienced weavers," Herm said. "I don't see the point to luring you into someone else's unconsciousness. What am I not seeing, Petra?"

I steadied myself to tell him, my words faltering when Lev stiffened. Breath held, I followed his gaze to the thumping on the stairs.

It was Marty, obviously, and as Pluck evaporated to ooze up the wall and hang from the ceiling, I wiped my nose and forced myself to smile.

"Hi." Marty scuffed to a halt at the wide archway opening to the hall, eyes red and looking miserable. "I heard voices."

Herm bounded to his feet, grinning from ear to ear. "You must be Marty," he said as he pushed forward, hand extended. "It's really good to meet you."

She took his hand briefly, clearly reluctant to come into the room. "Marty Mayson."

"Herm Ivaros," he said, gesturing for her to come in and sit, but she hung in the archway where she was, neither here nor there but in between. *That's about right . . .*

"Herm knows more about shadows and weavers than probably anyone who isn't one," I said, and she bobbed her head, starting to take an interest.

"Marty, you are so welcome here." Herm dropped back, clearly hoping she'd come in. "I'm sorry you found us under such trying circumstances. I'm starting to think change is a hallmark of a weaver's becoming."

He was smiling. I wasn't.

"I still don't know if I'm staying," Marty blurted, and I stifled a wince. Clearly her conversation hadn't gone well. "Petra said you could teach me how to keep shadow from following me. After that, I'm going home. I don't want to be a weaver."

"Oh." Herm glanced at me. "Ah . . ."

Yeah. That her boyfriend was a mundane had complicated everything. I took a breath, startled when Benedict shouted, "Hey, Marty? I could use your help."

"Sure." Head down, Marty retreated to the kitchen.

"Thank you," I mouthed to Benedict, and he nodded once. Turning away, he began talking loudly to Marty, clearly distracting her.

"You told her I could get rid of shadow?" Herm whispered, and

I hunched in sudden embarrassment. "Even if I could, she can't go home without a shadow to protect her. The separatists know who she is by now."

"You think?" Frustrated, I patted the couch for Pluck, but the shadow remained where he was, hanging from the hallway ceiling where he could see both rooms. "It's gotten complicated, and I had to tell her something to keep her from jumping the first bus out of here. She knows she's a weaver, understands we can help her, but her boyfriend is a mundane and there's no way of hiding that you're bound to a shadow. She's trying to decide between him or us."

The older man glanced at the kitchen, then slumped deeper into the couch. "Shadow spit. I can tell you right now the courts won't give a variance to tell him," he muttered softly. Sighing, he ran a hand over his stubbly salt-and-pepper bristles.

"None of this with Thoth is her fault," I said firmly, voice low and my head down. "She's safe for the moment, but—" My words cut off.

Pluck's guilt was fizzing through me like lava, and I forced my jaw to unclench if only to ease his thoughts. "Thoth thinks that weavers subjugate shadows," I said. "And since he can't harm a skilled one, he's trying to eliminate them lest they enslave his people again. That's why he lured me into Cameron's mind. It made a middle ground where he could damage me. Herm, he broke my ability to make fields." My gut clenched at Herm's sudden horror. "He, ah, knew exactly what he was doing. I'm more or less vulnerable to whatever he wants to dish out."

Over my inert plasma, Pluck thought from the hall ceiling, his anger as cold as winter.

"I haven't told Ryan," I blurted, thinking now that had been a mistake. "He'd have to tell the board. I don't want to start a panic, and if it becomes public knowledge that shadows can break a mage's ability to create fields . . ." I scrubbed a hand over my face. "I'm having a hard enough time already keeping the university from declaring shadows a clear and present threat and wiping them out."

"No-o-o," Herm drawled in disbelief. "You can't make a field? Show me."

Anger flickered. It was misplaced, but if I was angry, I wasn't crying. "Show you what? They don't form." Frustrated, I held the wire-wrapped chunk of moldavite around my neck. It wasn't tuned yet, and it felt almost warm. "I can hear dark matter bouncing off the back of the universe, but the echo of it in my head that I use to weave it all together is gone. No field, no magic."

"You can still fix dross inert," Herm said, and I shook my head. "You don't need a field to . . ." His words trailed off and his shoulders slumped. Eyes pinched, he turned to Lev, and the militiaman winced in confirmation.

I tucked my light green empty amulet behind my shirt. "Not only can't I fix it inert, I've got dross breaking on me. I may as well be a mundane."

That's not true, Pluck thought from the hallway. *Mundanes can't see dross. If you can see dross dust, your vision is as sharp as mine. Mundanes can't hear me, either.*

"I suppose," I said listlessly, and both Lev and Herm frowned.

"You suppose what?" Herm prompted, and I dangled a hand to encourage Pluck to come sit under me. I didn't like him blaming himself.

"Ah, I was talking to Pluck," I said, and the shadow darted under the couch and away from Herm's sudden scrutiny. "We can hear each other regardless of if we're touching or not now. Dross is brighter, too. You wouldn't believe the dross dust hanging about."

Marty came out from the kitchen, a bowl of rice and veggies in her hand. "Seriously?" she said as she went to sit on the hearth.

"Fancy that," Herm mused aloud, his bushy eyebrows high as he leaned to try to see the shadow under me. "So maybe Thoth left you not so much mundane as perhaps . . . shadow? Have you tried to do any magic?"

"You mean with dark matter?" My lips parted, and a spark of something lit both Pluck's and my thoughts. "What part of 'no fields' don't you get?" I said, surprised when Pluck flowed out from under the couch to coalesce into a dog form.

I don't use fields apart from holding a form, the shadow thought. Hope was fizzing through him—even if I didn't believe it. I couldn't do magic without fields.

Benedict came from the kitchen with two bowls. "Lev, you're not my girlfriend nor my girlfriend's mentor," he said as he handed me one and Herm the other. "You can get your own dinner. Bowls are on the counter."

"Fair enough." Lev heaved himself to his feet, struggling to get out of the beanbag chair.

"Thanks, Benny," I said, and he bobbed his head before following Lev into the kitchen. It smelled wonderful, and I began picking through the rice to find the peppers. *Yeah, he's one of the good ones.*

"Oh, this smells great," Herm said as he dug in; then louder, head bowed over his bowl, "Ryan told me you plan on using the old vault to lure him in." He glanced at Marty. "He's got the sweepers keeping an eye out for Thoth on their rounds, but this is far safer. Between you and me, I think the new university contact, ah, Dana, is it? I think Dana is petitioning to go into the memorial and flush out the shadows there in the belief they're working with Thoth."

"They aren't, and she knows it. I'm not sure what her motives are," I said between bites. Oh, God. Benedict had outdone himself in a good way, and it burned like dross going down.

"That's the feeling I'm getting from Ryan, too." Herm bobbed his head in agreement. "Apparently Dana is convinced that even if it's not one of the memorial shadows, the problem itself will move on at a show of force."

Benedict's flavorful rice went flat. Shadows could defend themselves with devastating results. They'd been in hiding for a millennium because they had no reason to fight. I'd given them a reason simply by existing. Mages wouldn't have a chance. Cameron was proof of that. Weavers were the only people who could best them—which in hindsight made it obvious as to why I was Thoth's target.

Lev came from the kitchen with an overflowing bowl. "Catching Thoth will end the problem." He looked at the beanbag chair, then sat beside Marty on the raised hearth. "Even better, once he's caught, we can force him to let Cameron go and tell us what he did to you"—he pointed his fork at me—"so we can reverse it."

Oh, it sounded great, but I knew it wasn't going to be that easy.

"The only problem I can see," Lev said between bites of his food, "is that we have to do it before anyone else can get their claws on said shadow and dump him in a vat of dross."

"Just us five in a race against the entire university's sweepers' guild?" Benedict held his bowl high as he gingerly sat down on the box of empty bottles beside me. "Great."

"We are the ones camped out over the only empty vault in the city." Lev shoveled his food in as if someone might take it. "Priority one," he said around his full mouth. "You want to tap anyone else to help? Ryan maybe?"

I shook my head, even as my guilt twined about Pluck's dark foreboding, knotting my stomach. I didn't want to risk Ryan. I didn't want to risk anyone.

"We should be able to handle it," Herm muttered as he ate. "The vault is safe enough, seeing as it takes a sweeper to open it." He wiped the heat from his lips. "Which brings me to my next question. How come Ryan isn't stuffing it full of dross? It was sound when they emptied it."

"I'm sure Dana wants to." Lips tingling, I looked at the kitchen, wondering if there was any milk in the fridge to tamp the peppers down. "So we are agreed? We keep what Thoth did to me quiet and tell everyone Cameron is okay but too deep to extricate at the moment?"

No one said anything. I took their silence as agreement. I'd tell Ryan the truth when this was over, but until Thoth was not an active threat, I couldn't risk letting the mages know a shadow could destroy their magic. Ryan wasn't a mage, but he answered to the board, and the board members were. Telling him would put him in a hard place I could avoid by keeping my mouth shut.

"I suggest shifts," Lev said. "Two awake at all times. We got Benny, Herm, you, me . . ."

My stomach hurt. Sure, sweepers could catch shadows, but one touch and Thoth might drive them insane or, worse, possess them. Only a weaver had any resistance to him, and we didn't have one.

"I can stand watch," Marty said, and my head snapped up. "I can't catch him, but I can stand watch."

"Marty . . ." Standing watch was about all I could do, too, but I had a shadow to keep me safe.

"I can stand watch," she insisted. "I brought Thoth here. I should help catch him." She took a slow, shaking breath as she looked at Pluck sitting next to me on the couch. "I don't need to know how to do magic to stand watch."

Let her help, Pluck offered, his mood as unsettled as mine. *It will leave her invested.*

He was right, but I didn't like it. "You don't have a shadow. I don't want you in danger."

"I'm already in danger." Her voice was low in guilt. "It's all because of me. The marshal, you, the threat on the vaults."

"It's not your fault," Herm said for both of us. "Marty, your help is very welcome, but if Thoth shows, I want you to stay out of it. You will be with Petra and Pluck."

"Ah, sure." I looked up from my bowl, not really liking the idea. It was safer than, say, hiding her in a motel, but not by much.

"Good!" Herm said cheerfully. "Benedict, Marty, Petra, and Pluck will have the day, when Thoth is less likely to show. Lev and I will take the night shift, seeing as we're used to being up then." His mustache turned in when he chewed on his lower lip. "I'll tell Ryan something. The less he knows, the better."

"Okay . . ." It was reluctant, and Herm beamed at me.

"I suggest you give a shout down the well at the memorial on your way home and tell those shadows what's going on and for them to stay hidden until we catch Thoth." Herm put his attention deep within his bowl, his thinning hair making an obvious ring. "Marty, you should take a chunk of moldavite that Pluck tuned."

"I don't want to be a weaver," Marty blurted, an increasingly familiar heartache furrowing her brow.

There's no dark matter within it to do magic, Pluck fizzed. *It is a useless gesture.*

"Having a stone around your neck doesn't make you a weaver," Herm said, but in truth, she already was one. "And you don't need a shadow to access a stone."

"Ah, it's not like a Spinner stone. Dark matter doesn't just happen," I started, and Herm waved his hand in dismissal.

"So Pluck puts some in there," he coaxed. "She might need it to defend herself."

Benedict's eyes flicked from me to Herm as I frowned at the older man. I knew what he was doing, using magic to lure her into staying. He'd done the same thing to me. I, however, hadn't had a murderous shadow trying to kill me at the time. It had only felt like it. "Pluck?" I said aloud, and the shadow dog pinned his ears.

I can fill the stone's lattice, Pluck fizzed, and my thigh went cold. *But should I? Marty may not be Thoth's weaver, but he can still use her against you.*

True, I thought. *But a little knowledge might save her life. Get her invested?*

I was using his own words against him, and Pluck's concern sank to an almost subliminal fizz, bubbling through my uncertainty like acid. "Pluck says it's a good idea."

It's an idea, he fizzed. *Not a good one.*

"We'll do that, then." Herm grinned, his thick, arthritic fingers fumbling for the two unwrapped tuned stones in the bowl and tossing them at me. They hit my palm with a soft thump, and I shoved them in my pocket to mute the roar of the universe.

"How long does it take to charge?" Marty asked, clearly reluctant.

Depends on how much dross is around, Pluck fizzed sourly.

"Few hours?" I guessed, my gaze going to Herm when he stood, empty rice bowl in hand.

"Ben, thanks for dinner. Lev, you're on KP. I'm going downstairs to look at the vault."

"Me?" Lev's fork scraped as he got the last. "What's wrong with you, old man? You got kitchen-itis?"

"Benedict made dinner, and Petra and Marty need to go home and catch up on their sleep." The old man's smile became fond. "Once I know what state the vault is in, I'll shift Henry's parameters." Herm took Benedict's empty bowl and handed it to Lev. "Senior staff only, if Ryan hasn't done so already."

Herm still has managerial access . . . I thought, surprised. Even when he went into self-imposed exile, they had left him in the system. Curious.

Mood sour, Lev settled the bowl into his own. "Fine." He took Marty's dish and his stack became higher. "Petra, you done?"

I stood to hand him mine, my side becoming cold as Pluck settled himself within the unwrapped stone. "Thanks, Lev."

"You're loving this, aren't you," Lev grumbled as he pushed past Benedict and into the kitchen. "My God!" filtered out. "Did you have to use every pan?"

"Welp, time to go." Benedict cheerfully gestured for Marty to head for the door. She glanced at me, then followed him.

Worried, I lingered when they went out and the sounds of the night slipped in. "Herm, I see what you're doing. I'm not going to trick her into staying. Besides, I'm not a teacher."

"You could be." He pushed me to the door, smiling. "Do what you can. We need her."

"Herm," Lev called loudly. "You want some coffee? Seeing as we are going to be up all night?"

"After that bodacious rice?" The older man blew his breath out in a soft exhalation. "I won't be sleeping for a week. Heartburn."

My long-stick was propped in the corner by the door, and I took it, not sure if it was Pluck's or my concern that was filling my thoughts. "Okay. I get how filling a lodestone with dark matter and teaching her how to use it might convince her to stay, but is it worth the risk?" I said as Lev's complaints and the sound of running water became obvious.

Herm scuffed to a halt. "You think she and that shadow are working together? That she's a spy? That doesn't make sense."

Thoth is chaos. Chaos does not make sense. Chaos makes destruction, fizzed through me.

"No," I blurted, very sure of it. "But Thoth has been ahead of us this entire time. He followed her here. He used Cameron to try to destroy me. Marty can't be the only weaver out there, but he chose to follow her, knowing she would never be a threat. Not because her fields are bad, but because of her boyfriend."

Herm's brow furrowed. He didn't get it, and I inched closer. "Okay, I teach her magic," I whispered. "But her thoughts are still two thousand miles away. Not only is she not paying attention, but I've made her a bigger, more vulnerable target."

The older man glanced out the open door to Benedict and Marty waiting by Benedict's convertible. "All the more reason to teach her what you can," he said. "Petra, if Thoth is using her, give her the tools to fall to a safe place."

Pluck was fizzing, but I could tell from the curious hesitation in his thoughts that the shadow wanted Marty to find her way despite Thoth, and slowly his hope began to overpower my uncertainty.

"Go. Get some sleep. See you in the morning." Herm gave my arm a last pat.

"You'll be okay?" I said as I took a backward step. It was hard to leave him, knowing what Thoth could do. Catching a shadow was hard enough, but one who ignored shadow buttons and wasn't opposed to putting you in a coma?

"With Lev?" Herm grinned. "Sure. Thoth is not even going to show. It's you he wants, not the vault. Breaking the vault is just a means to his end."

Like Cameron, I thought as Pluck shook himself and dark matter went flying.

"Pluck, keep her safe," Herm said as I turned to the car.

Better than you, Spinner, fizzed up through me.

But my good mood vanished, souring step by step as I headed to Benedict's car. Pluck was right. Chaos left destruction, but destruction was often the only way to move forward.

The question was, would it be worth it?

14

THE LONESOME, INSISTENT CALL OF A MOCKINGBIRD WAS A MUCH-APPRECIATED reminder of the desert amid the sound of traffic one street over as I stood on my balcony and breathed in the night. Lightning flickered in the distance, and I could smell the rain coming. Benedict's car was softly ticking below me as it cooled, and the murmur of Benedict's and Marty's voices was a comfortable come-and-go through the open sliding door. It had to be nearly midnight, and still the quad was bouncing light off the low clouds as if there were a game at the stadium.

It was dross I was seeing, not electrical light, and I stood with my elbows on the balcony railing, the beginnings of a headache threatening. Large drifts lit the trees as if it were Christmas, and dross dust sparkled like living pollen blowing in from the desert. I'd always been able to see dross well, but now I realized I'd been half-blind until Thoth had broken me and I could truly see. Pluck lived in a fairyland of burning hell.

It's not that bad. Pluck's thoughts percolated through my mind, hazing my thoughts like a wispy cloud hazes the sun, but I could sense both his wary disgust that mages kept making dross and his appreciation that there was an entire guild devoted to keeping the campus clean. The shadow dog lay curled up in a folding chair, not much more than a pair of eyes and pricked ears keeping me company as I worried about Lev and Herm. They knew the risks, but it felt wrong getting a good night's sleep when they were in potential danger—doing my job. I was the weaver. Bringing in rogue shadow was my responsibility, not theirs, even if I wasn't able to make fields. *How am I going to do that?*

The tickle of a bug traced down my arm, and I pushed from the balcony to brush it away. A heated pain flared at my fingertips, and I jerked, stifling a gasp when I realized it wasn't a bug but dross dust.

Panicking, I stupidly shook my hand to try to get it off, accidentally triggering the latent energy in a flash of heat. The dross broke and my elbow hit the wall—sending a zing of pain all the way up my arm.

"Oh, that stings," I said, and Pluck lifted his head. "I didn't even see it. How do you deal with this all the time? I mean, it's not as if it's a drift that you can avoid. It's everywhere."

I twisted my arm to look at my elbow, a sigh sinking my shoulders when Pluck's cold presence sifted through my uppermost thoughts. *Dross dust is breaking on me all the time,* he admitted. *I let it. Turn the released energy into dark matter and dump it into moldavite.*

"You can handle dross?" I questioned, and he dissolved back into a puddle.

I can handle dross dust. Anything more intense burns. It's akin to trying to funnel a gallon of water through a pinhole. Eventually it will all get through, but in the meantime, you drown. If it's only a trickle to begin with . . .

I licked my lips and glanced behind me into the brightly lit living room where Marty sat with her head over her phone, texting. Behind her, Benedict was in the kitchen again, and I winced when his lodestone flared and the three mugs before him began to steam. Hot tea would be pleasant; dealing with the dross drifting about on the counter would not. *You think I can do it?*

Pluck's hesitation sparked through me. *I've never known the weaver who would have thought to try, but it is breaking on you. Gather some dust. Encourage it to break. As the energy peaks, put your thoughts into the tuned glass you want to give to Marty. Either the energy will fill it via your mind, or it will break on you and the balcony will collapse.*

He wasn't serious about the balcony breaking, and encouraging dross to break on me wasn't a problem. I felt in my pocket for the square chunk of moldavite Marty had been drawn to. Gripping it in one hand, I exhaled to find a light, meditative state. I ran my other hand across the wall, not surprised when the dross dust clinging to it redoubled its glow like a phosphorescent alga.

Too much! Pluck protested, and I froze, quite sure I didn't want to try to shake it off again. A warm haze had begun to itch my palm, and I held my breath as the heat soaked in, becoming painful. *Put your thoughts into the stone. The dross is breaking, but we can minimize the damage. Petra, do something!*

I was afraid to breathe, tense as the heat on my palm began to prickle-burn. Put my thoughts into the stone? I could do that, and I dropped my awareness into the moldavite with a sighed *"Ommm."*

The ordered, icy lattice of the moldavite blossomed in my mind, dark, scintillating, ever reaching but finite. I felt myself shiver as the tantalizing thread of energy trickled through my brain and the lattice began to glow, electrons jumping to new shells as the energy filled it. Pluck's shock and satisfaction blossomed, buoying me up . . . until I realized he was right. There was too much. It was coming too fast.

And just like that, my calm vanished and the flow of energy pinched off. Before I could even think it had been a mistake, the tiny dust of energy rebelled, exploding in a flash of heat.

I gasped, my eyes snapping open as fire pulsed deep in my hand. I jerked, one hand reaching out to grab the railing to keep myself from going down, the other holding the moldavite crystal to my chest. A haze of dross drifted down like a water balloon in slow motion until it hit the weedy sidewalk and shattered into uncountable tiny drifts, only to re-form like a bead of mercury to make a drop of sun in the gutter. I might not have turned it all to dark matter, but I *had* condensed the dust into a drift that a sweeper could see and manage. The stone itself had become surprisingly dark. I didn't think I'd put that much into it. Giving it to Marty seemed harder now.

Leaning over the railing, I stared at the dross. "Pluck, I think I almost had it."

You do have it, resonated cleanly through my mind, his pride and wonder twining through my own. *It's a good thing you're not a shadow, or that drift would have damaged you severely instead of leaving a mild sensory burn. Next time, don't take so much.* His head coalesced and lifted, green eyes glittering in an almost dragon-like head. *You should go in. You're vulnerable out here.*

I'm not vulnerable, I thought, even as I stifled the horrible memory of my field unraveling and never taking form again. Okay, I couldn't do weaver magic, and I couldn't touch dross or fix it inert. But I could still manipulate dross with a stick and had just put enough energy into a moldavite stone to leave it almost black. *Energy that I can't use without a field.* But Marty could.

"Petra?" Benedict's call drifted out. "Tea's ready!"

Pluck's good mood tarnished. I went in, dropping the stone into a pocket and leaving the slider open a crack so I wouldn't lose the sound of the mockingbird. Marty was sitting by the unlit fireplace. Her feet were tucked under her and she looked pensive. Or worried. Or maybe tired. It was hard to know with her.

You need to give her that stone, Pluck thought dryly as he walked through my leg, turning it cold before trotting into the kitchen to flop on the floor in front of the fridge. The fan from it kept the floor dross-free, and he looked so much like his namesake that it hurt.

She can have it, I thought, smiling at Benedict as he threw the tea bag wrappers away. Dross clung to the flat of his arm, sparkling as if ready to break. Pluck huffed a warning when it pulled free and drifted down, one side of the shadow dog slowly dissolving to re-form on his other side, effectively giving the dross more space.

More dross glittered brightly on the counter, and Pluck's disdain merged with my fond acceptance when Benedict studiously wanded the area, utterly missing it. The better you were as a mage, the less likely you were good at seeing dross, and Benedict was one hell of a mage. I didn't see what was wrong with using the teapot, but maybe he was making dross as a Thoth deterrent. The shadow was understandably afraid of it, seeing as he didn't have a weaver to protect him if he ever stumbled into it.

And now, neither did Pluck.

Pleased, Benedict flicked his clean wand at the small tripod trap he'd set up on the counter. Anyone not in the know would think the slim wand he was returning to the cup of utensils on the counter was a pencil, and in fact, the best wands did have a sliver of graphite at the tip. But expensive wand or not, the dross was now on his elbow, not in the trap, and I sidled into the kitchen wondering if I could get the dross drift without him knowing—or it burning me.

"Thanks for the tea." I needed that wand to have any chance of getting that dross drift, but Benedict tugged me into him, his body shifting as he sighed, his breath moving my hair.

"You mind if I shut the slider? Thoth could just . . . come in. He wants you, not the vault."

Head tilted, I looked up at him, feeling cared for, feeling loved. My arms were around him, and grinning, I stood on my tiptoes, tugging him closer to whisper in his ear, "Pluck was with me. Why are you making dross in my nice, clean kitchen?"

"Because you don't have a microwave and I couldn't find a teapot," he whispered back, voice husky and low. "The sliding door—"

"Is fine." His earlobe was right there, and I took it between my teeth, feeling him start as I gently bit down, my reaching hand plucking the wand free of the utensil cup and spinning the dross from his elbow onto it. "I don't have a microwave because dross loves breaking in it." I pulled away, my teeth scraping his earlobe in a promise I was more than willing to fulfill—if we ever had a night free. "And the teapot is in the cupboard over the fridge."

Eyes coy, I slipped from his arms, the wand with the offending dross hidden behind my back. "Points for finding the herbal tea behind the oatmeal, though," I said as I flicked the dross to the trap, where it merged with a drift already in there.

Nice, Pluck fizzed as he trotted out of the kitchen—and relief brought my shoulders down. I wasn't helpless.

Oblivious to it all, Benedict leaned over the mugs and breathed in the steam. "I added some nutmeg. Hardly a pinch. Too much, and it overpowers everything else. Otherwise, it's just sticks and twigs."

Sidling close, I gave him a kiss. "You are the best, you know that? Thanks for staying with me tonight. I feel safer with an extra pair of eyes."

He bobbed his head, and feeling good, I took two steaming mugs in hand: one for me, one for Marty. The woman was studiously ignoring us as she flipped through a copy of the university's directory. It was a good sign despite the pinch of heartache in her eyes. Giving her the stone and telling her what to do with it seemed appropriate.

"I'd be nowhere else." Benedict took the last mug for himself. "With Thoth at large, I don't want you or Marty alone."

"She's in a hard spot," I whispered, still in the kitchen. "And I'm not talking about Thoth."

Show her what she gains by staying, Pluck fizzed from under the couch.

Benedict leaned his head toward mine, his gaze on her as she studied the class listings. "Is there something in that stone?"

"Yes, but I don't like that it feels like we're trying to trick her into staying."

It worked with you. The shadow dog sneezed, dark matter exploding out from under the couch.

Yes, well, I had a chip on my shoulder the size of a T. rex, I thought, giving Benedict a worried smile before going to set the two mugs on the low coffee table and sit on the couch kitty-corner to her. Giving her a stone might make her a target, but not doing so could be an even bigger mistake.

A wispy, whiplike tail stuck out from under the couch as the rest of Pluck remained in hiding. *I say teach her. It would have been easier to tame you if someone had given you guidance other than a Spinner working off hearsay,* he thought, the ache rising to fill my mind with an old regret. *Instruct her on how to use the stone. If Thoth kills her, we will avenge her memory.*

It wasn't the ringing endorsement I had hoped for, and I eased deeper into the cushions as Benedict plopped down next to me. It would take more than chamomile tea to lure me into sleep when Lev and Herm were across town waiting for Thoth, and since giving the young woman some way to protect herself was high on my list, I finally fumbled in my pocket for the dark piece of moldavite.

The tinnitus-like, rolling roar of the universe waxed painfully loud when my fingertips touched it, mercifully fading when I set it next to her mug. "You want to learn how to use it?"

"Now?" Her gaze fixed on the black rock with a familiar intensity. It was her future . . . if she wanted it.

Pluck hazed out from under the couch, puddling at my feet into his dog image, ears pricked, eyes level with my knees as he stared at her.

"If you're going to stand watch tomorrow, you need to know how to use dark matter." I took a sip of tea, trying to look sage-like and smart but not sure how it was coming off. I was only a few years older than her and all I had was a raggedy shadow dog beside me. "Don't mind Pluck. He's been waiting five centuries for this."

To destroy Thoth? A lot longer than that, fizzed through me, and I squelched it.

"I told you I'm not staying." Marty looked at the stone, clearly reluctant to take it. "You're trying to trick me into bonding with it."

That she didn't know that weavers didn't bond to an amulet like mages and Spinners somehow gave me confidence. Smiling, I nudged the stone closer to her. "You don't bond to moldavite. You just use it. It's nothing like a Spinner's stone or a mage's. I can use yours. You can use mine. But seeing as mages can make any scrap of glass into a lodestone, I guess it evens out."

Benedict chuckled, already knowing how this was going to end as he settled himself at the far end of the couch. The first time I had *intentionally* used dark matter from a stone, I had superheated a bottled water, exploding the cap clear off.

Brow furrowed, Marty reached for the stone, her fingers curling reluctantly around it. "Okay, but this changes nothing," she said as she took it in hand. "Soon as Thoth is taken care of, I'm leaving. You can have your stupid moldavite back. I won't need it."

Yeah. That was what she said, but her fingers were almost white-knuckled as she gripped it and her expression had gone blank. She was feeling energy in it. I'd bet my life that she'd never held a tuned stone before.

"Fine, but you need it now." I glanced at Benedict, not appreciating his grin. "Sorry about Herm. He thinks showing you how to use it will trick you into staying. That's how he tricked me into accepting that Pluck wasn't a savage, unthinking monster until I calmed my shit down long enough to see it for myself."

Thanks, fizzed sourly through my mind, and I dabbled my fingers in Pluck's chill.

"But that's not why I want you to know how to use it," I continued, and her chin lifted.

"And why do you want to show me?" she asked belligerently.

"Because if you are brave enough to help us with Thoth, you should be given the tools to survive him. What you can do with that stone might be the difference between all of us walking away from Thoth and not."

Benedict flicked his attention up from his phone, shifting in unease.

"But mostly because if you want to leave St. Unoc when this is over, you should have a fighting chance against the separatists."

Marty looked at the muddy-green stone, eyes down, head bowed. "I can hear the ocean when I hold it," she said. "In my head."

A faint smile quirked my lips. "That's the remnants of the big bang pushing on the back of the universe, like ripples on a four-dimensional beach," I said, and Pluck huffed, collapsing into a curled puddle at my side with only his nose and ears retaining any solidity. "The dark matter in the stone amplifies it. The more dark matter, the louder it is. You should hear a second one when you make a field, a little offset from the first."

Her head snapped up, eyes wide. "It's faster. Annoyingly out of sync."

"That's it," I said with a forced cheerfulness. I couldn't hear it anymore, and its lack was like the loss of a finger. "That's the echo of the energy in you. It's offset, bent like light bends when it goes through water. To use the dark matter in the stone, you have to bring the two sounds into alignment."

Her gaze flicked from the stone to me to Benedict. Pluck, too, was watching, nothing more than a dark haze with eyes. His thoughts, though, were whirling. "How?" she asked.

It hurt, watching her grow into something I'd lost, but if she did this, she'd be safer.

"Wait. Give me a second." Benedict heaved himself to his feet, dropping his phone on the table before going into the kitchen and filling a plastic cup with water. Pluck firmed up into his dog form when Benedict set it before Marty, his eager grin wide and honest. "Try that."

Better than warming already hot tea, Pluck fizzed, and I absently nodded.

"Put a field around it," I said, and Benedict retreated. "As if it's a dross drift."

Marty's expression fell. "You saw my fields."

"Your fields are fine," I assured her, stifling a grimace when Pluck's comment of *Barely adequate* drifted through me. "Hold your field around it as you bring the two chimes into one sound. You can modify the smaller one, and when they are in sync, you can use the dark matter in the stone like a mage uses light waves and a Spinner uses particles."

"Two chimes . . ." Marty cradled the lodestone in her hand and stared at the plastic cup.

An ache filled me. If I couldn't fix this, I'd never . . . *Oh, shadow spit. What about Pluck?*

I'm well, he fizzed. *Tell her what to do before she blows herself up.*

"Um, if you make the molecules in the water move faster, everything heats up. Slow them down, and it freezes. But don't use a lot of energy, otherwise you might boil it away."

You're good at this teaching, Pluck encouraged.

Well, you know what they say, I thought, and his tail flicked me, the cold stinging as it went right through my leg.

Oblivious to us, Marty exhaled as she concentrated on the moisture-beaded cup. A patchy field formed about it, and with a new wisdom born in seeing mine unable to take shape, I could sense the weft made by the very chime of the universe's beginning and the weave coming from Marty. *That,* I reaffirmed, *is what's missing from my fields.* The weave. I could still hear the universe. I just couldn't hear the echo of it in myself, and without that . . . no field.

"Good?" Tense, Marty waited for me. "Before I do anything, is my field okay?"

Petra . . . Pluck prompted, and I shoved my worries aside to deal with later.

"Your field is fine," I said, and she exhaled in a heady relief. "Give it a go."

Again Marty stared at the plastic cup. Pluck pressed closer, my leg going numb with prickles. *She's got it!* he crowed, and with a crack, the cup broke.

"It's okay!" I exclaimed as the thick plastic split in two and a cylinder of ice hit the table with a thunk. "Let go of the field!" I added when a skin of frozen condensation spread across the dark wood and inched down the legs. "Allow your attention to ease and bring your thoughts out of the stone."

"I broke it!" Marty sat before me, clearly distressed, and I leaned across the table to take her hand—the one with the lodestone—and force her to look at me.

"You did good," I said as the woman jumped at Benedict's whoop, her breath catching as she stared at the table.

"But I broke it."

She'd chosen to slow the molecules down. Much better than sending hot water everywhere, and I silently thanked her for her foresight. Beaming, I stood, giving her shoulder a thump of success before I gathered the broken plastic and ice. It was cold in my hands, but nothing compared to Pluck, and I took everything to the kitchen and set it in the sink to thaw.

"Marty, that's the coolest thing I've seen since Petra took out a drone," Benedict said, and the woman flushed. "All you need now is a shadow to take up residence in it to keep the levels of dark matter high."

Her confidence vanished. Her eyes shot to Pluck sitting on the couch, his ears flat against his skull as if he was displeased. I could have smacked Benedict.

"Or not," Benedict added, clearly feeling my glare. "It's just cool you can do magic."

I was happy for her, but my own loss was almost too much to bear, and I took Pluck's new, as-yet-untuned stone in hand. The rise-and-fall roar of the universe was loud, and I studied it, wincing when my head began to throb. And yet I inched my awareness deeper into the stone, searching for a twin echo as I tried to bring a field into existence . . .

Only to get that tangled knot of threads. I let them dissolve, disappointed as I went back into the living room.

Pluck lifted his head, little drifts of dark matter curling from him in interest. *We will find a way,* fizzed through me as I sat down, but I didn't see how. Annoyed, disappointed, and not wanting to hear the universe anymore, I took his amulet from my neck and put it on the coffee table.

"Well, um, it's going to be an early day tomorrow." Marty stood, hesitating a moment before stuffing her new lodestone into a pocket and picking up her mug. "Thanks for the tea." She edged past the couch, her expression sympathetic. "I'm sorry about what Thoth did to you."

It was a soft whisper, and I forced myself to smile. "It wasn't your fault," I said, quashing Pluck's faint insistence twining through me that it was his. "Don't stay up too late. If Herm calls, we are out of here."

She bobbed her head, giving Benedict a little wave before going to my spare room and shutting the door. A roll of thunder echoed off the nearby mountains and the blinds shifted in a freshening wind, but still no rain.

"Herm will be pleased," Benedict said softly. "You did good there, Petra."

The bright red, knotted silk tie of Pluck's new lodestone looked garishly optimistic arrayed on the coffee table. I should have chosen something darker. Shoulders slumped, I stood, taking the amulet in hand as I went to sit with him on the couch.

He sighed, shifting to put his arm behind my shoulder and tug me close. "You okay?" he asked, and I nodded. Pluck had vanished, but I could sense him under the couch, his thoughts twining in mine a mix of concern, support, and hidden worry as I ran the tie through my fingers, enjoying the silken coolness of the fine cord.

Tomorrow was going to be rough, especially if I told Ryan what had happened. He needed to know, if not for his insight into perhaps finding a way around the damage, then to work to keep both sweeper and mage from coming in close enough contact with Thoth to become like me.

But that decision was for tomorrow, and I set the moldavite on the arm of the couch and let my head fall against Benedict as my eyes closed . . . just for a moment. Cold cramped my ankle, then vanished, and I opened my eyes to see Pluck sitting beside the screened slider watching the rain like a giant cat—dog—thing.

Benedict was warm and comforting, and I could hear his heartbeat as I leaned against him. The click of the light going off in the spare room was obvious, and I snuggled deeper, trying to relax as his pulse slowed and his breathing became even. He was falling asleep.

I, however, was only becoming more awake. *What if there is no fix?* I mused, and Pluck's scintillating tip of a tail twitched at the slider. Guilt prickled along my thoughts—not mine, but Pluck's—and I wished I'd never thought it. *Pluck, I am alive. You are alive. If I had the chance again, I'd probably do the exact same thing. I for one am glad we can talk now without contact. Have there been weaver/shadow pairs in the past that could do that?*

No. The vaporous dog's definition blurred as he came closer until he puddled to nothing under the table. *We have always needed direct contact to converse.*

Then we are the first, I thought, remembering his pride that I could turn dross dust into energy. *Perhaps it means something.*

I quite like being able to feel you in my mind so clearly, Pluck fizzed. *I've not had to modify my thoughts so as to not hurt you since Thoth—*

His words vanished in a wave of remorse. Understanding, I put one of my hands out, palm up in invitation. "I didn't realize you needed to do that," I whispered, and Benedict frowned in his sleep.

It's not a tedious task, he thought. Again the thunder rolled, and the wind pushed the scent of rain into the room. The mockingbird had gone silent, hiding from the coming rain. Nothing more than a hazy drift, Pluck flowed up the arm of the couch and settled a glinting tendril about the last untuned piece of moldavite.

"Perhaps . . ." I whispered, and Benedict snorted as he resettled himself. Pluck was trying to tell me there might be something good here, but I still felt like crap. That is, until I realized the airy feeling that was suffusing me was him calmly reorganizing the molecular structure of the moldavite. He was tuning it. The feeling was almost a high, and I exhaled, letting the three-dimensional perfection chime through me.

Cheese and crackers, Pluck, I thought, and a flash of amusement from him lifted lightly through me. *Why did you wait to tune it? That feels amazing.*

You think that is amazing? Wait a moment.

For what? I thought, confused, and then I exhaled as Pluck's presence seemed to expand, pulling me deeper into his psyche. A bewildering twin vision hit me when he went wispy and thin, moving like an octopus through the crack in the door and out onto the balcony.

He was outside, and my eyes closed at the sudden sensation of warmth suffusing us both. The world was a dangerous fairyland of dark and light through his senses, and yet I relaxed against Benedict as Pluck wound his way to the roof, a sensation of anticipation and eagerness to show me something moving cleanly from him to me as he thinned himself to almost nothing.

With an effervescent hiss, an unexpected warmth dropped through him, tasting of lightning and ozone. Another followed, and then a third, until it was a veritable shower, the exhilarating sensation breath catching and pure.

Is that rain? I thought, and Pluck fizzed an affirmation, his own pleasure twining about my own. It wasn't a carnal sensation. It was something more, something deeper, something he'd never had the chance to share with anyone, not even his weavers of the past, and I drank it in as the feeling drummed into a mellow, hazy warmth of connection.

My worry melted away, and finally I could relax as I sat in Benedict's arms, my soul on the roof with Pluck, slowly falling asleep and wondering if a weaver was still a weaver if all of what made her one was gone.

15

THE NARROW STREET WAS BUMPY, AND I HELD ON TO THE OPEN WINDOW OF Benedict's sports car to even out the jolts. We were taking the back roads to the records building to avoid the busier, commute-jammed roads. The memory of the rain falling through Pluck drifted peacefully in my mind, easing my tension and coloring my mood—reminding me that there was good here. And yet . . .

"This would be faster on my bike," I muttered, and Pluck, currently a thin black snake wrapped around my wrist, fizzed a cold agreement. He was avoiding his new amulet despite the sun as he couldn't sense Thoth as quickly while within it. I thought we were safe enough in the daylight, but there was no reasoning with the shadow.

Benedict chuckled, his eyes firmly on the road. "You've seen me on a bike."

"Yeah, maybe you're right." I smiled, then slowly pulled my hand from the glare hitting my knuckles. The come-and-go flickering through the low buildings made an irritating warmth. *Shadow spit. Am I becoming a vampire?* I mused darkly, and Pluck fizzed, his thoughts mostly hidden. The sun seemed unusually hot. It wasn't bothering Benedict or Marty, the woman silent and pensive in the back, and I flipped the visor down to get the ball cap I'd left there.

Benedict turned onto a wide thoroughfare, and the light shifted to right in my face. Grimacing, I tugged the cap lower. The records building was just ahead, a black panel van with the sweeper logo on it taking up two of the three parking spaces. The side door was open and boxes filled it, spilling out onto the lot. There was more activity than I was comfortable with, and I twisted in my seat to reach my phone to see if Herm had sent me an update. He would have called if they'd caught Thoth, wouldn't he?

Thoth hasn't been here, fizzed as Pluck wrapped tighter around my wrist. *There are no ambulances.*

Right, I thought, mood darkening when I read Herm's text: **Went to check on the marshal. Ryan and Dana are watching the vault. Your call.**

I closed the phone down. My call. My call to tell him Thoth had the ability to destroy not just a weaver's ability to do magic but anyone who used a field—or keep my mouth shut and risk that Thoth might damage someone else.

"Lev and Herm went to check on Cameron," I said. Guilt rose and fell. How could I have just left her there? "Ryan and Dana are watching the vault."

Benedict jerked in surprise. "Is that a good idea?" Slowing, he flicked on the turn signal.

"No, but it does account for the increased activity," I said, not wanting to scare Marty.

"Are you going to tell them about . . ." He left his sentence unfinished, and I shrugged.

"I haven't decided yet. He's got plausible deniability right now."

Thoth is only interested in you, Pluck fizzed, but it didn't make me feel any better. *His goal isn't to destroy shadows or vaults, only weavers. He knows what will happen if it gets out, seeing as he was the one who orchestrated it before.*

Benedict's grip on the wheel tightened briefly before he put the car into park. "I say we keep Ryan in the dark until we get control of Thoth."

I nodded, uneasy as I reached for my door and got out. Marty practically bolted out after me, and I waited in the shade for Benedict, breathing in the cool, damp air smelling of desert. The universe was a constant thrum behind the noise of traffic, and eyes closing, I fingered Pluck's new amulet around my neck. The shadow had turned dross dust to energy all night, and it was almost black.

"Wow," Benedict said, and my eyes opened to see him staring at the building. "Look at that. No wonder Ryan and Dana came in."

My gaze followed his to the glowing bottles stacked up along the low wall outlining the property, the latent energy glinting brighter than the sun, burning. "It's better than it sitting in the gutter," I said, stifling a shiver as I headed for the door.

Marty followed, eyeing the bottles with a wary caution. Her hand was in her pocket, and I would sell my panties online if she wasn't holding her lodestone to find a sense of relief.

Head down, I continued up the narrow cobbled walkway and the front steps. I thumped my stick before me as I walked, first before my right foot, then my left as if I were blind, surreptitiously collecting any dross drifts that might have been drawn to the growing mass of glowing bottles. There was enough here to create a pull nearly a block wide, and I wondered if Ryan had considered that before inviting everyone to leave their dross.

The building's shade felt good, and my mood brightened when the door opened and Nog came out. "Here to help?" the somewhat raggedy man called out, a welcoming grin on his face. "We could use it."

"Old habits die hard." I fist-bumped his weather-beaten knuckles. Worry for the sweeper drifted through me, and I hoped Pluck was right that Thoth would see no threat in the older man.

"Ryan is in the front room." Nog glanced behind him to the low two-story building, then hesitated as he studied me. "Did you get a haircut?"

I touched my hair, bemused as Benedict and Marty waited at the open front door. Everyone seemed to be seeing me differently lately. "No."

The sweeper bobbed his head and eyed me. "Maybe it's that red lodestone cord. No dross in those knots, eh?"

"Not anymore," I said as we parted ways, and Pluck fizzed and bubbled, his thoughts carefully hidden. I wasn't sure what had sparked Nog's question. Sure, the lodestone cord was new. And yeah, it was kind of bright for my tastes. I had been wearing black a lot lately, but it felt more than that.

Benedict's brow was furrowed when I caught up to him, and he gestured for me to go first. "We're agreed? Don't tell anyone about me not being able to make a field," I whispered, and he sighed as he pushed the door open.

"Hey, hi!" I called out as we went in. The row of hooks in the hall was empty, but the stick trios and their associated knotted dross cords filled the racks taking up one entire wall in the old living room like katanas at a dojo. I propped my stick against the wall beside them, my fingers reluctantly leaving the reddish wood. My dad had made a set of five. I had one, Ryan had three, and the last was missing.

As promised, Ryan and Dana were in the front room, the low table between them covered with dross bottles. Spiky inert-dross nuggets filled a box at Ryan's feet, and even as I watched, he taped it up and set it on a stack by the archway. Clearly they'd been fixing dross into inert nuggets for a while.

"Herm told me you were here. I didn't know you were going to take a shift. Quiet night?" I asked when Ryan looked up, the tired man clearly glad to see me as he nodded. "For us, too."

Guilt twined with the urge to tell Ryan what Thoth had done, but it vanished when Benedict whistled long and low and I followed his gaze into the kitchen. Full dross bottles were stacked on every available surface, glowing to make it look as if the sun were setting between the fridge and the stove. Pluck darted for the safety of the overhead light, the shadow nothing but a hazy blur.

"*That's* what came in *last night*?" Benedict said, and Ryan straightened where he sat, his back audibly cracking. "Thoth won't show with this much dross here."

"None of it is going downstairs." Ryan folded a box closed and set it beside the low table. "Nog is moving it out nearly as fast as it's coming in, but we haven't seen the top of the bell curve yet."

"Benedict. Great." Dana tucked a strand of limp hair behind her ear and blew her breath out in fatigue. "Let me show you what I've been doing. You aren't going to sit and play with your phone while you're watching the vault."

Benedict's eyes widened. "Ah . . ." he stammered, and Dana patted the couch beside her.

"Benedict didn't come here to turn dross inert," Ryan said. "It's not his job."

"It's not my job, either," the woman complained.

Ryan chuckled, his tired expression scrunching into a smile. "True, but now that you know how tedious and skill-worthy it is, maybe you'll attach appropriate compensation to the job."

"He invented it," she said indignantly. "I want to see if he can do it better than me."

I knew for a fact Benedict could. There was one heck of a big nugget under the auditorium that said so, and my fingers touched his in a silent thank-you. He had saved Pluck's life, and by doing so, mine as well.

"Ryan, it's fine." Giving my fingers a squeeze, Benedict edged between the rows of bottles to reach the couch, leaving Marty and me in the hall and out of the way and out of the mess.

Ryan stood and stretched, ending the motion by scrubbing a hand over his morning bristles. They were more white than black, making him look even more tired. "I could use some good news. And a coffee."

"Breakfast is on me." Dana edged into the hall, clearly eager to leave.

I supposed I could pack up the spiky dross nuggets, and I edged out of the way, waiting for them to clear out so I could get in there. Marty, too, seemed to be waiting, and she turned from the dross-go board she'd been studying. "I froze a glass of water last night," she said shyly, her fingers touching her pocket as if she needed to confirm she'd done it with magic, not simply put it in the freezer. "Ah, I used my own amulet. You can have yours back."

"Marty! Congratulations!" Beaming, Ryan shifted his path, his relief almost palpable when he took his Spinner stone as she extended it, and looped it over his head. "That is fabulous." His brow furrowed. "Even if you decide not to stay with us, that new stone of yours belongs to you," he added, but I could tell he was truly happy for her.

Oh, yeah, I thought as my fingers found that third chunk of tuned moldavite, safe within my pocket. "Hey, ah, Ryan?" I said, quashing a feeling of possession as I gave it to Ryan. "We picked up a piece to replace the one that Fawn broke. Pluck tuned it. It's ready to go."

Ryan beamed, jostling Dana's elbow to make sure she saw. "Thank you! Pluck, this is wonderful. It's like Christmas today."

Maybe, but seeing as we were kind of responsible for the first one breaking, it felt like a wash.

Benedict dropped a spiky nugget into the empty cardboard box with a rasping clatter. "*All* this came in since last night?" he said again in disbelief.

Dana shrugged into a classy lightweight jacket. "Brought mostly by student mages. Dropping off bottles and driving away as if they were abandoning the Antichrist herself." She put the back of her hand to her mouth as she yawned, her eyes going to Nog when the large man came in to get more sealed boxes. "I've had to recharge my lodestone at least five times. Ryan, I concede. This is madder than a box of squirrels. Having one person do this is too much. It should be made inert at the site of pickup. Spread the pain around."

Nog chuckled, and the elegant woman slumped in fatigue scowled at him. "Absolutely, Dana." Ryan winked at me, clearly pleased. "Give me a list of about a dozen candidates. I'll pair them up with my thickest-skinned sweepers."

"You'll have it by the end of breakfast." Dana's brow furrowed as she watched Marty. The woman was fingering the colorful dross-go wands, weaving one as if to test its balance with more dexterity than her subpar fields would have suggested. "How about Petra and Marty?" Dana added as she tucked her clutch purse under her arm. "It will go down a lot easier if I can pair at least two of my rising seniors with the university's newest toy."

Seriously? I thought as Benedict sort of froze. *Did you just equate Marty and me to toys?*

Nog's pace to the door with another load of boxes faltered. Ears red, he hustled out.

Flushing, Dana met my eyes over her compact. "That's not what I meant to say."

It's what she meant, though, came Pluck's dry thought from the ceiling.

Ryan frowned at the flustered woman. "Marty isn't sure she's staying," he said, clearly insulted for all of us. "And remarks like that don't help."

Dana looked from my sour, high-eyebrow nonchalance to Marty's faint flush. "I am so sorry," the mage said, seeming sincere. "Neither of you are a commodity. God, I can't believe I said that. Petra, Marty . . ."

"Don't worry about it," I said flatly. "I've heard worse in the commons."

Ryan pointedly cleared his throat. "Dana, how about that breakfast?"

Still flustered, Dana held her purse close. "Great. Yes. Thank you for taking my foot out of my mouth." She took a step to the door, then hesitated. "Petra. Benedict. Marty. I will see you all later. Thank you for watching the vault." Grabbing a box, the woman walked out. "I can't believe I said that," she muttered, and then the door shut.

A sigh shifted Ryan's shoulders as he stuffed his arms into his jacket. "She's right," he said softly, and Pluck fizzed his agreement. "The job will go to rising seniors because of the skill needed. If we attach a lot of status to it along with a decent stipend, it will help separate the task from that of a sweeper's."

That didn't make me feel any better, and I flopped down on the couch beside Benedict. "Even though they will be doing the same thing?" I said. "I am not a trashman, and neither is Marty. No wonder she doesn't want to stay."

Marty put the wand down, her expression empty. "Ah, it has nothing to do with that."

"I know, I know." Ryan lifted a hand for patience, but his gaze was on the wide windows to where Dana was supervising Nog loading the last boxes. "Still . . . We need to make a place for you and Pluck, Petra, now more than ever. Show everyone your value. It's more than tuning moldavite to elevate more sweepers to Spinners. That might win over the sweepers, but it's the mages who have the loudest voice. People need to see you and your shadows doing something positive. I know it's not what you had envisioned, but you have to compromise to get anywhere."

"Compromise," I echoed as a thousand years of dissatisfaction fizzed through me. "Compromise should be an equal win-win. What you're asking is not win-win. It's win-survive."

The older man scrunched his face as if in pain. "Perhaps survival is enough at the moment?" Ryan's gaze flicked to Marty.

Benedict, too, eyed the woman now studying the pictures to either side of the fireplace. "Is it that bad?" he said softly, and Ryan nodded.

"This thing with the vaults," he said. "Petra, we have to catch Thoth before the mages collectively decide it wasn't the separatists and totally lose it. I'm worried about the shadows at the memorial, too. What they might do when some mage starts dumping dross into the well."

He should be, bubbled coldly through my thoughts.

"We will catch him," I said, but my confidence felt forced, and Marty looked a little ill, jumping when Dana honked the van's horn. Nog was in the driver's seat, reaming her out when the entitled woman tried to do it again.

"Go get some breakfast," I added, and Ryan took a big step into the hall.

"I brought Akeem up to speed. He will relieve you around three," he said. "Nog will be back with the van in about an hour. People have been leaving jars in the drive. Just let them. I'm not charging anyone at the moment." His attention went to Benedict, his expression softening. "Benedict, I appreciate anything you can do about this."

Benedict tossed a spiky nugget into the box. "No problem as long as the sun stays high."

"Okay, then." Clearly tired, Ryan walked out. "See you tomorrow!"

The door shut, and faintly through the walls, I heard him yell, "Hey! There's a noise ordinance here. Stop with the horn, Dana."

I blew my breath out, appreciating the new quiet. "As long as the sun stays high, huh?" I said, and Benedict looked at his lodestone ring.

"Yeah. I only have the one. Though I suppose I could make another." Nog drove off, and the house got even quieter. "That's a lot of dross in the kitchen."

"Mmmm."

Eyes on her phone, Marty sat in a nearby chair, brow furrowed as she scrolled. Pluck hung where he was at the ceiling, his satisfaction at his high perch out of the dross ringing through me.

"Dana has been freezing it within the bottle and then shaking it out," Benedict said as he put a capped bottle on the table before us. Exhaling, he stared at it. Energy swirled and his hands spaced around the bottle glowed—until the dross within the bottle spun into a knot, superheated into a higher state before he froze it so fast that it retained its condensed, shadow-repelling state. It was that last which had made his process so sought-after. It wasn't hard to turn dross inert, but dross expanded like ice when it was cooled—which attracted shadows. A definite no-no to most people. The spiky ball rolling around the bottom of the jar might be inert, but it still retained its condensed state. To shadows, it appeared hot.

It was an amazing feat of skill, one Benedict was indifferent about as he'd been working on it most of his life, and he shook the spiky dross ball into a box with the ceremony of tossing his undies in the washer. "Ryan didn't say where to put the empties," he said as he set the empty bottle down and took up a full one.

There hadn't been any empties outside. The kitchen, either. "The backyard?" I guessed.

Marty closed her phone and stood up. "I can check. I'm not doing anything."

"Thanks." Benedict handed her the empty bottle. Grabbing another, she wove through the mess to the hall. Pluck sensed my worry and he oozed from the overhead light, puddling into a snake to follow her.

Benedict hesitated until she was gone. "Her fields may be weak, but she's good with a wand. Did you see her check out the balance of the dross-go stick?"

"Yeah." I glanced at the empty hall, and faintly, as if from a distance, came Pluck's bubbly agreement, *Me too.*

I leaned closer, whispering, "You think she's sandbagging? That she knows more than she's admitting so we don't try to convince her to stay? She didn't have any problem freezing that water last night."

Benedict's smile went soft in memory. "Seeing as you exploded a bottle of water the first time you used a lodestone, I'm not sure how indicative that is of her existing skill." He glanced at the hallway. "I'm more concerned that if she doesn't have a shadow, the separatists will try to snuff her the moment she leaves St. Unoc. Whether he meant to or not, Thoth has probably been keeping them at bay."

His focus went to the haze within the bottle before him, and the glowing mist spiraled like a galaxy until it exploded into a spiny nugget. Saying nothing, I took the bottle, shook the dross into the box with the rest. "We need to find a way to make an exception for her boyfriend."

"That's not going to happen," Benedict said, looking up when Marty's shoes sounded in the hall.

"Nothing in the backyard," she said, voice cheerful as she came in, bottles in hand. "Maybe there are two vans, and the one toting the empties to the Surran building left already."

"They could be putting them downstairs," Benedict said as I moved the spent bottles out of the way.

"Mmmm, I doubt it." The hall was full, as was the kitchen. Much as I hated to admit it, Benedict's spiky inert dross took up a lot less space. The bottles were really stacking up, both full and empty. At a loss, I tucked the empties by the fireplace. "The loom here isn't much. Cement walls and a chemical hood that leads to a vault smaller than this room."

Spiders crawled over my spine as Benedict fixed another bottle of dross into a spiny nugget. I hadn't felt the others, and I wondered if maybe this was why Pluck hadn't returned with Marty. "I should check. Marty, you want to come with me?" I said, wanting to get out of the room, and Marty lit up. "I mean if you're good here, Benny."

"Sure, go," he said as he concentrated on the bottle and another spiky nugget took form.

Marty's obvious excitement held a thread of worry. "I've never seen a loom. We just left bottles at the door at my old job."

That sounded about right, and I managed a smile as I remembered the first time I'd gone down to St. Unoc's main loom. Darrell had been working it. My smile faltered. "Benny, I'll tape that up in a minute," I said as I moved a couple of full bottles closer to him, and he bobbed his head. "Stairs. I'm not sure where the stairs are," I added, and Pluck's presence in my thoughts strengthened.

Through the door, iced up through me. *That isn't a closet.*

Thanks, I thought, seeing the faded door between Akeem's and Ryan's offices.

"I thought you worked here," Marty said as I tried the door to find it unlocked.

"No, I worked at the loom under the Surran building." The door creaked open, and I flicked on the light. Wooden stairs went down, lit by an ancient bulb. "This is a temporary situation."

I headed down, Marty lagging behind, the two empties hitting the wall. Pluck padded along beside me, chilling my leg as he phased in and out of it. It was hard to tell who was more eager to see the vault—for different reasons.

"Yeah, this is it," I added when I saw the formidable fire door and lit keypad at the bottom. Pluck was waiting impatiently, clearly unable to get past the door. A quick rattle of the handle convinced me it was locked, but the keypad was glowing, and I tapped it awake. "Petra Grady, weaver third-class."

The door unlocked with a heavy thump. There was no cheerful voice announcing me, which I both appreciated and missed.

Let me check it out first. Pluck pushed past me, and in three seconds, *Good!* bubbled up through my mind.

Nose wrinkled at the scent of neglect, I fumbled for a light switch and clicked it on, scuffing to a halt just inside the door. "Good" wouldn't be my word choice. It was small, cinder-block walls with a cement floor. An empty floor-to-ceiling rack took up one wall, but there were no scales to measure what was being processed. The graciously named loom was nothing but a chemical hood with poke-through gloves and a swing door that presumably led to the vault.

"Wow, that's it?" Marty said as she set her two empties on the rack.

"This is really primitive," I admitted, tapping the glass hood with a fingernail. "Nothing like the loom at the Surran building. We had a full kitchen and showers. Somewhere to relax. The Spinners had their offices down there." I remembered Darrell's potted plants under full-spectrum lights and her strung loom now on display in the Surran building. "It was nice."

Marty swung the glass door open and shut, studying it before locking it. "It's not in use, is it?"

I shook my head. "No."

"And they used to put shadows in here?"

"Yes, unfortunately. But no one knew they were sentient back then." Which was sort of a lie. Shadow had been vaulted only when it was too "smart" to use for instruction. Which sort of begged the question of whether maybe the "dumb" shadow had pretended to be ignorant to avoid being vaulted only to be divided into wands and other repelling safety equipment. Cheese and crackers, what a choice to have been given—burned alive or cut into pieces so small you were lobotomized.

"St. Unoc was originally an artists' commune," I said, stifling a shudder of horror. "It grew into an artists' town, then a small university to provide dross traps disguised as artwork. St. Unoc University still is known for that. Our graduates are in high demand. It's one of the careers that's open to sweepers that actually pays well because it's still art."

"Huh." Marty ran a finger along the loom's door seals. "Are you sure it's empty?"

"Not without opening that wall door and looking, but it was supposed to have been emptied when the new vault went into service. They needed a large enough pool of starter dross to attract the stuff they were putting in. Pluck would know."

I scanned the floor, then the stained ceiling, not seeing him. "Pluck?"

For a heartbeat, I froze, listening to the silence. Not a fizz or bubble lifted through my mind. Actually, he had been missing for a while.

"Petra!" echoed faintly from upstairs, followed by a heavy thump, and then nothing.

16

I COULDN'T FEEL PLUCK FIZZING IN MY THOUGHTS. I TURNED TO MARTY, MY WORRY tightening at the outright fear on the woman's pale face.

"Pluck?" I sent my awareness out as if to make a field, knowing full well it wouldn't form, but it might help me to listen . . . to feel. Golden and scintillating, a casting of threads gusted out from me, visible only in my imagination. A second thump and crash came from the living room, and I stared at the ceiling as the thrum of the universe seemed to pulse, pushing on the threads I'd thrown—dissolving them.

For one agonizing moment I froze until I figured out what I'd just felt. Someone had broken the laws of nature. Someone had done magic.

"Stay here." Not knowing if Marty listened or not, I bolted upstairs, cursing myself for having left my stick by the door. I took the old steps two at a time, gasping as my foot slipped in some dross, sending me down, and I fell, palms breaking my fall. *Benedict . . .*

I clawed my way upstairs and ran to the front room, pulled by the sounds of desperation.

Fire burned my foot, dross snaking up my calf as I slid to a halt in the open archway. I tried to beat the dross off, and it clung to my hand like living fire. Bottles of dross lay broken between me and Benedict. The man was pressed into the far corner, pinned by a shadowy figure, but I couldn't move, in agony until I found a trap stick and used it to pull the dross from me.

The pain became bearable, and I stood, panting with a dross-coated stick in hand. Dross hazed the room, glowing on the floor, dripping from the ceiling. Nog was covered in it, out cold on the floor, but it was Benny I ached to reach as he fended off a wrathful shadow with my dad's old trap stick. It, too, was hazed with dross, and whereas the shadow clearly could shrug off Benedict's magic, the waste created by it was another story.

"Nog!" Benedict shouted, his face pinched in heartache. "Is he alive? Petra, is he okay?"

My stick dripped lava, and I picked my way to him between the broken glass and glints of living pain. *How does Pluck deal with this?* drifted through me, and then, *Where are you, Pluck?* Because that wasn't him weaving and dipping a threatening arc before Benedict.

Nog was breathing. "He's alive," I said as I pulled what dross I could from him, then yelped, my shoulder burning when a drop of it fell from the ceiling.

The shadow spun at my cry, the hazy outline coalescing into the shape of a man, hooded and cloaked, boots hazing to nothing before they touched the floor. Thoth.

"Where's Pluck?" I demanded, scared. My shoulder burned, and then relief found me when Benedict's field pulled the dross away and a spiny ball of inert dross plinked against the tiled floor. "If you have hurt Pluck, I will vault you myself," I vowed, then gasped, jerking when my foot found another drift of dross. *Damn it all to hell, this is misery!*

Dross was everywhere; I could hardly move without running into it.

Thoth pushed back his hood with a long-fingered hand to show a shock of black spiky hair. His face was darkly sallow, the only color to him being his eyes, the bright green of them finding mine when he took his dark glasses off and they misted to nothing in his hands. He was exactly how I remembered him from Cameron's dream, angry and disdainful, his feet hazing above the dross-covered floor as he stood between Benedict and me.

Be careful, Petra, fizzed through me, and I almost cried in relief. *He's most dangerous when cornered.*

Thoth sneered as his icy green gaze found Pluck twining about me in a weird mix of snake and cat. "You betray us again, Kahu," he said, his voice low and brittle, like dirty ice. "You call it balance. I call it death. And like dross calls dross, death calls death."

"Who the *hell* do you think you are?" I breathed, trying to keep him distracted as Benedict stood behind him, my dad's trap stick still in his hand when he drew his fists apart. A field so strong I could begin to see it formed between them, and Benedict's lodestone on his ring sparkled as he filled it with energy.

"Clear!" he shouted as he threw the spell at the shadow.

Thoth's expression melted, his entire construct collapsing in to avoid Benedict's spell. The energy hit the wall beside me to collapse the rack of sticks, pulling it to the floor with a gravity sink. Sticks rolled everywhere, gathering dross as they went. I could move again.

But so could Thoth, and I shouted a warning as the shadow coiled into a snake and lunged at Benedict. One touch, and he'd be comatose.

Face white, Benedict scrambled back, jabbing out with the dross-coated stick to keep him at bay. It struck Thoth, and the snake recoiled, thrashing into a tight ball, glittering, black sparkles of pain falling from him.

"Nog," I whispered, gingerly shaking his shoulder until he groaned, eyelids fluttering. What if he couldn't form fields? What if my silence had condemned him to a life without magic? Clearly Benedict still could, but Benedict hadn't been flat out on the floor.

Relief spilled into me when Nog sat up, his eyes widening as he saw Thoth writhing under the burning pain of a dross drift.

"Shadow spit. Is that . . ."

"Thoth," I said as Benedict gathered more energy between his hands. "Can you move?" But what I really wanted to know was if he could make a field.

He nodded, and I shifted to stand between him and Thoth as the older man slowly got to his feet. Dross clung to him, ignored. Seeing as it burned me like fire, it was a good assumption that Thoth hadn't broken him.

You okay? I thought, and Pluck's grip on my arm eased until pinpricks of sensation began to return, painful all on their own.

Yes, fizzed through me. *Use the freed dross. He's terrified of it.*

I ran the butt of the staff along the floor to gather dross and clear it from my feet. *So am I.*

Staff dripping pain, I faced Thoth. Behind him, Benedict stood ready. We couldn't catch him with only two sticks. There was a clear path for Thoth to leave, and yet he didn't, the shadow gathering himself again into a human form as if wanting to speak.

"I'm only saying this once. You need to leave," I prompted. "Or you're going to find yourself stuck in a bottle. We don't tolerate shadow attacks in St. Unoc."

A ragged, soul-shaking laugh bubbled up from Thoth. It pushed against my mind as if looking for weakness, and I exhaled, not to make a field but to let the chiming of the universe flow through me to array a tangle of threads between us. It wasn't a field, but it was something between his mind and mine.

His thoughts retreated, his hazy edges finding definition until he was again solid, ragged gaps showing where he'd been burned. The shadow took a step closer, his foot going indistinct to avoid a haze of sparking dross.

Nog's jaw was tight and his grip on the trap stick said he knew its power over Thoth. He hadn't brought in shadow that I knew of, but he looked okay.

Three, I thought, glancing at Benedict, the mage also beneath Thoth's concern. We had three trap sticks now, and Thoth was terrified of the dross they held. Three could hold him. Maybe.

"Nog, shift to my right to form a three-stick trap," I whispered, and the man's grim resolve changed to a confidence born in action. He instinctively knew my plan.

Thoth dissolved into a ribbon of blackness. I held my breath, thinking he was fleeing. But then he turned and headed for me.

"Get back!" I shouted as I swung the trap stick, spinning it right through the shadow to feel no resistance. Icy vibrations ached up my arm when it hit the floor, and the ever-present chiming of the universe seemed to hesitate. The solid hum collapsed into a wave that broke on me in a cascade of power and sparkles. Dross eddied in the unseen wind, and I panicked, snatching up a second trap stick.

Thoth jerked free, clearly shaken as the tear I'd put in him folded in on itself, sparkling as he burned.

"You will stop!" I ordered. *Pluck, get in the amulet,* I demanded as dross burned my fingers where they held the staff. *There's too much dross.*

Thoth took a step to the door, fear drawing him stiff when Nog shifted to block him. There were three of us. We could hold. With the dross clinging to the sticks, we could force him small enough such that Nog or Benedict could catch him in a field and, from there, a bottle.

"You would have us as thralls," Thoth burbled and hissed, not entirely solid. "Your life will be forfeit before I allow us to be betrayed by your like again."

I had time for a breath, nothing more. Thoth lashed out, his very substance parting to either side of me when I brought up a trap stick. His edges curled in around it, burning me as he touched my hand.

Blackness threatened my mind, and then his presence was gone and he was again cowering from the sticks we held.

"Nog! Benny!" I shouted, worried for Pluck even as he curled ever tighter about my wrist, his mind fizzing in my own. "We have him!" Pulse fast, I stared at the half man, half snake writhing on the floor trying to strike at us past the three sticks. "On three, we take one step forward. We're going to force him smaller. If we can contain him in a field, we can put him in a bottle."

Green, glittering eyes focused on me, hatred flowing from them.

"On three," Nog agreed. "We don't need a vault to burn you to hell," he whispered. "A bottle should hold you."

This wasn't who I wanted to be, but Thoth was out of control. I wouldn't burn him in a vault, but we'd catch him, bottle him, and try to calm him down. He had followed Marty here. He could be reasoned with.

Can't he? I thought, and Pluck's thoughts frothed icily; he clearly believed otherwise.

"Benny? One, two, three," I said when he nodded, and we all took a step forward, our trap sticks angled to keep Thoth from darting to the ceiling to escape.

Nog's wrinkled face brightened in hope as Thoth shrank, the shadow's cohesion vanishing as we pinned him in a smaller space. "It's working!" he crowed, arthritic hands coated in dross as he held his trap stick steady. "One, two, three!"

My fingers were burning, and I shifted my grip. The dross needed to hold Thoth was breaking on me, doing who knew what, but I couldn't let go. Benedict, too, was suffering, and I took a breath to warn him when the energy hazing his fingers burst into a sudden light.

"Benny!" I called out, but it was too late and his foot came down on a stray trap stick. The stick rolled and Benedict went down hard.

"Back! Get back!" the mage said, teeth clenched as he waved the trap stick at Thoth, driving him into retreat as Benedict found his feet and angled the stick to match ours.

My pulse quickened. We had to finish it fast. My hands were going numb, shaking. One more step, and the tips would touch, pinning him.

"Again!" Nog directed. "We almost have him. One, two, three!"

We stepped forward, setting the butts of the trap sticks on the tile floor as one and slowly angling them together.

Those sticks aren't balanced, frothed through my mind. It wasn't Pluck. It was Thoth. I could hear him, in my mind, and I froze. Dark matter wove upward through the stick in my hand, threads of an angry alien presence and energy moving like lightning to find ground.

Gasping, I let go. The stick remained, propped against the other two. But dark matter followed me, stretching until the distance was too great and it fell back into the stick. Threads snapped and recoiled—and then the pulse of the universe rebounded, pushing the gossamer lines of energy into an uncontrolled reaction.

Petra! Pluck fizzed, and then I ducked, turning to hold Pluck close when the stick exploded, bursting from the inside.

Pinpricks of heat, dross, and wood fragments peppered me. I stumbled, gasping when my foot rolled on a stick and I went down. My head hit the low table and I saw stars.

"Petra!" Benedict pulled me upright. Dazed, I watched from the floor as the tripod slowly collapsed and the remaining two sticks slid to a harsh clatter on the tile. Thoth was gone. "Petra, look at me. Are you okay?"

I put a hand to the back of my head, immediately regretting my nod when a headache exploded, throbbing all the way to the base of my spine. Shadow spit, we had trapped him, but I had a feeling Thoth had let us do it, knowing he could break out anytime he wanted. "I'm fine," I said, wishing Pluck would stop fizzing so loudly.

I could hardly hear real words at all. "I'm okay," I said again, then jerked when a drift of dross clinging to Benedict burned me.

"Are you sure?" The man was panicking, totally unaware that he was glowing like a lava monster to my weaver-sensitive eyes.

"Y-You're covered in dross," I muttered, and he dropped his hand, clearly at a loss. *Pluck? Amulet. Now,* I thought as I put a hand on the table and used it to stand up.

Not happening. Pluck renewed his coils around my arm like a tiny snake, numbing it all the way to my elbow. *He could return. I may not be strong enough to overpower him, but I can keep him out of your mind.*

Nog, at least, knew better than to try to touch me. Of the three of us, he had fared the best, seeing as none of the dross hazing the room would dare break on him. Which also meant he could still make fields. Thoth hadn't damaged him, and a knot of tension eased about my chest.

"We almost had him," the older man said. Expression pensive, he picked up the stick he'd used, eyeing it for possible damage before propping it against the wall.

"Hey, could you . . ." I waved to the room, embarrassed. "I'm, ah, really tired," I added to cover for why I didn't just make a field and de-dross the room myself.

"Sure." Nog glanced out the window as if looking for Thoth, then exhaled.

Sensation rippled over me, and Pluck's grip on my arm tightened. It was Nog's field, and I stifled a shudder when it passed over me again, this time going the other way as he drew in the dross from the entire room to leave the sporadic glints of dross dust too small to be caught.

Pluck? I questioned, but the shadow was humming his approval. Clearly he felt the cooling sensation that Nog's field had left behind as well—which made me curious. I rarely felt a field other than my own, but this had been obvious. How blind, I wondered, had I been?

"He broke the stick," Nog said in wonder, releasing his field when the glow it contained shrank into a rather large spiky ball of inert dross that fell to the floor thanks to Benedict. Nog picked it up, brow furrowed as he tossed it into the box with the rest. "That's the shadow who followed Marty here? Ryan said he's not bound to her. What's his problem?"

He has many, Pluck fizzed.

Is there a reason they have to become ours? I thought dryly, then gestured for Benedict to bring it in for a hug as I hobbled closer. "You okay? You had dross breaking all over you." It was a fact that Thoth had used to his advantage, I realized. Perhaps it was dumb luck that no one had been left comatose.

"Headache the size of Montana." Benedict's arms enfolded me, and my eyes closed as I soaked in his warmth. Pluck bubbled and fizzed his disapproval, but he never left my arm, even when Benedict pulled away, his eyes searching mine. "Pluck kept him off me until you got up here. Otherwise, I'd be in the bed next to Marshal Owens. Nog, too."

My lips parted and my focus blurred. *Pluck?*

You like the yeth. I did it for you, not him, Pluck fizzed, his embarrassment swirling through my gratitude. *Nog is useful in getting rid of dross. That's it.*

"Seems like I owe you my life, Pluck. Thank you." Nog sighted down each stick before carefully propping them against the wall. "We almost had him," he added in a mutter, but I knew better. Thoth had allowed us to circle him. It would take more than three random, unbalanced sticks manned by a sweeper, a mage, and a broken weaver to catch Thoth.

The sticks, I mused. *Perhaps if they were a balanced set . . .*

"Benny . . ." I said, my voice tight with a new idea, but my next words faltered when that same universe bubble of sensation pushed up against me. Pluck's grip tightened, and then he spilled from me to vanish into the hall, leaving only the memory of cold.

"Get away from me!" Marty shouted, her voice faint from downstairs.

Cheese and crackers. I'd forgotten about Marty.

"Marty?" I called, slipping when I tried to bolt. I grabbed a stick, almost rolling my ankle as I followed the faint fizz of Pluck's thoughts to the stairway.

Benedict and Nog were right behind me, and I thundered down the stairs. "Marty!" I exclaimed as I shoved the unlatched fire door open.

Marty was in the corner, crouched and cowering with her face in her hands. The door from the loom to the vault was open. A new crack etched the wall like lightning. Pluck was nowhere, and I went to Marty, jumping when I touched her shoulder and she shrieked.

Her eyes were wide, and I swear she didn't see me for a second before her expression cleared and she clutched at me, sobbing.

I knelt, holding the scared woman as she shook. "Marty, it's okay. He's gone."

"He'll be back . . ." she said between gasps for air. "He always comes back. Make him go away. Please, make him go away."

But I couldn't, and I held her as Nog and Benedict stared at the crack in the vault.

"He's gone," I mouthed silently, and the two men eased their stances.

"I'm so sorry," Marty said as I drew her to her feet, her head down and her eyes red. "I tried to stop him. I tried to make a field. He just . . ." Wiping her nose, she looked at the cracked wall. "I am less than useless."

"You're okay. It's a win," I said, and Benedict extended a hand to her. "Let's go."

She nodded, and he and Nog helped her up the stairway.

This is not good. Mages will say we cracked the vault, not Thoth, fizzed through my thoughts, and I tensed until I realized the black scintillating haze pushing its way through the crack in the wall was

Pluck, not Thoth. A shudder shook both of us, born in his horror at having been in a vault—broken or not.

"Yeah? Well, we saw him do it," I whispered as he coalesced into his dog form. The sound of Benedict's and Nog's voices filtered in from the ceiling, making the empty room even more creepy.

Pluck flicked an ear to send a drift of dark matter to hit the cement wall with a dull splat. *You opened the vault. Thoth came and destroyed it. He waited until you were here. Waited until you opened it, not Herm. They will say we are in league with him.*

Oh, for crying out loud . . . I closed my eyes in a long blink. He was right. Dana would be on this like hot on a pepper. Eyes opening, I shut the glass door to the loom and locked it. "I'm not taking the blame for this. Once we catch Thoth, we'll get him to admit he's working alone."

Pluck fizzed, cocking his doggy head to eye me sourly. *How? We just got our asses handed to us.*

My lips parted at the modern phrase, then I managed a smile. "Not as bad as it might have been," I said softly. "We're figuring him out." My gaze went to the soft sound of steps overhead, and then Nog's uneasy, comforting laugh. "Thank you for protecting Nog and Benny."

They were an unexpected asset, their liabilities amounting to less than the effort to keep them intact, bubbled faintly through my thoughts, and I started up the stairs, Pluck chilling my leg into a solid, cold nothing. *Perhaps trying to do this alone was my original mistake.*

"You mean like thousands of years ago?" I mused, my mind on what had gone wrong so I could piece out what had gone right. Three sticks had almost worked. Thoth's fear had been real. Had it been the number of sticks that was the failure, or that they hadn't been balanced? "I need to talk to Ryan."

17

NECK CRANED, I RAN THE TIP OF THE LONG RED STICK ACROSS THE CEILING, having only minor success in gathering the last of the glowing dust. Benedict cooked when he was nervous—I cleaned. And though Ryan hadn't said anything much when I'd called him, he and Herm were on their way back. This was going to be hard to explain, and the need to be honest with Ryan about my situation was growing.

Thoth isn't hard to explain, Pluck fizzed, the shadow hiding under the couch increasingly relaxed as I got the last hint of dross out of the room. *Thoth is a force of nature. Don't stand in the moonlight and call it the sun. Tell him. Ryan is the only person who might believe you.*

The metaphor was new to me, but it sounded a lot like don't make mountains out of molehills, and I studied the room for any hint of dross outside of the last six glass bottles remaining to turn inert. Nog was in the drive sending everyone and their jars of dross to the old gym, but Benedict wanted to finish this out and was sitting in the sun so as to keep his lodestone charged. Maybe he cleaned when he got nervous, too.

His head was down as his hands fixed around a glowing bottle, his gently curly hair catching the light when the hazy distortion within it swirled, condensed . . . and a spiny black nugget fell to the bottom of the bottle with a musical *ting*. Clearly bone-tired, he shook the nugget into a box, set the empty bottle aside, and took up another.

"Just a few left," Marty said as she set a trap stick with its two mates against the wall.

"Thanks for organizing those." I shook the haze of burning dross from my stick into the desk trap, my hands still red and aching from the dross burn. "If not for the broken rack, no one would know we had a party."

The woman smiled at my bad joke, but her expression emptied when she sat down, her fingers touching the pocket where her own lodestone was.

Pluck wisped out from under the couch and wrapped a cold tendril around my ankle. *She correctly sorted them into their balanced groups,* he thought, and I nodded, pretending to look for more hidden dross behind the blinds. Sensing the amount of dross within something was actually a high-skills art, and I began to wonder if Pluck was right. She was sandbagging. I'd be willing to bet her patchy, low-grade fields were pretense, too.

Can you blame her? I thought, and his fizzing indecision filled me. The woman wanted her old life, to return home, where her boyfriend waited, and forget this ever happened. I knew how she felt. I wasn't that far away from the sentiment myself. At least Marty hadn't blown up an entire auditorium and spread ten years' worth of stored dross over campus. Not to mention put hundreds in the hospital and several in the ground.

That was me, Pluck bubbled, but I wouldn't let him take the blame. It had been self-defense. I'd put him there, and I still felt guilty.

It shouldn't be this hard to talk to her, I thought, shoulders slumping when a familiar black van pulled into the tiny parking lot. "They're back." I let the blinds clunk into the window frame and turned.

Benedict shook another dross nugget into the box. "Shadow spit.

I wanted to be done before they got here." His gaze shot to Pluck. "Sorry, Pluck. I have got to stop saying that."

Like I care? fizzed sourly through me.

Dana's heels clicked smartly on the pavers, the woman outpacing Ryan and Herm to blow into the house like a summer storm.

"Hey, glad you're here," Benedict said with a worried cheerfulness, but the woman hardly acknowledged us, fast as she strode past the large archway, her intent obvious.

"No one leave," she said tersely, never slowing. "Not until I see the vault."

I felt like a kid who had broken Mom's best vase, and I winced, the butt of my staff thumping to the colorful tile when Nog, Ryan, and Herm came in, all three looking oddly mismatched but alike where it counted. I'd effed it up again.

"Petra, are you okay?" Herm pushed past Nog and reached for my reddened hand. "My God. You're burned! Like burned, burned. Did Thoth do this? Where's Pluck?"

"It was dross, and it's not that bad." My face warmed as I looked at my pink hand cradled in his sun-leathered, knobby-knuckled one. "Pluck is fine," I added as the shadow coalesced beside me, numbing my entire leg. When Herm saw him, his worry eased.

"Pluck, thank all that is holy," Herm said with a sigh, and the shadow hazed to almost nothing in surprise. "I would have bet my life that Thoth wouldn't attack the vault during the day. We never should have left you."

Pluck's green eyes blinked, surprise and gratitude bubbling through me at the man's relief. *We handled it,* he thought, then dissolved, vanishing under the couch as if embarrassed.

"Ryan," I started, and the man looked up from where he'd been talking with Benedict, Nog a silent presence behind them as he gathered up the empty bottles. "I am so sorry. I never should have gone down to the vault."

"Yeah, that will be hard to explain," the man said, his brow furrowed. "But everyone is okay. That's the important part."

"If there is one thing I've learned," Herm said, his gaze lingering on my burned fingers, "it's if a shadow wants to break something, it will." His lips quirked in a smile as he glanced under the couch. "Ryan is right. Everyone is conscious. I say you did good."

"Thanks to Pluck," Nog said brightly, empty bottles tucked under his arm as he made his way to the hall.

Ryan started, his conversation with Marty hesitating. "Really?"

Nog edged sideways into the hall, dodging the last bottles of dross. "Yep. He kept Thoth off me until Petra could get upstairs. Did the same for Benedict. Like an effing black tornado."

"Mmmm." Ryan patted Marty on the shoulder, completely missing the woman's terrified expression. "Thank you, Pluck. We can make another vault. We can't make another Nog."

The old sweeper snorted as he headed out the door. "Got that right. I'm a non-GMO-certified limited edition."

"I'm just glad you are all okay." Ryan sat beside Marty, his cheerful demeanor wearing thin. "I'm the one who should be apologizing for leaving you so vulnerable."

But the vault was broken because I had opened it, and my gut hurt.

Benedict dropped a spiky nugget into the box and set another empty bottle aside. "No one thought Thoth could get here in the full sun," he said with a sigh. "Now we know."

Pluck's form sparked from under the couch, his eyes glowing an evil green. "It wasn't a complete failure," I said as I sat on the arm of the couch beside Benedict. "I think we would have had him if the sticks had been balanced."

It's not the sticks, fizzed through me, and I started, surprised when Herm took my hand in his again, studying it. *I think it was the people holding them. The varying way they use magic.*

"Petra, you should get that looked at," the Spinner mused, and I pulled my hand away at the sound of heels on the stairs, embarrassed. I was a weaver, damn it, not a shadow.

"She's right. We had him until he busted a stick." Benedict fixed the last bottle of dross into a spiny nugget. But his hopeful smile fell when Dana came in, clearly frustrated.

"Well, how is it?" Ryan said.

Dana grimaced as she brushed a drift of new dross off her. Clearly she'd done some magic down there. "It would be easier to make a new one than repair it," she said, her gaze sliding to me. "If we could without interference."

"Don't blame Petra. I asked to see the vault," Marty blurted, clearly nervous as she perched on the edge of the couch beside Ryan. "I wanted to know what one looked like."

"I thought maybe you were storing the empty bottles down there," I said, and Dana huffed.

"That's why you opened the door?" Dana accused.

"Dana, relax," Ryan said before turning to Marty. "No one is blaming you or Petra."

Benedict stretched where he sat, clearly uncomfortable. "I'm still trying to figure out how Thoth got here."

Herm frowned at the haze Dana had discarded, his gaze going to the clean corners before he made a field to catch it. "Thoth had a lot of structure," he said. "I've noticed that Pluck has a stronger resistance to the sun when he's in a solid form."

Tell them it's not hard to move in the sun, the shadow bubbled from under the couch, and my ankle grew cold as he wrapped a tendril of presence around it. *There are always shadows.*

"Pluck says it's not as hard to get around as you might think," I said as Nog came in, but my thoughts blanked when Herm intentionally dropped the collected dross on Dana's back like a Kick Me sign. "Um, it might have taken something out of him to travel shadow to shadow, but all he'd have to do is sulk in the dark for a while to replenish himself."

"Not hard when there's so much inert dross lying about," Dana muttered, her voice heavy with accusation. "Good to know."

Benedict straightened from taping the last box closed. "Dana, if you have something to say, say it."

Nog scooped up the box, the older man's feet shifting nervously. "Hey, ah, Marty, you want to help me get the van organized?"

Marty took her gaze from the dross slowly oozing down Dana's back. "Sure." Springing up from the couch, she hesitated, stymied by the crowded front room until Benedict pushed deeper into the couch, arms over his chest, to let her slide past. No one said anything until the door clicked shut. That dross clinging to Dana was going to break on her. I could feel it.

"Say your piece, so we can tell you to eat shit and move on with our lives," Herm grumbled.

"Hey, hey, hey," Ryan protested, but it was obvious he, too, didn't put much store in her opinion.

Still oblivious to the dross, the woman stared us down, the confidence gained facing down an entire table of tenured professors in her stance. "After inspecting the vault, I have determined it broke from inert-dross expansion. Identical to what broke the university vault."

"Sounds reasonable," Herm said. "There's enough of it here."

"Which brings me to my point. Petra has made it clear she doesn't want a vault at all."

"Ah, hold up." Benedict stiffened in warning. "That's not true. She's been lobbying for shadow release valves, not a vault boycott."

My entire side went cold where Pluck pressed into me. "Once, maybe," I admitted, and Dana smiled as if she'd gained some points. "But even the memorial shadows agree that we need a vault to store the dross that the university is creating. That's actually half of Thoth's problem—that I'm advocating vaults. That's why he's cracking them."

Dana pressed her lips together. "So you say."

"Dana," Ryan interrupted. "I wish you would explain your thinking, because right now all your words will do is rile the university into a premature action that benefits no one."

Arms crossed over his middle, Herm leaned back against the folded Ping-Pong table.

"I think it's more than odd," the woman said confidently, "that in less than an hour after we leave, Petra opens the vault and somehow a chunk of frozen dross gets in there and it mysteriously breaks."

"Mysterious, hell," I said loudly. "Thoth blew it. There's nothing mysterious about it."

"A shadow that showed up when Marty did," Dana continued as if I'd said nothing. "A shadow who would need a weaver's help to even get here."

"I just told you he could get here on his own," I said, ignored, and Pluck's grip on my ankle tightened until my foot went numb.

"No, this all adds up just fine." The woman's eyes narrowed. "Marty and her shadow Thoth are the ones blowing up the vaults."

My breath caught as Dana twisted my words, using them to throw Marty under the bus.

"Marty?" Benedict blurted, and I was glad that she was out at the van with Nog. "Dana, are you serious? The girl can't even make a decent field."

I'm not so sure about that, Pluck fizzed, and my gaze went to the sorted trap sticks.

I licked my lips and shifted to the edge of the couch. "You weren't here," I said, remembering the young woman's fear. "Marty came to me looking for help. She was terrified down there. You can't fake that."

"Besides," Ryan said, his voice far more calm than mine, "the timing doesn't work for Marty to be responsible for any of this. The vault under construction was damaged before she got here. Petra and Pluck weren't here at the time, either."

"Yes?" Dana said. "We only have Petra's say-so about when Marty and her shadow arrived."

"Thoth is not her shadow," I insisted, but even Ryan looked worried.

"What's your point, Dana?" Benedict asked flatly.

Dana's unwavering gaze landed on me. "Petra, why did you open the door to the vault?"

"Stop right there." Herm pushed off from the Ping-Pong table, his weathered face creased in anger. "I see where you're going. This is bullshit. Petra did not blow the vault. It was an accident. At worst, a coincidence."

Anger and fear mixed in an ugly slurry, fizzing through me. "You can't seriously think I'm doing this," I said, but Pluck's thoughts fizzed miserably. He had seen it coming.

"Grady and Pluck did *not* crack the vault," Benedict said hotly. "Not this one, nor the one under construction. And if you want to hinge this on inert dross, it was *your* idea to centralize dross here to turn inert."

Dana shook her head, refusing to concede the point. "It doesn't change the fact that Petra opened the vault and then left it."

"Because Thoth was up here trying to kill us!" Benedict exclaimed, and my gaze flicked out the window to Nog and Marty standing by the van in the sun.

"You're right about one thing," Dana said confidently. "Marty is too inexperienced to orchestrate the destruction of a vault. But Petra and Pluck are not. Ryan, I want Petra and Pluck put into custody immediately."

"Are you out of your mind?" Benedict blurted as a pang of fear slid through me, heightened by Pluck's own dark thoughts. "She's the only one who can catch him!"

Cheese and crackers. I had gotten Marty exonerated only to put myself in the fire. Dana wasn't a separatist, but her fear coupled with her far-reaching voice would be just as devastating.

"To prove their innocence if nothing else," Dana added, as if that would make it right.

Ryan put both feet firmly on the floor, his elbows on his knees as he shook his head. "Accusations like that don't wash off, Dana. Be careful."

Herm was suddenly standing beside me, his hand warm as it touched my shoulder. "Go. Now," he muttered, but I couldn't even get my ass off the arm of the couch.

"If they're innocent," Dana continued, "there is no harm done."

"No harm?" Benedict blurted. "You're slandering a well-respected member of the university. Petra has done nothing but good for . . ." His words faltered. The collapse of the auditorium was my fault.

"If the attacks on the vaults cease while they are in custody—"

"Then we will all count ourselves fortunate," Ryan interrupted. "Petra and Pluck have no reason to see our society fall apart."

I exchanged a worried look with Benedict. Fall apart, no. Rearrange, yes, but for some people, change was seen as a destruction of what they held dear, not a betterment of it.

Dana, too, knew this truth, and she stood by the fireplace as if it were a dais, that drift of dross now sparkling at her heel. "Grady is advocating the reemergence of a shadow age the likes of which we've not seen since the dark ages," she said, and Pluck seemed to shrink deeper into himself. "Her so-called balance is a lie. This devastation has always been their true agenda. A return to shadow domination."

"Hey!" Benedict stood, his face red with anger.

"Or else why did their appearance begin with the destruction of the auditorium?" she said. "It was only luck that it didn't kill our entire graduating class and a large portion of our instructors. Fewer experienced mages to stand against them."

Holy cats, she was on a roll, and Pluck's anger fizzed through my own.

"Dana," Ryan said sharply. "Thoth is clearly responsible for this."

"And who is in charge of Thoth?" Dana said triumphantly. "By your own admission, Marty doesn't have the skill and, if you are to be believed, isn't bound to Thoth. That leaves Petra Grady. The only weaver known to exist."

"You think *I* did this because you believe a shadow can't work alone?" I said, and Herm's grip on my shoulder tightened in warning. Seeing Dana's trap, I closed my mouth. It was a lose-lose situation. Validating that shadows worked independently might start a shadow hunt. Lying and saying that I controlled them would put me behind bars. And she knew it.

"If the lodestone fits." Dana paced before the unlit fireplace as if lecturing. The dross on her sparked, broke, and the woman's toe snagged on the lip of a tile, sending her lurching. Arm flashing out, she caught herself, skinning her palm on the rough fireplace stone.

Clearly pissed, she stopped where she was and rubbed her raw skin. "Shadows have never acted on their own," she muttered. "At least not like this. Grady was, is, your employee, Ryan. Perhaps you should recuse yourself from any decisions regarding her guilt or innocence."

My what? I thought as I stood.

Pluck clung to me, winding into a snake about my arm and neck. *It's happening again,* he thought in panic, but I refused to believe. Dana was one person, and I had many who trusted me.

People who turned on me before, I thought, before quashing it.

Herm shifted to stand between me and Dana. "You need to get out of here," he whispered as Ryan began to argue with Dana. "You and Benedict. My truck is a few streets over out back. Leave your cells somewhere along the way. There's a burner phone in the glove box. Call me when you're safe."

"If I leave, what's stopping her from spreading her lies?" I said as Benedict sidled up beside me, his brow furrowed in worry. Thoth was getting exactly what he wanted. There would be no balance. Mages would attack shadows on sight. Who knew what the sentient energy would do now that they had been promised a little peace and found it ripped away?

"I will. Ryan will. You need to go," Herm insisted as Ryan's and Dana's voices gained strength. "I've seen this before."

So have I, Pluck bubbled and fizzed in agitation. *The Spinner is right.*

I glanced out the window to Benedict's highly identifiable car. "Cameron can vouch for me. Thoth told her everything. If I get her out—"

"You will go nowhere near the marshal," Dana said, interrupting both me and Ryan. "She's already been attacked by shadow once. There's no proof that you didn't do that."

Cheese and crackers, what was wrong with this woman?

Brow furrowed, Herm tugged on my arm for my attention. "Go. I've got this."

"You can't think Petra hurt Cameron," Benedict said, floundering for words. "Never . . ."

Dana nodded. "I think the marshal found something out. Thoth might have put her in a coma, but who told Thoth to do it?"

"I did not put Cameron in a coma!" I shouted.

"Well, you certainly did nothing to get her out." Dana turned to Ryan. "I'm going to talk to the board, and I will not leave until they agree that she and that shadow be incarcerated. It will look better if Grady comes in of her own volition."

My blood ran cold. I'd be in a cell, and Pluck . . . *I will not let them put you in a bottle,* I vowed, and his grip on me tightened until my arm went numb. Shadow spit. Herm was right. I had to get out of here.

"No!" Ryan shouted the word, and everything seemed to slow and still. "That is enough, Dana," he added, and Herm exhaled even as he pulled me a step closer to the hall. "As you pointed out, Petra Grady is my employee, and unless you have *proof* that she's broken the law, *I* decide when disciplinary measures are to be taken and what they are. Right now, all she's guilty of is questionable judgment in opening the vault after I told her the chances of Thoth showing up were nil." The Spinner met my eyes, wincing. "If anyone should be answering questions, it's me. End of story."

Dana took a breath.

"As long as I'm in charge of the sweepers and weavers, my word stands!" Ryan exclaimed, and the woman's eyes narrowed.

"Fine," she admitted. "But when I prove she is behind the attacks, it will become an issue for the mage courts."

Ryan's gaze flicked to me and back to her again. "As always," he said, and Benedict's shoulders slumped in relief.

"Glad we are in agreement," the woman said. "Until this is settled, Marty will have no more contact with Grady."

"What?" I exclaimed, and Dana brushed her scraped palm again.

"That is not helpful, Dana," Ryan said, and I pulled from Herm's grip.

"No, I think this is a good idea," Herm said, shocking me to silence. "And when Thoth follows Marty to Dana's house, she might realize Thoth isn't under your control."

"And when she ends up in a coma?" I said. "Ryan . . ."

Dana's flash of worry vanished. "I can handle a shadow. We'll be fine," she said, her motions fast as she scooped up Marty's hoodie. "Stay away from her or I will put you in a cell."

I looked out the window, longing to have just five minutes with Marty. "Tell her this isn't her fault," I said as Dana click-clacked to the hall.

"Oh, believe me, I will." Dana walked out, slamming the door behind her.

I allowed myself one sigh, then tightened right back up again.

Ryan watched them out the window, a sad, worried expression on his face. "Petra, Herm is right. Make yourself scarce. Stay in St. Unoc, but—"

"I'm not going into hiding," I interrupted, and his focus sharpened.

"Pluck, thank you for keeping them safe," he added, and Pluck, wrapped around my arm like a python, bobbed his snakelike head, green eyes glinting.

"We will need water . . ." Benedict bolted into motion to gather our few things plus some extras we might need. He'd gotten good at bugging out—thanks to me.

"You should leave before she comes back." Herm tugged at me until I had to take a step. "Ben, I have water in the truck," he said louder. "I'll get you clear of her. My junkyard safe house is known now, but I have somewhere in mind. You're going to love it."

Deep in thought, Ryan sat down before the small table, his elbows on his knees as he stared at the broken pieces of the trap stick. "How did she turn this against you so fast?"

I was kind of wondering the same thing . . . until Pluck fizzed, *Thoth.* The shadow was using us against ourselves. It was infuriating.

"Ah, my car is out front," Benedict said. He had a bag over one arm and a trio of trap sticks in the other, and I felt a surge of gratitude. "Petra can stay with me."

"No, you're going into hiding, too." Herm ushered us into movement. "Pluck will need help keeping her intact."

I do not, the shadow grumped as he flowed to the floor and shook dark matter from himself like dust.

"We're taking my truck," Herm grumbled, pointing to Ryan's office and the sliding glass door. "It's a lot less conspicuous than your go-faster car. I had to park a block away. I almost got towed the last time I left it at the miniature golf course. Go. Out."

I barely had time to grab my dad's oversize trap stick before he pushed me into the hall, but my gaze lingered on Ryan. Herm hadn't told him where we were going; Ryan hadn't asked. My life was out of control, but if Herm could hand me a life preserver to keep my head above water, I should take it.

"Wouldn't it be better to concentrate on proving Pluck and Petra didn't have anything to do with the vaults?" Benedict asked as Herm led us to the back door in Ryan's office.

"Thoth is not a wild shadow," Herm said, and Pluck fizzed a sour agreement. "He's got an agenda and is setting you up to take his fall. Quite well, actually."

"Tell me about it." Ryan's office was hot from the sun pouring in, and I hesitated, my feet edging the light as Benedict tugged the sliding door open and the warmth of a late-November day spilled in. Pluck dove for his amulet, and as I held the dark green glass, the slight burn on my palm disappeared. "That doesn't mean we can't catch him."

Breath held, I forced myself out into the sun, wincing as the initial flash of heat dulled to something tolerable. *Huh,* I thought as I compared it to the initial jolt of connection I'd once felt when handling dross.

"I'm not so sure." Herm worked the sticky door shut and ushered us to the far gate. "Thoth took your ability to make a field but let you live to take his blame. That vault had to have been locked and unlocked three times last night. He waited until *you* unlocked it before destroying it. His plans stretch into the next century, and you and Pluck are not in them."

I glanced at Benedict, a flicker of fear that he might be right sparking through me. Pluck had said the same thing.

"It's going to be okay." Benedict's fingers brushed mine as Herm opened the back gate, his uncomplicated figure looking at home among the recycle bins and empty totes. "You have a lot of friends here." Benedict shifted the pack higher up his shoulder. "Besides, Herm is exaggerating."

Imagine my disappointment, echoed in Pluck's and my memory, *when I found it was an accident and you would have shadows burn in the hell of your making. Petra, the yeth.*

"Maybe," I said, and Pluck fizzed sourly. "I still think waking up

Cameron has merit." I shifted to skirt a drift of dross, and the thought that I hadn't told Ryan what Thoth had done to me bubbled up from nowhere. Maybe it was just as well. If he knew—or Dana knew—she'd find a way to use it against me.

"This is so unfair," Benedict said, and we hustled to catch up with Herm. "None of this was your fault."

But as I pulled my cap lower, it occurred to me that maybe it was. Being naive wasn't a crime, but perhaps it should be.

18

IF HERM'S TRUCK WAS DUSTY ON THE INSIDE, IT WAS POSITIVELY FILTHY ON THE outside, and a thick layer of desert-road dirt caked everything—especially the license plate. Still, he fit right in between the high-end convertibles and the oversize ranch trucks, driving sedately through St. Unoc's streets as if he were in from his spread for the day.

Benedict was to my right, my staff between us. Herm was driving, obviously, and my knees were high as my feet were over the drivetrain. Pluck had parked it in his lodestone, and I fingered the knotted cord about my neck as Dana's accusations swirled through my mind.

Shadow spit, I thought as I ran my nail over the rills of glass created not on earth or in space but somewhere in between, suspended as we were between mage and Spinner.

Do you have any idea how irritating that is? fizzed through me, or us, rather, and I let the amulet go.

"Sorry," I whispered. "Maybe I should have taken that dross drift off her."

Benedict took my hand in his and gave it a squeeze. "What dross drift?"

Herm, doing a slow thirty-two mph behind a landscape truck, snorted.

Sighing, I gripped Benedict's fingers tighter in mine. "She can't really believe that Pluck and I are responsible for this. I don't understand where Dana's attitude is coming from."

"I do." Herm eased to a halt, brakes squeaking as his eyes fixed on the truck before him slowly running the red light. He didn't say another word, but his expression was clear. Pluck and I were guilty until they found someone else to blame, and even then, I might take the rap because the university didn't want the expense of putting in shadow escape valves. Catching Thoth might not even make a difference because as a weaver I'd carry the stigma from his actions, and retractions seldom got the attention of the original sensational lie. No, if I wanted to find a balance between shadow and light, I had to prove my innocence. And Marty's. Now.

Grimacing, I let go of Benedict's hand to push the hair from my face. "Herm, is the hospital on the way to your safe house?"

"No-o-o-o . . ." Herm's drawl was full of thought as he ran a hand over his bristly chin. "But finding a way to sneak you in to see Cameron is high on my priorities." He glanced in the rearview mirror in suspicion. "Settle in at your safe house first. Get yourself acquainted with the locals. Give me a couple of hours to coordinate with Lev. He's been there most of the day."

"Locals?" Benedict questioned when Herm pushed the accelerator and the truck roared, trying to pick up speed so he could make the next light.

Pluck's worry tangled through my thoughts and I rubbed my wrist, remembering the snapping sensation. We'd have to go into Cameron's dreamscape again. If Thoth was there . . .

Grinning, Herm pulled to the curb and put his truck into park. "Here we are."

Benedict's brow furrowed. "Ah, Herm?"

I followed Benedict's gaze across the street, realizing we were behind the memorial gardens. *Is he joking?* I thought as his "locals" remark finally made sense.

"I suggest avoiding the stairs." Herm leaned across Benedict and me, smacking the glove box until it opened. "Henry will ping university security until I take the garden off the system." He blew out his breath as if tired. "I'm going to need a nap after this."

"The auditorium?" I questioned, and Herm slammed the glove box shut, a small bag with an electronics store logo on it in his hand. "With the memorial shadows?"

"How are we supposed to get down there if we don't use the stairs?" Benedict asked, choking when Herm's grin widened. "The well?"

But Pluck fizzed happily at the idea. *It's perfect. Even when they realize you're there, which they eventually will, they won't dare follow you.*

For good reason, I mused, worried.

"Down the well, yes," Herm said confidently. "Benedict, you're good with earth magic. You can't tell me you haven't jumped out of a two-story window before."

Benedict flushed. "Okay, I can slow our fall to where it's safe, but the shadows . . ." His words faltered, and he glanced at me for reassurance—reassurance that I didn't have.

"Ah, I don't know, Herm," I said as Pluck bubbled and fizzed, eager to get into the dank space. "Going down to ask a few questions is one thing. Staying there is another."

"Petra, I don't know where else to take you." Worry pinched Herm's eyes. "For all his skills, Pluck is vulnerable. He can destroy anyone who tries to touch you, but doing so enforces their very fears. He's fighting with one hand behind his back, far too easy to put in a bottle, chained by his desire to become a part of society, as are you."

Suddenly my protests and reluctance to spend the night in the dark seemed petty. I owed him. Owed him big. "Thank you, Herm. It's a good place."

His shoulders slumped in relief. "I'll have the security system offline in about an hour. You have your phone?" he asked.

"Yes." I touched my pocket. "I'll need a charger by tonight, though." I looked at the auditorium's rear gate. "And somewhere to plug it in," I finished faintly. Where was I going to find a plug? The only power to the auditorium ran to the salvaged bathrooms.

"Give it to me," Herm said, hand outstretched. "Ben, yours, too. I'll drive them around with me today and turn them off on the expressway going east."

I took a breath, then exhaled, feeling stupid.

"Use this in the meantime." Herm handed me the bag. "Ben, that water I mentioned is in a cooler in the truck bed. It won't be cold, but you can fix that."

That he could, and I looked in the bag to see the phone still in its box. Herm was good at this. "Thanks," I said as I handed him my phone, and he tossed it up onto the dash with Ben's.

Motions slow, Benedict got out. I slid across the seat, feeling as if everything was moving too fast. There were only three cars in the huge lot, the parking space not yet repurposed, and yet I felt as if we were being watched. Tugging my cap lower, I scuffed the butt of my staff on the warm pavement and squinted at the shade by the door. Pluck was hiding in his amulet, and I held it, taking the brunt of the sun for both of us.

"See you in a few hours," Herm said loudly as Benedict slammed the door shut. Saying nothing more, he drove away.

Benedict squinted at the sliver of the quad visible between the buildings, a small cooler in hand. "You put dross on Dana? When?"

Heat billowed up from the pavement, but my fingers were cramped with cold from the lodestone. "Herm put it on her. She brought it up from the basement. Remember when she skinned her hand on the fireplace? I guess he didn't like her assuming one of us would pick it up."

It was my life in a nutshell. Uncomfortable, I headed for the small rear service door that opened to the garden itself. Benedict met my pace stride for stride as he scanned the area, but no one came back here and it was likely we'd gain the grotto unseen.

There were no cameras, and the tiny door in the brick wall was little more than a way to satisfy the fire codes. Benedict broke the lock with a well-placed piece of magic, and we went in, being careful to shut the door behind us. It was nearing noon, and the gardens with their shady nooks and cooling water fountain made a pleasant place to eat one's lunch. Today, though, it was empty thanks to the university having shut the grounds due to it being a high-shadow zone.

"Looks clear," Benedict whispered, and we eased out into the sun.

No cameras, Pluck fizzed as I followed Benedict to the well set over the original floor of the sunken auditorium. *Aasta kept breaking them until the university got the hint.*

Aasta, I mused. I liked knowing the shadow's true name, but it wasn't her that my mind went to but the half-drowned slim man who had pulled me from the floodwaters to the top of Cameron's car. Kahu, Thoth had called Pluck, both there, at the tunnel, and again at the records building. Clearly it was an image that Pluck had used before, attached to a name he no longer wanted to be known by.

Thoughts swirling, I touched Benedict's hand as we made our way down the walkway running between newly planted cacti and succulents. The aggressive chatter of a hummingbird was familiar and soothing. Benedict laced his fingers in mine almost shyly, and our pace slowed.

Hey, is Benny going to be okay down there? I asked Pluck as I remembered Aasta's reaction to Cameron.

He will be tolerated, fizzed and bubbled through me. *Every city shadow knows he made the inert dross that hides under the floor. But I doubt they have returned.*

I scuffed to a halt at the raised edge of the well, propping my staff against it before peering down into the blackness. *You sure?*

His concern laced through my query, and I wasn't surprised when Pluck hazed out of his lodestone, puddling onto the top of the wall briefly before slipping into the well and clinging to the shadowed side like a bat. *I will check,* tangled about my thoughts, and then he was gone.

Oblivious to our conversation, Benedict set the cooler atop the wall. "That's more than two stories down."

"Is it too far?"

"No." He squinted at where the surrounding walls met the sky. "Herm was right. I've jumped out of windows before."

"Somehow, that doesn't surprise me." I stared into the well as Pluck's presence became faint. I thought it odd that from here, it looked pitch-black down there, even with the spot of sun at the bottom.

"Okay." Benedict exhaled, the lodestone on his ring suddenly sparkling. "Sit on the wall. Legs in. On the count of three, I'm going to give you a little shove and you'll fall. It might seem fast, but it's about half speed. You'll land as if it's only three feet down."

My eyes widened. "Shove me? I don't think so. I will *shove* myself."

He winced, his hand on my shoulder. "This is kind of tricky," he admitted. "If you want to jump, that's fine, but if you hesitate when I say go, the field won't be around you and you'll drop like a stone."

I peered into the darkness. "Fine," I whispered. "You can push me."

Staff in hand, I worked my way up onto the well's edge, feet dangling. My pulse quickened when Benedict exhaled and a field, presumably, took shape between his hands. I couldn't see it, but I could sense it as a threadlike trace of something warm settled about me. It was the weft and weave of the universe, harnessed by Benedict's skill to make a space where gravity was less.

"Three, two, one," Benedict said, and I stifled a gasp at his firm shove.

I fell, losing the light. Darkness was a cool, soothing balm, and I held my breath. It was akin to being on a swing, hesitating at the apex before the plunge.

And then my feet hit the oak boards of the stage with a solid thump.

My legs flexed as my muffled grunt echoed against the unseen walls. Pulse pounding, I stared up at the bright spot of light. Benedict's silhouette was a sharply defined shadow. "Made it!" I called up, and then I laughed. *Never in my imagination . . .* I thought, and Pluck's fizzing relief that I was again in the dark found me.

"I'm good," I said, more softly now as my voice hissed eerily against the far walls. My eyes were adjusting, and I stepped out of the small circle of light, immediately feeling better. It was stuffy and closed, but not hot. At least, not until I put my hand in the beam of light.

Heat burned all the way to my elbow, knots of it tightening like a vise. I pulled back, thinking it more than odd. I hadn't felt any pain at all when I had been in full sun thirty seconds ago.

"Stand clear. I'm coming down!" Benedict called, and I shifted deeper into the dark.

If it had been strange falling under the influence of Benedict's spell, it was even odder watching him drop as if in slow motion. The cooler was tucked under his arm, and he squinted into the shadows to find me even before his feet hit the stage.

No one is here, fizzed through my uppermost thoughts, but it was faint, as if Pluck was still ranging about.

"That was way cool," I said as he yanked me into a relieved hug. "You must have had a fun childhood."

"Not especially." He sighed, and my shoulders relaxed. "It wasn't too fast, was it?"

"Perfect," I said, and he let me go.

"I still can't believe they left the chairs." He set the cooler down and spun in a slow circle. "Right up to the new ceiling."

"And the ghosts." I propped my stick against the podium.

Benedict sighed, his gaze on the silent, dusty blue chairs, his thoughts clearly on that day. "Temp isn't too bad," he said, but his expression was tinged in heartache. It had been awful, not knowing who was hurt and who we'd never see again. "This is not a safe house," he grumped. "It's not even a house."

"No dross, though." I took his hand and gave it a heartfelt squeeze. "Not even any dross dust."

He turned, me in the shadows, him still in the sun. "Dross dust?"

I tugged his hand until he joined me in the dark. "Don't worry about it. I'm really glad that you're with me," I said, thankful that Pluck was too far for our thoughts to mingle easily.

Smiling, he leaned down, head tilted, until his mouth found mine. Warm and tasting faintly of coffee, his lips moved against mine, sending a jolt of emotion through me. "I wouldn't want to be anywhere else," he whispered when he broke free.

"Still . . ." My grip around his waist lingered until it began to feel awkward.

Sighing, he rocked from me. "You want a water?"

He had moved back into the sun, but I stayed where I was, wondering if it was a portent of things to come. "Maybe later."

Benedict's motion to open the cooler hesitated, and he sat on it instead, his knees almost to his ears as he stared at the rows of chairs. His lodestone glittered in the sun, probably gathering energy, and I sat where I was against the podium. My toe shifted in and out of the sun as I fidgeted. Light. Dark. Light. Dark.

"You think this is an old nugget, or new?" Benedict asked as he flicked a spiny chunk of dross into the orchestra pit.

"Old." My higher voice hissed in the damp air, and I pulled my knees to my chest. Herm's burner phone was an uncomfortable bump, and I worked it from my back pocket and set it beside me. "There might be two, maybe three years' worth of space down here, but it's a mistake."

"A second mistake, Petra Grady?" a strong feminine voice called out, and both Benedict and I started, our attention going to the far wall. It was Darrell—or rather, Aasta animating Darrell's rez—and I scrambled up when Benedict stood, the man clearly uneasy.

Pluck, I called, getting a faint acknowledgment in return. He was on his way back.

Aasta curved Darrell's lips into a smirk, and her tightly corded hair bedecked with beads clinked as she took step after heavy step down the aisle toward us. It was eerie how much she looked, acted, and sounded like my old mentor—but there was a sly darkness in her that the woman I'd known had never possessed. "One mistake I can forgive," she said as she halted a mere two rows from the stage. "But two?"

She was staring at Benedict. Cold cramped my ankle as Pluck materialized at my side, his tail stiff and ears pricked, green eyes glaring at the shadow among the chairs. *Sorry. She wasn't here when I checked,* fizzed in my thoughts, his worry merging seamlessly with mine.

Benedict was ashen as he stood in the patch of sun. "Darrell . . ." he whispered, and the shadow animating the rez twitched her woven skirt.

"Not hardly," she said wryly. "But I like this energy pattern. It comes with an inborn sense to expect obedience."

Benedict edged closer to me, never leaving the security of the sun. "Sorry," he said, head bobbing. "You surprised me. I know you're a shadow."

Aasta lifted Darrell's chin to recognize his words, then turned to me. "Why is he here?"

"We're hiding," I said, and Aasta's attention flicked to Pluck as if she was annoyed.

"From the light?" she said, moving with Darrell's broken grace to the stairs rising to the stage. "No doubt."

"From everyone." I brushed the dust from my jeans and inched closer to Benedict. He almost glowed in the focused beam of light, but I couldn't bring myself to join him in it. "Um, Thoth cracked another vault, and until we can prove it was him, it's better if I stay out of sight."

The image of an old woman paused on the lowest stair, staring up at us as if tired. "Is that your first mistake's idea? Blame you for Thoth's ills?"

Benedict's brow furrowed. "First mistake's idea?" he whispered.

He was almost blinding in that spot of sun, his lodestone winking in a show of strength and surety. "That's what she calls Cameron," I said. "My mistake, and no. That isn't Cameron's idea," I added, talking to Aasta.

Benedict grimaced. "I am not a mistake."

Aasta began to rise up the stairs, moving slow as if pained. It was an act pulled from the remnants of Darrell's psyche imprinted upon the rez, and now, the shadow. "If we can't catch Thoth, Pluck and I will go down for it," I said, and Aasta's attention flicked to me, a wry expression furrowing her brow. If we were jailed, there'd be no hope of finding a new balance.

Darrell's hunched form reached the top step, pausing to frown at Benedict hiding in that spot of sun before continuing on to the podium. "Catch Thoth?" Aasta said as she scuffed her slippers. "It would be better if you were here to clean dross."

Annoyed, Pluck flicked an ear to send a drop of dark matter to hiss against the stage, inches from her not-there foot.

"I am surprised you are alive, weaver Grady," Aasta said as she reached the podium and leaned heavily against it. "Thoth has either made a mistake or a brilliant, strategic move."

He has made a mistake, Pluck thought firmly, but his ears had gone misty, and his feet were nothing but hazy drifts. His mind, too, was closed to me, and I dangled my fingers against his skull, ice deadening their tips. *And you will capitalize on it. Tell her I said that.*

"I can still direct dross," I said, and Aasta sneered at Pluck, the expression totally wrong on Darrell's face.

"You *let* Thoth break your weaver. Fool yeth. You know he is uncatchable. You should have hidden her. Like the rest of us."

Pluck lifted his lip to show his teeth, but the warning was directed at Aasta, not me. *That's not what happened. Petra, tell her.*

Benedict's grip on me tightened spasmodically. "Petra is not broken," he said, voice holding a hint of worry. "She'll learn how to make fields again. Even so, we almost caught him."

Aasta sank deeper into the shadows, the green of her eyes glittering until it was all I could see. "And that is why you are hiding in the dark. No, if you caught him, it was because he wanted you to," she intoned. "He must have more blame for you to take if he left you alive."

Pluck's frustration fizzed through me. The shadow drew away from me with an uncomfortable raking sensation, his mass swirling and coalescing until, with a shifting of booted feet not really there, he became the dark, slim man I'd seen in Cameron's coma. Clearly uncomfortable, he glanced at me before staring at Aasta in obvious defiance. He could have taken a human shape right from day one. Why hadn't he?

"You fool yeth," Aasta muttered as she looked Pluck up and down with a disinterest that said she was familiar with his image. "You, Kahu, of all of us, knew best who Thoth was, what he is capable of, and you allowed your weaver to engage. Her failing is your fault. All of it."

"Hey!" I snapped when Pluck's guilt lit through me. "This wasn't Pluck's fault."

"Petra isn't broken," Benedict insisted, gaze darting between Aasta and Pluck's new form. "And when we catch Thoth, we will find out what he did and repair it."

Aasta waved a hand, mimicking my dead mentor perfectly. "There's no fixing that," the shadow pronounced, and Pluck's shoulders rounded. "No field, no magic. How can she do anything if she can't even touch dross?"

I curved my fingers to hide my burned palms, and Pluck lifted his chin, his green eyes hazing into a mist. "The mage is right," he insisted, his voice holding that same faint accent it had had when in Cameron's coma. "Petra isn't broken. She can hear what no weaver before her has. Our thoughts mingle without my touching her, or she me."

The beads in Aasta's coiled hair weren't real, but they clinked as she squinted at me. "Threads," she said, and Benedict leaned into me, tugging me closer. "There are threads between you. I can see them in the sun." Her hand stretched out, and I shuddered when she curved her fingers in one by one as if plucking them, and an odd sensation shivered from me to Pluck—echoing back and forth. "How?"

Maybe . . . I thought as I squinted at the light between Pluck and me. It wasn't anything I could see . . . But something was there. I could feel Aasta tugging on it.

"It has been such since yesterday." Pluck glanced uneasily at me. "When she lost her ability to create fields, she gained the ability to see the threads making the universe's weft, to manipulate dark matter. She might not be able to weave it anymore, but last night, she tuned dross dust to energy as if she was a shadow." He took a slow breath he probably didn't need. "It was only to find relief from the pain, but she did it. No weaver has ever done that."

Aasta dropped her hand, and both Pluck and I shuddered as something fell back into place. "Truly." The shadow's gaze lifted to the lodestone around my neck. "You turned dross into energy? Stored it?"

Benedict's hand on my shoulder tightened, and I leaned into him, needing his support. "Um, I lost it at the end . . ."

"Because you took too much," Pluck said quickly. "But you tuned it. Stored what you could. Your skill will grow. I did not arise knowing what I do now. None of us did."

Shadows had a beginning, I mused, and Pluck fizzed an absent agreement, his thoughts clearly focused on Aasta's agitation.

But the shadow remained unmoved, her head slowly shaking in denial, beads clinking. "You cannot gain enough skill in a hundred lifetimes to best Thoth," she said to me, and Benedict took a breath to protest, hesitating when her green eyes narrowed on him. "His hatred is all-consuming. Thoth will snuff out your existence if you continue your goal of finding balance. And you . . ." She focused on Pluck. "You will be alone, scavenging for scraps like the rest of us."

Benedict leaned to whisper worriedly in my ear. "Petra . . ."

"Not this time." Pluck's edges hazed, then returned all the sharper. "Thoth took something from her, but now she can hear, and see, and manipulate dark matter. Aasta, if she can do that, maybe she can be what we've been missing. Maybe she is what's needed to finally catch Thoth and stop him. She can see the threads holding the universe from collapsing and still withstand dross to some extent. It burns, but it does not consume. That means something."

Aasta's shoulders slumped. "You would risk your weaver in a yeth's hope."

"It's not a yeth's hope," Pluck insisted, his gaze holding a hard determination. "Not if she can create dark matter from dross."

Benedict shifted uneasily from foot to foot. "You made dark matter from dross dust?"

"Yes, I guess," I said as I fingered Pluck's old amulet. "Last night. But what good is it if I can't make a field to do magic with it?"

Aasta's hope vanished. "Even your weaver knows it's a yeth's dream." Head down, she shuffled to the stairs. "She is one. You are alone."

"She is not alone!" It was a thunderous, icy statement, and I winced at the soft headache beginning at the base of my skull at Pluck's cry. The shadow shifted awkwardly as he glanced at Benedict, then me, a soft pleading in his eyes. "We will find five."

One stick, two sticks, three, four, five. Stand them straight to stay alive . . . "That's right!" I said, gaze darting to Benedict. "We almost had him with three sticks. If we could find five balanced sticks—"

"There is no strength in five!" Aasta blurted, an old pain crossing her. "That's a myth, a story to console ourselves. We have tried and failed before."

She already knows? I wondered. *Then it's not just a nursery rhyme. Pluck?*

Pluck pressed forward, his eyes alight. "Aasta, together we will bring him to task. We can catch him within a circle of five. Petra is not broken. She is the linchpin, the catalyst that will make it possible. What we have been missing."

The shadow made a bark of laughter. "Thoth will break any weaver or mage you send at him, like he broke Petra."

"I am not broken!" I exclaimed, and Benedict's hold on my shoulder strengthened even as Pluck's emotions flooded mine, spikes of cold stabbing through the last of my doubt. I might not be able to make fields, and dross broke on me, giving me bad luck and burning my skin, but I could wield a long-stick and tune dust to energy. That wasn't broken. That was just . . . being different.

"Those able to touch dross and make fields were never able to catch him," Pluck said, and Aasta spun away, clearly done arguing with fools. "Weavers always failed. But by trying to damage Petra, Thoth has given her something that might snare him. He doesn't know her skills. Blending it with others might be enough." He stared at me, his enthusiasm diluting my doubt until it was gone. "Five can snare him."

"It's a fable!" Aasta shouted, voice echoing, and Pluck stiffened.

"It's a promise," he vowed, but Aasta became only more agitated.

"A promise of failure," she said bitterly. "We tried five shadows and all were lost. Five weavers were the same. Spinners, mages, any combination. It makes no difference. We have tried every permutation. It only ever adds up to death."

"We have never tried with her," Pluck said, his surety fizzing through me. "She is something new. Five aspects of magic. We have only ever had four. It will work with her." He took a slow breath. "I know it."

Shadow, weaver, Spinner, mage, and whatever I am? I thought, feeling Pluck's enthusiastic agreement blending with my desire for this to work.

You are the medium, iced through me, and I stared, wondering if I could see the threads connecting us after all.

"I don't need to be able to touch dross to wield a stick," I said, and Benedict groaned softly. "We almost had him before," I added, pulling away to see the mage's desperate worry that I was going to hurt myself beyond recovery. "No, listen," I protested. "Even if he had only allowed us to trap him knowing he could break free at will, we almost had him. Benedict, you were there. Tell me I'm wrong."

Benedict hesitated, then nodded. "Perhaps if the sticks had been a balanced set."

Aasta huffed. "If you believe that, then you will die beside her." Motions holding an arthritic stiffness, she took the stairs slowly, woven skirt swaying. "I will not be a part of this."

"We've never had a weaver who could tune dross to dark matter," Pluck said, and Aasta waved at him dismissively. "She will master it," he added firmly.

"She is broken. There's nothing to master." Aasta walked through the empty orchestra pit, a disparaging huff coming from her. "You are fools," she added as she began to make her way back up the low steps between the rows of chairs. "We will abandon St. Unoc. To stay invites destruction as mages target us again."

At the last row of chairs, Darrell's image began to rock, her gaze going distant as the shadow started to pull from her. "We wanted to believe, and now pain lives with us again. No hope is worth this. No love is worth the grief it leaves." She took a breath, hunched in heartache. "It will destroy us." Darrell began to go misty, Aasta spilling from the rez like a dark fog.

"Why are you afraid, Aasta?" Pluck shouted, shaking almost, and I winced as ice stabbed my skull. "You have nothing left to lose, and still you will not hope?"

"Aasta, wait," I pleaded as Darrell's image blurred, but she was gone. As if a switch had been thrown, the apparition was empty now, soulless eyes staring at nothing, and the rez began to weep, a great gash in her forehead trickling blood into her eyes. It was just a rez now, repeating its empty litany as it slowly vanished.

Benedict took a slow breath, exhaling in relief. "At least she took the rez off the stage before leaving it," he said softly. Smile waning, he brushed the hair from my eyes. "You okay?"

"Ask me tomorrow." I glanced at Pluck, his stance stoically stiff. His emotions twining in mine were in turmoil. "Pluck thinks this will work, and so do I." I took Benedict's hand, my grip tightening when Pluck noticed and looked away.

Benedict nodded as he tried to pull me into the sun. "Five sticks carried by five aspects of magic. Shadow, weaver, Spinner, mage, and . . . you." His hand slipped from mine when I refused to step into the light. "Are you sure?" he said, his worry obvious.

"She's not broken," Pluck practically growled. The shadow had settled himself on the edge of the stage, feet dangling.

"No, she's not," Benedict agreed. "Hey, thanks for animating a rez so I could hear you."

Pluck's shoulders misted as he shrugged, the shadow clearly distracted.

"That's not a rez," I said, my worry twining about Pluck's making it worse.

Benedict's eyes widened. "You can become a person now?"

Pluck didn't shift his gaze, and a hidden pain drifted through me. "I like the dog better."

"Mmmm." Benedict glanced at me, then Pluck. "Me too."

Pluck listlessly threw a spiny chunk of inert dross into the chairs. He was positively depressed and I didn't know why. So what if Aasta didn't help us?

Worried, I went to sit with him. Pluck never glanced up as I lowered myself, but I knew he felt my question twining in his mind.

"I shouldn't have chastised Aasta," he said, the shadow watching Benedict stare at the hole in the ceiling. "She has a right to doubt. To be afraid. I don't want to talk about it."

I reached out until my pinky touched the haze of his presence. Ice cramped my hand, but I didn't care. "Maybe Aasta is right. If it's too much of a risk, we could hide."

His form dissolved into a bright haze and I jerked my hand away, silent as the black sparkles fell back into Pluck and he coalesced into his more usual dog form.

Not again, fizzed angrily through me. *I can't let Thoth ruin what we have started. We are so close. Thoth might have taken your ability to make fields, but you're stronger without them. You can hear the universe chime, see the threads of dark matter forcing it to expand so time moves as it should. You have tuned dross dust, turned it to dark matter so as to build your strength. No weaver has done that before.*

Strength I can't use, I thought as Benedict gave me a bottled water. "Thanks, Benny."

Not yet, Pluck thought as the mage heaved a sigh and sat down on my other side. The man clearly knew Pluck and I were talking—and he seemed content with that. *But you will.*

"I don't even know what I am anymore," I said aloud to both of them. "I can't be a weaver if I can't touch dross."

"It's okay, Petra." Benedict bumped my shoulder, the cheerful man probably trying to shake me from my pity party. "I can't touch dross, either. That's why they invented dross-cored sticks."

You can touch dross, Pluck fizzed, a part of him melting to nothing when Benedict curved an arm around me and tugged me closer. *It may burn and break on you, but you can already tune more than I can. With practice, you might regain your ability to touch it entirely.*

Like changing it to dark matter instead of fixing it inert? I questioned. It felt a little close to using dross as an energy source, but that was what shadows did.

Thoth left you alive to take the blame for his actions. He's never done that before. It's given you skills he's becoming afraid of. Aasta is too mired in her memories to help, but you will not face him alone. We will find others.

"We will find a way to catch him," Benedict whispered as he felt me tense. "Once Thoth is in a bottle, he will reverse whatever it is he did to you or burn in a vat of dross."

It was a rather grim thought for Benedict, gaining a heady agreement from Pluck, the sentiment flowing through me as the shadow dissolved into a puddle. Oozing away, he left me to find solace with Benedict. Sighing, I pretended that Benedict was right to hope if for just a moment as I molded myself to him, my head pressed into his shoulder.

There was no going back, only forward. I had heard it in Aasta's words, certain and hard. Pluck was right, though. I wasn't facing Thoth alone. Together we were stronger than our sundry skills. If it took five balanced sticks, we'd find five balanced sticks and the magic users to wield them.

19

BENEDICT'S FIDGETING WAS SLIGHT BUT TELLING, HIS GAZE IN THE MIDDLE DIStance and his arms over his chest as he stoically stood dead center of the hospital elevator. I wasn't much better, fingering Pluck's new moldavite amulet until I realized what I was doing and stopped. As promised, Herm had come shortly after four to pick us up. The Spinner was insufferably pleased with himself, not only successfully taking the garden security offline but arranging to meet with Dana so as to get her out of Cameron's hospital room.

I, though, was worried that the subterfuge would backfire on him. Pluck and I hadn't been charged with anything, but we'd been told to stay clear of the marshal. If we were caught, Dana might have the ammunition to put me in custody.

And yet here we were.

Pluck huffed, and I dangled my fingers between his ears, enjoying the chill cramping my hand. There was a faint glitter of dross in the corners and where the walls met the floor, missed from the last sweep. *Too tiny to catch?* I mused as I swung my stick into play, running the silver-shod end along the seams to collect the dross dander into a small dust bunny. Maybe it was overkill, but I didn't like messing with elevators.

Silent, Benedict moved so I could reach behind him.

"I'm surprised you brought your stick," he said, and I shifted the dross-cored staff a hundred and eighty degrees until I could eye the admittedly small, glittering drop of latent energy. The microparticles were probably remnants of larger dross issues.

"Yep."

"It makes you easily recognizable," Benedict grumbled.

"Probably." We would likely have to go back into hiding after this stunt, whether it worked or not. "But if Thoth shows, it will keep him at arm's length. You saw how scared he is of dross." Not that I blamed him. That stuff hurt.

My fingers dangling in Pluck's effervescence grew even more cold. *You should try tuning that.*

I eyed the glow on the tip of the stick, dueling feelings of anticipation and dread making an ugly slurry in me. "Seriously?" I said aloud, and the elevator chimed.

Benedict pushed past me when the silver doors opened. "Wait here," he said, gaze on the nurses' desk halfway down the hall. "Give me a few minutes to plow the road."

"Ah, sure." I glanced over the elevator lobby, the walls covered with informational placards and watercolor pictures of poppies. There was a bench, and I sat, waiting for him to distract the nurse so I could slip past. From down the hall, Benedict's cheerful hail rang out.

It's one nurse, Pluck fizzed. *How hard can it be to evade one nurse?*

"Depends on the nurse." I eyed the dross trap doing double duty as a trash can. Sighing, I angled the tip of the stick toward it to get rid of the dross dust, and Pluck's thoughts quickened with a sudden urgency.

Don't . . . he thought, and I jerked the stick away, a haze of dross pulling from the trap until the attraction faded and it fell back under the tripod. *Tune it,* he encouraged.

I slowly set the butt of the staff on the floor. It put the haze of dust almost at eye level. *Now?* I asked nervously, and a wash of reassurance flooded me.

Put your thoughts into your lodestone . . .

I knew what to do, and I glanced to where Benedict was chatting up the nurse. It clearly wasn't going well. I had time. Slipping into a meditative state was easy, and I centered my awareness on the unassuming muddy-green stone in my hand and exhaled. Its latticework shimmered at the edge of my mind's eye, a faint green glow of dark matter lighting it.

In comparison, the dross dust was on fire, and I gingerly pulled it free, fingers burning. It puddled in my hand as I set the stick aside, and I hardly breathed, feeling it scorch my palm, threatening to break on me.

Gently now, encourage it to break, letting it funnel through your mind and into the stone, Pluck suggested. *It's not enough to hurt you.*

Sure, that was what he said, but what I wanted to do was throw the stuff into the trap and be done with it. Instead, I rolled the glowing sphere in my palm until it began to prickle in protest, little darts of agony jolting through my hand.

Watch now. It's breaking. Catch it. Direct the released dark matter into the stone, Pluck encouraged, and with that, the dross dust completely fell apart. Heat flashed through me as it tried to randomly change the universe. I pulled it into me instead, feeling it sear my thoughts until it found the lodestone. With a sudden plink of sensation, the energy wave flashed through the entirety of the moldavite and elevated the lattice to a new energy level.

The heat in my palm vanished. My hand was empty and the lodestone perched in my fingers glittered a darker green.

Pluck? I thought, but his pride and excitement were already spilling through me. Clearly I'd done it—done it right this time.

Outstanding! he praised, and the image of the glowing latticework in my mind vanished as his thoughts eclipsed everything. I was not a shadow, but this would make my life a lot less painful. Especially if I could train myself to do this without thinking, as Pluck did.

"It's going to take a lot more practice before I'm as good as you,"

I said, and he made a wolfy huff, his ear flicking to send a splat of dark matter hissing against the wall as he stared down the hall.

Ah, I think they called for security, Pluck fizzed, and my elation faltered. He was right. Two bulky orderlies were flanking Benedict, large enough they made even his wide shoulders and height seem small.

Ever the elitist, he began to protest, and a smile found me. I didn't think this was what he had had in mind, but it would still work. Standing, I went to the trap and used my stick to knock it apart. The trap's shorter sticks rolled and bumped about the floor, freeing the previously collected dross.

What are you doing? Huffing, Pluck jumped up onto the bench as I danced back, avoiding the mini flow even as I wrangled all three trap sticks free of it.

"There's only one person without a hospital ID who can go anywhere without question," I said as I shook a stick until the clinging dross let go. "And I know all the passwords." My fingers burned, the pain ignored as I shook the other two until they lost their dross as well.

They will recognize you, Pluck warned, and I gathered the three sticks in a tight bundle.

Better than a clipboard . . . "That's the point."

No disguise was a thin disguise. I'd be relying on props and attitude, and I had plenty of both. "Amulet?" I prompted, and Pluck shook himself, dark matter flying.

Only until you get past the desk.

"Then let's go." The moldavite around my neck grew cold when Pluck ghosted into it, and I tucked the stone behind my shirt, not liking the growing knot of people. Benedict was going to get himself kicked out.

Chin high, I sauntered to the supply room next to the nurses' desk. Benedict's argument faltered when he spotted me, and I shrugged.

The mage took a breath, channeling his inner entitled tenured professor. "I have every right to make sure that the marshal's needs are being met!" he exclaimed. "I know she's on this floor. I demand to know what room!"

We already knew what room thanks to Lev. Head down, I opened the supply room door, waiting as the lights flickered on. The hospital-grade bottles were right where they should be, and my heart gave a little thump when the nurse looked up from her argument with Benedict.

"Thank you," she mouthed, distracted but relieved when I came out with an empty bottle. She didn't care what I was cleaning up, just that someone had come from the sweepers' guild to take care of it.

It had been a while since I'd felt that gratitude. It almost hurt—the realization of what I'd lost when I'd gained Pluck. Things were tense on campus, but my sweeper friends would always be appreciated. Me? Not so much anymore.

I'm sorry for the way things are, Pluck fizzed, and I shifted the bottle under my arm.

"Don't you dare apologize," I muttered. "I'd rather be a misunderstood weaver than an underappreciated sweeper any day. If I wasn't here cleaning up their mess, I'd get the stink eye."

And with that, I boldly walked past Benedict and the two orderlies and headed down the hall.

"This is not over," Benedict said loudly. "I'll be sitting right there until Dana comes back, and then I expect an apology. I am not a criminal."

"Mathis, will you escort the professor off the grounds?" the nurse said, but her voice was already going faint as Pluck and I continued down the hall.

Sticks and a bottle get you anywhere, I thought, and Pluck bubbled, a faint haze of nothing taking shape at my heel when we turned a corner. Nervous, I dabbled my fingers in his chill presence. Anxiety kept my pace fast, and I didn't put the jar down. I had to get Cameron free. I thought I was the only one who could do it. *Or am I overinflating my own value . . .*

You are not, Pluck fizzed, but doubt clung to me, and my pulse quickened when I spotted Lev sitting in a chair next to a door. Seeing me, he stood, his stance furtive.

"I heard yelling. Where's Benedict?" he said as Pluck and I closed the gap, and a feeling of kinship flowed from me to Pluck, surprising the shadow.

"Arguing with the orderlies," I said, and Lev gave Pluck a nod. "Probably getting kicked out as we speak."

"Not the plan, but whatever works." He glanced down the empty hall, then ushered me to the door. "She still hasn't woken up."

Guilt laced his voice. He was blaming himself. I understood why, but it hadn't been his fault. My relief that we'd gotten past the nurses' desk vanished when we entered the room. It was bright with the low sun, and Pluck hazed to nothing, disappearing under the bed.

"You sure Thoth isn't here?" I said as I took in Cameron's pallor. Someone had propped the bed up so she was nearly sitting. Almost, I could believe she was sleeping.

He's gone, Pluck fizzed as Lev shrugged. *But he left a web to snare us. It will not.*

Good, I mused, then started when Lev pushed a chair forward for me.

"Thank you for this," Lev said, expression grim. "I'll keep watch in the hall. I'm not supposed to come in, and if they see me gone they might investigate."

"This wasn't your fault, Lev," I said, but he shook his head as he left, jaw clenched in frustration as he shut the door with a soft click.

Truly it wasn't, and I set the empty bottle and trio of sticks aside before going to pull the vertical blinds. *Much better,* I thought in the golden haze as I scooted the chair closer and gingerly sat, my knees touching the hard frame of the bed. Pluck fizzed and bubbled, his thoughts coming so fast that I couldn't parse out anything but a rising worry. Cold seeped upward from my ankle as he slipped deeper into my thoughts until even my chest cramped and my arms became icy. I took a deliberate breath, feeling odd as I exhaled a cold mist.

And yet for as cold as I was, I wasn't shivering. Even the chill of dark matter had lost its bite.

I can sense her, Pluck fizzed, his thoughts in mine seeming almost warm. *If we can get through the web he left to snare us, we can pull her consciousness free of it.*

My eyes closed, and I took Cameron's hand. It was hot, and I strengthened my grip, relishing it. *Then let's do this.*

Indecision colored his confidence, spilling into me until I banished it for both of us. Slowly the smaller sounds of the room gained a new importance: the hum of equipment, Lev's foot scraping in the hall, the TV in a distant room playing. Until faintly, almost not there, came an echoing ring of the universe at odds with the constant chiming tinnitus in my ears.

Is that Cameron? I mused, and Pluck's light presence in mine brightened in affirmation. Relief spilled through me. It was a double blessing as the slow rise and fall of her presence gave me something to follow deeper into her thoughts, but more importantly, if the roar of the universe still echoed in her mind, Thoth hadn't taken away her ability to make fields.

More confidently now, I let myself dissolve into the muzzy nothing that filled Cameron's mind. Slowly a glittering network of twined threads took precedence, Pluck's bright humor and sour acceptance making it obvious what was Cameron's mind and what was his. Sparking nodes of thought blazed within her, but there were far too few. I had to wake Cameron up. Not just for me but for her. Somewhere, hardly recognizable, I felt my hand tighten on Cameron's.

Cameron sleeps beyond the snare, he fizzed. *She's trapped in the same dreamscape as before. Are you ready? I can take you through Thoth's trap.*

I didn't see any trap, but that was the point. Pluck could. *Yes.*

Then take a breath.

He didn't mean literally, but I still found myself doing just that as my thoughts shrank down to a tiny point, and I followed Pluck's presence, letting Cameron's mind grow closer, larger, until a glowing mass of threads took shape between it and us. A second hum became obvious, vibrating through me, the soft rise and fall coming in ever-larger waves until it was a roar. This, I realized, was Thoth's snare, and I had no idea how to get past it.

I looked for the way out, realizing I was trapped.

Panic spiraled through me until Pluck wrapped his presence around mine, muffling the chaos, his thoughts growing more solid as the pulse of energy swelled and ebbed. It was telling me I was no longer real, and I believed it. How could I be?

Of course you're real, Pluck thought, clearly having caught my musings. *You are as solid as the chair you're still sitting in, but you are also just as much the spaces between your mass as your mass itself. Concentrate on the spaces. Like you, the sound of the universe isn't solid, it's many parts moving in concert, just as light energy is. You must pull yourself into the spaces your mass possesses to slip through. That's all this is.*

Spaces, I mused, listening for the emptiness amid the clutter of noise. They were there, and the more I concentrated on them, the bigger the gaps grew until the rising echo all but vanished.

You have it, Pluck thought. *Go. Take us both through.*

It wasn't so much moving my awareness as it was falling inward. Vertigo spiraled through me, through us. My mind seemed to hiccup, and with a crack that was more felt than heard, something broke. And with that, everything seemed to implode, taking me with it.

I gasped, suddenly floundering in that brown, warm, gritty river of Cameron's nightmare.

"Pluck?!" I called, choking on a mouthful as I treaded water. A log was to my right, sinking under me as I grasped for it and I, too, went under. Water roared with the echo of the universe, and then I found the surface.

"Got you!" Pluck sang out, and then a hand gripped my shoulder and dragged me to a floating car.

We were back, and I pulled myself up onto the roof, hacking and coughing out stardust disguised as dirty brown water.

"You mastered it," Pluck said, and I looked up, more surprised at the pride in his voice than at seeing him as he had been before, in jeans and a lightweight shirt, dry this time right down to his soft shoes. *He must have appeared on the car,* I thought, then jumped at the sudden hammering on the front window.

"Cameron!" She was there inside the car, the frantic woman armpit-deep in water as we floated and spun down the river. "Open the window. We can get you out! Thoth made a mistake. Let's go!"

"Grady?" she shouted, voice muffled as she put a damp hand to the dash. "Oh, my God. You've got to go. Now! Before he knows you're here. He's going to break the vault!"

"He already did. Put the window down," I insisted, and Pluck grabbed my arm as I leaned over the hood to see her better. "We're getting out of here."

"Not the vault at the records building," she shouted, making me wonder how she knew. "The one here at the hospital!"

The one full of dross?

"Ah, Grady?" Pluck's grip on my arm tightened. "We've got a bridge coming up. I think it's our way out."

I looked up, blanching. "Are you serious?" I blurted. The floodwaters were smashing up against the bottom of the bridge with the force of a car hitting an overpass. Angry water frothed and boiled, and I watched in horror as an entire tree crashed against it, spinning violently, roots over crown over roots, branches snapping, until it was sucked under. The maelstrom would pull us down before we had a chance to climb onto the bridge, but seeing as we were headed right for it, I knew this was it.

"It's a trap!" Cameron shouted from inside the car. "He will know if I escape. It will trigger him into blowing the vault. He won't do it until you're here. Just go!"

What? No! I thought, sensing Pluck's sudden anger and . . . chagrin? The net around Cameron's mind hadn't been the real trap.

Damn it all to hell . . . I wasn't sure who had thought it, and I straightened, scanning for another way out. Frothing water and dangerous, slippery shores: I wouldn't leave her a second time. "Cameron, you need to get out. Now!" I demanded. "The car is about to get sucked under a bridge, and if you die here, you die in that bed."

"That's what I'm saying!" Cameron slammed her fist on the dash, her neck craned to see me on the roof. "Go before he knows you're here. You have to catch Thoth. Once he's contained, I will wake up."

"Petra . . ." Pluck's green eyes pinched in worry. "I misjudged him again. The bridge was triggered into existence when we got through his trap. He put it here to force us to take her out. She either comes with us and alerts Thoth to crack the hospital vault, or she stays here and dies."

Cheese and crackers, I thought, cold as I looked at Cameron's suddenly frightened face. I was not leaving her here to die. "Cameron . . ." I started, gasping when the car hit something and spun into a sickening swirl. I fell to my knees, holding on to the wet car in a panic until it freed itself and we lurched back into the current.

Pluck hadn't moved, his balance perfect as he stared downstream. "You see that bridge?" he said, and Cameron's expression faltered. "This car is going to hit it in forty seconds. When it does, we will have three seconds, tops, before the current pulls the car down and drags it under. It won't resurface." His eyes met mine, the green of them giving away that he wasn't human. "The only way to hide that we were here is to let Cameron die."

That was so not going to happen. "Cameron, get your ass out here!"

"But everyone will blame you for the vault—" she started.

"Open that damn window and get your ass out here!" I shouted.

"If you don't, I will stay and all three of us will die. Not just here, but for real!"

The woman looked tearfully up at me, her jaw clenched. "I order you—"

"I outrank you here!" I exclaimed. Shadow spit. The bridge was almost on us. "Open the fucking window or I'm going to bash it in!"

Finally Cameron turned to the window. Floodwater poured in as she lowered it, and the woman panicked. Arms flailing for me, she reached for help.

"I've got you!" I cried as her wet hand found mine and I gripped it, pulling her up and out onto the roof. The small woman hung half in, half out for a moment, her feet struggling to find purchase until Pluck grabbed her shoulder and hauled her higher. Gasping, she lay on the roof, legs akimbo as she struggled to sit up.

Tearstained, she blinked at us both. "Everyone will blame you," she said, even as she reached out to us to help her stand. "They won't believe me when I say it was him. Dana will say you forced me to say it in return for getting me out."

I pulled her to her feet, staggering as I took her weight. The car slowly spun, and I inched to the edge to balance it out. It was sinking fast now that the window was open. "We will deal with it after you wake up. Ready? Pluck says if you get on the bridge you'll wake up."

"Are you fucking kidding me?" she whispered, eyes riveted to the frothing water.

"Okay," Pluck said, eyes on the bridge. "Brace yourself!"

I clenched my teeth, holding Cameron up, holding her close. I would not let her go. She would make it. I would not allow Thoth to use people against me. Never.

We hit with a bone-shaking thud. Cameron gasped as we were flung forward. My wet hands grasped for the cold stone, slipping.

"Climb!" Pluck shouted, and then I yelped when he boosted me up. My arms felt like noodles as I hooked one in the stone railing and reached down for Cameron, only to find Pluck standing alone on the sinking car.

"Cameron!" I panicked until I saw she was already on the bridge, face creased in effort and a hand out to help pull Pluck up.

Together we grasped his raised hands just as the car was pulled under the bridge, metal grinding and twisting in a frothing madness.

"Up, pull him up!" I groaned as we struggled to draw him from the current until, with a sodden scrape of wet clothes, he was on the bridge.

It might only be a nightmare in Cameron's mind, but it felt real, and I was too exhausted to laugh, or cry, or anything as I stared at Pluck, his eyes wide as the water continued to beat on the bridge, rumbling like thunder under us.

"I can't believe we made it. Are you okay?" I asked, and he jumped, startled when I touched him. He looked like a person, and I suddenly felt ashamed for ever seeing him as a dog. Uneasy, I turned to Cameron. But she was gone. "Where . . ."

Pluck smiled, the expression looking rare and beautiful. His eyes, I realized, were the same hazy green as moldavite. "She's starting to wake. Let's go. We slipped his snare."

He touched my shoulder and I gasped when the scent of the universe hit me. A thunderous peal of noise pushed me tumbling through a net of spider silk. Like a rabbit hole in reverse, the universe flowed through me as if I wasn't really there.

And then I jumped, startled when my eyes opened.

Shocked, I grasped the roll bar of Cameron's bed. I took a fast breath, but she didn't move, quiet and still, and as dry as a bone in the desert. The sun still shone on the blinds, but the harsh glow had faded to a warm haze. It had been a dream, but it had been real, too. We'd done it. I think, even if she didn't look awake. "Cameron?"

"Oh, thank God," Lev said, and I spun to see him just inside the door, his eyes wide in hope. "I was getting worried. Did you find her?"

"Y-Yeah," I stammered. My leg was freezing. No surprise, seeing as Pluck was pressed against me. Shadow spit, my leg was almost inside him.

My lips parted as Cameron's living dream flashed through me. He had pushed me to safety first, even knowing if he had died there, he would have died here. Gratefulness spilled from him to me, and relief that we were both okay. Under it was a lingering worry, but before I could form a thought, he dissolved into nothing and hazed under the bed. *Pluck?*

I leaned down to look for him, recalling his worried smile and his wet hair plastered to his face. Dross dust sparkled everywhere, so much more than I'd ever seen before.

"Go," Cameron rasped, and I jerked upright.

"Cameron!" Lev blurted, knocking me aside as he put a hand on her shoulder and the woman opened her eyes. "Look at me. Cameron?"

"She's okay," I said as he gently shook her and she pushed on his hand, trying to get him to stop. I rubbed my fingers together, remembering the cold feel of the threads and the echoing emptiness beyond.

Eyes open, Cameron fumbled for my hand, squeezing it until I looked at her. "Get out of here. Now. They can't blame you if you aren't here."

"For what?" Lev asked.

I took a breath to answer, hesitating when something shivered up through me: a tangle of lines, a pressure, a pause in the constant hum of the universe. "Ah, Pluck?" I said, and then I reached for the wall when the floor shook.

I spun, staring at Lev and Cameron as multiple distant alarms began going off.

"For that," I whispered.

20

LEV'S EXPRESSION BLANKED WHEN THE BUILDING TREMOR FADED ONLY TO BE replaced by the faint hooting of alarms. "Time to go. Cameron, do you know where your clothes are?"

"Do I know . . . Are you serious?" Teeth clenched, Cameron eased the IV out of her arm. "Ah . . . shit, that hurts."

The ex-military man stooped over her, flipping her blanket back with a decisive motion to slip one arm around her shoulders, the other under her knees. "Gown and wheelchair it is."

"Hey! Get off," the woman demanded. Angry, she gave him a smack. Lev immediately backed away, his hands in the air and a scowl on his face. "I have been out for a day. I can walk," she insisted, looking breathless as she swiveled her feet to hang over the bed. Her hospital gown had ducks on it, and she was clearly embarrassed. "Turn around. I have to get my catheter out."

"Um . . ." Lev started, and I put a hand on his shoulder to spin him to the window.

Pluck? I thought as Cameron exhaled, clearly feeling some discomfort. The oddest sensation was rippling over my skin. It felt like a spiderweb blowing into me, and I shuddered. *The vaults are full here. Thoth wouldn't risk a dross flow by cracking one. Would he?*

Pluck swirled out from under the bed, a flicker of solid mass showing for a moment as he pushed past the vertical blinds to look out the window. *I'm sensing free dross. Moving. A lot of it.*

He'd blown a full vault. *Shadow spit. Not again.*

"I told you to leave me there," Cameron said. "You can turn around now."

I spun to see her sitting on the edge of the bed, clearly trying to catch her breath. Lev, though, had joined Pluck at the window, standing to the side to peek out past the blinds.

"Ah, guys?" he said, voice tight. "I think the hospital vault just went."

My attention lifted from Cameron and a sick feeling swirled through me. The hospital vault was under the three-story parking garage—the same one that Lev was looking at.

"Go." Cameron still sat on the edge of the bed, her head low as she tried to gather her strength. "If no one sees you, they might believe me when I tell them it was Thoth."

"It's too late," I said. The nurse hadn't recognized me, but she could identify me. Benedict, too, had been detained. Drawn by Pluck's horror, I went to the window, aghast when I saw a thin stream of brightly glinting dross pouring out of the garage's exits, strands of it clinging to the landscaped cacti like plastic bags in a flood.

"Ah, I think the structure is cracking," Lev said, pushing the blinds all the way open, and we stood watching as a little blue car tore out of the parking garage as if it was on fire, which it sort of was. "See the supports?" he asked, sounding almost pleased when he added, "Pluck, you are better than a demo espionage team. You sure you won't come work for us?"

"That isn't helping, Lev," I muttered.

"Well, the university isn't going to want you after this." Lev ran a hand across his chin in approval. "They've known shadows can take out vaults since Pluck destroyed the one under the auditorium. Your promise that they wouldn't do it again is running thin."

All because of one deluded shadow, I thought, my sick feeling growing when a spiderweb of cracks raced up the pilings. It was like watching two hundred years condensed into thirty seconds. *Please . . . No one be in there,* I thought at the approaching sirens. A scattering of people ran from the garage, and I jumped, horrified at the muffled thump of uncountable tons of cement hitting the earth.

Dust billowed, looking worse than it probably was with the setting sun gleaming through it. Lev swore softly when it was followed by a glittering mass of dross, vomited from the structure to flood the street. It was my living nightmare come again. Fear clenched my gut. *Please. Please let no one have been in there.*

Cameron scuffed to a halt behind me, a pained, heartbroken expression pinching her features. "I'm sorry," she said. "You should have—"

"Let you die there?" I finished, and Lev's eyes widened. "Dana would have blamed me for that, too. Get dressed." With a panicked quickness, I pushed past her to rummage in the dresser until I found a clear plastic bag with her things. "You're coming with me to Herm's safe house."

"I'm not going to hide in a safe house," she said as she dumped the bag on the unmade bed, frowning at Lev as she stuffed her feet into her pants and hiked them up under her gown. Her breath was fast as she struggled, and I stared at the growing crowd on the hospital lawn, everyone staying clear of the receding flood. Across the street, a hundred-year-old cactus slowly tipped and hit the ground.

"I need a phone," Cameron said, voice muffled as she probably tried to get her shirt over her head. "Bring in some backup. Damn it, why am I so weak? I was only out for a day. It's only been a day, right?"

"They had you on some wicked drugs," Lev said, and then we both jumped when the second floor of the parking structure fell into the lower one. Alarm sounding, a car slid from the garden level into the street, nose first.

"My phone is dead," Cameron said in disgust as she stuffed it in her pocket. "Lev? Give me yours."

"I have a burner." I felt sick, and I tried to get her moving. "You can make as many calls as you want from the grotto. We gotta move."

Cameron's brow furrowed as she pulled away from me, catching her chancy balance against a wall. "Grady, give me your phone. Now."

Lev yanked her into motion. "I can understand you being a little confused, ma'am, but Thoth just took out the hospital vault full of dross. He's changed his modus operandi and is therefore unpredictable. You're the only one with firsthand knowledge of his actions."

"Me hiding won't solve anything," she protested as he pushed her to the door.

"Yeah?" I scowled at her. "As long as you are alive to say he busted the vault, he'll come for you. It would be smart to be a little less accessible."

Cameron stopped fighting Lev. "The grotto?" she whispered, worry pinching her expression as she looked at the setting sun. "At night?"

"Aasta is down there, but she knows you. Better, she hates Thoth." I lifted my head, searching. "Pluck?" I could feel his dread from here, and I touched the amulet around my neck in invitation. There was so much dross out there. Sure, it would burn me like the sun, but I wouldn't dissolve like Pluck. "Where's my stick?" I added, snatching it up as Pluck hazed my feet.

"Okay." Lev cracked the door and an excited chatter filtered in. "I had to park out at C lot. Some good luck there. Cameron, when we find a wheelchair, you're in it."

"I can walk," she grumbled, and he looked at her hospital slippers, a sly smirk curling his lips up. Her shoes hadn't been in the bag, and I wondered if they were still in my apartment.

Lev glanced again into the hall, then gestured for us to move. "Ladies?"

Cameron pushed forward, clearly struggling. Pluck was a cold chill wrapped about my wrist, his every emotion pinging against mine as I followed her, balking at the chaos. What had been an empty hall moments ago was now full of people clustering at the windows. The sound of sirens persisted, and reflected lights were flashing against the ceiling.

"Go back to your rooms!" a harried nurse demanded, ignored. "The hospital is not being evacuated. You're safe here."

But as I caught a glimpse of the collapsed parking structure and its moat of burning dross, it was hard to believe her. *Please, no one be in there . . .*

Lev's hand cupped Cameron's elbow, a subtle help her pride could accept as we made our way down the hall pretty much ignored. The chatter was loud, and head down, I paced as quickly as we dared, my remorse pinging against Pluck's as we both remembered a day just like this on a larger scale when the auditorium collapsed under a thousand little things going wrong with its construction. Death by a million cuts.

Shadow spit. I bet he used Benedict's frozen dross to break it from the outside. Can't we go six hours without a major breach? I thought, and Pluck fizzed, his coils on my wrist tightening.

Not if they keep storing dross like this, he thought dryly.

But "this" was how they had always done it, and I tensed as we passed the nurses' desk.

"Stairs," Lev said. "I'm not getting in an elevator. Cameron, you doing okay?"

"Have I said anything to imply otherwise?" Cameron panted, and Lev tucked his shoulder under her arm and took her weight.

"You've got her?" I yanked open the fire door, and he nodded. Cameron was gripping him in a white-knuckled strength. If I hadn't guessed it before now, it had become obvious that Lev felt responsible for Cameron. I understood why, though I didn't agree with it. He'd left her where she lay in my apartment for who knew how long, thinking that Pluck had downed her. He could have gotten Thoth off her far sooner, but the reality was that the damage had probably already been done by the time she hit the floor.

"They will have a wheelchair in the lobby," I said, trying to hide my stick when someone raced past us on the stairs, the woman yanking the fire door open so hard it slammed into the wall. She was gone in an instant, and the sounds of sirens and someone on a bullhorn slowly faded with the door closing.

"You think she recognized you?" Lev asked when we reached the landing, and I shrugged, pulling the fire door open.

It was even more chaotic in the lobby, and Pluck's grip on my arm tightened. Knots of people clustered before the tall windows, and I had a thought that Thoth's stunt had one good outcome: we could walk right out the door and no one would notice.

The cameras, though, were not so distractible, and I kept my head down as I scanned for a chair. "There," I said in relief, and Lev waited by the wall when I went to get it.

"I'm not riding in a wheelchair," Cameron protested when I returned with it, the woman white-faced as she gripped Lev's arm. "I can walk."

"Pretend you need it." He almost pushed her into it. "It will help us get out of here," he said as she glared up at him.

Her gaze went to her feet, and finally she relented. "You are such a bullshitter," she grumbled, and Lev took control of the handles. The wheels had never been locked, and with the slow, steady pace of an orderly paid by the hour, he angled the chair to the huge revolving door.

Pluck dove for his new amulet when the setting sun hit me, and I tucked myself in behind Lev, shuffling in the revolving door's half circle . . .

. . . until we were outside.

I almost ran into Lev when he made a quick right. People lined the drop-off zone and a man with a bullhorn shouted garbled instructions, mostly ignored. The scent of broken rock, oil, and gas was thick. Dust billowed from the rubble to haze the sun, and a few car alarms continued to sound. A flashlight-lit triage had formed on the lawn, and my relief twined with Pluck's when I realized it was only minor scrapes and bruises. There was no line of covered bodies, and I stifled a memory of the disaster at the auditorium.

"Everyone with a patient wristband needs to be inside," the man insisted, ignored. "There's no evacuation at this time, but we are asking visitors to leave and for arriving off-duty employees to report to their managers for instructions."

"We're all the way in C lot," Lev said, frustrated at the people in his way. "Petra's luck strikes again. The car ahead of me got the last spot in the parking structure."

Cameron managed a smile, but I failed to see the upside. A hundred and fifty people had thought themselves lucky for having snagged a spot so close, and now their cars were totaled.

My skin prickled at the pool of dross now flooding the nearby parking lot. Tires were already beginning to rot as the freed potential energy began to break on everything. A veritable whirlpool of it spun like a shining galaxy over the drain, and I winced at the coming damage to St. Unoc's infrastructure on the way to the desert.

Behind us was a growing knot of angry people. I reached for Herm's burner phone, quickly texting both Benedict and Herm that we were okay, that we'd gotten Cameron free but Thoth had blown one of the hospital vaults and we were on the way to Herm's safe house.

Safe house, I mused, and Pluck bubbled a sour, worried agreement. Safe for me. Safe for Benedict. I wasn't sure how Aasta would react to two more "mistakes" seeking refuge in the dark.

Dross, Pluck warned as we began to go downhill, and I swung my stick to intercept the hotly glowing mass.

"Little bump," Lev warned as he worked Cameron up onto the sidewalk. The heat of the day blew in from the desert, and both the sound of the bullhorn and the smell of burning gas and oil began to fade. I shook my stick to try to get rid of the dross, but it clung to it, and I carried it like a sword, unwilling to chance it sliding down to my grip and burning my knuckles.

More dross, Pluck fizzed again, and I spun the stick to catch it. I must have missed some, because a fluttering of broken threads seemed to brush me and I tripped on the sidewalk.

"You okay?" Lev half turned to me, eyebrows high in question.

"Dross," I said, annoyed. There hadn't even been a crack in the sidewalk. I'd tripped on my own feet. Flustered, I walked beside them with my stick pointed downward and at the ready.

"It broke on you?" Cameron squinted at me in disbelief. "Thoth was telling the truth?"

Pluck bubbled in guilt, and I absently soothed him. "Yeah," I said, unable to look at her.

Lev's pace was even and smooth. "She's been developing some new skills he doesn't know about."

That woman is watching you. Pluck's thoughts fizzed through mine in a sharp warning.

My head snapped up, and I flushed, trying to hide my stick when the woman at the bench set to the side amid the tended cacti and succulents saw it. Dross slid down the staff, burning when it found me, and I yelped, flinging the glowing stuff everywhere when I shook my hand.

"Weaver," the woman said bitterly as we rolled past. The hatred in the single word shivered through me. *She's going to remember me . . .*

"That stick is attracting attention," Lev said. "Can you leave it, Grady?"

"Soon as you leave your lodestone," I shot back. I needed it. I needed it and the other four to catch Thoth. The sticks had to be balanced, and they needed to be held by the right people.

"Point taken." Lev grimaced, his gaze fixed on the parking lot ahead. Solar panels made a shading roof, and Pluck's relief was almost palpable.

Dross, Pluck fizzed, and I jerked, shifting direction only to come down on more dross. I jerked free as my ankle burned, but I knew it was too late when a fluttering of threads brushed through my soul and my hair snagged on a low tree branch. Frustrated, I extricated myself. Where the devil was it coming from?

"Oh, my God," Cameron whispered, and I followed her horrified gaze to a pipe at the edge of the lot spewing a flood of glowing energy only a magic user could see. It was the outlet to the whirlpool above, and it was eddying through the cars like an ill fog on its way to the desert.

"Ah, yeah." Lev slowed, brow furrowed. "I think my car is still free of it. Let's take the long way."

"This is stupid," Cameron said as Lev angled up the cracked sidewalk skirting the entire lot. "Lev, let me use your phone. One call to DC and I can clear this up."

"Sorry, ma'am," he said cheerfully. "I ditched my phone at the beginning of this raid."

"Raid," she echoed, her gaze going to my pocket. "Grady?"

I shook my head, and the woman tightened in frustration.

"Marshal Owens?" Lev said smoothly. "You are an endangered species. We have to wait for the wind to blow the right way before you make your statement. You talk now, Thoth will know where you are and snuff you. We have to catch him first."

Cameron's gaze fixed on Lev in disbelief. "He wouldn't dare."

"It's a risk we don't need to take." Lev slowed to get over an uneven spot. "Not when we have a place to find refuge and wait for the drugs in your system to work their way out."

Petra . . . Pluck fizzed, and a drop of fire hit my shoulder.

"Damn it, how do you people live like this! Off! Get it off!" I shrieked as the dross burned, and Lev ducked, my stick narrowly missing hitting him as I pulled it from me. Panting, I stared at the length of reddish wood and the dross clinging to it, afraid to move. There was no spiderweb of threads snapping against me, but it had been a lot.

Lev looked me up and down before pushing Cameron back into motion. "If you're done?" he said dryly.

Sheepish, I started to follow, dragging the stick on the ground to wipe the dross off—jerking to a halt when I ran into Lev. "Hey," I complained.

Perhaps we should go the other way, Pluck muttered, hiding himself deeper.

I followed Lev's attention to the parking lot, every last thought I had vanishing at the rumble of a van door opening. It was Dana, Herm, and Ryan, as yet oblivious to our presence. I took a breath to shout that we had rescued Cameron, choking on it when Pluck fizzed a heady warning.

We haven't done anything wrong, I thought when Marty got out as well, but my defiance faltered when Herm spotted me and jiggled Ryan's elbow.

"Turn around," Lev said, but it was too late, and Marty froze, lips open as she stared at us.

Don't you dare leave that amulet, I thought when Pluck's frustration twined about my own, making it ten times worse. *I don't need defending.*

That's a matter of interpretation, he fizzed icily.

Lev exhaled long and slow. Never taking his eyes from them, he locked the wheels of Cameron's chair, lodestone glinting. "Dana. Just who we were coming to see. Good news. Petra and Pluck woke Cameron up."

Dana's expression was grim. "Looks like that's not all the weaver did," she said as Herm reached for his phone. "Surrender your lodestones," she added, her gaze rising to the dust and sirens behind us. "All of you. Don't make this difficult."

"Dana, it wasn't her," Ryan said persuasively. "I've known Petra her entire life. She wouldn't harm anyone, much less do it with dross. She woke the marshal!"

And yet I thought his smile looked forced. "Thoth broke the vault when I was getting Cameron out," I said.

"Something I distinctly told you not to do," Dana said, and Cameron sputtered.

"You told her to leave me trapped in there?" Cameron said, clearly not liking being in a chair when everyone else was standing. "Ms. Vean, I am the lead investigator. Petra and Pluck are not suspects. This is Thoth's doing. All of it."

"You saw this?" Dana asked. "You saw him break the vaults?"

"No," Cameron admitted. "But he has an agenda and he liked to talk about it. You need to get on board."

"He's here?" Marty shrank back. Her hand was wrapped around her new lodestone, the square chunk of moldavite now hanging around her neck on a length of silver.

"I doubt it." Ryan moved to stand protectively beside Marty. "There's too much dross."

Herm was inching away, expression worried as he motioned me to do the same.

"So, Ms. Vean. First thing I'd like to know is why you took steps to keep me in my coma." Cameron struggled to a stand. Lev lurched forward, halting when the woman glared at him.

"You were attacked by shadow," Dana said. "I'm not going to let another one near you lest they try to finish the job."

"I'm not trying to kill Cameron!" I shouted, and Marty went pale, gaze searching the outskirts of the parking lot.

"She saved my life!" Cameron insisted, angry now. "Despite your interference. It's a militia matter now, not university. I expect you to surrender your findings and resources to me immediately. Thoth is the main suspect. Do I have your compliance?"

Lev winced. "Yeah. That ought to do it."

"You do not," Dana said, stiff with anger. "By your own words, you are compromised."

"Dana, she's right," Ryan coaxed, and Dana spun, her lodestone twinkling.

"You seriously expect anyone to give an ounce of credit to anything Cameron Owens says she learned while in a coma? That Petra and Pluck are innocent because they 'helped' her escape it? The coma *they* put her in?"

My jaw clenched, but I managed to stay quiet. It was just too stupid.

"That's *Marshal* Owens," Cameron intoned. "And I might have gotten my information while in a coma, but I did talk to Thoth. This is his doing, and he's setting Petra up to take the blame. He followed Marty here to destroy the rising balance, and failing that, the weavers themselves."

My gaze went to Marty slowly retreating to the van.

"It was a dream." Dana put a hand on Marty's shoulder in support, stopping her. "A nightmare. Nothing there was real, and I'm not going to act on it."

Ryan scrubbed a hand over his chin. "Ah, Dana? That's not entirely true."

Herm motioned for me to leave. Pluck, too, was fizzing in indecision, but I couldn't move. Dana couldn't protect Marty. She was coming with me.

"If anyone should be detained, it's you!" Cameron shouted, shaking as she stood before Dana. "Don't you *dare* tell me I am misremembering."

"Marshal, your memory is compromised," Dana said. "By your own words, your witness is immaterial."

Cameron's jaw clenched in defiance. "I will immaterial your ass from here to DC, you smug, entitled—" And then she hesitated, furious as she tugged from Lev's support. "That bastard of a shadow put me in a coma," she said, pointing to the hospital. "Trapped me where I couldn't be reached, then used me to try to kill the only two people who could stop him. He will destroy anyone and anything he sees as a threat to get what he wants. I am a marshal of mage law, and you will—"

Petra! Pluck warned, and I yelped, my foot suddenly engulfed in fire. Dancing free, I instinctively swung my stick down to draw it off me, almost passing out at the agony.

"Dana, don't!" Ryan shouted, and I looked up, freezing when I saw the woman holding a mass of threads, weaving them into a field between her hands. Alight with the creation of the universe, the weft and weave was singularly beautiful. Pluck had said spells looked recognizable to him, but never had I dreamed they'd be so stunning. And so I stupidly did nothing as Dana harnessed the energy . . . and threw it at me.

Herm's lodestone flashed, but Ryan was faster and his spell smashed into Dana's, the two energies hissing and bubbling as they twined together and canceled each other out inches from reaching me.

She's trying to hurt you, Pluck said in anger, and Cameron stood weaving on her feet as she shouted at everyone to stand down.

"I've been hurt before," I whispered, but at least I knew how far she'd go.

"Calm down, Dana," Ryan soothed, hand raised as the magic they had both thrown flickered and went out. "Everything is circumstantial at this point. You can't—"

I yelped at the sensation of spiderwebs breaking on me. It was that damned dross again, and I shook my foot like I was doing the Hokey Pokey, trying to get it off.

Tune it, Grady. Dump the energy!

It was far more than the dross dust, but I frantically allowed the energy to filter through me, shunting the organized dark matter into the amulet as it burned and hissed. Little licks of flame burned the both of us from the inside out.

It was too much, and I smacked the stick into the ground to get rid of what I could.

With a thump I felt more than heard, the sidewalk cracked. Cold flashed through my arms, then heat, vanishing with little tingles. I gaped at the curls of spent dark matter rolling up from the new crack, shocked.

The stick felt hot in my grip. Everyone was staring at me. Marty was gone. That hadn't been weaver magic, and by the way Herm was frowning, he knew it. I had tuned an entire drift of dross, stored some, used the rest to break the walk. It was shadow magic. "Uh . . ." I started.

"You still believe in Petra's innocence, Ryan?" Dana accused, clearly oblivious that I'd just done something utterly unprecedented. "Maybe I should bring you in for questioning as well."

"Get out of here," Herm mouthed, and then his expression changed to a jovial cajoling as he stepped between me and her. "Dana, we all want the same thing."

Marty had left. Maybe I should, too, and I began to edge away. Expression grim, Lev took Cameron's arm to pull her into a slow retreat. *Holy crap. Did I just . . .*

You did, Pluck thought, his pride washing through my doubt. The fear, though, remained, and I didn't think it was mine alone. *You tuned an entire drift, Petra.*

Scared, I reached for the stone about my neck. It was warm in my grip, but my fingers were blue with cold . . . *How? I'm not a shadow.*

No, he agreed. *No shadow can touch that much dross, much less tune it. But you're not shadow. You're a weaver. Petra, you are* still *a weaver.*

"Dana, I've had enough of your conspiratorial garbage," Herm said, his back to me as he held his hands behind him and gestured for me to go. "You're not touching Petra and Pluck without solid evidence."

"I don't need . . ." Dana's words faltered as she realized Marty was gone. Worry flickered, smothered by a hot anger. "I don't need evidence to detain. Just probable cause. Grady and Pluck were here when the vault cracked. They are coming with me."

Petra, run! Pluck's thoughts thundered through mine. Stunned, I froze when Dana's lodestone gleamed and I felt the threads gather.

"Go!" Herm shouted, throwing himself at Dana.

The woman shrieked as she hit the ground, her spell sputtering to nothing.

Never! Pluck frothed, and I gasped when the shadow poured from his amulet, growing into a snarling, snapping dog from hell.

"Now would be good, Ryan!" Herm yelled, grunting when Dana shoved him off.

"Dana, stop this!" Ryan demanded, wading into the fray.

Bending low, Lev flung Cameron into a fireman's throw over his shoulder and began to run. The small woman protested, an odd huff-huff to her words in time with his thumping steps.

"Pluck!" I pleaded, unable to leave him. Savage and wild, he stood between Dana and me, his skin torn and pus dripping from where bone protruded. Shaking his mane, he roared; the echo coming back from the surrounding buildings made it sound as if we were surrounded.

Ashen, Dana stared at Pluck. He was as she saw him, and she saw a monster. I suddenly realized why she was so hell-bent on blaming me. For all the platitudes and smiles, she was scared of me. I was the one who she wanted bound by law. I was the threat to her peace of mind. *No wonder she has all those lodestones . . .* My old roommate, Ashley, had been the same.

"There is your truth, Ryan," Dana whispered, and I reached for Pluck, my grip falling through him with scintillating tingles of cold. "Detain her, or I will."

"Pluck, not like this!" I shouted, and a third eye formed at the back of his head, looking at me. I hadn't seen a third eye from him in a while, and it threw me. "Cameron," I said, hoping she and Lev had made the car. "She's our only alibi." I reached for Pluck again, this time feeling some resistance. "If Thoth finds her, Lev can't—"

Pluck's third eye vanished. His presence swirled, caving in on itself until he faced the other way. Muscles bunching, he sprang after Lev.

"—protect her," I finished. Dark matter from Pluck coated my hands, and I shook them. The cold spat of energy hitting the hot stone brought a gasp from Dana.

"You're wrong," I said to Dana as I began to back up again. "About everything."

I spun, dodging drifts of dross as I ran through the parking lot following Cameron's shrieks of anger. From behind me, I heard a disgusted, "Dana, you are a first-class idiot," and then my side went cold as I caught up to Pluck.

Pluck loped along beside me, his feet never really touching the ground. *I have forgotten how useful fleeing is,* he said, and I choked down a laugh, worried it would sound hysterical.

"Do you know where Lev's Hummer is?" I said as I jogged through the cars, and the shadow dog flicked an ear in indecision. A wisp of him twined about me as I ran, and my pace faltered when his rising emotion of protection flashed into warning.

"Dana, no!" Ryan yelled, and then the asphalt turned to liquid beneath my feet.

Gasping, I went down, palms scraping the hot pavement as I was suddenly calf-deep in the earth. It was as if I'd fallen through the ice, and I panicked, lurching to pull myself out of the spell before I was trapped here. Dana, I remembered, was a world-class airologist—air not as in flying, but as in able to manipulate the spaces between mass.

"Go!" I shouted to Pluck as the tingling wave of threads snapped through me. Eyes wide, I got one foot free, then cried out when her spell solidified around my other. Frantic, I twisted, my butt hitting the pavement. Two cars away, Lev froze in indecision. Behind me,

Dana's low heels thumped as she closed the distance between us, and my fear for Pluck intensified. If they caught him, they'd kill him. It wasn't illegal to kill a shadow.

"I said go!" But neither Lev nor Pluck moved, my big, beautiful shadow standing between me and Dana running toward us. "Pluck, Thoth's plans are wheels within wheels. He wanted us here to take the blame. We have to get ahead of him. Keep Cameron safe. Aasta will let her stay if you're with her. Come and get me when you can. They won't hurt me."

His shaggy head dipped and he breathed stardust into my soul. *I can't.*

Tears pricking, I held his ruff, our foreheads touching as I breathed his ice in. "I will be okay," I said, my breath coming back warm. "They won't hurt me. They're just going to put me in a box." Fingers fumbling, I took my phone from my pocket. "Give this to Lev. Call Benedict. Please, Pluck. She can destroy you in thirty seconds and the law will let her."

Ice cramped my hand as he took the phone, and I felt Dana's charm redouble, the pavement under me becoming putty. *If she hurts you, I will drive her insane. Slowly.*

I tugged, unable to free my foot. "Go!" I said, and he vanished in a swirl of sparkles.

"Lev!" Cameron yelled from the Hummer. "Don't you dare leave her!"

Lev floored it, the engine noise drowning Cameron's protests until they were gone.

Dana paced forward in the new silence. Hands at her hips, she stared down at me, and I looked up at her, one foot stuck in the pavement. "Hey!" I protested when she bent low and yanked my lodestone from my neck.

"They left you," she said as if that proved she was right. "Even your shadow," she added as she stuffed the moldavite into a pocket. "Why am I not surprised?"

"Maybe because you're a one-talent hack of a cretin," I said, and her eye twitched.

"Dana!" Herm protested, but her hands wove a net of the universe and hit me with a sleep charm. She could have done a lot worse, and yet all I felt was a frustrated anger as my consciousness snapped.

Benedict was going to be really pissed.

21

THE UNIVERSITY'S LOCKUP HAD NO WINDOWS, MAKING IT BOTH STUFFY AND warm. Depressed, I sat on the edge of the cot with my back hunched and my elbows on my knees. After months of Pluck's presence and opinions bumping up against mine, it felt decidedly odd not having him fizzing through my thoughts. I didn't like that our new reach had limits, and I missed him.

My view from the three cinder-block walls was of the empty, room-long cell across the hall, but there was another smaller cell next to mine. It, too, was empty. I had a suspicion that they'd cleared the small cellblock for me, either not wanting to risk me obtaining a drift of dross or, more likely, not wanting me talking to another detainee and possibly starting a sympathy campaign. I might be on the outs with most of the campus right now, but there'd been a time when everyone was glad to see Petra Grady the sweeper.

The silence was relieved only by the garbled band scanner and the occasional comment from the front office. It had gotten quieter after eight, when half the staff had gone home.

Earlier tonight, I had entertained a sporadic parade of stern faces and terse questions from both the university cops and a few board members. Most wanted to know what Pluck and I had been doing at the hospital, where Pluck was now, whether I knew where the marshal,

Lev, and Marty were. That Lev and Cameron were at large was a relief. That Marty was alone was not.

When I realized they weren't actually listening but looking for discrepancies to point to and say "liar," I quit talking to them. That had been hours ago.

I stood and stretched, bored out of my mind as I recapped my empty water bottle. Putting my arm through the bars, I tossed it to the nearby trash can. "Two points, yay!" I said sourly when it landed and went in.

Frustrated, I leaned against the bars to look at the window set in the door leading to the front offices. It was frosted, so I couldn't see anything, but I could tell by listening that it was almost empty out there. The university's holding facility wasn't actually a jail. Jail would have more amenities and adhere to the basics of lawful restraint. I'd gotten no phone call, no official declaration as to why I was being detained. There was, however, a toilet and a sink half-hidden behind a partition, which I was extremely grateful for. The cell was set up for a comfortable two or a crowded six. But it did have something a regular jail didn't, which was why I was here and not at the city lockup: no-dross protocols.

Thanks a hell of a lot, Dana. She'd seen me turn a drift of dross into dark matter and crack the sidewalk. Now it would be harder to escape—but I was going to have to.

Peeved, I leaned against the bars, arms around my middle. Being stuck here was bad, but not knowing how everyone else fared was the real punishment. I was worried about Herm, who had tackled Dana. I was worried about Ryan, who I knew would call in all his favors for me and then some. I was worried about Marty, and I was *really* worried about Cameron and Lev, who I had sent to hide under the city with a mercurial shadow who hated mages to the point of blindness. And I was worried about Benedict, who was likely still in some hospital office for having snuck me in.

Mostly, though, I was worried about Pluck. Which was odd. Of everyone, he could likely take care of himself the best, having been a loner for the last handful of centuries. Now, though, he had something to fight for. He'd take risks—foolish ones. If they caught him . . .

I pushed the ugly thought away and went to sit down, bringing one foot up to rub my ankle when the memory of getting stuck in asphalt lifted through me. It was shortly followed by the image of Pluck facing down Dana. Fear and anger had tripped him back to the terrifying beast that I'd first encountered, right down to the broken bone protruding from half-decayed flesh and the dark matter dripping like pus to burn and crack stone. Had it been Pluck's idea or Dana's fear that had made him so? I wasn't sure which would be worse.

And why, I wondered as I drew my other foot up, *does he want to be a dog when he could be so much more? Something like . . . Kahu?*

Sitting cross-legged on the cot, I brought my palms together and apart as if I were making a field. As before, it was all weft and no weave—the chime of the universe immediately dissolving into a messy tangle of energy threads without my own echo to give it form. Pluck maintained that he liked being a dog because no one expected anything of him and everyone already had a framework of wary trust when it came to dogs—the perfect attitude for dealing with a shadow. It made sense, but people had to be treated with that same suspicion as well. Why not be a person?

Like Thoth?

A burst of noise from the front drew my attention, and the tangle of threads between my hands broke along with my concentration, fragmenting into nothing. Someone had come in, but they were staying up front, so I conjured a new tangle of threads between my hands, feeling the energy pull tight like a cat's cradle between my fingers. Pluck tuned dross dust that plagued him into a usable energy, storing it in a moldavite lodestone. I'd done the same thing in the parking lot with an entire drift, using the energy to crack the sidewalk.

Clearly being a weaver allowed me to handle more dross than a shadow could—that is, if it didn't break or burn me while I was doing it. Deep in thought, I brought my hands together, shivering at the rising tingling chill cramping my fingers.

A mocking laugh sounded through the heavy door, drawing my attention when the muffled conversation grew louder. They were processing someone, by the sounds of it, and I went back to the threads of dark matter tangled about my fingers with the cold of space. It was as if I could feel the energy shift from a lower shell to a higher as I wiggled my fingers, a hint of spiderweb, a brush of butterfly wing, the cold found on the far side of the moon: it was all an expression of energy.

I wonder, I mused as I shook my hands and felt nearly all the threads fall from me to leave a singular chill that was somehow more defined, stronger now that it wasn't competing with untold others. My breath was a cool mist as I focused on the single thread of dark matter, wondering if I could do anything with it. Pluck used dark matter straight from shadows. It was only weavers who had to use the tuned stuff they left behind in moldavite—the energy found in dross dust stored there as a matter of convenience.

I closed my eyes, shivering as the full sensation of the chiming universe flowed to the forefront of my awareness. The slow rise and fall was the echo from the big bang, pushing the edges of reality out in an ever-growing space. The phenomenon was there all the time now, ringing between my ears, but if I focused, the energy tingling in my hands seemed to mimic it.

Exhaling, I pinched the single thread between my fingers and my thumbs, pulling it taut. The gossamer thread of dark energy was too tiny to see, and yet I knew it was there, slowly deadening my fingertips with an aching cold. *Hold up. The sound changes when I stretch it,* I thought as the thrum shifted to a high-pitched whine.

My eyes flashed open and my lips parted. There, between my pinched blue fingers, was a glowing light. I was freakin' making a light. Though the thread of dark matter stretched between them was invisible, a sphere of light had blossomed from it, and when I squinted, I could see an impossibly thin trace of a more certain glow, like the filament in a glass bulb.

"Wow," I whispered as I made the glow brighten and fade by drawing my hands apart and closer together. Breath held, I pulled tight, tighter . . . tighter . . .

An ache began to thrum between my ears as the singular sound began to split into two, a half note apart—until I reached the limits of its capabilities and a burst of light flared and was gone.

I jerked, my muffled yelp of surprise huffing from me in a cold mist. "Shadow spit," I whispered, glancing at the door as I held my now-frozen hands to my middle to try to warm them. I'd been too excited to care, but stressing the thread of dark matter into glowing had left my fingertips blue with a cold that was quickly spreading up my arms, settling in me to feel as if I'd spent the night sleeping on a rock. There was probably a way to use the dark matter threads to do magic directly, but I didn't know it. I needed dross. The stuff right from the universe was too unwieldy. And cold.

"Hey!" I yelled in the general direction of the door as I awkwardly tugged the thin blanket from the cot and wrapped it around me. "Can I have another blanket?"

No one answered, and I slid from the cot to stand at the bars. "I know you can hear me," I said, almost to myself, as I thunked my forehead against the gate. Okay, I had told Pluck it was only a box and no one was going to hurt me, but how was I going to get out of here?

I exhaled, brow furrowing at the new, unexpected flush of cold rushing to my head like an ice cream headache. "Ow . . ." I whispered as I put a hand to my forehead. What good was being able to make a light from nothing if it froze you solid and gave you a headache?

"Put him in the box," someone said from the front room with a cruel bitterness.

I flicked my gaze to the closed door. Wondering who they had brought in, I retreated to the cot, not wanting to engage with the guards. I'd find out soon enough. The awful cold was finally abating, and I shuffled out of the blanket, tossing it to the cot when the heavy security door opened. Marty would be my preference, but she was probably halfway home by now. I was guessing it was Herm, seeing as he had sat on Dana to help me escape.

I heard the lock to the cell next to mine snick shut, and then a terse, "Hands."

I'd gone through the same procedure, and I tensed at the clink of handcuffs being removed. The cop leaned to look in my cell before he walked off. "Have fun, kids," he said, then yanked the door shut behind him.

There was a masculine sigh. "Way to use your big mouth, Strom," Benedict said to himself from the next cell over, and I practically flung myself at the bars.

"Benny?"

Feet scuffed, and a familiar arm pushed through the bars. It was all I could see. "Are you kidding me? Petra? Shadow spit, they didn't tell me you were here." He was silent for a moment, and his hand withdrew. "Why did they put us together?"

I pressed my head against the bars, but I couldn't see past the plane they made. Twisting, I put my hand through the cell gate. "They've been trying to get me to talk. Maybe they think if they put us together we'll tell them something."

"You mean like bugging the cells?" Benedict's hand touched mine, and our fingers laced. "Nah. They aren't set up for that. I think they put me here because they didn't want me talking to anyone else."

The thought of which had its own perils. My throat tightened, and I held my breath. I wasn't going to cry, and I sure as hell wasn't going to cry in campus jail. But my arm was twisted, and I finally pulled away when my fingers began to cramp. I felt bad he was here, but man, I was so glad he was. "Is everyone okay? Last I saw, you were arguing with the orderlies."

"They detained me until after the parking structure collapsed," he said softly. "It gave me an alibi at least. I'd still be free if I hadn't tried to talk to the board. Cameron and Lev are with Herm at his safe house. Pluck too."

"Good." My brow furrowed. That only left Ryan. "Marty ran off. No word on her, I suppose?" He was silent, and I added, "Dana says Cameron's intel is suspect because I am the one who got her out. She thinks I implanted a memory," I muttered.

Benedict chuckled. "Well, to be fair, most comas *are* fever dreams."

I slowly slid down the wall until my butt hit the floor. "It was real," I said, brow furrowed as I recalled Cameron's terror, her demand that I abandon her a second time. Maybe Aasta was right that we were in over our heads. Thoth used Cameron to lure me to the hospital so I'd be there when he broke the vault there. My hubris had given him the vault at the records building, too. How was I going to get in front of his destruction when he knew what I was going to do?

"What about Ryan?" I asked.

"Ah-h-h." Benedict sighed, and I heard him sit as well. "He's trying to smooth things over with Dana," he continued, voice soft as he put his face right next to the bars. "He is calling in all his favors to get you out. I made the mistake of arguing with her, landing me here."

"Which I'm selfishly glad about," I said, worried. This sucked. If I had a little dross, I might be able to do something, but there wasn't even any dross dust in the corners. *Fool dross protocols* . . . "What did you do?" I prompted when he said nothing more.

He took a breath, held it, and let it out. "Went too far," he said softly, and then added, almost shouting, "I called Dana an antiquated remnant and an academic hypocrite afraid to explore a new way to handle an old problem." His tone eased. "But what probably got me in here was trying to contact her superiors behind her back. She doesn't have any, by the way. Whatever she says, goes." He chuckled. "No wonder Cameron is ticked."

I stifled a shudder, pulling my heels closer to my body at the memory of finding myself sinking into asphalt. "She could be anywhere. What is she doing here?"

"Anything she wants." I heard him scuff his feet. "I think Ryan would be in here, too, if not for tenure. Which he's probably going to lose."

I rested my chin on my knees. "Not likely. He's a Spinner. And you can't lose tenure."

"You can if you violate the morality clause."

"That's a matter of interpretation," I protested.

"Which is also part of Dana's job," he said sourly.

Depressed, I began to play with the dark energy between my hands, not to make a light—which would freeze me to the floor—but to see how fast I could find a single thread. Not that I could use it. Just exciting it enough to glow had nearly frozen me. "And you?" I said as I flicked my hands, dislodging most of the threads with a sharp snap. Benedict didn't even have tenure.

"I didn't resist arrest, so who knows?" There was a moment of silence. "They took my lodestone," he added softly. "Searched me for anything I could use to make one. Not that there's any sun in here."

"Or dross," I whispered. Grimacing, I collapsed the softly glowing thread between my hands before they went numb. "Well, thank you for sticking up for me."

"I do *not* like being without a lodestone." Benedict continued his train of thought, his words almost inaudible. "Makes me feel like a mundane. Dana is hell-bent on proving that you and Pluck are cracking the vaults using my frozen dross. I could almost believe her myself."

I thumped my head back against the wall and clasped my arms around my drawn-up knees. "She's scared of change."

"More like scared of how important you and Pluck will be if you can create a viable way to get rid of dross. Something other than putting it in a hole in the ground to wait for it to dissociate naturally."

"That doesn't give her the right to stop it," I said, but I didn't think he was listening.

"Unfortunately she's not the only one who is afraid. It's a mess out there. The sweepers are refusing to pick up. Ambient dross levels are rising. Accidents are happening. To tell you the truth, the parking garage collapse hardly made the news after the pileup on the interstate and a six-inch gap formed in the train tracks." He hesitated. "It's clean in here, though," he finished sourly.

I gazed at the ceiling. "The one time you need some dross. You saw the news? Did everyone get out of the parking structure?"

"Yes."

I blew a sigh of relief. No funerals was a *very* good thing.

"Cameron made a few calls," Benedict said. "But I'll be honest. It's not looking good. Most of the people who can help you are turning a blind eye. Cameron is pissed. But that might be because Herm won't let her leave to find Marty."

"Yeah?" I inched closer to the bars. "I have to believe she knows enough not to take this home to her boyfriend. Benny, I have to get out of here and find Marty. She came to me for help, and I tried to trick her into staying. Into being something she doesn't want to be."

Something she was already, I thought glumly. "It's scary enough finding out that you are capable of bonding to another sentient creature who kind of desperately needs you, but that it's one that we've been told is an indiscriminate, mindless killer sort of throws a person." I pulled my knees tighter, feeling even more alone. "We have to get out of here."

"No argument," he said. "Dana is not having it, though. Ryan is having zero luck."

I'd thought getting news would have eased my anxiety, but it had only made my mood worse, and I pushed back against the wall and stood.

"Petra?" Benedict's shoes hiccuped on the concrete as he straightened his legs. "Lev said you tuned a drift of dross and used it to break the sidewalk." He took a slow breath. "You really did that?"

"Yes," I whispered, rubbing my fingers together as I wished I could handle the cold born from working with dark matter right from the source. Pluck could, but I wasn't shadow. I was flesh and bone, and I think the only reason I could use the dark matter I tuned from dross was because the heat of the dross and the cold from the dark matter canceled each other out—mostly.

"Huh," Benedict said, a new lilt to his voice. "Um, you think maybe you could do it again? Like to get us out of here?"

I felt myself sigh. "You have any dross on you?"

There was a scuff as he got to his feet as well. "No," he said softly as he reached through the bars for my hand. "But I bet I could find a way to get one of those school cops out there to do something stupid and make some."

I met his fingers with my own, emotion tingling right down to my toes.

"You have to get out of here, Petra," he said as he gave my hand a squeeze. "No one besides Ryan will risk their job to prove that you aren't responsible, and barring that, you and Pluck will take the blame. Thoth will walk, and Marty? Who knows where she will end up."

Lure a campus cop in. Get them to do some magic. Use the dross to get out of here. It wasn't much of a plan, but it was a plan, and I inched closer to the wall, whispering, "What do you have in mind?"

22

RESTLESSNESS PRICKED AT ME AS I RECLINED ON THE COT, STARING AT THE ceiling and listening to the muted come-and-go conversation from the front room. Benedict was right. Unless we shouted, no one was going to hear us.

It had to be after two in the morning and I was surprisingly awake. Fewer guards would increase our chances this ill-thought-out plan would actually work. I missed Pluck like I might miss a foot, and I was determined that Benedict and I would get out of here before any new decisions came down from the university board in the morning. We had to find Marty and prove Pluck's and my innocence.

Our escape hinged on getting someone to come in here with more than dross dust clinging to the soles of his or her feet, and in the absence of that, maybe get someone to do magic to make some. Benedict would collect it in a field, get it to me, and from there I could maybe break the lock or something.

Maybe. Too much maybe. Nervous, I shook my hands out. *No pain, no gain,* I thought, imagining Pluck's confusion as he tried to pick the idiom apart. The reality was, when it came to magic, if it hurt, you were doing it wrong—which was why I knew better than to try to use conjured threads between my hands for anything other than making a light.

"I think we're down to two guards," Benedict said from the corner abutting my cell. "That's probably the best we're going to get. Petra, I still don't see why they would come in here, much less do any magic. Pretending to have a stomachache won't do it."

"Tell them Thoth is attacking me." I sat up and moved to stand at the cinder-block wall between us. "I figured out how to make a light using threads of dark matter. It will look convincing."

"You what?" Benedict barked, and I settled myself beside the bars. "When?"

"Just before you landed in the cell next to me," I admitted, flushing. "If they bother to look through the window, they will come in." Yeah, it sounded good, but it was just as likely the guard would stand well clear and hose me down with a fire extinguisher. "Give me a second."

"Why didn't you tell me?" Benedict asked.

"Because making a light is the limit of what I can do," I admitted. But the truth of it was he would have wanted to see me do it, and I wasn't keen to experience that bone-chilling cold again.

"This changes everything," he muttered, but it felt as if he was making more of this than it was. Exhaling, I resettled myself, sitting cross-legged before the bars, right next to the wall between us. As before, I drew my hands apart to pull a mass of threads into play. There was no glow, no tickling of power between my fingers, but I could feel the threads all the same, and I shook my hands to flick off all but one little trill of the universe.

This time, instead of pinching the ends between my thumbs and fingers, I spun my middle fingers around the ends like dental floss—and pulled, smiling when a tiny light blossomed. Benedict swore softly, and I squinted as the shadows of my prison bars spread over the floor and into the cell across from me. The cold felt sharper, more painful than before, and I eased the strain between my hands, glad when both the light and cold diminished. *I can do this.*

"That's amazing, Petra," Benedict said, and I clenched my teeth to keep them from chattering. "I could always see the light in you," he added, clearly impressed. "And now everyone else can, too."

It was a nice thought, but I was too cold to appreciate it. My hands felt like ice. "You're up," I said, and he cleared his throat.

"Hey! Hey!" he shouted, and I leaned my head back against the wall between us and closed my eyes to try to appear incapacitated even as I held that glowing thread between my hands. "Thoth is attacking Petra! Somebody get in here!"

I listened, my chest aching with cold. "They aren't going for it."

"Hey!" Benedict stood and rattled the gate. "Thoth is in here! Someone help!"

"Effing two in the morning?" came a muffled complaint, then the scuff of a chair. My pulse leapt, and I doubled the light. The numbing cold spilled to my core. An odd feeling of disconnection threatened, and wispy thoughts flitted at the edges of my mind like sleep.

The door opened, and I shifted my fingers to make the glowing thread wax and wane to get the guard's attention. "If this is some sort of—holy shit!" the guard blurted, and I let myself slump, careful to keep the string taut between my fingers and the glow going. "Aaron! Something is wrong with the weaver. She's turning blue!"

"Blue!" Benedict rattled the gate again. "Petra? Petra!"

Cold. I was so cold, and I cracked my eyes, shocked to see that my breath was making a frozen skin of condensation on the bars. *Sweep him for dross, Benny,* I thought, my groan real as I looked up at the guard. "Help me . . ." I rasped, starting when a wave of warmth rippled over me. It was Benedict's field, but it fell back to him empty. Not a hint of dross decorated the guard's shoes. They were being extraordinarily careful.

"Aaron!" the guard shouted through the open door. "Get in here!"

"Seriously?" Aaron said from the front room, and I let my eyes slip shut when I heard the second guard's chair scrape. "Don't unlock her cell, West.

"What the hell?" Aaron whispered as he scuffed to a halt beside West, both men well clear of the bars. He, too, was dross-free. I had to get them to do some magic. Muscles creaking with cold, I watched through slitted eyes as West fidgeted in indecision. Desperation closed my throat, and I increased the light, making it pulse with my finger motions. I shook with cold, and with a sudden fear, I realized it was getting hard to keep my lungs moving.

"She was trying to call her shadow," Benedict ad-libbed, but a real fear colored his voice. "I think it's Thoth." He hesitated. "Do something! That shadow is killing her!"

"I don't know . . ." one of them said, and I let my hand fall to the bars.

A sudden surge of energy shocked through me as I touched the metal and the light between my fingers went out. I hadn't done it, and I jerked, startled when a frozen rim of skin stuck to the bar when I pulled away. I'd frozen my knuckles to the metal like a tongue to a flagpole, but the debilitating cold was easing and I could breathe again.

Shaking, I sat slumped where I was. I had done everything I could, and still they hadn't done any magic. We'd failed.

"She looks okay now," West said with a dismissive laugh, and then he yelped.

My eyes flashed open at the sudden scuff and thump.

Benedict's arm was wrapped around Aaron's neck, muscles tense as he pulled the guard to the bars and the man flailed, trying to get away. He had him.

"Aaron!" West yelled, and then I sat up, elated when the sensation of broken spiderwebs trailed over me. Someone had done magic.

Benedict yelped in pain. His arm vanished back in his cell and Aaron flung himself clear, his hand to his throat and an ugly look in his eye as he shouted at Benedict. Benedict, though, had the guard's lodestone. Better yet, there was dross on the floor.

"Petra?" Benedict said cautiously, and I coughed.

"Okay," I said, but I sounded shaky even to me. My light was long gone, but enough of the debilitating chill remained to make me slow and achy. I stood, my pulse fast when I felt Benedict's field settle over the dross from West's magic, condensing it into a little spot of fiery horror—right within my reach.

Smirking, I reached through the bars, relishing the prickles of heat as I took it in hand. *Don't break yet, my lovely,* I mused as the dross tingled against me, the heat of it driving the last of the cold away.

"You can't use that," Aaron said, clearly angry. "It's tuned to me."

I heard the tinkle of glass. "Now it's not," Benedict intoned.

West sneered. "Seriously? The sun is down. You can't bind it."

The second guard was smarter, though, and I watched Aaron's expression blank. "You stupid fuck, West," he whispered. "You gave her dross!"

Aaron bolted, shoving West aside in his need to escape. Gaping, West did nothing as I smashed the dross against the floor to encourage it to break. Painful flares of heat pulsed against my fingers in warning until finally . . . it did.

Fire engulfed my hand, burning. I gasped, almost losing the echo of the universe. My hands were glowing with it. Frantic, I pulled the energy into me, into my mind. First cold, now heat, and my mind sizzed with the unruly energy. I had nowhere to put it.

Panicking, I focused on West. Flinging my unburned hand out, I sent a burst of energy from me. I gasped at the sudden flash of light, brighter than the sun, as my hands and mind hummed with the power of the universe. The man slammed into the bars of the cell across from me, pushed by whatever I had released. His head hit with a disturbing thump and he collapsed.

The light vanished and I hunched over my aching hands—staring at them, wondering how they could still be whole and unblemished. *What have I done?*

"Petra?"

My hands shook; they were red, but they weren't burning anymore. I wasn't cold, either. I had tuned the drift, used the dark matter directly. But what had I done? The torrent of focused energy had been instinctive, a blast of power that had pushed the university cop down. He was breathing, though, as he slumped on the floor. I had to believe he'd be okay. I had to believe that I hadn't fried his mind or burst his heart. *He is okay, isn't he?*

"Petra." Benedict's voice was closer and I looked up. He was standing outside my cell.

"How did you get out?" I said blankly. I reached through the bars for him, then realized his hands were bloody. "When did you . . ." I said, my eyes going to West.

"I made a lodestone," he said, and then I saw the shard of glass in his hand, glowing with a faint light. "When you downed the guard, the light was bright enough to use not only to bind a shard but to energize it." He smirked, gaze going to the outer office and the sound of Aaron frantically calling someone. "Be right back."

"Benny? Benny!" I rattled my locked cell when he darted out. "Don't you leave me here!" He must have used his lodestone shard to break the lock. It was Pluck's goal of balance, where mage, shadow, and weaver work together. It worked!

Except I was still behind bars.

"Hey! How did you—" Aaron exclaimed from the front room, and then I jumped at a thump. Little whispers of broken thread brushed against me, lifting through my hair like wind . . . I was sensing Benedict's magic, feeling the universe working contrary to its usual laws as the mage wrung power from the raw substance of light and left dross in its wake.

Until Benedict's magic ran out and he strode back in, a set of keys in his hand.

"I can't believe that worked," I said, relieved beyond belief when he fitted a key card into the panel and the cell door buzzed open. And then I was in the hall, my arms wrapping around him in a quick, desperate hug. "Are you okay? How bad is your hand?"

Grinning, Benedict looked at it. "It's fine. We need to get out of here. I brought him down with a gravity spell, but he called someone."

Nodding, I glanced at the open door. I had felt his spell as if I had created it myself, but that was nothing compared to the fact that the dross he had left behind was a growing presence, niggling at my thoughts in a weird mix of warning and opportunity. It was a room away, and I could feel it. What the devil had Thoth done to me?

"If your hand is bleeding, it's not fine," I said, my head snapping up when a familiar fizzing bubbled through my thoughts. "Pluck!"

Benedict's eyebrows rose in question. "He's here?"

The guard is waking, the shadow warned, and then I saw him in the doorway, a great sleek dog, black ears pricked and green eyes flecked with gold. He was okay. And if he was okay, then Lev and Cameron were probably good, too.

"Pluck!" Benedict pulled from my grip as if embarrassed, and the shadow dog flicked an ear to send dark matter hissing on the cold cement floor.

You mind if I . . . Pluck dissolved into a haze that skated across the floor to the guard. Nothing more than a glimmer of sparkles, he sent a tendril around the man's arm, the shadow's distortion brightening until the man slumped against the floor again. *Lev, Herm, and Cameron are outside. We came to get you free. I am the vanguard. Looks as if you didn't need us.*

I grabbed Benedict's unbloodied hand and headed to the outer offices. "I will always need you, Pluck," I said; and then to Benedict, "Our ride is out front."

Benedict stumbled, walking sideways so as to talk to Pluck. "Ah, this isn't what it looks like. I didn't mean to get her out by myself. It just kind of happened. I don't think I've ever been so happy to see a shadow in all my life. Thank you, Pluck."

I jerked to a halt when I spotted the guard Aaron face down beside a desk and unmoving. Unlike the cellblock, here dross dust and hazy drifts were like cobwebs in the corners, and I began to pick my way through them. Benedict was oblivious to it, striding forward and kicking up drifts as if they were snow. Pluck, though, was as careful as I, the living shadow dissolving into a haze of sparkles that coalesced into a black raven-like bird.

I didn't expect Benedict to be here, fizzed through me as Pluck hopped from desk to desk, wings extended. *He left the grotto to talk to Dana.* The crow chortled, eyeing me sharply. *I made him promise to not try to free you alone.*

"He didn't have a choice," I said softly. *I had to get out before Dana signed your death warrant.* I froze as the main door opened—but it was just Lev and Herm.

"Benedict?" Lev exclaimed, clearly pleased as the two men closed the distance and fist-bumped. "What are you doing here? You promised Pluck you wouldn't."

"It's not what it looks like." Benedict glanced out the dark window. "Give me a sec. I want my ring."

"Wait." Lev's eyebrows rose. "*Your* ring?" He began to laugh. "Dana put you in jail? With Petra? She won't make that mistake again."

Herm scuffed to a halt before me, his wrinkles sliding into each other as he smiled. Beaming, he gave me a sideways hug, the scent of coffee making him as comforting as home. "Everything okay?" the older man said, and I nodded, wincing when my burned hands twinged. "How did you get out?"

"Benedict," I said, and Pluck fizzed sourly through me, clearly wanting to know as well.

Eyes alight, Benedict handed me my staff. "Sorry, I think the university has your lodestone."

"Go! Go!" Herm gestured for the door. "Truck is out and to the left."

We went. It was loud, messy, slow, and awkward—nothing like the slick precision actions I was sure Lev was used to—but I'd never been happier in my life.

"Seriously." Lev waited for us to go first. "How did you get out without a lodestone?" He glanced over his shoulder to Pluck. "At night?"

Benedict yanked open the door and the desert night sounds slipped in. "Grady made a light to lure the guards in."

Pluck's thoughts in mine seemed to choke. *You did what?*

Suddenly he was tangling about my feet, making them ache with cold as I went out into the parking lot. A single security light buzzed overhead, and I gripped my dad's staff tighter and headed for the shadows. "I pulled one string of dark energy taut," I said softly.

A single string? Pluck fizzed in agitation. *You isolated it? How?*

I shook it free from the rest, and when I stressed it, its latent energy shifted and it gave off light. And cold, I added silently, and Pluck vanished into a puddle of sparkles.

"One got too close to the bars," Benedict continued as we hustled forward in a muddled knot. "I got his lodestone. Untuned it by breaking it. It might have ended right there, but Grady brought down a guard with his own dross. The light that gave off was strong enough for me to bind the stone," he said, as proud as if he'd done it himself. "From there, I broke the lock."

"You tuned dross?" Herm pointed at his truck, lights off and about a block down the alley. "Like a shadow? No lodestone intermediary? How did you do that?"

I was glad it was dark and they couldn't see my face. Pluck, though, could feel my worry. Tuning dross felt really close to a mage using dross to do magic, a "dross-eater." They were reviled and shunned. "Um, Pluck taught me how to tune dross dust. It's the same thing."

It is, and it's not. Pluck fizzed, little rills of energy curling off him like fog. But the fact remained that I'd used dross to do magic, and the light from that had charged Benedict's lodestone. We had made Pluck's balance real. It was happening, and I think he was annoyed he hadn't been there to see it.

"Great. You did shadow magic." Lev put a hand on Benedict's shoulder to push him into a faster pace. "Tell us all about it in the truck," he said, pointing to where Cameron stood in the driver's open door, waving for our attention. Relief spilled through me. We were free.

"That was fast!" Cameron said, then ducked back inside. "Load up!"

"Shotgun!" Lev dove for the front seat. "They didn't need us. They were out already."

"Slide over, missy," Herm demanded. "My truck, I'm driving."

"I am not an invalid," Cameron protested when Lev pulled her to the middle.

The engine sputtered to life. Benedict vaulted into the truck bed, hand extended to help me in. "Like hell we didn't need you," he said as he half lifted me in, my stick clattering.

The truck lurched into motion. Smirking, I wedged myself in the front corner behind Herm. Benedict sat close to help even out the coming bumps, and Pluck, once again a dog, wedged in on my other side, numbing my thigh as stray, spiky thoughts of pride and worry fizzed through me.

"Wow, you're still cold," Benedict said as the truck bounced onto the dark street. "At least you aren't blue anymore."

Blue? Pluck questioned, and I tried to wall off my thoughts. We were moving, and that was all that mattered. *Petra, why were you blue?*

"From the cold," I said to Pluck as I pressed closer to Benedict. "I'll be fine." And for the first time all night, I thought I would be. It was almost three in the morning, the skies dark and cool, and the wind in my hair felt wonderful.

The little window at the back of the cab slid open with a bang, and Benedict jumped. "Everyone okay?" Cameron asked, the small woman sitting almost sideways so she could see us.

Benedict looked up from trying to get a sliver of glass out of his palm in the glow of the sporadic streetlights. "I could use a Band-Aid. Herm, you got a piece of untuned glass in here?"

"Check the glove box," he said, and Cameron spun to do just that.

Dana had taken my lodestone. Unless I wanted to risk getting the one I gave to Ryan, there was no easy replacement apart from perhaps the rock and gem show. But I had one stick out of five, and my friends. It was a start.

"Got 'em!" Cameron sang out, and Benedict sighed in relief when she stuffed her hand through the window to drop three marbles, two Band-Aids, and an antiseptic wipe into his palm.

"You want to bind to them?" I asked as he stuffed the marbles in a pocket.

"It can wait," he said quickly, and from up front Herm called out a loud "Yes!"

I'd like to see you make a light as well, Pluck fizzed through my thoughts, and I winced.

"It can wait," Benedict said more firmly as he tore open the antiseptic wipe and gingerly swabbed his palm. "Petra turned blue from cold the last time. Sunrise is soon enough."

"If you're sure," I said, and he nodded.

"Could you . . ." he said as he handed me a Band-Aid. "It's awkward."

"Sure." I tore it open and put the Band-Aid on. He sighed and tugged me closer and I felt his entire body relax against mine. I didn't really care where we were going—unless it was to one of Herm's desert bunkers.

"Hey, ah, is there a plan we're working from?" I asked, and Lev turned where he sat so he could see everyone.

"I suggest we check in with my superiors. They can give us sanctuary."

Cage, drifted through my mind, but I wasn't sure if it was me or Pluck.

"Absolutely not!" Benedict protested. "Petra already has too close a tie to them. Going to the militia for help will make it tighter."

"I'm not taking Petra to the militia," Herm agreed. "Next suggestion."

"Herm, you can drop me off anywhere in the quad," Cameron said with a huff. "I have to jam some knowledge down Dana's throat. She practically called me a liar. I am not delusional. I know what I experienced."

"Which is why I say the militia," Lev said, and Cameron frowned. "We have specialists who can vouch for what you experienced. You want court-worthy testimony? That's where you'll get it. They've been working on this since Petra first showed up."

"Actually," Herm said thoughtfully, "that's not a bad idea."

Pluck fizzed, the wind raking through his form as he tried to take on definition.

"But not for Pluck or Petra," he added, and the shadow subsided with a soft grumble. "I'm taking them off-grid."

"Ah . . ." I started, ignored.

"I can have you tucked away in six hours," Herm continued, the light catching the bristles on his chin when we went under a streetlamp. "And when Thoth breaks the next vault and you aren't even in the same country, they will come to their senses."

"Hey!" I shouted, and Benedict hid a smile a heartbeat too late. "I am not going to Mexico. Or Canada. Or anywhere other than St. Unoc. I have to find Marty. None of you know what she's going through. We are asking her to leave the man she loves, and for what?

This mess? No one wants her here except the people in this truck and Ryan. All we've given her is grief. No wonder she ran off."

Mmmm . . . Pluck asserted, and I elbowed his semicorporeal state to be quiet, wondering if the tingling jolt felt warmer than usual.

"And selfishly speaking, we need her." I took a slow breath, remembering the feel of Benedict doing magic in another room. "I don't think I'm a weaver anymore, and we need one to catch Thoth. That and five balanced sticks."

Benedict took my hand in his. "You really want to trust her to help catch him? Put your life in her hands? You're ignoring the facts, Petra. She's not reliable."

"I am not ignoring the facts. The fact is that we need her!" I barked.

"Enough!" Herm exclaimed, and I scowled when he pulled into a night-emptied parking lot, bringing the truck to a squeaking halt and putting it into park. The engine stilled. Hands still on the wheel, Herm looked out at nothing. "What is this about five balanced sticks?"

I glanced at Benedict, and he shrugged. "I didn't have time to tell him," he said. "I was more worried about getting you out of university jail."

Pluck was fizzing enthusiastically, and I shifted to face Herm more fully. "Pluck and I think Thoth can be caught by five people who use light and shadow in unique, distinct ways," I said. "Thoth won't be able to adapt." Cameron stared at me, and I added, "One stick, two sticks, three, four, five. Stand them straight to stay alive?"

Her eyes widened. "You want to snag a clinically insane shadow with a children's rhyme?"

"It's not a children's rhyme," Benedict said, and Pluck's gratitude twined a glittering fizz about my own. "It's an instructional manual in a world that doesn't know we exist."

Lev's incredulous expression began to ease. "Yea-a-a-ah . . . Jimmy

Tross is the modern equivalent." His head tilted. "Five balanced sticks makes sense. So . . . mage, Spinner, weaver, sweeper, and shadow? I call dibs on the mage."

Benedict bristled, and I put a soothing hand on him. "Not quite," I said. "I don't think the type of magic user is as important as them using magic differently. Water, air, earth, fire, and ether." I took a slow breath, hesitant. "Which brings me to my next trick," I added faintly.

Herm chewed on his lower lip in thought. "I don't know. Your weaver abilities are compromised."

I flushed. "It will work *because* my weaver abilities are compromised. I am not broken. No one has ever been both weaver and shadow and yet neither."

Cameron, too, shook her head. "If it could be done, they would have done it eons ago," she said. "Herm is right. Thoth almost killed you."

"He woke something up in me." I leaned toward the window between us. "I lost my fields," I said, finding it easier to admit. "No fields means no inborn shadow protection. He thinks that makes him safe, but he's wrong. Not being able to turn dross inert has forced me to learn how to tune entire dross drifts. It gives us an edge, and we need to act before Thoth figures that out."

Benedict's hand in mine tightened. I wasn't broken, damn it! So what if dross went out of its way to burn me. I could tune it now. Use it. "I am exactly what's missing," I said. "We can catch Thoth." I hesitated, knowing they weren't going to like this next part. "But we need to find Marty. It's my fault she's in danger. She was helpless when he followed her here, but I gave her a stone. She's learning how to use it. She's becoming a threat to Thoth, and if we don't find her, he will."

Herm's brow furrowed. "You think he will hurt her?"

I nodded, and Benedict's arm went more securely around me. "I'm in," he said.

Lev scowled. "Me too."

Herm's sigh was loud and long. "Okay, you two, out," he said to Lev and Cameron, and the two mages stared at him. "Go get the court-worthy evidence from the militia to keep Petra and Pluck on this side of the bars after we bag Thoth. While you're doing that, Benedict, Petra, and Pluck will find Marty."

I was going to find Marty, and a thrill of relief fluttered through me. Cameron, too, grinned, clearly pleased as she punched Lev in the arm, saying, "Just remember I still outrank you, Evander, even if we are in your clubhouse."

"I'm going to regret this." His expression holding a mock horror, Lev opened the door and got out, Cameron quick behind him.

Motions slow, Herm got out, too. "Petra, take the truck. You need it more than me."

Immediately Benedict vaulted out of the truck bed and spun to lift me down. It was happening, and Pluck's excitement fizzed through me. "You're not coming with us?" I asked Herm, and then my attention fixed on Benedict as his hands found my waist and he gently settled me on the ground. "Thanks," I almost whispered, and Pluck bubbled, impatient to be away.

"I have to talk to Ryan," Herm said. "He's got three of your dad's sticks. He might know where the last one is." His stubble caught the faint light as he chewed his lower lip. "Odd that your dad made five to begin with. Maybe he knew something?"

I gave Herm a quick hug. "Be careful."

"You too." Herm's gaze went from me to Pluck, the shadow's ears pricked and his tail nothing but a drift of dark matter. "Do not take on Thoth without us. Okay?"

"Okay," I said, even as Pluck phased in and out of solidity in excitement.

Herm was patting his pockets absently, but the keys were still in the truck. "Lev, you do not speak for Petra or Pluck. Let me hear it."

Lev put all his weight on one foot in a show of annoyance. "I do not speak for the shadows or weavers."

I didn't like us breaking up like this, and my gut hurt. "Thank you for trusting me on this," I said, and Herm patted my shoulder.

"Always," he said, rusty voice rumbling. "I made a mistake not trusting your dad. I won't do it again. Be careful, Petra."

"Always," I echoed, but the old man was looking at Pluck, not me.

Benedict was already in the front seat, adjusting everything to his height. Ice cramped my ankle as I got in, shortly followed by Pluck's grumpy bubble and fizz. But Benedict's reach for the key hesitated when Herm leaned in on the open window. "Everyone funnels their intelligence back to me," he said. "I will disseminate it."

"Ah, old man . . ." Lev started, voice tight, and Herm's gaze shot to him.

"I've been off-grid longer than you have been alive, Lev Michael Evander, and I have pioneered three stealth techniques that you militia brats can't detect, much less get around."

Lev's humor evaporated. "How did you get my middle name? My real one."

Herm pushed from the window. "Use the burner phones I gave you. Everyone talks to me. I talk to everyone else. No cross talk unless I go silent, and in that case, someone come get me out of jail. Lev and Cameron will get the professionals to validate the marshal's report. I get the tools to successfully snare Thoth." His gaze came to me holding an equal mix of worry and pride. "You three find Marty." I nodded, and he added a terse "Go!" Herm smacked the window frame twice, and Benedict put the truck into drive. "Pluck, take care of her."

It's what I do, grumbled coldly through me. *Though it's hard when she doesn't listen.*

"Good luck!" I shouted, and Lev gave me a wave, even as he walked away with Cameron. We were just outside of campus. One call, and someone from the nearby militia outpost would come get them. They'd be fine. Herm was gone when I looked back.

"I suggest we try the tunnels and aqueducts," Benedict said.

I agree with the mage, Pluck thought. *With Benny,* he added belatedly, making me feel better. Benny, he had called him. It was a start.

"You mind if we hit the bus station first?" I said. "I want to rule out that she's left St. Unoc, and they have a camera in the ticket kiosk we can check."

Benedict's expression lightened. "Huh. That's a really good idea," he said, then did a U-turn right there in the middle of the four-lane road.

My arm rested on the open window and I looked out at nothing. We would find her, and somehow I'd teach her enough magic to survive Thoth.

23

BENEDICT DROVE THROUGH ST. UNOC'S NIGHT-EMPTIED STREETS WITH ONE hand, looking as comfortable behind the wheel of Herm's dusty truck as he was in his own sporty go-faster car. Maybe more so. Pluck was nothing but a haze of possibilities, his glow eddying into a tiny coiled snake beside me. We were only a few minutes out from St. Unoc's bus station, and the buildings had begun to get that wide space between them that said city's edge. The desert beckoned, and a part of me longed to just keep driving.

"It's too bad I don't have her phone number," I muttered. "Not that she'd pick up."

"I don't know. She might." Benedict glanced at me, and I took his free hand—the one with the cut—and gave his fingers a gentle squeeze. "She ran off to get away from Dana, not you. If she hasn't left, we can at least trim our search down to St. Unoc." Benedict's eyes roved the dark side streets as we passed. "Unless she rented a car or bummed a ride."

Pluck fizzed at the top of my brain, his opinion a slurry of concern. "We'll find her," I said, talking to both of them but mostly Pluck. His hard and ugly past with Thoth colored his mood, but my hope blended smoothly through it. We would find her.

My elbow slipped into Pluck, and the sudden chill woke me up fast. The night already glittering with dross became brighter. If it wasn't truly bad luck made real, I'd say it was pretty. "Thank you for trusting me," I said, and Benedict turned his hand to grip mine, bringing it to his lips for a quick kiss. Little streamers of Pluck's essence fell from my elbow, sparkling to my more sensitive eyes.

"Petra, there is little you could ask of me that I wouldn't do."

So says the mage . . . Pluck bubbled sourly.

The truck's lights suddenly threw back a haze from a pothole full of dross. I took a breath to warn Benedict, but it was too late and he drove right through it, the thump loud and obvious. Contrary to popular belief, it wasn't the hole that usually caused damage but the dross hiding it.

"Yeah," I continued when our ride smoothed out. "But I can tell you're worried about what comes next. I know I said we need her, but I won't push Marty into this once we find her." I fiddled with the hole in my jeans, right at the knee. "She doesn't owe us anything, even if Thoth followed her here."

Her want to flee is well-founded, the shadow mused, and my shoulders dropped as his agitation eased. *Thoth might not be her shadow, but he's been manipulating her as much as he's been manipulating you.*

"I say points to her for running away from Dana," I added, gazing at Benedict in the come-and-go light.

"Herm told me to trust your gut feeling. I told him I already did." His grip on the wheel tightened. "Me accidentally giving Pluck the tool to blow up the auditorium was lesson enough."

Pluck hazed a brilliant green, his snakelike head hooding as he stared at the man. *You find yourself dropped into a live volcano and see what you're willing to do to get out.*

"That wasn't your fault," I said, talking to both of them. "And you know it."

"That's what everyone keeps saying, but that's not how it feels." He hesitated. "Why do they always put the bus station in the worst part of town?"

"It's not that bad," I said as Benedict slowed, both hands on the wheel as he eased to a halt under the single glaring light at the bus depot. Set between two distant manufacturing buildings and a shuttered food truck, the depot was little more than a twenty-by-twenty building at the edge of the desert. There was a quick-eats place across the street, closed, and a laundromat next door, open but empty. I would be willing to bet the camera focused on the small parking lot was recording us. Dross levels weren't bad, but it probably didn't get a lot of traffic.

I will see if Thoth is here, Pluck fizzed, and I stifled a shudder when he slithered out my open window. Looking like a snake with pricked dog ears, he wove past the dross drifts to vanish inside.

Thoth, Pluck had thought, not Marty. I just hoped his gut feeling was better than mine. After all, he knew the shadow.

Unfortunately, hazed through me, hardly discernible, and I smiled. Our reach had grown.

"Pluck is doing a quick check," I said, and Benedict nodded.

"Thanks, Pluck," he whispered as he got out, his motions slow with fatigue. The truck door shut with a loud thump . . . and he rested his forearms on the hood to stare at the building as we waited. The front glass wall made it a veritable fishbowl. There were restrooms in the rear and an empty counter that might have once sold tickets. The vending machine looked old, but the ticket kiosk tucked into the corner was probably new.

"That was fast," I said as Pluck slithered out under the door and headed our way. His entire body glittered as he crossed the parking lot, his form growing until, ears slapping, he took his customary dog shape. I knew everything was fine by the way he carried his thin, whiplike tail curved up over his back. He might not *be* a dog, but he had a canine's mannerisms down to perfection. But then again, it was how he chose to communicate. Almost everyone could speak dog.

Worry and guilt that I was holding him back flickered through me.

I told you, tingled through my mind. *Being a dog is easier than being a human. I don't want to talk to anyone else, and no one expects anything of me.*

I reached for my stick and got out. *But you're not a dog,* I protested. *I would totally be okay with you as a person.*

At the curb, Pluck's one eye focused on me, and then he dissolved into a puddling, dripping haze. *I took your dog companion from you,* fizzed through me, his embarrassment twining equally with my own. *I'm not Pluck, but you feel good when you remember him, and you remember him more when I wear his shape.*

"Lev shot him, not you," I whispered.

I frightened the mage into it.

I grimaced, wondering why we were having this conversation now. *Only because I saw you as a slavering beast,* I thought. *That was totally not your fault.*

Perhaps, he thought. It was his way of saying agree to disagree, and I slumped when he hazed to nothing, sinking into the dark to pretty much vanish.

Fine. Be that way. "Pluck says it's clear." Mood bad, I ran my stick around the truck's wheel well, my lip curling when I pulled a good-size burning blob from hell from it. My hands ached as if the energy was looking for a way to break on me, and I angrily spun the stick to send the hazy heat flying into the night to hit the dry desert earth with a momentum-laden splat.

"Ah, thanks." Benedict came around the front, keys jingling. "Here," he said as he handed them to me. "In case you need to leave fast."

Clean stick in hand, I eyed him sharply as we headed for the front. "What do you think is going to happen?" I asked as I stuffed them in my pocket. It wasn't only Herm's truck keys but about six others, not one of them similar to the next.

Benedict bumped my shoulder with his. "No idea," he said cheerfully. "But you run faster than me. Get it started. I'll catch up."

Head bobbing, I shifted my hand so our fingers would touch. He was headed right for a glowing dross drift, and I surreptitiously pulled him clear.

"Thanks," he whispered as he gave my hand a squeeze and let go, clearly embarrassed. Most mages could see dross, but Benedict had always had problems. *Maybe,* I thought suddenly, *it's because his fields are so damn strong.*

Possible, Pluck agreed as we followed Benedict to the door. *But you could see dross even when you could make them.*

Not like this, I thought as I studied the pockets of light glowing in the desert. Even the saguaro cacti sported a fine haze of dross dust. My sensitivity had increased tenfold since I'd lost the ability to make fields.

"The kiosk should have a video record of everyone who used it," I said when he opened the door and gestured for me to go first. It was an ugly room, and I lagged behind as Benedict strode forward. The floors were dirty and the lights were bright. A dross trap disguised as a trash can sat overflowing with both mundane and magical garbage, and I gave it a wide berth.

Benedict faced the machine, ignoring the screen asking for the requested destination as he studied the lock on the front panel and access to the video-monitoring equipment. "I suppose I could bust in with a spell."

Tell Ben there's a USB port to access the video log once past the panel. The cable Herm gave you to charge that phone will work, and you can watch it on your screen.

"Pluck says there's a video port inside," I said as I felt in my pocket for the coiled cable. "I bet the charging cord will work."

"Inside. Good." Benedict put his palm to the lock. I stifled a shiver at the sensation of spiderwebs brushing my mind, then took a step back at the drift of dross snaking down from the machine. There was a sudden click of breaking metal, and Benedict pried the panel open. "Sorry about the dross," the mage whispered as he peered at the inner workings.

Pluck huffed, the shadow dog flicking an ear in annoyance before dissolving to a ribbon of energy and going to an orange chair to sulk. I gathered the dross with the butt of my stick with a sigh.

Totally oblivious, Benedict fitted the phone cord into the USB port, then his phone. Immediately both screens lit up, and he frowned. "I need to get an app."

Of course you do. Tired, I went to sit in the chair directly over Pluck. My ankles went cold, and I eyed a drift of dross rolling like a slime mold in the far corner. The dross I'd gathered from Benedict glowed, and I smacked the stick on the floor until it fell off.

"Got it." Benedict tapped, swiped . . . then frowned again. "Update," he muttered, and I smiled.

You should try tuning that, Pluck fizzed, the shadow having slipped up onto the chairs to sit beside me. He was again in his dog form. I guessed we were good.

My gaze went to the drift I had just freed. *Pluck, why did I get so cold when I made that light from a strand of dark matter? I seriously thought I was going to freeze.*

Pluck didn't answer, a thin haze of green skating over his almost-there surface like lightning. *I don't know,* he finally admitted. *I didn't think it was possible to manipulate a single strand, and I am over three thousand years old.*

That kind of makes sense, I thought, my fingertips barely touching him. *Why would you want to make a light in the first place?*

True. His ears flattened to his skull, and a hint of his concern lifted through me. But I was guessing it wasn't so much a lack of knowledge as it was that Pluck was already ice-cold. Maybe if he tried to make a light, he'd go solid right through.

"Done," Benedict said, head down over his phone. "Who bought tickets today?" His fingers manipulated the phone, and he sighed. "This might take a while. It's not set up well."

I leaned my head back against the wall, staff scraping the floor as I looked out over the parking lot. I couldn't see the coming dawn, but I could feel it behind my eyes, sort of a faint zest to the ever-present tinnitus that was the ringing of the cosmos. Slowly my eyes closed.

"Woman with a baby," Benedict said, voice preoccupied. "Couple of students. Wow, four, no, five students going to Vegas." He chuckled. "That won't end well."

Eyes closed, I listened to the universe, hearing the light creep across the skin of the world, the sensation becoming ever stronger, ever more turbulent. No wonder the light burned me. It was unmitigated chaos forced into tight bands of waves. "I don't know how we are going to find her if she's left already. I don't want to bring the militia into it, but we are all she's got, Benny."

I agree she needs to be found, Pluck fizzed. *Teaching her how to use a lodestone might not have been the best idea.*

"I didn't expect her to run off," I said softly. "She's just scared."

"Of Thoth?" Benedict said, not having heard Pluck. "Me too."

Frustrated, I opened my eyes, losing the feel of the coming sun. *Pluck, if we find her, can she keep him out of her mind? I know I said weavers were exempt from shadow attacks, but Thoth got through my defenses.*

Pluck flicked an ear, then flowed to the floor. *She can. She likely already has. She and Thoth do not mesh well. Thoth had to lure you into Cameron's mind to damage your ability to make a field.*

I quit swinging the stick between my ankles. *Still, am I asking too much of her?* I thought, and Pluck turned into a snake. Body hazing, he climbed the side of the kiosk until he hung his head over the top to watch Benedict's screen.

No, prickled through me, but it only made me more worried.

Thoth might not be able to mesh his mind to hers and take her as his weaver, but they are alike enough that he found her. Followed her here. I will take that as a good sign, seeing as one of Marty's defining characteristics is fear.

You think he's afraid? I guessed, and Pluck's snake head lifted.

I do. He made a mistake. He's never done that before. Finding Marty is the smart thing to do even if it makes her more vulnerable.

Because we would teach her how to survive Thoth and help catch him. Looking into the future, we had to find a way to bend the rules for her boyfriend—but I didn't see how. I couldn't even get the board to admit that shadows were worthy of consideration.

"Nothing today," Benedict said, completely unaware of our conversation. "I think she's still here." He yanked the cord from the machine. "She'd need a credit card to take the train or rent a car."

Still atop the kiosk, Pluck's green eyes glinted. *I suggest trying the aqueduct tunnels. It's getting close to daybreak, and I would appreciate being hidden. Dana is probably looking for both of you.*

I glanced at the dark windows as I stood. Stashing Herm's truck might be a problem.

"I'll drop Herm a text," Benedict said, and I started when he gave me a consoling, sideways hug. "We will find her."

"As long as Thoth doesn't find her first." My shoulders slumped, and he tugged me closer yet. "I don't know where to look," I said, then stiffened when Pluck's alarm fizzed through me.

Try behind you.

She's here? I spun, my elation and Pluck's worry making a sickening slurry of emotion in me. Marty stood just inside the door—it hadn't even closed yet—and I smacked Benedict's arm to get his attention. She was scared. That much was obvious. And alone.

"What?" Benedict muttered, and then he looked up from his phone. "Oh!" He took a breath. "Oh . . ."

Gently now . . . Pluck's warning lit through me. *She's here to flee, not join our cause.*

But I was too excited to care, and I pushed Pluck's thought aside. "Oh, my gosh, I'm so glad to see you," I said, my grip on Benedict's arm tight in hope.

Marty's eyes widened. "I didn't know you were here," she said, her gaze darting nervously from me to Pluck to Benedict.

She's going to run, Pluck thought as she took a step back.

"Marty, wait," I pleaded as the young woman reached for the door.

"I never should have come." Marty fumbled for the handle, unwilling to look away from us for even a second. "Dana said they were going to make Victor forget about me . . ." she said, voice rising in panic.

"Just . . . wait," I pleaded as I stepped between her and Benedict. "You are a weaver. You have no idea how important you are. She's trying to scare you, but you have power. You can make demands."

Benedict made a rude snort. "She's telling the truth. Petra does it all the time."

"We will work something out. I promise. Cheese and crackers, Marty. I blew up the auditorium and they gave me a promotion and a raise."

It wasn't you, it was me, Pluck fizzed, ignored.

Marty's breathing was fast, eyes wide as she clutched her coat close. "What if you're lying to me? What if you make me forget about him!"

"Please. Please," I begged her, desperate. The moldavite we'd given her was still around her neck. It was a pale green. *Empty,* I thought in relief. "I think we have a way to get rid of Thoth. But we need your help."

She took another half step back. "You expect me to trust you?" she accused softly. "You said you could get rid of him. And look what happened!" In a quick motion, she tugged the lodestone over her head and off, holding it out as if it was to blame. "You lied to me.

Maybe once, I could have gone home, but now? Now I know too much. I don't want this anymore!"

"Marty, no!" I shouted as she threw it.

Benedict lurched, diving for the glittering green glass. He hit the floor with an *oof*, sliding to narrowly get his hands under it. Relief spilled through me, doubly so for Pluck's emotion, and I exhaled, eyes darting to Marty. It was safe.

"Marty—" I pleaded as the woman retreated to the door. "I'm so sorry. I only wanted you to see how wonderful it could be."

"Wonderful!" Marty barked, her gaze going to Benedict as he got to his feet, stone cradled protectively. "There's a monster following me!"

No argument there, Pluck thought.

And yet her eyes never left the amulet when Benedict handed it to me.

"You know full well that Petra and Pluck aren't destroying the vaults," Benedict accused. "She can't help you if she's hiding from a crime she didn't commit."

Her hand fell from the door. "I told Dana what I saw in the basement," she said, a flicker of anger giving her a hint of strength. "She thinks I'm lying for you." Her jaw clenched. "Or that I can't tell one shadow from another. She says we're in it together. And you think I want to go to school here? Well, screw that!"

"Damn you, Dana . . ." Benedict whispered as I tried to wrap my head around it. Marty had told Dana the truth, and she still blamed me and Pluck?

The mage is a yeth, Pluck fizzed. *She won't believe unless she hears it from Thoth himself. Thoth, though, is a confident shadow spit. He will admit to the destruction and trickery if we can catch him, if only to prove how smart he is. He has never been contained and will expect to gain his freedom at the moment it's most devastating to you.*

I put a hand to my head, trying to figure this out. If Dana didn't believe Marty, she sure as hell is hot wouldn't believe Cameron's testimony whether supported by Lev's militia experts or not. Catching Thoth was the only way Pluck and I could prove our innocence. "Marty, please," I begged. "We almost caught Thoth with three sticks, but they weren't a set and Thoth found a way to break one and escape. All we need are five balanced sticks and the people to hold them. I know we can catch Thoth. It's the only thing that will discredit Dana, and once the board stops listening to her, we can change their minds about Victor, too. There's no reason he can't be told about magic."

"Ah, Petra . . ." Benedict started, and I rounded on him.

"There's no good reason!" I shouted. "She is a weaver! If he talks, her shadow will leave him clinically insane and no one will believe him." I turned to Marty. "But he won't. Not if he loves you."

Marty's impetus to leave faltered. Hope pinched her eyes, a quiet desperation that I might be throwing her a rope with which to pull herself to a happy ending. "I can't . . ." she said, clearly scared, until she looked at the stone in my hand. Gaze fixed on it, she rubbed her fingers together as if feeling a tingling of power. Slowly her chin lifted, making me think she might have only now believed she had value—that what she wanted mattered.

"Thoth first," she said, breath shaking in her. "Then Dana. I will not allow anyone to hurt Victor. Promise it."

"I promise," I whispered, and then she nodded.

"What do you want me to do?"

24

THE HUM OF HERM'S TRUCK BLENDED SEAMLESSLY WITH THE EVER-PRESENT rise and fall of the universe in a mind-numbing drone. It rumbled up from the floorboards and into my bones as I drove us back into town, eager to return to the memorial garden. To the east, a faint light threatened, visible in flashes through the low buildings.

Benedict was having a hard time keeping his eyes open, but I felt wide-awake—though that might be from the coming prospect of trying to sleep in the grotto. The truck's front bench seat wasn't long enough for three people and a shadow, but I wasn't going to ask Marty or Benedict to ride in the truck bed.

Head down, Benedict was texting Herm between his yawns. Marty was to his other side, pressed against the passenger window as she stared out at nothing. Pluck had surprised me by volunteering to park his shadow ass in Marty's amulet, currently around my neck. He had wanted to put some usable dark matter in it, but he was uncomfortable, if his sporadic fizzing was any indication.

You okay? I thought, and Pluck's agitation sharpened.

A new stone is scratchy, bubbled up through me. *There are no comfortable spots.*

I glanced at Benedict, wondering if he would mind shifting a little, but he was oblivious to the world as he texted Herm that we'd secured Marty. *You can sit on my shoulder if you don't mind being small.*

My lips quirked as the image of Kahu the size of a saltshaker drifted through my head, quickly banished. I had a feeling that Pluck caught it when an odd sensation of reluctance colored our joined moods as he fizzed, *Benedict would notice.*

I had no idea why that mattered, but I let it go.

Benedict made an unhappy noise. "Ah . . . Herm says not to go to the grotto."

My foot lifted from the accelerator in a moment of surprise. "Does he say why?"

Benedict closed his phone out. "No. He says to meet him at Brown's lab. You think he means Professor Brown?" he asked around a yawn.

I bit my lower lip, worried. Dr. Brown's lab was more of a woodshop. There was only one reason to meet there.

"Why would he want to meet at—" Benedict's words cut off as his gaze darted to my stick wedged between us. "Oh," he said, slumping. "He couldn't find the last stick."

"It was a long shot anyway," I said, and Pluck fizzed sourly.

Marty had perked up at the mention of sticks, and little ribbons of potential sparked through Pluck's mood at her sudden interest. His belief that she was more skilled than she let on was obvious, but who was I to take the last shred of comfort from her? Grip tightening on the wheel, I slowly drove through a blinking yellow before making a U-turn. Early rush hour would start in a few hours, but right now, the streets were empty. Camping out in Brown's lab wouldn't be much better than sleeping on a wooden stage, but at least there wouldn't be any shadow-rezes about.

Your thoughts are mixed. Eagerness and dread. What's at Professor Brown's lab? Pluck asked, clearly interested at my memories of belonging crashing against a new feeling of dismay.

I majored in trap development and construction before I decided to become a sweeper. It was a good group of people. I had fun there. Felt a part of something. I glanced at Benedict. *The concern is because Herm wouldn't send us there unless we needed to make a new stick.*

"Five minutes," I said aloud to ease Marty's worry. "It's a good place to catch some sleep, seeing as we're on Thanksgiving break and no one will be there. Professor Brown knows me. I doubt he believes Dana's tripe." I smiled softly.

Benedict put his phone on the dash. "Word is Brown never forgave Ryan for luring you away to be a sweeper." He chuckled. "You were one of his best students, I hear."

Marty turned, clearly interested. "You know how to make trap sticks?"

"And knotted cords," Benedict said proudly as I winced, wanting to downplay it. "She was exceptional at it. *Is* exceptional. Takes after her dad."

"I was okay," I said. Making a new stick balanced to the other four would slow things down. It had taken me a week to craft three for my final exam. "It was good I shifted majors when I did," I said, scanning the long street for any sign of traffic and finding none. "I was filling my sticks and knotted cords with inert dross. That's how I found Pluck. He ripped one apart for it."

Marty leaned past Benedict to look at me, eyes wide. "You couldn't tell it was inert?"

That did confuse me, Pluck thought, and a fizzing mirth bubbled through me as I pulled into the empty lot. The university building was long, low, and covered with solar panels, and I parked at the edge under a paloverde tree at the back, where the truck would be hard to spot from the main road.

Benedict leaned forward, studying the lot. "I doubt Herm is here yet. I can bust the lock."

I opened the door, relishing the cool night air spilling in. "No need," I said as my feet hit the pavement. "Sweepers have a code to get in."

He chuckled as he followed me out. "Sweepers could steal the world if you wanted."

"And don't we know it."

Marty was slow, taking the time to ease her door shut and then knock her hip into it to close it completely with hardly a sound. Benedict handed me my stick, and together we headed for the front glass doors.

The building itself was open. I went in first, my shoulders slumping at the memories filling me. There were no mage studies here, and it was blessedly clean of dross right down to the corners. Pluck, too, seemed to relax, and I wondered if maybe Herm had chosen our new hiding spot better than I had originally thought.

"Man, I'm tired," Benedict said, stifling a yawn as we made our way down the corridor.

Marty, too, looked beat as she shuffled one step behind us, but Pluck's nocturnal nature was overshadowing my own, and my steps sounded crisp on the old tile floor.

"Locked," Benedict said when he tried the door to Brown's lab, and I punched in the sweepers' access code. Immediately the light on the box turned green, and I went in.

"It doesn't ping anyone's office when you open it?" Marty asked, the woman giving the hallway a last look before following us.

"Maybe Professor Brown's?" I guessed. "Herm wouldn't send us here if it wasn't safe," I added, eyes closing briefly as I brought the scent of cut wood deep into my lungs, holding it for a moment before breathing out contentment. The long room looked exactly as I remembered, with its eight workstations, tidy and pristine under dark shop lights. Each one was equipped with both woodworking tools and dross-handling equipment. Windows took up one entire side facing the parking lot, and Benedict was already closing the blinds.

I smiled at my old workstation at the back. Professor Brown's instruction table was at the opposite end of the room, eight high-top swivel chairs surrounding it. A more conventional desk sat to the side of it—empty since he appreciated a clean work area—and behind that were the locked cupboards of bottled instructional dross, raw trap sticks, wands, and countless spools of the tightly woven silk with which to make the needed matching ties and long-cords.

"We're good," Benedict said, and I flicked on Professor Brown's desk lamp. "But I'd keep the big lights off."

Marty grimaced at the hard workbenches. "Maybe we could bring in a couple of the couches from the lobby," she suggested, and Benedict exhaled to puff his cheeks out.

"I'm so tired I could sleep on the floor," he said, then sighed. "Oka-y-y-y . . ." he groaned as he shuffled to the door. "One last push."

Someone is in the building. Pluck's thought darted through mine, waking me up fast.

"Wait," I said, and both Benedict and Marty froze at the warning in my voice. Pluck had already phased out of Marty's surrendered amulet, and the young woman jerked when he darted to the door, nothing but a dark ribbon skating along the floor. "Pluck says someone is here."

Benedict's expression blanked. "Light," he whispered, and I clicked it off before he carefully peeked past the blind to the parking lot. "A car parked three spots down from Herm's truck," he added. "I don't recognize it."

Concerned, I gestured for Marty to come stand with me. "I thought you said Herm was going to meet us here," she whispered, and I shrugged.

It's Herm and a short man I don't recognize, Pluck fizzed through my mind. *He smells like redwood and silk.*

"Professor Brown?" I said aloud, and from the hallway came a distant, frightened shout.

"Great God Almighty, Pluck!" Herm yelled, voice echoing. "Give a person a little warning. I almost dropped everyone's dinner!"

Dinner? I smiled in relief at Benedict and clicked on the light again. Timing put it more like a very early breakfast, but I could eat.

"Are you sure it's him?" Marty asked, and I nodded. With Ryan's three and my one, we still had to make one stick really fast. Fortunately Professor Brown was a three-state expert. It wouldn't be as elegant or beautiful as my dad's sticks, but as long as it was balanced to the rest, it would work.

Twin shadows appeared behind the frosted glass in the door. Herm came in as if he owned the place, his annoyance at Pluck obvious. Professor Brown was with him, and the slight man met my eyes and beamed, clearly pleased to see me. Moving with a wary quickness, he set a bag of food on the desk. His almond-shaped eyes were bright, and he ran his scarred fingers through his short dark hair in worry as he studied Marty. An elaborately knotted cord held his Spinner lodestone about his neck.

"Great green eyes staring at me from under a chair," Herm griped, as he handed Benedict a second bag of takeout. He had my dad's three sticks from Ryan in his other hand, and my worry eased. *One to go.* "It's a wonder I didn't have a heart attack. Petra, Benedict, good work. Marty, I'm glad we found you. Safety in numbers and all."

Marty fidgeted at the edge of the light's easy reach. "Petra promised she'd help change Dana's mind about Victor, but she can't do that if Thoth is free."

"Ah, sure." Herm acknowledged my glare telling him not to argue with her. "Marty, this is Professor Brown."

The man in his early sixties nodded to Marty, his gaze immediately going to Pluck when the shadow dog made a doggy circle and flopped to the poured-cement floor at my feet. "Petra, it's good to see you."

"Hi, Professor B." Mood soft, I closed the distance between us and met his fist with my own. "My gosh, it's been years. Your lab looks the same, though."

His gaze went to the dark corners as if seeing more than the quiet, tidy space. "I never forgave myself for losing you to the sweepers' guild." Eyes bright, he looked past me at Pluck. "Clearly it was a good move."

Benedict had taken both bags to a workstation, head down as he rustled through them.

"You met Pluck?" I asked.

He did. Pluck flicked an ear to send a wad of dark matter to splat next to Benedict's foot. The mage noted it with half his attention, more interested in the food.

"Ah, yes." Professor Brown watched the haze of spent energy evaporate in an evil-looking ribbon of smoke. "Um . . . I've not been able to bring myself to work with shadow since the auditorium collapsed. That energy could have an intelligence . . . agency." His eyes held guilt as they found mine. "Perhaps it was easier to ignore what was in front of me. Us. Dana . . ." His words cut off, and he rocked back a step to include everyone. "I make it a practice to not talk ill of others, but it's an honor to give you all sanctuary," he said, voice louder. "Not everyone is against this new balance of shadow and light."

"Thank you," I said, but in all honesty, as a Spinner, he had everything to gain and nothing to lose.

Pluck sat up, whip-tail waving. *I approve of this Spinner. Tell him I won't ever drive him insane.*

Timing, Pluck, I thought, and the shadow flopped onto the cool cement again.

"Ryan says to stay out of sight." Herm's gruff expression eased when he came close and handed me the three sticks. "I'm sorry, Petra. He doesn't know where the last stick is."

"No, this is great!" I looked the three over, silky against my fingers. "I thought we'd have to make an entirely new set. One stick won't take too long. Marty has agreed to help. Our chances at catching Thoth just got better."

Herm pinched the bridge of his nose. "Can I talk to you for a moment?" he said, gaze going to Marty.

I stifled a sigh. He doubted her. Whether it was her skills or loyalty made no difference. And that I might doubt her, too, sort of irritated me. "Sure." I propped the sticks up against a counter, and Pluck fizzed that there was no need for Marty to see his uncertainty. He was right.

"Um, Benny?" I said loudly, and the man looked up from the bags of food. "Could you and Marty go find a couple of couches to drag in here? I'll unpack everything."

Benedict hesitated, and I widened my eyes and sort of nodded to the door.

"Oh! Right." Benedict glanced at the bags reluctantly. "Sure. Marty, where did you say you saw them?"

Marty slid from one of the high-tops and set her waxed cup down. "The front. I'll show you." But it was obvious by the way she left that she knew that she was being gotten rid of.

"Thank you," I mouthed to Benedict when he looked back, and then he was gone.

"Herm, Marty has better skills than she's admitting to," I said as I went to unpack the bags. "She wants to help. You told Benedict to trust me. So trust me."

The old man sighed, and when Professor Brown gestured, he settled himself on a high-top with a familiarity that reminded me he had been a student here once, too. "I do," he grumped. "I just don't like us all scattered like this. Lev and Cameron are still working to get the court-worthy affidavits."

"Good." I moved to take the seat next to him. "We're going to need them. Marty told Dana that Thoth was the one blowing up the vaults and she called Marty delusional."

Professor Brown looked up from trying to engage Pluck. The shadow was being unusually accommodating, making extra eyes on stalks to freak the man out.

Herm grunted his opinion. "Yeah, well, Dana being a hypocritical bureaucrat was my big news. Petra, you can't promise Marty that they will make an exception for Victor. He's mundane."

I crumpled up the first bag and tossed it to the center of the table. "Then we lose her." I glanced at Professor Brown, clearing my throat when Pluck flicked an ear and the man jumped with a nervous laugh. "Herm, she has to tell him. You can't hide a shadow. If Victor and Marty are both here, we have some sort of control. Not to mention if he blabs, there's an entire university of people who can cover for his mistake."

Head down, Herm nodded, forcing a smile when Professor Brown came to join us.

"Petra, Herm said you plan on capturing Thoth with five sticks." The older man winced. "Five would certainly make a tighter net than three, but it still feels chancy."

"We almost had him with three." I drew a folder of cold fries closer and began to pick at them, looking for the longest. "With balanced sticks and the right people manning them, Pluck thinks we can force him into a pure energy state and capture him in a field."

Guilt pinched my gut. I couldn't make a field. Couldn't help catch Thoth. It was my idea, but I wouldn't be the one taking the risk.

You can wield a stick, Pluck fizzed. *And you can tune dross better than any shadow.*

Only if I stop and think about it, I mused. *I'm sure Thoth will wait for me.*

Don't be a yeth, Pluck fizzed, his presence in mine taking on a disgruntled tone. *You're tuning more dross than any shadow alive. Practice imparts speed.*

I couldn't exactly ignore his sour fluster twining through me, but I tried, and the salt from the cold fries stirred my appetite despite the general sogginess of them. Okay, maybe I could be of some help. Keep the area clean if nothing else. Benedict was exceptional at manipulating heat. Lev was good with gravity. Herm was good with water studies, and Cameron claimed she was an etherologist, which would be helpful in her marshal duties.

Worried, I glanced at the three sticks Herm had brought. "So, Professor B. How long will it take to make a fifth stick?"

Professor Brown ran a hand over his chin, his expression having that same distant look I remembered from when I'd been his student. "Making a stick isn't a problem. Matching the dross balance of the other four might be an issue."

Herm unwrapped a burger and lifted the top bun, sighed at the mess, then put it back on. "Her dad made them here, didn't he? I thought you kept records."

Professor Brown's gaze went to the door as Benedict and Marty shuffled in, an ugly, institutional-looking couch between them. "Yes," he admitted. "But I have no idea of the amount of dross decay that has occurred."

I ate another fry, a small noise of understanding slipping from me. "I forgot about that. Shadow spit, none of them are alike anymore, are they?"

"Dross decay?" Herm prompted as Benedict and Marty left to get a second couch.

Professor Brown clasped his hands before him, his index fingers coming together to make a little steeple. "Dross is energy, and like any power source, it loses potency over time and use. Think of it like a radioactive substance, but unlike, say, carbon 14, which decays at a fixed rate . . ."

He looked at me to finish his thought and I smiled. He was in teaching mode. "Dross decays at a variable rate dependent upon how much there is and how often it comes in contact with other dross. That's why you have to keep your sticks together."

"And whereas," Professor Brown continued, "your dad's sticks have been scattered the last few months, they had been stored the previous ten years in a controlled environment that promoted stability. They won't be as far off from one another as you might think."

"Mmmm." Herm took a bite of his burger and chewed. "Can't you run one through one of your apparatuses here to figure out how much dross we're talking about?"

The smaller man looked at the sticks in question. "Sure. But to get an accurate measurement through a quarter inch of wood, I'd need twenty-four hours. Unless you want me to destroy one. That would take about an hour, but require making two new sticks."

My shoulders slumped. *Twenty-four hours?* Pluck fizzed, clearly not wanting to break one of the sticks, either. *We don't have that long.*

"Meanwhile, Thoth is free to do what he wants," I said softly, attention going to Benedict and Marty bringing in a second couch. "There has to be a faster way to do this."

Marty's end of the couch hit the floor with a thump. "Sticks? Is that why we're here? You can pick them up at any secondhand shop. I should know."

"They need to all have the same balance of dross," I said as Benedict came forward to claim a paper-wrapped burger. "My dad's old set is the only one I know of, but we just have four." *Did he prepare for this?* I wondered. *Or was it because, as Darrell claimed, he went through them fast?*

Marty came closer, clearly more interested in the four sticks than eating. "Oh. Dana has one just like these," she said, and Herm grunted.

"Dana?" he said, swallowing hard. "Are you sure?"

Marty ran a finger down one of the sticks to trace the esoteric symbols my dad had carved into them. "Absolutely. They're beautiful, and I thought it weird she had only the one."

Where the hell *did Dana get one of my dad's sticks?* I thought.

More importantly, why did she retain it? Pluck fizzed. *She couldn't have known we needed it. We didn't know until yesterday.*

Benedict noisily pulled a stool closer to me and sat down. "That's lucky. I don't think there's another stick on campus that is shod in silver. It's probably your dad's."

Herm bobbed his head. "Agreed. Petra, your dad was my best friend, but he was an odd duck for sure. Those symbols don't do a damn thing other than making it obvious they're a set."

Marty was still looking at my dad's sticks, and remembering how she had regrouped all the scattered sticks in the front room of the records building, I twitched my foot to touch Pluck. She had more skill than she knew. Enough to be of real help. More help than me, probably.

So I wasn't surprised when Marty picked one up and took a step back, spinning it like a baton to gauge its weight and rough dross level. "Yeah, that feels the same," Marty said as she set it down. "Your dad made this? It's beautiful."

One stick, two sticks, three, four, five. Stand them straight to stay alive. The poem echoed in both Pluck's and my thoughts as my ankle cramped with cold, and I held a hand down in invitation, dabbling my fingertips into his tingling concern. If Thoth knew her real strength . . .

Benedict took a bite of his burger, jaw moving slowly as he chewed. "Why would Dana have one of your dad's sticks?"

"I'll ask her." Herm sighed at his flattened burger, then took a bite.

"I'll help." Benedict slid from the stool, his fatigue becoming more obvious.

"I'd like a word with Dana myself." I upended the fry folder to get the last of the salt.

"Hold up, campers." Herm chuckled. "I like the enthusiasm, but if Dana has one of your dad's sticks, I will get it. You're both staying here."

"Hey! I can steal stuff," Benedict complained, and Professor Brown laughed.

"Duly noted, Professor Strom," Herm said dryly. "But you and Petra are wanted for questioning."

I slumped, not pleased that I was trashing Benedict's career along with mine.

"No, you will sit tight with Petra and Pluck in the shadows where they belong," Herm continued. "Practice using the sticks in tandem. Lev has a light touch, and I wouldn't mind bringing in Cameron's expertise, either. Five sticks need five handlers."

In the shadows where they belong? I wasn't sure what to think about that, but Pluck fizzed happily at the idea.

Professor Brown patted his front pocket as if looking for something. "Herm, your situation isn't that secure, either. I'll ask Dana," he said, finding his keys. "Give me until ten tomorrow. You should be safe here until then."

Herm eyed him sourly. "I have been ostracized before, Steven. I know what I'm doing, and you asking Dana about the stick is a bad idea. If she has it, then it's because she knows its value. You asking about it will only tell her you're involved." Herm shoved the last bite of his burger into his mouth. "Lev, Cameron, and I will liberate it tomorrow without her knowing," he said around his chewing.

"Fine," I muttered, and Benedict put his elbows on the table, clearly disappointed.

"Okay, then." Professor Brown jiggled on his feet, then swooped to his desk. "I will defer recovering the last stick to you." Head down, he shuffled through his top drawer until finding a thick Sharpie and pad of paper. "Keep the lights off," he said as he began to write in big, bold letters. "I'll put a note on the door in case one of my students tries to get a foot up on next week's classes, though that would be highly unlikely." He ripped the paper free and straightened. "Petra, you and Pluck are getting a raw deal. It's obvious that Dana doesn't care who pays for it as long as things go back to normal. I'm going to make a few inquiries. See who thinks Dana is being criminally shortsighted. There may be support out there that you don't know about."

Herm slid from his stool, shaking his hand as the man prepared to leave. "Good luck," Herm said, smiling. "I never found the knack to get the university board to admit they were wrong. Thanks, Steven."

My old instructor beamed confidently. "My pleasure. I'm headed home. Let me know if you need anything." He smiled fondly at me, then nodded to Benedict. "Strom," he said, as if parting with an equal, adding in a lighter tone, "Pluck, Marty, good to meet you. Petra, take care of yourself."

Pluck flicked an ear, delighting the professor, and I dangled my fingers into the shadow. "You too," I said, not happy that everyone I cared about was likely going to take a hit if we could pull this off.

We had to pull it off.

Professor Brown chuckled ruefully as he headed for the hall. "I never should have let you drop that class," he said as he walked out and closed the door. His silhouette before it hesitated as he taped the note, and then it was gone. "A shadow wrangler," came faintly from the hall, and then even the sound of his steps vanished.

Focus distant, Benedict unwrapped a second burger and took a bite, jaw moving slowly. "Shadow spit, I'm tired," he said, then glanced up at Marty. "There's lots here, Marty. Dig in."

She lifted her nearly empty cup and jiggled it to make the ice shift. "I'm good. Not hungry this time of night." She looked at the blinds. "Or is it morning now?"

It *was* closer to morning, and I yawned as the first hints of fatigue began to steal into me.

Marty glanced at the couches, really nothing more than long benches with a thin layer of foam on them. There were only two, but I felt awake enough to stand watch.

"I do not want to cut up one of my dad's sticks," I said, and Herm grunted, wadding up his burger's paper and throwing it away.

"You won't have to. We'll get the last one." He beamed at Marty as she went to a couch.

"I would bet my life it's the same." Marty hesitated. "Ah, should we look for more couches?"

Herm waved her to have at it. “I’m standing watch.”

“Me too,” I blurted before Benedict could.

“No, you need your sleep,” Herm said, and Benedict’s coming protest faltered. “I need the time to plan out how to get in and out of Dana’s apartment.” He reached for his phone, his thoughts already on it. “Two of you can share a couch. It’s big enough.”

Marty immediately claimed a couch, stretching out with her face to the wall. I could hear her sigh from where I was, and Benedict looked from the other couch to me.

“It’s not your queen, but I think we can manage,” he said, and a smile quirked my lips.

Shadow spit, Pluck grumbled, and his presence faded from mine as thoughts of Benedict pressed up against my length flooded both our minds.

“Mind if I have the inside?” I said as I gathered up the trash, and Herm chuckled, sighing in what might be a fond memory.

The couch was indeed as hard as it looked, but as I curved into the shelter of Benedict’s body, I decided that for having started this night with a cinder-block wall between us, this wasn’t bad.

Not bad at all.

25

A MURMUR OF VOICES PULLED ME FROM MY DREAM OF HAZY SUNLIGHT AND lapping waves. Stretching where I was, I cracked my eyelids to see an empty couch. I could hear the soothing rumble of Benedict's voice, and for a moment, I stayed where I was as the last remnants of sleep fractured and fell away. Slivers of light ran long lines across the floor through the blinds, and I sat up, swinging my feet to the cement only to start at a sudden painful tingle.

Dross, I thought in annoyance, but when I looked down, it was only the glint of the low sun. Worry washed through me, quickly followed by a faint fizzing.

You okay? Pluck asked, and I cautiously stuck my foot back into the sun to feel only the expected warmth.

"Fine," I said, but he had felt the echo of my pain from the initial contact and he was concerned.

Pluck looked almost solid as he sat with ears pricked watching Benedict and Marty playing paper triangle football on one of the empty workbenches. Sticky-looking cellophane wrappers sat at the corners, and two more wrapped pastries waited on the adjacent bench with my dad's four sticks, tied into an easy-to-carry bundle with a knotted long-cord. Clearly they'd found a vending machine, and I stifled a surge of jealousy when Marty scored a field goal and both of them laughed.

Pluck flicked an ear, a saucy glint to his green eyes. *You are the one he was pressed against last night.*

My shoulders slumped and I quashed the stupid feeling. "Morning," I said, surprised at my rough voice.

Marty started, going to sit on one of the high stools with a guilty quickness, but Benedict visibly brightened. "Good morning!" he said, his gaze flicking past me to the window blinds glowing with light. "Didn't mean to wake you up."

"You didn't." I sighed, still feeling tired. "Did Herm leave already?"

"Yep." Benedict fiddled with the paper triangle, finally setting it by the makeshift goalpost since Marty was clearly done playing. "About five minutes ago."

I stood, pace wobbly as I went to sit with my elbows on the workbench and my chin in my cupped hand. "He knew I wanted to go with him to get that last stick," I said, and my ankle went tingly and cold until Pluck swirled up to sit next to the dross separator bolted to the corner. There were three empty paper cups in the trash, and I could smell coffee. *Just how long,* I wondered, *has everyone been up?* Benedict looked positively chipper.

"That's why he hustled out of here," Benedict said as he flicked the triangle to Marty and she caught it. "He'll call when he knows something."

Typical. Tired, I dragged one of the unopened pastries to me and struggled with the cellophane. "Any more coffee in that break room?" I guessed, relieved when the bag finally opened. *Shadow spit. Why am I so tired?*

Marty slid from the high stool with a reluctant slowness. "I'll get you a cup. It's just down the hall." She patted her jeans pocket, then winced. "Uh . . ."

"I got it." Benedict took his wallet from his back pocket and handed her a five-dollar bill. "Can it handle this?"

"Yup." She flashed me a smile. "Won't be long."

She practically ran to the door, but I *had* just caught her flirting with my boyfriend. "You don't know if the vending machine can handle a fiver?" I asked Benedict when the door shut and her shadow vanished.

He wouldn't leave you, Pluck thought. *I'm starting to admire his unthinking zeal to keep you safe—which is a strange feeling in itself. Speaking of which . . .*

Pluck shrank to a thin ribbon, skating to the door and puddling under it to follow her. *Good idea,* I thought, getting a faint response. Marty had said it was just down the hall, but no need to take chances.

His good mood obvious, Benedict began to disassemble the goalposts, each one made from pencil-size sticks destined to become desk traps. They had tied them together with silk ribbon and propped them up with sticky tack.

"Is Pluck with her?" he asked as he picked the silk knots free.

I ate a bite of the pastry. It was sweet, but that was its only redeeming feature. "Yup."

The tiny sticks clattered as he set them back in their bin. "I was being nice. That's it."

I looked up at him, eyebrows high. "You sure?"

He smiled, his even teeth showing in a flash of mirth. "You're jealous!" he exclaimed, and I scowled when he tugged me close and gave me a long hug.

I couldn't stay mad at him. Giving up, I set my pastry down to put both arms around his waist. "You need to do something to make me unjealous," I suggested, and Benedict grinned.

"I'd give you a kiss, but I haven't brushed my teeth."

"Neither have I."

He leaned down and I looked up, our lips meeting for a full-on, satisfying kiss that was just about as far as I wanted to go without a toothbrush. My grip tightened about his waist, and a thrill raced through me when I broke from him, a little breathless. That Pluck was far enough away that he couldn't hear my thoughts was appreciated, seeing as they were decidedly earthy.

"Still jealous?" he asked.

"Not sure." Playing coy, I drew just out of his reach. "Might need more convincing."

Benedict dragged a tall stool closer so he could sit right beside me, his attention going to that last wrapped pastry. He ripped it open with a practiced ease. "She's had a rough week. And she really misses Victor."

"Tell me about it." I bumped my shoulder into his before giving his neck a solid kiss . . . which turned into biting his ear.

"You are wicked, you know that?" Benedict glanced at the door, then peeled the cellophane from his pastry. "I'm glad you woke up. I was waiting to eat with you and I'm starved."

I glanced at the closed door, wishing I had my coffee. "So . . . Herm has a plan?"

Benedict shrugged. "He sent Lev and Cameron to get Dana out of her apartment on a wild-goose chase so he could search her apartment for that last stick."

I nibbled at the sticky bun, hoping the coffee would be better. "Simple works best."

"We should get a call in about twenty minutes, I'm guessing?"

I nodded, wondering what was taking Marty so long.

Benedict pulled a ribbon of dough free and ate it. "Which leaves us to figure out how to either find Thoth or lure him into a trap."

I followed Benedict's gaze to the four gathered sticks lying on the workbench. Saying nothing, I picked at my pastry, not really enjoying it.

"Hey," he said, clearly trying to change the subject. "Those dross bottles are shadow rated, right? Maybe we should empty one to put Thoth into. I mean, *I* should empty one. Or I could do it here and you could tune the dross. Fill Marty's amulet, maybe."

My fingers touched the squarish stone around my neck. I knew without looking that it was a muddy green from storing the dark matter I'd put in it. There was room for more. "That's not a bad idea." I slipped from the high stool, my thump from finding the floor going right up my spine. The cabinet latch was simple, and the old glass door creaked as I swung it open. "I'm sure she'd appreciate getting it back."

A shudder rippled over me as I looked at the stored bad luck, shining like bottled miniature suns. But when I drew a wide-mouthed jar from the rack, I hesitated. My fingers were tingling. Not only that, but the sensation was growing, becoming a soft burn. Shadow spit, I could feel the dross right through the glass!

Breath held, I paced quickly to the nearest workbench and set the jar down. Benedict stared at me as I wiped my fingers on my jeans to rid myself of the memory. It had been that same burning feeling that I'd gotten from the sunbeam, but unlike the heat of the sun, it had gotten worse the longer I had held it.

"What?" he asked when I didn't say anything.

"Um." I made a fist to hide my fingers, nervous. "I can, ah. I think I can feel the dross through the glass," I admitted, and his eyes widened. I shouldn't be able to, and I backed away from it, wishing it was some special dross or unique bottle—but I knew better. It was me.

It was one of the unbreakable rules that dross couldn't pass through glass and, by association, shadow. That was how the bottles and vaults worked. Something, though, was getting through the glass, or I wouldn't be feeling the tingle of energy.

How the sweet ever-loving hell am I doing that? I thought, wishing Pluck was here. "Maybe it's the dark matter from dross's natural decay?" I guessed, not wanting it to be me.

Benedict's eyebrows rose high. "Seriously?"

Yeah, it had been a dumb idea, and I shrugged, studying the way the dross seemed to pool against the glass when I got too near. It was almost as if it was attracted—which sort of tracked. Breath held, I pressed a finger against the bottle, shivering when the faint chime of the universe became louder. Disturbed, I curved my finger under and away. "I need to talk to Pluck."

"It doesn't take this long to get a coffee," he said, brow furrowed.

Pluck? I called, senses straining.

"It was just down the hall," Benedict said, adding, "Ah, stay here. I'll go check," when I slid from the stool.

"We'll both check. Bring the sticks," I said, my thoughts on Thoth as I flung the door open—

Only to stop stock-still in shock. Dana stood there, accompanied by three men with rifles and another with a handheld battering ram.

"Grady!" Dana exclaimed, quickly finding her aplomb as the three men brought their mundane weapons to bear. "And Benedict, too. Is Herm here by chance?"

I backpedaled, face cold, and they came in, faces grim and lodestones winking.

"No?" Dana stopped just inside, motioning with a curt gesture for them to surround us. "Too bad. Can't have everything. We'll find him."

No, they wouldn't, and I swallowed hard as I bumped into Benedict. The four balanced sticks were slung over his shoulder, but they weren't much good unless I wanted to hit someone with them. "Where's Pluck?" I said. They knew he wasn't with me or they wouldn't be so brazen.

And with that, I got it. *They have Pluck.* The thought struck through me like fire, terrifying me.

Smug, the mage held a glass lodestone draped around her neck, little glints of light leaking from between her fingers. "Resisting will only make you look guilty," she said as we kept backing up. "I'm detaining you both for questioning concerning the recent vault destructions." Her eyes narrowed. "Amulet, Grady," she added, voice harsh. "Set it down. Now! Strom, you too."

If you have hurt Pluck . . . Benedict was at my shoulder. I had to get out of here. Find Pluck. Fear tightened my spine. "Think about what you're doing, Dana," I said as Benedict guided me around a workbench. "We know Marty told you Thoth was destroying the vaults. So did Cameron. You keep this up, people are going to think you're with Thoth." *Pluck!*

Dana's eye twitched. There were too many rifles pointed at us. Benedict might be able to explode the shells in the chambers but not all at once. Not spaced out as they were.

"Lodestones off! Now!" Dana barked. "I won't tell you again."

She'd already taken my lodestone. I wasn't going to let her take Marty's. My foot burned. I glanced down expecting dross but seeing only sun. Benedict's lodestone glittered and I froze, startled when the sensation of breaking threads rolled over me like a wave. He was doing magic.

"Benny . . ." I reached out, fumbling to take my dad's sticks when he shoved them at me. The knotted dross burned as it bumped through my fingers, and then my head snapped up when his lodestone flashed into play and one of the mages facing us cried out and dropped his rifle. It hit the cement floor with a crack and broke in two, condensation icing the metal. He'd quick-frozen it. His practice in freezing dross was paying off.

"Take them! Move!" Dana shouted as she ducked behind a workbench.

The four men rushed us. I panicked, slipping as I spun to flee. Arms flailing, I hit the floor, gasping when a spell zipped over my head where I'd just been. "Let go!" I shouted when someone reached for me, and I swung the bundle of my dad's sticks at him. They hit with a solid smack, breaking the tie and sending sticks rolling everywhere.

Benedict bellowed in anger. Someone grabbed my ankle when I tried to stand, yanking me down again. Kicking out, I stretched for a stick.

My breath exploded from me as I got it. Turning where I sat, I swung my stick. It hit the man's shoulder with a pop of magic, and I gasped when Marty's lodestone, safe around my neck, flashed green. Dark matter iced through my mind, my hand. I hadn't willed it to come forth. I wouldn't even know how. But I felt it pour from me to the guard.

The man cried out and fell back, wreathed in a green haze.

Pluck? I thought, but it hadn't been him. It had been me. I had done it. How?!

I watched in horror as half-seen threads coiled and hissed about me with the transparent color of the aurora borealis, lashing out with the cold crack of ice breaking until the heat of the room evaporated them. The man lay face down on the floor, ice rimming his ears and hair.

Stunned, I did nothing even when someone yanked me to my feet and pried the stick from my hand. I looked up, startled when I realized it wasn't Benedict. "Wait," I protested as the chain raked across my ear and they took Marty's lodestone. The man I'd downed shuddered, taking a gasping breath and curling into a ball, cold. He was okay. But what in the sweet hell had I done? I wasn't a mage. I didn't know how to make a cold spell.

And yet I had. Twice now. First to escape that cell, and then now.

"Benedict?" I warbled, surprised to see him kneeling with his hands behind his head in a tiny patch of sun. Dana had his lodestone as well, but she didn't seem happy as she stood before us dabbing a shop towel against her jawline.

"Get the sticks. Put them with her amulet," she demanded. "And don't let Strom near any glass!" she barked when one of the mages with her went to gather them. He was limping. Benedict must have kicked some serious mage ass.

"You just keep digging yourself in deeper," she said to me, but I was still trying to figure out what I'd done. I had been holding a stick and had an amulet full of dark matter, and then . . .

"Where's Pluck?" I whispered at her mocking expression. "What did you do with Pluck!" I shouted, and the man who had taken my amulet nudged me to be quiet. I spun, glaring at him. I was not going back to that cell. "What . . . did you do to Pluck?" I said again, and Dana came closer, thinking she was safe, that I needed a lodestone to do magic.

That's right. A little closer, babe, I thought, eyes narrowed.

"He's been bottled," she said, standing just out of my reach. "Like every shadow should be. He will be parceled into little tiny bits and put into dross-go sticks."

Ice infused my spine, spreading to my fingers and toes until the air touching my face felt hot. The chiming of the universe rolled over me in waves, each one a demand to do something. Anything. My eyes flicked to the dross hazing the floor, undoubtedly created when they brought us down . . . and a feeling of avarice slipped through me. It was not bad luck. It was power.

And I could use it.

"Petra . . ." Benedict whispered as my hands clenched.

"Get them to the van," Dana demanded. "If they don't tell us where Herm and the rest are, we burn the shadow right in front of her."

"You can't do this!" Benedict shouted, stumbling when someone pushed him, and I rocked into motion when one of the mages shoved me as well. "Pluck is smart. He thinks. He talks. Dana, it's murder."

"It's not murder. You have to be a person for it to be murder." Dana shoved Benedict into taking a step. "Tell me where Herm is and I might let it stay in a bottle."

Someone pushed me with the end of my dad's stick and I stumbled forward. My senses tingled. Benedict was helpless without his lodestone, but I wasn't, and I eyed the dross the mages had created curling up like heat waves in the desert. None of it was close, and I couldn't make a damn field to catch it.

"She can't do anything without her shadow," Dana said when someone shoved me to the door. "They can all go into the same van."

I had to get to the dross. I didn't care if it burned me or not. Pluck was in a bottle, and nothing else mattered.

Eyes narrowed, I looked to see who had my dad's sticks. It was the guy I'd frozen. Hunched and clearly still feeling the cold, he had them in a loose bundle. My gaze slid to Benedict, my eyebrows high in question. Benedict nodded, grim. We were almost to the door to the hall. There wouldn't be any dross out there. I had to move now.

"Be ready," I said soundlessly to Benedict, and he tensed, not knowing what I was going to do. Hell, I didn't know what I was going to do. Pluck wasn't answering me, and I wasn't sure I could intentionally duplicate what I'd done.

I stopped stock-still just before the door to the hall. Dross glittered out of my reach. This was the closest I'd get to it . . . and then my chance would be gone. "Where's Pluck?"

Impatient, Dana stood next to the doorway. "Get her moving," she said to the two mages behind me.

Either they would make the mistake of pushing me with their hands, or they would make the mistake of using one of my dad's sticks. One would get the mage thrown into Benedict so I could reach the dross, the other would give me the reach I needed to get the dross with a little more finesse.

"Out," one of them demanded, and the hard butt of the stick jammed between my shoulder blades.

Stick it is . . . I lurched forward, spinning to grasp the silver-shod end. Feet shifting, I found my center and yanked the staff with all my frustration, my grip sure because of the symbols my dad had etched into the smooth wood. The man let go, staggering until he fell, his lodestone clutched in fear.

"She's got a stick!" someone yelled, and Dana ducked, thinking I was going to hit them with it.

"Damn it, Anderson!" she shouted, and then dark matter seemed to burst into existence in my mind's eye as I inhaled. Elated, I slammed the stick into the dross. The latent energy burst into heat, breaking as I willed the threads of dark matter through it. Heat flooded me; I tamed it as I inhaled, bringing more threads of dark matter into play, binding the power the breaking dross released until it was entirely mine.

"Down!" I shouted, and Benedict dropped, slipping from his guard's grip to hit the floor.

Exuberant, I spun the staff to draw the released energy into me. It hummed louder than the universe. My heart beat once . . . and with a twist of thought, I tuned the breaking energy, turning it into something I could use—and shoved the force right back out again through the stick.

A fog of ice crystals exploded from the whirling stick, carried by a cold green light. The boom of energy was soundless, but the chime of the universe rocked with the release as everyone still standing was shoved backward by a burst of driving snow.

Dana hit the wall by the door with a cry, eyes closed and slumped even before she hit the floor. I watched to make sure she was breathing as the snow settled, covering her in a faint white. Three of the four men were down as well, but the fourth, the one I'd downed before, had dropped at my warning. Eyes wide, he stared at me from the floor.

"Well?" I said, and he rolled the remaining three sticks to me.

Ticked, I scooped them up, fingers cramping at the icy chill that had taken them.

"Petra," Benedict croaked.

I spun, sticks an awkward tangle as I lurched to help him. His head was down, and his eyes were streaming. *Shadow spit, he had his eyes open,* I thought as I grabbed his shoulder. He jerked, shoving me as I shouted, "It's me! It's me!"

His breath came in with a rasp, and he blinked as he wobbled to his feet. "I couldn't look away," he said, his sight clearly returning as he focused on the man still conscious. "Petra. You tuned the entire drift."

"And then exploded it," I added, wondering if doing magic would always leave me this cold.

Dana groaned, a shaky hand rising to touch the back of her head. Lips pressed, I tugged Benedict toward the hall. *Pluck* . . . "We have to find Pluck."

But Benedict pulled from my grip to bend low over Dana, roughly searching her until he found both our lodestones. The woman was beginning to come to, and Benedict tossed Marty's moldavite amulet to me before putting his lodestone ring on. Grabbing the woman's shoulder, he shook her awake. "Pluck!" he shouted, and she ineffectively pushed at him, little breathy swears passing her lips. Her eyes, too, were blurry and red as she tried to focus.

"Where is Pluck!" he asked again, thumping her shoulder against the wall to get her attention. The snow fell from her, leaving wet marks.

"Van," she said, and I jammed Marty's amulet into my pocket, anxious to leave. "You're going down for this, Strom," she panted, and Benedict backed off.

"Yeah?" he said bitterly. "If you have hurt Pluck, I'll crush your lungs to wet paper myself."

"Benny," I whispered, not liking this side of him.

He gave her a last look. The mages were beginning to move; that is, all but the one who had ridden the blast out on the floor, ashen faced as he watched us.

"Van." Benedict took my elbow to draw me into a quick jog. I could feel him tapping into his lodestone, sensed the energy gathering in his hands like spiderwebs on my face.

"Anderson! Get up!" I heard Dana demand faintly from the lab when we pushed through the double doors and out into the parking lot.

The sun hit me, and I faltered. I couldn't feel Pluck, and I staggered after Benedict as the heat from the pavement spiraled up through me, driving the spell's chill away.

"Wait," Benedict said as we neared the black van and he drew me to a halt. "There might be someone here," he added, and I nodded. The van looked empty, but we settled to either side of the sliding door. On the silent count of three, Benedict yanked it open. My pulse hammered. *Pluck?* Nothing.

"Marty!" Benedict blurted, then lurched up and into the van. "Where's Pluck?"

"I couldn't stop her!" Marty shrieked, and I pulled myself in to see that Benedict had practically pinned her to the middle bench seat. Her hands were zip-tied before her and she'd been crying. "I tried. She won't listen."

"Where is Pluck!" I demanded, then followed her gaze to the front of the van.

There in the cup of the console was a small thick-walled bottle. *No . . .* I reached for it, feeling the icy hint of something within. It was tinted black. I could see nothing past the glass. Someone had sealed the lid by melting the glass top. Experience said I could drop the thick-walled, lab-grade bottle from a one-story building onto pavement and the glass wouldn't shatter.

But I was really pissed. I'd break it. Somehow.

Hang on, Pluck. I'm here, I thought as I lurched out of the van, glancing at the silent building before setting the bottle clinking onto the pavement. This might be messy, but it was going to take one hell of a tap and I didn't want to break our ride.

"Start the van," I said as Benedict snapped Marty's zip-strip and the woman rubbed her wrists. "Wait. I need dross."

He took a step down onto the pavement and into the sun. "Um, sure."

Hang on, Pluck. My head snapped up when the main door to the building slammed open. It was Dana, yelling for the mages with her to stop us, demanding that we get away from the van. I felt the universe pulse when Benedict did something . . . and a cooling sensation of breaking threads whispered over me.

"It wasn't me," Marty pleaded. "I didn't tell her where we were. I tried to stop her!"

Dana staggered into a slow run. The three men with her didn't look eager to engage. "Start the van!" I shouted as Benedict's dross burned my hand. This was going to be close.

Benedict made a frustrated noise, but he vanished back into the van. Exhaling, I twined threads around the dross he'd left behind, wringing it like a wet rag until it broke. Energy flooded me and I took it in, tuning it just slow enough that it wouldn't burn me, fast enough that I could use it. Green and pale, light streamed from my hands as I settled them around the top of the bottle and willed the cold to snap the glass. Heat didn't work for me, but cold? Cold I could do.

Please, please, please . . . Be okay, Pluck. My fingers turned blue and ice coated the bottle. My hands began to shake, and still I drew it colder, colder, until with a ping, the bottle shattered.

"Pluck!" I exclaimed, then cried out in pain as his presence slammed into my thoughts.

Hand to my head, I staggered, struggling to see as the shadow boiled up, pissed to the ends of the earth. From the building, shouts rose, but I couldn't take my eyes from Pluck as he made a quick swirl around me. *You are alive. You are unhurt,* he thought, his relief twining through mine as my ice cream headache vanished. *Where. Is. Marty?*

"Van," I said, and he was gone.

"Pluck! Thank God!" Benedict shouted over the roar of the engine. "Petra, let's go!"

I reached for the opening and pulled myself in, but my motion to roll the door closed faltered when Marty shrieked in fear.

"Pluck?" I froze. Marty cowered on the middle bench seat, pressed into the wall of the van with Pluck standing over her. He looked like a human, and his hands shook.

"It wasn't me! I didn't tell her where we were!" the scared woman said as a sparking green haze flickered over the shadow's clenched fist.

"If I thought you had, you would be dead," he intoned, then turned to me. "Warn Herm. Now," he added. "He's walking into a trap."

Oh no. Herm . . . I glanced at Marty curled up on the seat, then rolled the door shut. Out the front window, Dana skidded to a halt twenty feet back, yet another lodestone winking as three of her men clustered behind her. "Benny, go!" I shouted, but he'd already put the van in motion, and I clutched the seat, wobbling as I sat in it and buckled up.

"Call him." Pluck glared at Marty, his eyes flecked with rage. "Before it's too late."

Tires squeaking, Benedict spun the van. I gripped the dash, breath held until we were facing the right way and racing across the parking lines for the road. Through the side mirror, I watched Dana stand where she was, her head down over her phone even as she yelled at the men.

"Wow. That was close." Benedict leaned forward to look both ways before bouncing out onto the road. "You okay, Pluck?" Twisting, he worked his phone from his back pocket and handed it to me.

My fingers shook as I tried to unlock it. Herm. I had to call Herm.

"I'm so sorry," Marty half sobbed from behind Benedict. "Pluck, I am so sorry. I didn't know what to do."

"So you ran away?" Pluck shook, his frustration twining about my shock. "You left Petra and Benedict to be caught!"

"I'm sorry!" she wailed, making me wonder why Pluck was being so harsh. He had a right to be angry, but it felt displaced.

Feeling my question, the shadow turned from her, his balance perfect even when the van hit a pothole and bounced. Kneeling behind the front seats, he wouldn't meet my eyes. Benedict's burner phone didn't have a password, but my fingers were too cold to register on the screen and I rubbed them on my arm to make some friction heat, cursing the delay. *Shadow spit.* "Do you think Marty told her where we were?" I asked, trying to figure out where Pluck's anger was coming from.

"It wasn't me!" she shouted, pressed into an almost fetal position in the middle seat. "They had guns! I didn't know what to do, so I ran!"

Pluck's anger, frustration . . . and a hint of chagrin flooded me. Overlaying it was a solid belief that she hadn't called Dana. He believed her, but as I saw his furrowed brow and pinched eyes, I could tell it was tempered with the shadow's bitter opinion that Marty was a coward. She had run away when she could have run to warn us. His eyes met mine, and a feeling of guilt sparked through him as he realized that the betrayal he felt wasn't aimed entirely at Marty but someone else. Someone in his past.

Pluck? I thought, and he turned away.

Head down, I texted Herm to abort.

why? pinged onto my phone's screen, and my shoulders eased. He was still free.

trap, I texted, then added, **see you at aasta's place**.

"We're good," I said when Herm's inventive swearing popped up onto my screen, banishing my worry that it wasn't actually him texting me back. Relieved, I set Benedict's phone on the dash. No one swore like the old Spinner.

"There's a stick in Dana's house," Marty whispered, utterly

miserable. "I know I saw one. It's real. I'm not a liar. And I didn't tell her where we were."

His shoulders tense, Benedict scanned the oncoming traffic for any sign of blue and amber lights. Depressed, I glanced out the window at the passing buildings. "Pluck, it's okay."

"I should not have taken my hurt out on her," Pluck whispered, hints of betrayal hazing our joined thoughts. "It's an old pain, and though she did abandon us, she is not its cause."

I shifted to sit sideways so I could see both Marty and Pluck. The shadow was hazing, his green eyes holding a deep regret as he looked at Marty snuffling in the corner. "Pluck . . ." I started, and then he dissolved into a shadow and slunk under my seat. *Please talk to me,* I thought, and he closed his mind.

"Did you get to Herm in time?" Benedict asked, and I nodded, fingers tightening on Marty's borrowed lodestone until they cramped with cold. "Where are we going?"

My brow furrowed. That Marty had abandoned us to capture hurt. I wasn't sure how much we should expect from her, though. She didn't owe us anything. Did she?

"The memorial garden," I said, and Benedict flicked on the turn signal.

We had lost the fifth stick, but we would face Thoth all the same.

26

BENEDICT STOOD NEXT TO THE SPOTLIT STAGE, HIS CLOTHES WRINKLED AND A frown pinching his brow as he scrolled through his local-news feed, sneaking pensive glances at Marty in the first row of dusty chairs. The mage had been pleased to find the sun was shining all the way down here when we had arrived, but the longer we cooled our heels in the dark, the brighter and more uncomfortable that ray of sun felt to me.

Pluck, too, wasn't happy, puddled at the back of the room as far from the light as he could get, almost in the unsafe area behind the stage. I couldn't see him from where I sat on the top step, but I could feel him, his emotions unusually closed. Clearly he was trying to work something out, something he didn't want to share with me.

Rush-hour traffic was a faint rumble through the dirt walls, and a bright spot of sunlight poured through the well to pierce the gloom like fiery vengeance. We'd been here about twenty minutes, having ditched the van almost immediately and walked in on the bike paths. Just three "friends" with their off-leash dog. Herm, Lev, and Cameron were on the way in, all of them having easily evaded capture. Even so, I was nervous. Pluck had been with Marty when Dana had found them in the break room. He might be avoiding me, but he had made it clear that she wasn't to blame. I believed him. Otherwise, Marty might be dead.

It was obvious that people had begun to dump their dross here. It wasn't a lot yet, but it would get worse. A rather large ball of it lurked near the opposite set of the stage stairs, and I wondered if I should use it to refill Marty's amulet before returning it to her. That I'd used it as if it were my own tracked, seeing as Pluck had tuned it. Giving it to her felt like a mistake, though. Thoth might take her to be a bigger threat than she was, and I tucked the stone into my pocket.

As expected, the tinnitus in my ears eased the moment my fingers left it. The more dark matter I carried, the louder the echo of it was on the back of the universe. I'd begun to sense waves of sensation seeming hours long, and in the quiet parts, the whispers of Pluck's thought seemed clearer. It was like being on the swells on the ocean, where if two boats were at a crest at the same time, they could see each other, but if one were in a trough, you might as well be alone.

Eyes closing, I created a tangle of dark matter, ordering the threads into bands before sending them out from me, listening to them hit the world like ripples of sonar.

How can anyone be so selfish?

I jerked, losing the threads entirely. My gaze shot to Pluck, but I'd swear it hadn't been him. *Pluck?* I thought, and the puddled shadow quivered, shuttering his thoughts even more . . . but not until I recognized his embarrassment for having gotten caught and leaving me helpless—his thoughts, not mine—and his anger at Marty for not living up to his standards of what a weaver should be. He called her a coward, and I think that bothered him more than being bottled. Underneath it all, though, I sensed an increasing agitation at himself as he relived something from his past, triggered by Marty's failings.

Pluck, will you talk to me, please? I thought, and the black puddle by the archway rippled a hazy green. *None of this is your fault,* I added, frowning when he pulled his thoughts even further from me.

"I can get the stick from Dana," Marty said, startling me. Her words whispered against the dusty walls, and Aasta's hazy shape at the ceiling tightened into a hard black knot. The shadow had been here since we had arrived, watching. "I know where it is."

"It's not worth putting you in danger," Benedict said, voice tight.

Marty cringed, and a twinge of guilt sparked through me. Mine? Pluck's? It didn't matter. Pluck's outline had gone hazy, and a decidedly not-me emotion of regret and self-shame had become strong in our shared thoughts.

Just wanting Benedict to stop glaring at her, I stood from the top step, hands in my pockets as I inched closer to the spot of sun. *I swear, I can feel it from here . . .*

"Hey, Benny," I started, words faltering when ice swirled around my ankle.

I will be . . . somewhere else, Pluck fizzed, and then he was gone, his hint of a sparkling haze disappearing behind the stage.

Benedict watched him go, brow furrowed. "Is he okay?"

My gaze lingered where he'd vanished, but it was hard to see past the beam of light. Pluck was remembering things he didn't want to. I didn't know how to help him. Torn, I hesitated. "I'm not sure. I'll go talk to him. Let me know when they get here." I flicked my attention to Marty, my gaze drawn to Aasta at the ceiling when a bolt of green sparked through the shadow. "Ease up on her, will you? Being afraid doesn't make you a bad person."

"I know. But she could have warned us," he muttered.

"We found her in the van as much a prisoner as Pluck," I reminded him, and he nodded, his shoulders finally slumping.

Smiling, I gave him a quick hug, then went to look for Pluck.

I'd only been in the back area of the stage once, and that had been before the collapse. The harsh light streaming in through the well didn't go very far, and I inhaled, palms tingling as I brought a mess of threads of dark matter into my forethoughts. Pinching one between my fingers and thumbs, I stretched it, satisfied when a soft glow appeared, the dark matter protesting the manhandling.

Repurposing the auditorium into a memorial had necessitated a bare minimum of rubble removal if for nothing more than inspecting the support structure, and much of the false ceiling that the gardens were based on was really nothing but a large dome to redistribute weight to the edges. Most of the nonsupporting walls had been knocked out, leaving ragged edges and scratched floors. Dross glittered here as well, but it was old and faint, and the damp feel of water touched my face as I picked my way through the shattered backstage areas following a faint sense of sadness.

Pluck? I thought when I turned a corner to find a wall of rubble fronting me.

Here, came faintly from beyond it, and I searched out a good-size opening through the clutter at the ceiling. There was a space beyond it. I could almost see it through Pluck's eyes.

Moving slow so I didn't lose the light, I worked my way up the rubble to the ceiling.

Mind the dross, Pluck fizzed, and I jerked, the sudden heat on my elbow driving away the light-born chill. The haze of latent bad luck had been hiding in the broken concrete, unseen in the glare from my own light.

"Aww, shizit," I whispered when a tingling cramp raced up my arm and the dross broke. The rock I was standing on shifted. I yelped, but when I reached to catch myself, my light went out. More rocks slid from under me and I slipped to the bottom in the new, utter darkness.

You okay? fizzed through my thoughts, a ribbon of guilt and heartache twining through it.

My pulse hammered, but I had only gone a few feet, and now that my light was out, I could see the dross better. Actually, I could see everything better, and I sat up, wondering at the glow coming through the hole near the ceiling. *I'm fine,* I thought as I carefully stood and rubbed my elbow. *Is that light from dross?*

A faint sense of agreement drifted through me, but if Pluck was in there, then there had to be some open space free of it. Careful now, I made my way back up to the opening and looked through.

It was a large area left fallow after the work crews cleared it, lit by the dross that Benedict's spell five months ago had missed. Movement drew my gaze to the ceiling where reflected light rippled as if shining through water.

I looked down, lips parting as I realized that was exactly what was going on. I had been told that St. Unoc had been built to take advantage of a natural underground river, but until today, I'd never seen any evidence of it other than the washes filling in the rainy season. The water must have been forced up after the auditorium collapsed. Dross glittered up from the depths, going down into a subbasement. Ripples ran the surface, giving the very air a transparent, glowing feel.

"Pluck?" I whispered, my attention pulled to a sudden movement and *sploot* of water. It was Pluck in his human shift, his dark hair catching the light and narrow face creased in thought as he sat on an enormous chunk of concrete beside the underground reservoir. Even as I watched, he threw another pebble, his motion somehow listless and depressed.

He glanced sidelong at me, green eyes blinking. It wasn't much of an invitation, but seeing as he could have evaporated and vanished, I took it as one. Moving carefully, I worked my way through the gap at the ceiling, and from there, down to the floor. It must have been a practice room for the orchestra, as the ceiling was high and there were no walls to mar the large, cavernous space.

Worried, I sat down beside him, feet dangling almost to the water. Little fish clustered, drawn to the movement. They had to be either pet-shop flushes or an almost-extinct native species. I was betting it was the latter. Fish in the desert. It made sense if you knew that the continent had once been divided by an enormous inland sea.

"Did you know this was here?" I said when he remained silent.

"I found it when looking for Aasta." He threw another pebble. "Is she still out there staring at Marty?"

I nodded. It was odd. His spoken voice held the same accent as his words fizzing in my mind, and I swung my feet, scaring the fish. "It's beautiful down here."

Saying not a word, he tossed the hair from his eyes and scanned the far side of the underground pond.

It was difficult to hear him in my mind, seeing as he was working hard to keep me out, but his body language said it all. "Pluck, I know it won't be easy without the last stick, but if we do nothing—"

"The world will not change," he said, lifting his hand to study his fingers. "I may as well wear this form, seeing as I'm making the same mistakes again."

I looked at his hand pressing into the fractured cement beside me, wanting to take it in mine. The regret tickling my thoughts was his, and I wished he'd solidify up a little more so I could give him a hug or something. "It's not your fault Marty ran away," I said, fishing.

It is, echoed in my thoughts, bitter and sour.

If he wasn't saying the words aloud, I was probably getting close to what was bothering him. "How so?" I said softly. "She's not your weaver."

Pluck tossed another stone in with hardly a splash or ripple. *I . . .* fizzed awkwardly in my mind, his confusion flooding me. *I . . . I demanded too much and frightened her. I was angry that she wasn't more than she is, and I shamed myself.*

A small smile quirked my lips. "She was caught as much as you were. I think you're being too hard on yourself. You didn't hurt her."

"No," he agreed, and then, *But I wanted to punish her. I . . . I used to be more like Thoth.*

I turned to him, trying to keep my shock hidden. "You were against weavers?"

No. Never, he thought with a pained decisiveness. *But I did questionable things for ideas that I thought were worthy. Hurt and killed people to protect an idea. Not a person, but an idea. When I thought you were in danger, I became what I had been before.* He took a slow breath. "I don't want to be that again," he said aloud.

I picked a pebble free of the cement and tossed it in to scatter the minnows. "Ideas are often fragile and deserving of more protection than we give them," I said, and Pluck grimaced.

"They're nothing without the people to uphold them," he said. "I want a return to the balance, but I've seen the cost in both myself and the world. Perhaps it's more than I'm willing to pay again. It was clearly more than Marty was willing to give. She knows her limits, and I berated her. I'm no better than Thoth trying to manipulate others to fulfill his own needs."

"She's fine," I insisted, and he shook his head.

"It's not what I did, but what I didn't do. I could have helped her find her courage. Instead . . ." He hesitated, his almost-there skin phasing. "I wish you'd never seen me as a person."

I leaned into him until my shoulder went numb. "What does that have to do with anything?"

He wouldn't look at me, but his emotions churning through mine were chaotic. "It was as a person that I did the most damage," he finally said, eyes lowered. "When I wear that form, I feel as if I'm being drawn back into a life I don't want . . . and dragging you with me."

My breath slipped from me as I finally got it. "That's why you avoid a human form."

Pluck was silent, but the guilt rising through us both was answer enough.

"I'm sorry," I said. "But it's not the same. It can't be. We know what Thoth is doing."

"And yet people are again ignoring the truth because change is uncomfortable." Grimacing, Pluck threw a pebble. It made hardly a splash, golden and green as it sank to the bottom. He looked depressed and resigned, and a sigh shifted his narrow shoulders. "Thoth is behind all this misery, but in Thoth's mind, I am to blame for it. If I had done nothing, ignored you and let you believe you were a Spinner, none of this would be happening."

"Yeah? Well, Thoth is psychotic. You haven't done anything wrong." I tossed a pebble in. It hit with a heavy *sploot*, the ripples mesmerizing as they caught the light coming up from the bottom. The tiny waves were like the pulse of the universe, all swells and troughs. "I'm the one who confronted Thoth and let him damage my ability to make a field. But, Pluck, maybe it's not that bad."

Pluck turned to me, his expression resolute. "Petra, I could hear you," he said, and my lips parted at the guilt in his thoughts. "When Dana trapped me in the bottle? I could hear you through the glass, but you couldn't hear me."

"You could hear me?" I flushed, remembering my thoughts. All of them.

A faint, understanding smile flashed and was gone. "Not everything," he said. "Just what you directed at me. I . . . I tried to reach you. I couldn't." His head dropped. "I lack the innovation, or the skill. I'm not enough. I thought I was, but Thoth is going to—"

"Pluck, stop." I touched his arm, and he looked at my fingers. "You were in a bottle. Shadow . . ."

"Can't get through glass," he finished sourly. "But your thoughts did."

I took my hand away, rubbing my cold fingertips together to warm them up. "I'm not a shadow." I hesitated, a sick feeling dropping through me. "I'm not a weaver, either, if I can't fix dross inert and it breaks on me."

Pluck's head snapped up. "That's not what I'm saying."

"Then what *are* you saying?" I demanded.

He stared out over the water, struggling for words. "I don't know, and that's the problem. I've always known, and now?" He looked at my hand again. "You're using energy in ways I know nothing about. Can't even sense. You're at the top of a wave, and I'm at the bottom."

I rubbed my fingers together. "I could feel dross through a glass bottle as well, and I swear, I thought I heard someone else in my head a few minutes ago."

Pluck's eyes hazed as he looked over my shoulder. "Benny?"

It wasn't jealousy pinching his eyes. *Is it?* "No," I said, flustered, and he grimaced.

"Are you sure?"

"No," I said again, remembering the stray thought that I had first assumed was Pluck's but knew in my heart wasn't. "Maybe?" I added, and at his gesture of encouragement, I closed my eyes to better hear the rise and fall of the big bang echoing against the edge of the universe. *Benny,* I thought, sending it on the back of a single twisted thread.

Nothing returned to me, and feeling silly, I opened my eyes. "No," I said, and Pluck's lips twisted in a sour knowing.

"Mmmm."

It was bland, almost accusing, and I followed his attention to the sudden light flickering at the hole near the ceiling. It was a mage-made light, and my pulse hammered. "Benny?" I called in disbelief when I heard a small rockslide.

"Shadow spit!" came faintly from the far side of the rubble. "Petra, where . . . Oh!" There was more clinking, and the light brightened. "How did you even know this was here?" he said, voice loud as he peered in through the opening.

"I followed Pluck," I said, but I felt unreal as Benedict moved a few chunks of concrete to make the opening bigger and came in. Had he heard me? On some level, had he sensed my call? "Is everything okay? Are they back?"

"Ah, Herm is. He's fine. Talking to Marty." He hesitated, then committed himself to the slow slide down, the dross from his light looking like ocean phosphorescence trailing behind him. I'd be worried it might bring the ceiling down on us, but it was nothing compared to what already lurked in the corners lighting the space like candles.

"Whew, made it." Benedict held his light higher. "Wow. Where did the water come from? It's not city water, is it? This is amazing. You think it's safe?"

"I wouldn't drink it," I said. "It's got fish in it."

Pluck began to haze. His feelings of guilt and heartache lifted through me, and I reached for his hand, flooding his thoughts with acceptance and forgiveness. He was my shadow, and there couldn't possibly be anything I couldn't understand.

Benedict's shoes ground the grit as he came closer. His eyes flicked to Pluck's hand in mine, and Pluck pulled away. "So . . . you don't mind being a person anymore?" Benedict asked, and Pluck made a noncommittal shrug, his hands a hazy nothing. "That's cool. I'll admit I was feeling left out when you and Petra talked."

Pluck's silhouette flickered when Benedict sat on my other side, and not wanting him to go shadow, I elbowed him, accomplishing nothing but freezing my funny bone.

Oblivious, Benedict dangled his feet beside mine and stared into the water. "Huh. Fish," he said. "I'd heard there was a reservoir under St. Unoc. That's why they built the artists' commune here in the first place."

Ask him, fizzed through me, and I started.

Ask him what?

Ask him why he came down here, Pluck insisted.

I glanced at Benedict now using a stick of rebar to play with the fish. The dross created from his light dribbled into the water, looking like a living thing as it coiled downward in search of more dross. *He was clearly checking on us.*

That he was there when you called him is inconclusive, Pluck insisted, his green eyes squinting in annoyance. *Take his hand and think on him as if you were trying to touch his thoughts.*

This was really uncomfortable, and I huffed.

Please, Petra. Humor me.

Fine. "Ah, hey," I said as I fumbled for Benedict's hand. "You think we can hide out here for a while? Maybe everything will blow over if we just do nothing."

Smiling, Benedict lifted our joined hands and kissed my knuckles. "I'm game."

His fingers were warm in mine, and exhaling, I listened to the universe, joining my thoughts to a ribbon of dark matter, feeling it catch the wave that flowed over us. *Benny* . . .

Benedict gasped, startling me. I looked up as he scrambled to his feet, his hand pulling from mine. Eyes wide, he stared at the water, not me. "Where did it go?" he said. "I saw . . ." His gaze dropped to my hand. "Um."

His expression sour, Pluck leaned past me to take my hand and put it in Benedict's. *Again,* fizzed through me, and I exhaled once more, using a single thread of dark matter to cast out and find . . . Benny.

Again Benedict started, his hand in mine spasming. "Shadow spit," he whispered, and his light went out as he stared into the water. "Is that dross down there?" His gaze came to me, flicking to Pluck and back. "It's beautiful." He looked at the ceiling and the rippling reflection. "I—I'm seeing . . ." he stammered, and then his attention fell to me. "Is this what the world looks like to you? My God. I'm blind."

I winced, embarrassed that I had made him feel less. "No, you're not."

Brow furrowed, Benedict looked at our joined hands before turning his attention to Pluck, the shadow decidedly listless as he threw pebbles into the water. "How?"

Pluck rolled a pebble between two fingers, and the rock vanished behind a swirl of black. "It's a shadow skill," he said softly.

Benedict's grip on my fingers tightened, and the shadow chuckled darkly. "Relax, favored mage," he said, then flicked the rock. "Our Petra is not a shadow. But she's not a weaver, either. Since Thoth damaged her, she's begun to use her other senses, like a blind man. If it helps, you can think of her as an etherologist."

"Manipulating ether is a mage skill," Benedict said.

The stone Pluck threw hit the water with an ungraceful *sploot.* "She's not a mage."

"But dross is breaking on her like she is one." Benedict's gaze lifted from our twined fingers. "You have lost the ability to fix dross inert. If that's not a mage—"

I shook my head. "I'm not a mage. I don't know what I am."

"I do," a familiar raspy voice rang out, and both Benedict and I jumped, spinning to see Darrell standing between us and the way out. The beads on her tightly coiled locks clinked faintly like a lost memory, but it wasn't Darrell, it was Aasta.

"Shadow spit," I swore, shifting to include the shadow. "We need to put a bell on you."

Benedict's fingers reluctantly slipped from mine. "Aasta," he said in respect, but the vision of my old mentor ignored him.

"I see you found your war uniform," the shadow said sourly to Pluck, and he grimaced.

"You have seen this before? What is she?" Pluck asked, and my breath caught.

Aasta pointed a finger at me. "She gave sight to a mage, but she's not shadow. She can't turn dross inert, so she's not a sweeper. Dross breaks on her—she is no weaver."

"We know what she isn't," Benedict complained, and I twined my fingers in his again.

"She got *you* into a form that can verbalize," Aasta continued. "Making her capable of miracles. She's something new. New might be able to catch Thoth. Let me . . ."

I pulled away as she reached for me. "No." I didn't want her to touch me, and both Pluck and Benedict stiffened in warning.

Aasta's hand dropped, and she twisted my mentor's face into a familiar expression of annoyance.

"We can't even try until we secure five balanced sticks," Benedict said. "Without access to Professor Brown's lab, it will take at least a week to make them. We can't hide down here for a week."

Well, Pluck could, but the rest of us?

"You don't have a week." Aasta's gaze went to the opening at the ceiling. "Thoth is making you dance on his string, take the blame for his actions. The more you delay, the better his manipulation."

They are here, Pluck said suddenly, and I followed his gaze to the rockslide.

The sounds so faint I wondered if I was perceiving their voices through Pluck, I heard Cameron and Lev arguing. "They're back," I said, and Benedict's shoulders pulled out of their worried slump.

"We should probably get up there." Benedict stood and extended a hand to help me up. Pluck evaporated, flowing like a snake over and up the rubble to vanish after Aasta. Not a single rock shifted under either of them.

"Go on ahead," I said somewhat sarcastically. "We'll catch up."

Benedict chuckled as we followed, carefully picking our way through the chunks of concrete. "Is everything okay with Pluck?" he said softly. "He looks a little depressed."

"He is." I let go of Benedict so I could half crawl, half walk up the fallen concrete. "I, ah, found out the reason he doesn't take a human form often."

Benedict's eyebrows were high when I reached the opening and turned. He was right behind me. "Which is?" he prompted.

"He went to war in it." It was a gross simplification, but a distant agreement fizzed through me and I felt better.

"Oh."

I was first through, and I waited, listening to Lev and Cameron argue as Benedict wedged his wider shoulders past the opening to stand beside me. Together, we half slid, half walked down the crumbling pile until we found solid ground again.

"They're at it already," Benedict said as we followed the beckoning light until we reached the front stage.

Herm saw us immediately, the older man giving Marty a comforting pat on the shoulder before leaving her sitting in the front row to make his arthritic-slow way to the stage's stairs. Her amulet felt heavy in my pocket, and I gave her a distant smile, wondering at her worried expression. That is, until I noticed Pluck lurking under her chair . . . almost as if in . . . protection?

Aasta was nowhere to be seen, but Darrell's rez lurked among the chairs by the ceiling, the soft, mindless litany making eerie hisses of memory against the dusty walls.

"Then we find her," Lev said, his back to us. "And beat the truth out of her."

My eyes shot to Marty. *No wonder Pluck is underneath her.*

"Is that your answer to everything?" Cameron said. Next to her on the stage was a small military task bag. She'd changed, too, looking sharp in black jeans and a leather jacket. "*Beat* it out of her? No wonder you washed out."

Herm looked embarrassed as he gave me a quick hug. "I can't tell you how glad I am that you're here," I said. "Is Professor Brown okay?"

"Fine." Herm's wrinkles slid into each other as he frowned. "The university is watching him, but he's pleading the Fifth as to you being in his lab. He'll be okay." Herm gave Benedict a nod in greeting. "Well done for evading Dana. Both of you."

But it didn't feel well-done, apart from our goose being cooked.

"I didn't wash out." Lev dropped a worn knapsack noisily on the stage. "I chose not to be the courts' dumb muscle."

Fist on her hip, Cameron furrowed her brow. "I don't like the way you said that."

Herm ran a hand over his head in exasperation. "Can you two romance each other later? That stick is still at Dana's apartment. We need to decide if it's worth another go."

"Oh!" Lev's face reddened as he looked at the woman sitting meekly in the first row of chairs. "That's right. Marty." His eyes narrowed. "You set us up, you little liar."

"I didn't set you up." Marty stiffened when Lev strode forward, his intent clear.

"Whoa, whoa, whoa!" Cameron jerked the man to a halt. "It wasn't her."

"Why? Because she said so? Seriously?" Lev reached for his lodestone.

"It wasn't me." Marty cringed, starting when she realized Pluck was under her.

"Knock it off, Lev!" I shouted, immediately regretting it. Voices carried, and anyone might be in the garden. "Marty didn't give us away. Pluck was with her when Dana showed."

Lev jerked out of Cameron's grip, his expression livid. "You're both siding with *her*?" he said, making the last word an insult. "Help me out here, Herm."

Herm chuckled. "Dana has her people out with the sweepers collecting dross. Anyone could have seen us going into the building," he said, and Lev glowered.

"I'm not siding with anyone," Cameron said with a huff. "But you will not browbeat Marty because she's an easy target. Ben says she was being held prisoner as much as Pluck."

Stymied, Lev dropped back a step. He looked mean in his frustration, but I was starting to understand Pluck's self-recrimination. This wasn't Lev, or rather, it wasn't the man that Lev wanted to be. This was what anger had pushed him into—and he would regret it. Like Pluck.

"Are you and Pluck okay?" Herm said, startling me out of my thoughts when he touched my elbow. Cameron and Lev had begun to argue again, and I leaned against the side of the stage.

"More or less," I said, not having any hurts to catalog. "Pluck is depressed. Dana had him in a bottle. Benedict and I got him out."

"No!" Herm said, aghast as he found Pluck under Marty's chair, and a green haze lifted and fell from the shadow as if in agreement.

"He thinks he overreacted to Marty running away. Personally, I think he exhibited an enormous amount of restraint. They had guns, and I had her amulet."

But Pluck's fizzing in me was faint, as if he'd closed himself off again.

"I'm glad she's unhurt," Herm said, and I flicked an annoyed glance at Lev and Cameron arguing. "This probably doesn't help," he added.

"This is a waste of time," Lev said loudly. "Cameron, do your Vulcan thing and find out if Marty is lying."

"Seriously, Lev?" Clearly not liking his callousness, Cameron gave Marty a weak smile. "We can make a new stick."

Herm ran a nervous hand over his chin. "If we had access to a lab and materials. Lev, doesn't the militia have some sort of workshop we can tap into?"

"Ah, I'm not comfortable going to the militia," Benedict said, and both Lev and Cameron looked up, their argument forgotten.

I pushed off from the side of the stage as their voices twined together in persuasion, Lev and Cameron finding common ground in arguing with Benedict. The sun was giving me a headache, and I went to sit with Marty in a show of support. So she tried to run away. So what? The woman had been thrown into the deep end of the pool with a leaky air float. That didn't make her a pariah. It made her human.

My ankle went cold as I sank into the musty cushions beside Marty. Herm was perched on the top step across from us, the older man clearly uncomfortable but his mood brighter than I would have expected. "Petra, thanks for that warning text. You and Pluck really saved my ass." He puffed all his air out. "I usually can sense it when things are about to go bad, but I was so worried about that damned stick that I wasn't paying attention."

A stick we no longer have access to, I mused sourly. "I'm just glad we figured it out in time."

"I'm thinking that even though we know where that last stick is, we should take the time to make a new one or try to catch Thoth with four."

"I can get it," Marty said softly, her gaze on the four propped up against the podium. "I know right where it is. She will never know I'm there."

"You?" Again Lev cut his argument short, and all three of them turned to Marty. A flicker of green at the ceiling caught my eye, but it wasn't Pluck. He was chilling my ankles. The shadowy shape evolving into what looked like a plate-size spider had to be Aasta.

Why is she still here? I thought, and Pluck fizzed a sour nothing.

"I know where she hid it," Marty said, pale and wide-eyed. "If she catches me, I'll tell her you thought I gave you up and that I had to escape. When I get the chance, I'll bring it here." She swallowed hard. "I can do that. I don't want to be afraid anymore."

"Seriously?" Lev barked, and Cameron glared at him to be nicer.

My ankle throbbed in a sudden cold snap, and I looked to the ceiling, drawn by Pluck's interest. Aasta had taken a solid form, twisted and wrong. Half spider, half crow, she let herself down from the ceiling on a thread of her own making, six legs and a pair of wings all working together until she found the top of a row of chairs and dissolved into an abhorrent vision of fangs and eight eyes. *My God, that's the stuff of nightmares . . .*

"You need that stick," Marty said, oblivious to the shadow skulking behind her. "*We* need it. I can get it. It's my fault Thoth is here. I might not be skilled enough to fight him, but I can do this." Eyes wide, she knotted her hands into a tight ball. "I am not a coward. I didn't know what to do is all."

"Huh." Lev pretended to open a book. "Let me look up the definition. Oh! Here it is. Coward. See Marty Mayson."

"Lev, that's enough," I said as Pluck fizzed in guilt and heartache. The man was being more than mean. He was being cruel. True, as militia he expected those he worked with to give all, risk everything for each other. But Marty wasn't militia. She was a civvy. She hadn't signed up for this. Any of this. Pushing her nose into her limits wouldn't make her brave. It would cut her off from the very people who could help her become more.

"Okay." Benedict put up a hand to try to calm everyone. "Five sticks are better than four, but I'm not sure risking Marty is the right way to get it. If Dana catches her, she won't let her out of her sight."

Herm bobbed his head, his elbows on his raised knees. "Marty, I'm sorry, but I agree with Benedict. The risk is too high. We will get a set of balanced sticks another way."

Cameron cracked a bottled water. "Why not just ask her for it?"

"Dana?" Herm said, clearly surprised, and Cameron came up from slamming half the bottle and nodded.

"She wants Thoth in a bottle, too, doesn't she? The world returns to normal."

Pluck fizzed and bubbled. *Dana doesn't want normal. She wants everything to return to the way it was five months ago: no weavers bucking the system and shadows destroyed on sight.*

"Dana doesn't want Thoth in a bottle." I relayed his thoughts, no longer feeling the need to goad Pluck into taking a human form so he could talk. "She's made it clear she wants everything to go back to the way it used to be, whatever the cost. If Pluck and I take the fall, everything we are pushing for goes away."

Marty fidgeted, her breath fast and her face pale in the shadowed light. "I can get it. Please," she said, and I stifled a shudder when Aasta stretched one long, twitching spider leg out to inch herself a row closer. "I need to do this. To make amends."

"I'm sorry, Marty," Cameron said when Herm stoically shook his head. "Herm's magic gives him a good feeling about risk and benefit. If he says it's too risky, I believe him."

I wasn't so sure, though, and I dangled a hand into Pluck's icy presence. *What do you think, Pluck?*

The dross dust gathered at the corners brightened as Pluck settled deeper into my thoughts. *I believe Marty wants to help,* he thought. *But she ran away once. Trusting her not to do it again seems chancy, and one of us going with her might result in even worse.*

Benedict was silently looking at me, the man correctly guessing I was talking to Pluck. "I'm sorry. Pluck and I agree," I said, and he seemed to deflate. "It's a brave gesture," I added. "But we aren't going to put you in that much danger."

Marty's hopeful expression vanished. Motion fast, she stood. "I suppose I deserve that," she said tartly, jaw set as she went to sit halfway across the auditorium. Behind her, the twisted spider/crow melted into a puddle . . . and followed.

"Marty, you are a nice person," Lev said loudly. "But I won't trust my continued freedom to you."

It was harsh, but the panic I'd felt when Pluck had been in a bottle sort of kept me where I was, silent as Benedict sighed and Herm studied his shoes. Aasta was creeping toward Marty, jerking to a halt four seats away when the young woman noticed her.

"Marty, we will find a way for you to help," Cameron said, but Marty's face was creased in self-recrimination.

Herm pulled his head up, resolute. "Okay, kids. Let's talk about what we can do."

The mood was still uncomfortable, and Benedict brushed at a spot on his jeans. "I can talk to Dana. Convince her Thoth is too disruptive to ignore."

Head shaking, Herm extended his legs, clearly stiff with arthritis. "Ah, I don't know. You and Petra hit her crew pretty hard. I was thinking more like going into Tucson to find a set of matched sticks. Maybe hit the secondhand shops. We might get lucky. Marty, you have some skill feeling that out. I would appreciate the help."

The woman shifted to turn her back to us, oblivious to Aasta waving her forelegs at her in agitation like a jumping spider.

Pluck, can you tell Aasta that a spider is not the best image for making friends?

It's not Aasta's idea. It's probably Marty's, the shadow thought, reminding me of the time my fear of him had made Pluck appear like a slavering dog from hell with matted fur and broken bones sticking from pus-oozing skin. Pluck had once said he hid from people because it was too difficult to appear as he wanted, not how people believed him to be. Marty clearly had a few issues.

Cameron forced her gaze from the plate-size spider and sat on the edge of the stage by Lev, her small feet dangling. "Lev and I are the only ones not wanted for questioning. If anyone goes into Tucson, it should be us."

"We're safe here for now," Herm said, gaze roving over the ceiling. "Let's get some rest. Do some thinking. Dana might be more inclined to listen if another vault goes, as awful as that might be. Meantime, Ryan might know someone with a home workshop. I'll give him a call." He twisted to reach his phone, frowning as he stared at the screen. "Cameron, you're right about not being wanted by the authorities. If you think you can keep Lev from doing anything counterproductive, take him and get some supplies. Then park it up top and keep a lookout."

"Water," Benedict interjected. "Lots of water."

A smile blossomed on the small woman's face. "Sure," she said, drawing Lev's attention from Marty and Aasta. "You going to do what I say, Master Ranger?"

"No." Lev pushed from the stage, clearly eager to go. "You can drive, though."

"I'll stand watch in the garden until you return." Herm stood, groaning as he held his lower back. "I have to make some calls. And before you say anything, Lev, I'll ping them off a tower on the other side of town."

Halfway to the stairs, Lev jerked to a halt, his annoyance gone in a flash of curiosity. "What app are you using?"

Herm laughed. The sound filled the forgotten space as he patted the younger man's shoulder as if pushing upon his lingering frustration until it fractured and vanished like fog in the sun.

Until the fire door clicked shut behind them, leaving only the echo of Herm's belief that the day would end better than it began.

Pluck pulled himself into a tight knot, his thoughts cycling further from me until I could hardly sense them.

"I guess we stay here." Benedict squinted as he looked up to the spot of light at the ceiling.

I stood, slapping the dust from myself. "Cameron is right," I said loudly, and Marty looked up from where she was eyeing Aasta. "We'll find a way to get what we need. I don't want to risk you anymore, either, Marty."

"It's my fault Thoth is here," Marty said, chin high as she tried to balance her fear against her need to make amends. "For once in my life, I'm not going to walk away. I have to do something."

"You are doing something." Benedict scrunched down in the chair, legs outstretched and head on the back of the seat. "Sit tight," he said, eyes closing as he yawned. "Let the militia do what they do. We'll get what we need in a few days."

I nodded my agreement, but inside, I wasn't so sure.

Thoth could do a lot of damage in a few days.

27

I KNEW I WAS DREAMING: SLUMPED IN ONE OF THE DUSTY CHAIRS, LEGS OUTstretched, breath moving easily in and out in the stuffy darkness of the grotto. But I was also drifting, suspended in a haze of icy darkness that spread in every direction. Long-stick in hand, I surveyed the rise and fall of sound and pressure pushing out the edge of the universe to make time.

Like a superhero, I hung within it as I drew the peak of one wave to another, joining them together to collect the energy released when they met and became as one. Once joined, the waves continued their motion to the edges of the universe as if there had only ever been one wave. For all the energy I took, nothing changed.

Petra, wake up.

The three-dimensional cloth of the universe spread before and around me, my thoughts a needle stitching it together to fill my chunk of moldavite with stored time. Time was an expression of energy, and that was what my lodestone held. Creating light made time, and time was what pushed the edges of the universe wider, a drop of nothing in an even larger, incomprehensible nothing. Look close enough, though, and nothing was everything.

Petra, Marty snuck out to get the stick. Wake up.

Pleased to see him with me, I spun to Pluck. The shadow was

here and not, more of a concept than an actual presence. That was okay. It was a dream, and I stretched in the icy comfort.

If she's going to run, we can't stop her. Stick extended, I stitched the top of a swell to another, running the seam for light-years until by chance it hit a star and broke it into a sudden supernova. *We were lucky to find her the first time.*

She's back. She got it, Pluck fizzed. *Petra, wake up!*

I snorted awake, blinking at Pluck coiled up like a snake atop my chest. "Dude." My fingers went numb in cold as I touched him. "I was just dreaming about you."

Pluck bobbed his hooded head, green eyes glinting. *It wasn't a dream for my part in it.*

He evaporated, hazy as he flowed to the floor to coalesce into a dog. His annoyed emotion sifted through my muddled confusion as he shook his head, ears slapping as tiny drops of dark matter popped against the floor of the auditorium. The sun had moved away from the stage to make a weak, oval glow on the distant wall. I'd slept for hours.

Voices came from the steps to the stage, and I sat up to see Marty, Herm, and Benedict. As Pluck had said, there was a stick in the woman's hand. Still fuzzy, I looked at the podium to where I'd left the other four, all of them propped together.

Damn. She'd gotten the stick from Dana?

"I . . . I have to go," Marty was saying, and I slowly stood, wobbling until I found my balance. "You can stop Thoth now. You don't need me."

Herm caught my eye, then turned to Marty. "I didn't even hear you leave."

"Me either." Benedict shifted to make room for me, and I stumbled over, trying to figure out why I was so freaking sleepy. It was warm, sure, but to have fallen asleep?

Sorry, Pluck fizzed as if it had been his fault, and my side went cold when he flicked his tail right through me.

"Hey, Marty," I said as I joined them, collapsing on the stairs as if it were four in the morning, not four in the afternoon. "You got past Lev and Cameron? I'm impressed." Grinning, I raised my hand for a fist bump, which she nervously exchanged. "Yeah, I don't listen to Herm, either."

Benedict squinted at the dimming circle of light at the ceiling. "You weren't followed, were you? I wouldn't put it past Dana to let you take the stick just to lead her back to us."

"Dana didn't *let* me do anything, and I wasn't followed."

Herm chuckled. "If she slipped past Lev and Cameron, she probably got past anything Dana could muster. I think we're in the clear."

The pinch to Marty's brow eased as she extended the stick to me—but she still looked worried. "I . . . I have to go," she said, clearly distracted as Pluck hazed to nothing on the step beside me. "I'm not a fighter, and you have what you need to catch him."

"Marty, I told you. You are a golden child." I took it, immediately knowing it was a match to the others. A haze of dross dust tingled at the end, and I propped it up next to the stairs where it might draw the drift lurking under the rows of seats. "The board will make an exception for Victor to keep you."

"She's right." Benedict's dusty shoes scuffed on the stage. "Nothing you could do is worse than what we're standing in now, and they gave Petra a promotion. Besides, it's not safe for you to leave until he's caught."

"It's not about Victor. I have to go!" she said loudly, and Herm winced, the older man looking at the ceiling as if someone might hear.

"Marty . . ." Benedict coaxed.

She's not afraid of me anymore, Pluck fizzed suddenly, and my lips parted as I realized it was true. Marty was agitated, nervous, and clearly upset. But she wasn't afraid of Pluck. At all.

Marty took a step away, a hint of panic in her. "Dana caught her. She's going to drop her in a vault." Her eyes widened as she locked with my gaze. "I didn't even know she was there!" she said. "She let Dana catch her so I could get away with that stupid stick. I have to go back for her!"

Her? I thought. And then Pluck's sudden elation swirled through me, stunning.

Aasta is gone, Pluck thought, his chaotic emotion making me ill. My breath caught as my gaze shot to Marty. She was afraid, but not for herself. She wanted to go back. Not home. Back. To Dana's? Shadow spit. Had Marty and Aasta . . .

"Caught who?" Herm said, but I stared at Marty, already knowing the answer. An undeniable thread of determination and self-sacrifice twined through her panic. I had felt that before. I remembered.

Pluck . . . I thought. Pluck had gone completely hazy, little sparks of dark matter fizzing from him. *I thought shadows could only bond with weavers who had similar thought patterns* . . .

Aasta swore . . . Pluck thought, still not believing. *She swore she'd never risk the pain again. She was so afraid* . . .

And with that, understanding lit through us both, drawing Herm's eyebrows high as he stared at me in question. Aasta had been afraid to trust anyone since losing her last weaver. Marty had been afraid to trust at all. The emotions engraved within their thought patterns were the same. There was common ground with which to grow.

"Marty," I whispered, elated as I stood. I wanted to take her hands and spin her around. Instead, I stayed where I was on the hard steps, almost afraid to move. I could see her misery. Her heart ached for having lost Aasta—just as she found her. Guilt and regret pinched her features—the same feelings that Pluck knew moved Aasta. They were both broken, but together they were whole.

Except that Dana had captured Aasta. Shadow spit. This wasn't going to end well.

Herm's brow furrowed as he looked at me, the old Spinner clearly trying to figure out the emotions parading over my face. "Mmmm. Either Dana wasn't expecting us to make another go for the stick or she thinks it won't do us any good," he said, fishing.

"Um, Marty," I said, but the woman was focused on Herm.

"She has six mages posted outside her apartment," Marty said. "I got past them once. I can do it again."

"You got past six mages?" Benedict moved to get between her and the stairs, and Marty's brow furrowed in anger.

"Not all at once. Excuse me. I have to help Aasta." Her eyes went wide, and she turned to me as if looking for understanding. "I didn't know she was there. I ran right into her. I thought she was Pluck until . . ."

Marty's lips parted and she flinched in a remembered pain.

"Aasta?" Herm made his mustache bunch. "What was she doing there?"

"She was in my head!" the woman wailed, and I came closer. "How can you stand the cold? I could hardly move!"

"She'll get better at it," I promised as I took her hand. "She's several thousand years out of practice. Pluck says working through rezes is like working through stone, but she'll get the knack."

"No . . ." Herm's gaze darted from Marty to me. "Marty . . ." he said, a huge smile finding him before it vanished in the same worry that had taken me. "Dana has Aasta?"

Marty nodded, head down. "I ran into her outside. She was waiting for me, I think. Or maybe she was there spying on Dana, because she went in to hear what Dana was saying about storing the university's dross in the vaults at 'their failed, great test.'"

I had no idea what that was, but I think Herm might have, as his frown deepened.

"She told me to run," Marty was saying. "But I couldn't. My head hurt so bad. Dana saw Aasta. Put her in a bottle," she practically whispered. "Aasta made me promise to take the stick to you. She said if Thoth fell, so would Dana and she would be free. She said that you could do it. I never should have left her. Aasta is worth more than a stupid stick. I have to go."

"Wait!" I made a grab for her hand, missing when she jerked away. "Marty, you're right. Aasta comes first." I glanced at Pluck, and the shadow dog nodded. "But you're not doing it alone."

"You can't stop me." Marty took a step back.

A small part of me cheered for her new courage even knowing the possible heartache it stemmed from. Benedict still didn't get it, and I caught his eye. "Could you get Lev and Cameron? We need to make a plan to get Aasta free."

I'll get them. The shadow dog leapt from the stage, hazing before he reached the floor.

Benedict rocked to a halt as Pluck flowed up the fire stairs. "Why? We've got the stick. Once we take care of Thoth, we free Aasta."

I took a breath. Let it out. Gave Marty a reassuring smile. "Aasta comes first. I think she followed Marty there. She sure as hell protected her."

The mage started to say something, catching his words when he figured it out. "Seriously?" he said, voice hushed as if to say it louder might break their tenuous bond. "Marty. I can't believe it. Yes. Aasta comes first."

The woman blinked furiously, her desperation easing a notch. "Thank you. I didn't think you'd help."

Herm could hardly contain himself, shifting from foot to foot and not knowing who to congratulate first. "Petra, I'm so happy for you," he said, giving me a sideways hug. "Marty, congratulations."

"For what!" the woman exclaimed. "Everything is wrong. I can't go home. I can't stay here. I am scared to death of that shadow, but I know who she is now and I can't walk away!"

I nodded, totally getting it. "It sucks at first, but it will get better. I promise."

But Marty only shook her head, continuing to back up until she found the edge of the stage. "I want to get Aasta free. That's it. Once she's free, I'm gone. I'm not a weaver. This is not what I want."

"Fine," I said, knowing she'd have to come to it herself. "Do what you want. But we don't really have a choice. They pick us. They're kind of in charge."

We are not, fizzed distantly through me, even as I heard steps on the stairs. *We need you more than you need us.*

"But it's worth it," I said, aching to give her a hug, but she looked too angry.

Marty shook her head. "You tricked me."

"No, Aasta tamed you." I jumped when the fire door slammed open and Lev came in, trailing a haze of dross as usual.

"At least you weren't the first." Benedict shifted to make room for Lev. "Petra and Pluck made a mess of their, ah, tuning?" he added, using the familiar word in a new way.

I nodded to tell him that he'd used it right, but as I looked around the dusty grotto, I couldn't help but wonder. Somehow we had brought Marty to a place where she could accept her full potential—leaving Aasta in danger of being burned alive. That sounded like a mess to me.

"Cameron is keeping watch." Lev flipped one of the chairs down to sit. "What's up?"

Herm put a hand protectively on Marty's shoulder. And whereas the woman had shirked from me, she accepted his touch. He was everyone's grumpy uncle. "Marty snuck past you. Twice. Got the stick. Aasta was with her and got herself caught protecting Marty. We're planning a rescue before we tackle Thoth and thought you and Cameron might like some input into it."

Lev looked up from the dusty chair. "You got past me? Twice?" Admiration pushed out his initial disbelief. "Damn, girl." He glanced at me and away. "And Aasta is your shadow?"

"She's not militia," I warned him, but Lev's eyes were glinting in avarice.

"She made me promise to leave her there," Marty blurted. "She made me promise to get the stick to you. She said that she didn't deserve a weaver. That someone else would merit me." Her jaw clenched. "I appreciate the help, but I'm leaving right now."

Benedict grinned, wisely quashing it when I glared at him. Marty's desperation wasn't funny. It was real; even if it had evolved in the blink of an eye, it was real.

"Lev, stick, please," I said, and the man followed my gaze to where I'd left it propped against the stage. That dross he'd brought in with him was bothering me and I wanted to put more dark matter into Marty's amulet. I could return it to her now. Aasta would protect her against Thoth. "Marty, tell us what you know. We are rescuing her. All of us."

Marty exhaled in relief, watching with a new interest as I used the butt of the stick to pull the dross from Lev's ankle. I shook the stick to get the dross to break, finally having to slam it against the floor. Fire cramped my hand and I pulled the energy into me before it could give anyone bad luck, funneling it into the moldavite. The glass's latticework shifted to a higher state as the light it gave off dissipated. *Done.*

Pluck sat by the podium, a doggy grin on his face. *Told you,* he fizzed smugly, and I sighed as I gave Marty the pitch-black stone.

"You might need some dark matter to play with until we get Aasta," I said, and the woman nodded, looking decidedly tumbled and lost as she put the stone around her neck and tucked it behind her shirt.

"Thank you," she whispered. "I have to get her out of that bottle." Her gaze went to Pluck. "If I had known, I never would have run away when Dana put you in one."

Tell her thank you for me, Pluck fizzed.

"Pluck says thanks." Marty knew who she was. She was clearly not happy about it, but she was free to become whatever she would be. Aasta too. "I would move a mountain with a teaspoon for Pluck. We will rescue her."

"That we will." Herm twisted as he brought his phone from a back pocket. "Let's see where things sit at Dana's." He chuckled. "Slipped right past her bodyguards, eh?"

"Until I ran into Aasta." It was a regretful whisper, and I shot a sidelong glance at Pluck when a hint of his remorse twined through me. "She scared the crap out of me."

And then made it worse trying to get into her head, probably, I thought, and Pluck's ears flattened to an embarrassed slant. Sometimes shadows were their own worst enemies.

Lev inched closer, brow furrowed as he stared at the phone. It was a burner, but it could still be tracked with magic.

"Relax," Herm said as he scrolled. "It will bounce off the tower across town. As far as Dana will know, we are in Tucson."

"Someday you are going to tell me how you do that, old man," Lev grumbled.

Marty touched Herm's arm. "I'll give her anything if she lets Aasta go."

"It won't come to that." Herm hesitated, one thick, arthritic finger poised over an icon. "Does Dana know it was you who stole the stick?"

Marty shook her head. "No. She never saw me."

"Good." Herm jabbed at the icon. "She probably thinks it was Pluck and Petra. We can use that."

For what? Pluck fizzed as Dana's voice came faintly through the speaker.

"Dana!" Herm beamed though the woman couldn't see him. "How's your day going?"

"Ivaros," Dana said as Herm put her on speaker. "Why am I not surprised? You want Pluck? I want Petra. Either Grady turns herself in or I drop the shadow into a vat of dross."

Marty gasped and I took her arm, whispering, "It's okay. She thinks she has Pluck. She won't hurt him. Aasta, she might. Don't say anything to change her mind."

Angry and tearful, Marty nodded, and I took my hand away.

Herm exhaled to puff his cheeks out. "As pleasant and direct as always, Dana. Is Pluck hurt?" he added, looking at the shadow by the podium, and Pluck stood, stretched, and trotted closer.

"No," Dana said. "Do the right thing and it will stay that way."

"The right thing?" Agitated, Herm shifted his weight. "A desert full of shadows might have a problem with you damaging a weaver/shadow pair."

"Don't threaten me, Ivaros," she said, but I could hear a soft commotion behind her and figured someone was trying to trace the call. "If the desert shadows were a real danger, they would have shown it by now."

"So . . . you admit the vault destructions aren't caused by St. Unoc's resident shadows?" he said, and she laughed.

"Not at all."

But she seems to know it, regardless, I thought sourly, and Pluck fizzed his agreement.

"Not going to let that go, huh?" Herm said. "Either way, I think we can both agree that the situation is becoming dangerously close to breaking the silence. Despite your interference, we have what we need to catch Thoth now. Let that shadow go so we can do it."

"Out, out . . ." I heard her whisper, and then the shutting of a door. "I will release Pluck if Petra admits she riled up the memorial shadows into breaking the vaults."

"Like hell!" I said, and Lev nodded, his brow furrowed in thought.

"But that's not what happened," Benedict protested. "Thoth cracked the vaults."

Herm held the phone to his chest to muffle Benedict's words. Too bad the mic was actually on the rim of the phone. "Will you two shut up?"

"Dr. Strom," Dana said, her confidence returned. "I'm glad you're there. I'd like you to surrender yourself as well."

"To make a false confession?" Benedict said hotly. "Not likely."

"Dana, be reasonable." The Spinner glared at Benedict to be quiet. "I won't throw Petra under the bus so you can look good. It was Thoth. Both Cameron and Marty say so. Why don't you cut the crap and help us catch him? We could use your help. The truth will out."

"The truth is what I say it is," she said, and Marty went pale. "I'm not going to waste my time trying to catch a shadow while Petra and Pluck destroy the last few vaults we have."

"That's not what this is about," I protested. "Why do you think we stole that last stick? We have all five. We can catch him now."

"Five . . ." Dana said, tone distant in thought. "You risked everything on a children's rhyme? I thought Ryan was kidding. No, you will turn yourselves in," she continued. "Admit to helping the desert shadows to destroy the vaults. I want a written apology for breaking into my apartment. The university has already agreed to limit Dr. Strom's punishment for his involvement to probation provided there are no more disturbances."

But with Thoth free, future "disturbances" were a guarantee.

"And Petra and Pluck?" Herm said, one hand motioning for Lev to hold his thought. The man had become decidedly antsy.

"Pluck will remain in custody," Dana said.

My breath caught. "You said you'd release him."

"I'll release him to a bottle, where he will remain alive," Dana said.

Not bloody likely, Pluck fizzed, ears hazing.

"Ms. Grady will serve a minimal sentence for her part," Dana was saying, but I wasn't sure if anyone was listening. Marty, too, was watching Lev whisper to Benedict, the man pantomiming some sort of military maneuver. It was all finger and arm gestures, none of which made any sense to me.

"I can arrange for her to stay in St. Unoc," Dana continued. "Minimal security. Six months if the desert shadows behave. If not, she stays where she is."

Benedict's gaze flicked from Lev to me. "She wants to use you as hostage for Thoth's behavior? How does that even work?"

It doesn't, fizzed coldly through me.

"As a show of goodwill, I won't press charges against Petra for stealing that stick, provided there is an apology," Dana finished.

My lips curled in disgust. "Just so I have this straight, Dana. You want me to say that I incited a group into destroying the vaults, the same group that you want to burn alive, as if they are trash? You can't have it both ways. If you assign them agency to make decisions, then you assign them the same rights as a person. We can catch Thoth, Dana. Don't help him destroy everyone's future. You're an airologist. We could really use your help."

Dana made a small noise of negation. "Grady, surrender yourself before I lose custody of the shadow in question."

"His name is Pluck," Herm said forcefully, and the shadow's skin rippled in and out of reality. "And we want to see him first. Make sure he's okay."

It would be a chance to free Aasta if nothing else. Too bad Dana knew that, too. "Sorry, Ivaros. You will have to trust me," she said smugly.

"We don't have to do anything of the sort," Herm shot back. "We see the shadow, or nothing happens. You want this to go away? So do we. Once we know Pluck is safe, we talk."

"Fine." Dana sighed. "I will bring the shadow, but I'm not letting it out. You can ascertain the health of it through the glass."

It wasn't the best situation, but it gave us a chance, and I nodded my agreement. Marty seemed to shudder in a mix of relief and anticipation.

"Tonight," Herm said, and Lev frantically waved for him to stop. "Somewhere neutral," Herm continued, his eyes fixed questioningly on Lev. "The records building, perhaps?"

"Tomorrow," Lev mouthed, but it was too late.

"The Surran building," Dana said, and I frowned. It was just across the street. Close. We might lose our hiding spot. On the upside, the Surran building was university property. Any magical mishaps would be contained and wouldn't end up on the news. "But our conversation will have to wait until tomorrow. Tonight I'm inspecting an old vault for possible use."

Both Lev and Benedict sighed in relief, making me wonder what they had been plotting while Herm set this up. Marty, too, was pleased, which made no sense at all unless . . .

We are liberating Aasta tonight, Pluck fizzed, and I eyed all three of them. Figured. But it was a good idea. Marty wouldn't wait around, and if she went alone, she'd be caught. Probably.

"Fine. Tomorrow noon," Herm grumped, and Lev gave Marty an extravagant thumbs-up, grinning from ear to ear. "But if Pluck is not in that jar, the deal is off."

"He's in the jar, and he's going to stay there," Dana said. "Ivaros, I expect you to—"

Still staring at Lev, Herm ended the call. "Why tomorrow, Lev," he said flatly.

Lev brushed a nonexistent dross drift from his shoulder. "Because I am going to free Aasta while Dana is busy inspecting that new vault."

My gaze shot to Marty. The woman looked ready to bolt, damn the risk. Herm took a breath to protest, exhaling in surrender when I nodded my agreement. "She'll be expecting that," he warned instead. "I doubt she'll leave Aasta sitting on a shelf. There will be security."

"Nothing a small team can't handle." Lev grinned at Marty. "I figure two rangers and a weaver can handle it."

"I am not useless," Benedict grumbled, and I bumped into his shoulder.

"Good, because I need you with me," I said, and both Herm and Lev turned from their infant argument. "If Dana leaves some of her security with Aasta, she will have less when she goes out to inspect the vault. I want to talk to her," I added, gut tightening. "Face-to-face. Convince her Thoth exists and that we could catch him if she'd get off my back."

"Ah . . ." Herm said in anticipatory understanding.

I glanced at Pluck for his opinion, and the shadow flicked an ear. *Dividing our resources may be a good risk, given the return. Dana may still choose not to believe, but if Marty liberates Aasta, it will remove the mage's hold on us.*

"I'm coming with you, too," Herm said, and Pluck hazed in annoyance. "I have a few things I'd like to say to Dana as well."

Lev was decidedly smug. "All you need to do is figure out what vault. I don't know of any more in the area large enough to make a dent in the dross problem. I doubt it's military. Cameron might know."

Marty fidgeted. She was flushed, but it was in hope. "Aasta said Dana was talking about it being at 'their failed, great test of their time.'"

"Like I understand wise-old-shadow-speak," I grumped.

"Soon as we free her, we'll find out," Lev said, but Herm made a satisfied harrumph.

"She's talking about Biosphere 2," Herm explained, and my eyebrows rose. The then-state-of-the-art facility had made news in 1991 when eight people locked themselves in a sealed structure in the Arizona desert to study if long-term space travel or planetary colonization with self-renewing food, air, and water sources was even possible. What most people didn't know was that it wasn't just air and food they were watching in a contained system. It was dross. Which, as Aasta had said, failed miserably. When the university bought the facility, they emptied the twin vaults, having to treat the accumulated tinkered-with dross with more care than atomic waste. The vaults, though, remained.

"Those vaults are empty . . ." I mused. If Thoth knew about them, they'd be broken by now. "Herm, we have to get out there before Dana does."

The old Spinner bobbed his head. "Marty, she's your shadow. It's your call."

She didn't even hesitate. "Yes," she breathed, gazing at all of us in relief and gratitude. "Thank you for helping me."

Lev brought his hands together in a loud *pop*, then hopped from the stage to the floor. "I'll tell Cameron. I know she'll go for it. Marty, can you sketch out what you remember of Dana's apartment? I'll be right back."

"Ah, wait up," Benedict said as Lev hightailed it to the stairs. "Shouldn't we have a contingency plan or something?"

"That would be the grotto," Herm said. "We leave in five minutes. Dana didn't say when she'd be out there and I want to get there first. Hey, Lev! Bring the truck around, will you?"

"Got it, old man!" filtered down the stairs, and then the fire door slammed.

Benedict's gaze went distant. "We should bring water . . ." he whispered, then darted off.

A fond smile quirked my lips. *You get stranded in the desert one time . . .*

I turned to Marty. "You going to be okay working with Lev?" I said, and she nodded, breathless but eager. "He won't let you down," I added, glad to see the new strength in her. She was going to need more than a mystical bond with a sentient energy source to see this through, and I put an arm around Marty, giving her a half hug. "But if this doesn't work, you, me, and Pluck will sneak out together and do it ourselves," I whispered. "Okay? You are not alone."

Marty's gaze flicked to Herm's hunched shoulders, then Benedict's worried frown as he counted our water bottles. Pluck sat beside him, panting like the dog he wasn't. Up to now, I'd been the bad guy. Up to now, she hadn't understood.

But this time, finally, Marty nodded as if she had begun to believe.

28

MUSCLES BUNCHING, BENEDICT DRAGGED THE HEAVY METAL DOOR OPEN, WINCing at the creak of metal on metal. "Wow," he whispered as the harsh sound echoed painfully in the dark before us. The automatic lights clicked on one by one, and we clustered at the threshold, taking in the large building set off from the main facility. There was a vault here—I could feel it.

"This is . . . huh," he added, neck craned as he went into the enormous circular space that functioned as one of Biosphere's two "lungs." Pluck, in his human shift, went hazy at the edges as he mentally searched the place. Herm, too, seemed impressed, hands on his hips and mustache bunched as he squinted at the strange ceiling. The lights did little to alleviate the almost claustrophobic feel of the huge building linked by a long tunnel to the main facility.

I lifted my feet, being careful not to scuff them as Herm's steps hissed like a hundred snakes. The huge circular room had a flexible ceiling that moved, inflating and collapsing over the day like a lung when the facility was sealed, giving the warming air a place to go so the pressure wouldn't break the glass. Right now, the heavy black material hung like the top of a circus tent attached at the walls and the silver disk at the center.

Underneath our feet was one of the facility's two vaults built to house the experimental dross created by the eight people living in a closed system. That Dana wanted to use it to temporarily store the university's dross made sense. One vault could be used for active dross, the other for Benedict's spiky inactive stuff. The drive was nothing compared to having to truck the stuff out of state.

Herm's phone hummed, and I jumped. It was embarrassing, but I had a feeling that I could lay the reaction at Pluck's feet. The shadow was tense, and his anxiety was spilling into me like a cold draft.

"I remember reading about this," Benedict said, studying a flickering light on the wall. "I had no idea they were testing how to balance dross in a closed system as well as oxygen and food."

"My dad told me about it." I kept my voice soft, not liking the hint of an echo it was creating. "The only reason he knew was because they asked the sweepers' guild for ideas on how to safely break dross." My gaze went to the floor as if I could see the enormous, glass-coated room under it. "Maybe if they had included a sweeper or Spinner in the personnel mix, things might have gone differently."

Maybe. But as it was, there would never be a mage in space. Dross was deadly in zero-g. Every. Single. Time.

"It's not still here, is it?" Benedict's attention came back from the roof.

"Dross? No." I hesitated, not sensing any, but who knew how much concrete was between us and Biosphere's old vault. "Is it?" I asked Pluck, and the shadow fizzed coldly, his agitation swirling through both of us as he stood in his human form, dead center of the huge room with his hands on his hips.

"No."

Herm made a satisfied noise, gaze on his phone's screen. "Lev says they have Aasta and are on the way to the grotto."

It was done. Relief cascaded through me. Pluck, too, seemed to breathe easier, and even Benedict blew his air out in a long, noisy breath. "Marty is going to be okay," I said. "And Aasta."

"All the more reason to take care of Thoth." Herm tucked his phone in a tattered back pocket. "He also said that Dana left about forty minutes ago. She had only one other person with her. He thinks he was a driver, but we might be dealing with two mages."

"Better than the six she left guarding Aasta," Pluck said, and Herm started, the man clearly not used to seeing him as a person. His war uniform, I remembered Aasta saying. "I distrust this," Pluck added, his concern fizzing through me. "If Dana sees your truck, she will call in reinforcements."

"You want to go wait for her?" I suggested, already knowing the answer, and Pluck nodded. The unseen vault below our feet clearly made him nervous.

Herm looked at the ceiling, running a hand over his bristly chin in thought. "I would appreciate knowing when she gets here," he said. "How far away can you be and still communicate?"

Pluck hesitated. "We shall find out." A burst of angst for leaving me lit through both of us, and then his outline went hazy. In a breath, the image of a man evaporated to an inky swirl glittering with green highlights and flowed to the door. I could feel a rasping of unequal energy between him and the steel and I shuddered.

"Ah, our reach is pretty good now," I said, and Pluck fizzed his agreement. He, too, didn't like the sensation and had slithered to the ceiling to make his way among the pipes.

I will go no farther than I can hear you, twined in my thoughts, and the knot in my gut eased. At least until he added, *This air holds a foul phasing.*

I jumped, startled when Benedict bumped into me, his smile faint and forced. "So now we wait. Probably a good idea you didn't bring a stick. Dana would likely try to take it."

"Yeah." He was right, but I missed it all the same. "She's not going to go for this, but I have to try." I turned to Herm. "Thank you for coming with us."

"No need," Herm said gruffly. "I have a few things I want to say when I know I'm not being recorded." His wandering gaze came to me. "And you never know. If you play on her ego enough, you might convince her to help catch him."

"Thoth has done a good job setting you up for the fall, though." Benedict eyed the single rickety chair set against the wall by an electrical panel. "You got to give the shadow props. Waiting until you were at the records building *and* the hospital before cracking the vaults."

"But I've publicly stated we need a source of containment until we find a new balance," I said softly. "Why does everyone believe her?"

"Because like most people, she doesn't want a balance. She wants a return to normal." Herm shifted his weight as he settled in beside us, his gaze on the door over my shoulder. It was the only way in or out. "I'm getting too old to stay off-grid and remain healthy. I'll bring her around." His attention remained over my shoulder. "Even if I have to draw a picture for her and color it in."

"An airologist could put Thoth in a bottle without forcing him to evaporate," Benedict said, his brow furrowed in worry. "Shadow spit. I'm going to have to be nice to her. After she lied and put me in jail."

"And you all wonder why I don't go to the university parties," Herm grumbled. "Ben, you've been eyeing that chair since we got here. Either sit in it or bring it over here for me to sit in it."

Benedict pushed into motion, feet making hardly any sound.

"Welcome to my world," I said, but I wasn't sure I could let go of the fact that Dana had put both Pluck and Aasta into a bottle and threatened to burn them if I didn't do what she wanted. The same bottle that we were going to put Thoth into.

Don't feel pity for him, fizzed through me. *He has destroyed many shadows and an entire demographic of people who loved them. If I could sunder his bonds and scatter his energy to the edges of the universe, I would.*

I stifled a shudder, jumping when Benedict dropped the chair beside Herm.

"Thanks, Ben." Herm's cheeks puffed out as he shifted the rickety thing to face the door and sat in it, as happy as a clam at high tide. "I'll keep watch if you two want to relax."

Benedict nodded, shoulders rounded as he came to stand with me. "I suppose we could lean against the wall," he said dryly, and I chuckled.

Dana is here. Pluck's thought came clear in mine, and I froze. *She's not happy. It's likely she knows Aasta has been liberated, though that it wasn't me might still be unknown. I also think she knows you are here. She's heading your way.*

Thank you, Pluck. Missing my lodestone, I took Benedict's hand and gave it a squeeze.

Try to convince her, but we don't need mage Dana. Pluck's thoughts came clear, his hatred obvious. *We have the sticks. Thoth goes into a bottle and the truth will out. We don't need a lodestone to do it, either.*

Shuddering, I pulled from Pluck's thoughts to find Benedict staring at me as if he had heard them, too. "Um, she's on her way. Pluck is following her."

"Benedict, be ready." Herm shifted on the chair and made it groan. "Dana will want to arrest you both, probably even after we demonstrate that's not going to happen."

The mage blinked as if trying to place himself, then glanced at his lodestone ring on his hand, clasped with mine. "I'm good." He shifted his weight, then leaned toward me, whispering, "If we fail to catch Thoth, it won't be because of you." His smile held love. "I think I was in Pluck's thoughts just then. You've got this, Petra."

I wasn't so sure, but I nodded, my focus blurring when a wave of sensation tripped over me. It was Herm's field, its spiderweb feel sparking as it lifted through and past me. The old Spinner held his lodestone as he sent his awareness out to look for threats and possibilities. I'd always been impressed at how he managed to stay one step ahead of any capture. Sensing his class-five field push out past the room and into the desert, I was even more so. Herm could have done anything with his abilities, and he had chosen to use them to hide me. Keep me safe.

He still was.

Herm's field reversed and pulled back over me, the weft and weave tighter than before. "She's close," he said, his expression holding concern, persuasion, and hard refusal all in one as he tugged his worn shirt straight. I could hear Dana's heels in the tunnel, her sure pace definitive and loud. "Here we go."

The desire to cluster together was heady, but I gave Benedict's hand a quick squeeze and moved a few steps away. If she was going to start throwing magic, it would be better to give her three targets, not one.

"Dana!" Herm said with a forced warmth as she came to a halt in the threshold, lingering just inside the tunnel. Her white dress suit was spotless, and with her purse over one shoulder and her sunglasses in her hand, she could have been going out to a five-star restaurant.

Yes, she had put Pluck in a bottle, but if she helped us, I might forgive her for it.

You might feel differently if it was you she trapped in glass, Pluck fizzed.

We need her to admit it was Thoth, I reminded him, and his sizzing became sullen.

Hand extended, Herm paced forward, scuffing to a halt when the woman held up her hand to stop him. "Ah, we were hoping to find you here," Herm added.

Dana pursed her lips as she eyed the ceiling as if the room might be a trap. "I wish I could say the same." Her gaze landed on me. "You. I thought you'd take the opportunity to free Pluck." Her eye twitched. "That wasn't Pluck in the bottle, was it."

It really wasn't a question, and I shook my head.

"Where is he?" Dana's jaw clenched. "Is he here? I swear, if you broke the vaults—"

"We didn't break the vaults," Benedict interrupted. "We haven't broken any of them. Thoth did."

"Hear us out." Herm pushed at the air as if asking for her patience. "We know how to catch Thoth, but we could use your help."

Still in the hallway, Dana crossed her arms over her chest. Her lodestone ring twinkled in an obvious threat. "Where is Pluck?"

"Staying clear of you," Benedict accused, his hands clenched in a protective anger.

"He's behind you, actually," I said, wanting her to commit to the room. There was only one way in and out of the lung, and she was standing in the threshold.

Stiffening, she moved into the room. "So who is that in the bottle?"

I glanced at Benedict and he shrugged. "Ah, a memorial shadow."

Her lips parted. "What was a memorial shadow doing in my apartment?" She stiffened. "You were going to addle my mind?"

"No!" I blurted, wincing when my shout seemed to roll a circular path around the edges of the round room until it was gone. "Um . . ." I glanced at Benedict, and he nodded. "It followed Marty there. She was stealing the stick we needed and . . . ah . . ."

Dana thought about that for a second, and then she slumped. "Fuck," she whispered, and my eyebrows rose. "Another weaver with shadow? I can't stop this, can I."

Herm chuckled, his likely concern that I'd played my cards too soon vanishing. "Nope. You'd be better served helping Petra and Pluck than persecuting them." His brow furrowed when she reached for the wall. "Um, this is a good thing, Dana. You want to sit down?"

"No." It was a breathy, half-hearted sound, but her lips were pressed when she swung her purse around for her phone. "That whiny little girl attracted a shadow? I thought you had to have a strong will to handle one."

That's not how it works, Pluck fizzed from the tunnel, but I was more worried about Dana, her fingers flying as she texted someone. Benedict took a step forward, halting when she looked up, her clenched jaw and winking lodestone warning him to stay put. "I am nothing if not open-minded," she said as she finished and dropped her phone into her purse. "You have thirty minutes to convince me you have a viable way to catch Thoth. Otherwise, I'm taking you in. Thoth has agreed that if I can contain you and Pluck, he will leave St. Unoc alone."

"You made a deal with Thoth?" I blurted. Gobsmacked, I looked at Benedict. Herm, too, was clearly shocked.

An agreement that will hold until it suits him no more, Pluck fizzed, his bitter disappointment and betrayal twining through my utter disbelief.

"You know he destroyed the vaults," Benedict whispered, and the woman had the decency to look embarrassed. "You knew, and you made a deal with him? He walks free and Petra takes the blame? *Why?*"

"It was my best choice," she said, and Herm pushed his fingers into his temples. "Twenty-nine minutes to give me a better one or this conversation never happened."

Benedict's hands clenched and my stomach tightened into a hard knot. Thoth had been manipulating everything from the moment I'd returned from Chicago. Probably before. The only thing the shadow hadn't been able to control was Marty and Aasta. *Perhaps it's their existence that can break Thoth's hold . . .*

Herm's expression was hard in disgust. "I never pegged you for a coward, Dana. Political prostitute, yes, but never a coward."

"You have a shadow standing in your living room threatening to break your mind, and you tell me you could do better!" she exclaimed, flushed as she looked at me. "I *saw* what he did to Grady. *She* can't even make a field anymore, much less handle dross. And you have the gall to stand there and tell me you can catch him? With what? Five balanced sticks?!"

A wave of doubt hit me. Behind Dana, Pluck dropped from the ceiling in a ribbon of black sparkles to coalesce into his human shape. Grim and brow low, he shook his hands and dark matter hissed on the floor. His belief in me, though, was as bright as the sun.

"If you think they're so ineffective, why did you hide the last stick?" Herm asked.

Benedict's shoulders hunched as he came to stand beside me. "Petra is fine," he said. "And she can touch dross. She uses it now like a shadow."

"Ahhh . . ." Herm warned, but if we couldn't convince Dana we had a chance to catch Thoth, we'd be back in custody. I doubted she'd been texting for takeout. There would be mages, and there would be a lot of them.

"Lies. All lies," she said, and Pluck's frustration fizzed. Or maybe it was mine. "You are helpless, Petra. I saw dross break on you."

You are not helpless. Pluck stood in the tunnel, little streamers of energy lifting from him like a fog.

Benedict put his hand on my shoulder. "It's not a lie. I've seen her do magic," he said.

Dana glanced at her phone. "How? I've still got her lodestone."

My chest clenched. Herm looked ill, but Benedict nodded to me in encouragement, his eyes warm in pride and admiration. I was simply scrambling to survive, but he thought I was amazing, and I took a steadying breath. "Ah, when Thoth damaged my ability to work a weave in the weft of the universe and create a field, it allowed me to create alternate ways to manipulate dark matter. Like a shadow, sort of."

"You can work with threads directly?" Dana said, surprising me, and I nodded.

Herm made a confident huff. "Not a shadow, but something between a shadow and a weaver and a mage. Furthermore, she's learned to passively touch another's thoughts, but unlike a shadow, she's not powerful enough to cause any damage."

Like Thoth? I wondered, and Pluck soothed my flash of panic. I was nothing like Thoth.

"You can do magic?" Dana said, her eyes wide in shock. "Without having to put the spell in a field?"

"Just like a shadow," Benedict said, and Dana's astonished gaze returned to me.

"But I'm not one," I said, seeing fear in her.

"Dana." Herm took a nervous step to Benedict and me. "What Thoth did to Petra doesn't matter. Do you believe Thoth is responsible and should be contained, or not?"

"Oh, he's responsible, I agree," she said. "But I won't risk the stability of the university and the continued silence on it. You're down to twenty minutes."

"You're not looking at the long term," Herm pleaded.

Petra, I sense Thoth is close, fizzed through me.

My attention flicked to the tunnel. Pluck evaporated, dissolving into a hazy blot that darted away. I took a breath. Held it. The ceiling was one big shadowed space. He could be up there, and we'd never know.

Benedict leaned close, gaze fixed on Herm and Dana arguing. "What?"

"Pluck says Thoth is on-site," I whispered, and the mage made a frustrated groan. "If he cracks the vault while we're here, everyone will believe we did it." Shadow spit, Thoth had done it again!

"I'll check the room." Benedict touched my arm in support before he sidestepped away. His lodestone ring was winking, and Dana cocked her hip, her suspicion growing.

Senses reaching, I studied the walls, ceiling, floor. Pluck's thoughts fizzed against mine as he ranged through the facility. *Pluck?*

Searching . . . came back, faint and agitated.

"Dr. Strom . . ." Dana called suspiciously, and Herm cleared his throat to distract her.

"Petra has become exactly what we need to snare Thoth," Herm said, his words tumbling over themselves. "We know Thoth can't be bested by another shadow, or a mage, or any number of sweepers or weavers, but Petra is functioning as something between them, and we think that with your help and the five balanced sticks, we—" He hesitated. "Dana?"

The worry in his voice pulled me around to see she hadn't moved. Head down, she stared at the floor, her shoulders rounded and arms hanging slack—until her head snapped up and she stiffened.

"My help?" she said as she ran a hand down her front as if smoothing her thoughts as well as her clothes. "Why do you need my help? You have an entire university of mages with which to *try* to best Thoth."

Benedict turned from his distant inspection. Herm, too, sensed a shift, and the old Spinner exchanged a worried look with me. "True." Herm scratched his jawline, bristles making an echoing rasp. "But you're the most skilled airologist this side of the Mississippi. You can put him in a sealed bottle while the rest of us distract him, pin him down, and befuddle him."

Eyebrows rising, Dana shifted her weight to one foot, a finger going to her jawline in a show of confidence and understanding. "Ah. I see. All five aspects of magic working together," she said, motion fast as she rocked into a smooth step-click, step-click to block our way out. "That's why you risked everything for a balanced stick. Five would enable a more secure connection. And an airologist would certainly widen your choice of . . . bottles. What would the damaged weaver be doing?" she asked, almost simpering at me. "She can't protect you from him dipping into anyone's mind and leaving them . . . addlebrained."

Damaged weaver? I thought, not so much insulted as wondering why she didn't use my name. *Pluck, any progress?*

I know where he isn't. I'm circling in.

Benedict returned to my side, the mage clearly not liking Dana's sudden shift in mood. "She and Pluck are the catalyst that will keep us all working together," he said guardedly. "Through Pluck, she can communicate and coordinate our actions to hold Thoth safely until you can put him in a bottle."

"Indeed . . ." she drawled. "And you're certain it will work?"

"Enough to save your job," Herm muttered.

Something was wrong. I could feel it—a shifting of threads, drifting as if in a fell wind.

Benedict's presence beside me was as sure and confident as always as he frowned at Dana's callous disregard. Herm was a few steps away, and both Dana and I stiffened when I felt a haze of threads brush against my awareness. Herm had sent out a field.

And Dana felt it?

Suddenly I had no idea what was going on, but I knew I wanted Pluck with me. Apart we were vulnerable; together, we might have a chance. *Pluck!*

Thoth is close, Pluck answered, his worry twining with mine as he saw my thoughts. *Petra, be careful.*

Face pale, I looked past Benedict to Herm. "We have to go," I whispered. "We can convince her later. We have to go. Now!"

Herm spun to me. "Now?" he blurted, and then his expression hardened when saw Dana blocking our easy exit, the woman standing confidently with her hands loose at her sides—waiting. "Thirty minutes, Dana?" he said sourly. "You couldn't even be truthful about that?"

"The clock has stopped," Dana said, and Herm squinted at her in anger. "I have decided to help you. Yes. Of course."

"You'll help?" I said in surprise, but there was no relief. She didn't look scared, or hopeful, or eager, or even afraid that Thoth might have a problem with this.

"I have no choice," she said, her smile looking oily and fake. "Where is Pluck? Sealing him into a bottle at the stick lab was a mistake. I . . . would like to apologize," she said, her words faltering as if it was hard for her to do. But she was an elitist mage. It probably was. "I *need* to apologize. Especially if we're going to work together."

"He's on his way," I said, mistrusting this.

"Good!" It was almost a shout, and I frowned at the soft echo hissing about.

I don't feel Thoth anymore, fizzed through me, and that sinking sensation grew.

Did he leave? Is he cracking the other vault?

And then Dana beamed when Pluck walked in, my shadow's glower of apprehension growing when he saw Herm's unease, Dana's confidence, and how close Benedict stood beside me. "I see you found your uniform," Dana said sarcastically, and my lips parted. I'd heard that before. Aasta had said it. "Too bad it's a little too late," she added—right before she wound her arm in a circle, gathering power.

"It's him!" I shouted, voice echoing harshly as I backed into Benedict. "He's in Dana!"

Petra! Down! thundered in my head as Pluck launched himself at me.

He hit and we crashed to the cold floor and out of the reach of Thoth's magic. *It's him!* I thought as the floor where I'd been sort of went fizzy and indistinct under Dana's magic, but Pluck already knew. Thoth had taken the woman over, wearing her like Aasta wore a rez, knowing all the right responses because he was living rent-free in her mind. *Fool yeth,* I berated myself. I'd known he could possess another without leaving them insane. But to take her over so fast, with only a small shudder to show for it? No wonder no one could catch him.

Worse, we had just told him how an airologist could catch a reluctant shadow.

"Pluck, no," I whispered, sitting up when Pluck coalesced into a snarling dog, dark matter hissing as it dripped from his jaws and spiky darts of energy hazed over his black skin. He stood between us and Dana, a sure and obvious threat.

Herm and Benedict were down, struggling to move with their feet stuck *in* the floor, having been snared by Dana's abilities to sink them into it. It would take another airologist to get them out, and one hell of an etherologist to befuddle the memory of any mundane who saw.

I scrambled up. "Pluck," I whispered as I tried to pull him to safety, but my hand went right through him.

Confident and sure within Dana's body, Thoth walked toward me. I could see it now, but he wasn't trying to hide it anymore. "I took you out of the game," he said, Dana's voice holding the shadow's haughty cadence. "You were supposed to live out your pathetic life pining for something I stole from you. And yet you leave me impressed. Your skills are not weaver, nor shadow. It almost pains me to do this, such a harsh sentence for one with so much potential. But I suppose it's just, if you were going to do it to me."

My expression blanked. He was going to put me in a bottle? How?

You will not touch her, Pluck threatened, his thoughts icy in mine.

"That's Thoth!" Herm shouted, the man sitting on the floor as he struggled to unlace his shoes. "Benedict . . ."

Thoth smacked Benedict's magic down with half a thought even as the threads of Dana's magic began to swirl about Pluck and me like migraine stars.

"You will never win, Pluck. You want a perfect balance, but mages kill perfection," Thoth said through Dana, and then I gasped when Thoth harnessed the woman's magic and the energy from her lodestone cascaded over us. Vertigo hit me as I felt the world shift. I gasped as the world turned inside out and I was floundering. Energy poles flipped to align mass and make the space within them line up—and I sank into the floor.

"Pluck!" I shouted as I scrabbled for a handhold that no longer existed. Triumphant, Dana watched as I felt myself slip . . . And then I fell, sinking through cement and rebar as if they were clouds.

I hit the floor of the room below with a painful thump.

I struggled to breathe; my breath was knocked out of me. I couldn't see, and I forced myself onto my hands and knees and blinked to try to make my eyes work. The echoes of my breath came back from distant walls, but there was no light. There was nothing. All I could sense was a smooth perfection under my hands.

"Benny?" I rasped, thinking I had passed out, but he didn't answer.

More rasping hisses rose as I shifted to sit. My head hurt, but I managed to inhale to create a mass of threaded dark matter between my hands. Choosing one strand, I pulled it tight, feeling a surge of cold when the light reflected off the glistening distant walls.

"Oh no," I whispered as I looked up, not at the expected silver disk and collapsed diaphragm of Biosphere 2's lung but at the shiny, smooth nothing of what had to be a vault, a glass-lined, unbreakable, sealed vault.

"Pluck?" I called, and then I saw him as he sat, knees pulled to his chin.

"I know of no way to get out," he said.

We were caught, both of us, like shadows in the noon sun.

29

NECK CRANED, I STOOD UNDER THE OPENING TO THE VAULT, BRACING MYSELF against the cold as I stretched my fingers apart and the single thread of dark matter wound between my index and pointer fingers like dental floss glowed brighter. The light barely reached the distant ceiling, but I could see enough to tell that the once one-way valve was now a no-way valve, having been both soldered shut and coated with hot liquid glass. We weren't getting out that way. Not without some help.

And help, I had reluctantly decided as hunger pinched my middle, wasn't coming.

The valve was shadowproof, even if that shadow had hands and a frustrated expression on his narrow, angular face. Pluck would survive as long as they didn't remove the glass coating and start pumping dross in here again—which they might. Biosphere 2 was considered too far from St. Unoc to make an easy dump, but seeing as there was no other large vault in a fifty-mile radius, it was a good option. Much depended on how the fight upstairs had ended.

Thirty minutes, my ass . . . Thoth had played us, and my naivete had let him.

Cold to the bone, I eased the tension and the light dimmed. If I kept it to a soft glow, the chill was tolerable. It was hard to tell, but I had a bad feeling that the air was beginning to get stuffy in the huge, echoey, shiny space. The light in my hand made weird shadows, and the rippled layer of glass on everything reflected gold and black alike. I didn't have a phone, and I doubted it would connect to anything if I did. Lack of a watch meant I had no idea how long we'd been down here. There were no escape valves, no new air intakes. Without air, I wouldn't live long enough to dehydrate.

"Pluck?" The shadow sat at the far end of the glass-walled room, staring at literally nothing. He was still in his human shift. Still fighting, I guessed. "Pluck, I can't reach the valve. Will you just . . ."

The fizzy thread of his emotion billowed as if given a sudden wind: frustration, heartache, dread, but mostly anger. "There's no need," he said, his words echoing as they bounced off the wall in front of him. "We are in a vault. It's shadowproof by definition."

My light faded and I tried to muffle my own thoughts as confusion joined Pluck's feelings. No one was coming to get us out or it would have happened by now. The not knowing was awful, leaving my imagination to invent all sorts of ugly scenarios. Thoth had succeeded in quashing the truth. Benedict helpless in a mage jail. Herm on the run or in the cell next to him. Lev and Cameron on trial for the gall of telling the truth. Marty . . .

My heart ached at the thought of Marty and Aasta. They might be safe in a militia compound, but they would be used, turned into a weapon.

I scuffed across the featureless glass floor, the glow of light coming from my fingers running like fish before me. Pluck tilted his head to acknowledge me, and yet his eyes never met mine as I sank down beside him with a heavy sigh. "You shouldn't be down here," he said, and I stifled a shiver at his low, rumbly voice.

"You think?" Sitting so our knees almost touched, I played with the single string of dark matter between my fingers, making the energy *ziming* and *zoumong*, *ziming* and *zoumong*, feeling the cold swell and ebb with it.

"I do." The shadow stared at my fingers until I quit and held the light steady. "He had been willing to let you live until I encouraged you to find a way around the damage. You shouldn't be down here."

"Finding a balance was my dream, too," I said, trying to ignore his anger bubbling like acid.

"You will die because of me." Pluck's lips pressed into a thin line. "Thoth would have let you live if not for me."

"Oh, yeah?" Ticked, I pulled my fingers apart to make the thread sing. "I've got news for you, shadow. This saving thing goes both ways." He said nothing, and I added, "Hey, when I'm good and dead, promise me you will use my leg bone to beat a crack in the glass. One of us should make it out of here."

"Stop!"

I jumped at his shout, the light in my hand faltering as his voice reverberated until it subsided into an uncomfortable hiss. "I have had this conversation before," he added, head bowed as he refused to look at me. "Though not at the bottom of a glass-walled hell."

My own anger flared, now that his was lost in an ancient heartache. "Oh, I'm sorry," I said bitterly. "I'll just go over there and try not to breathe."

I gathered myself to stand, slumping back down when he put a hand on my knee.

"Stop," he said again, whispering it.

More cold seeped into me where we touched, but it was a familiar sensation, and a melancholy thread of his grief wound through it, little sparkles of his unshared memory coloring it. My anger slowly faded, and for a moment, we were both silent. "I never realized how devastating an air mage could be," I said as an odd peace seeped from Pluck to me. "I hope Thoth took Benedict and Herm out of the floor before he left."

Pluck's shoulders shifted in a breath he really didn't need. "I'm sure he did. Dana called for reinforcements. He would have to adhere to basic human decency laws to maintain his deception."

I glanced at the ceiling, trying to estimate how much air was in here. "How long do you think we've been down here?" I'd drowsed and slept and drowsed again, but the pinch of hunger in my gut said it had likely only been the better part of a day.

"Too long," he said, gaze flicking toward my makeshift latrine.

"I should have worked harder getting those shadow escape valves put in," I muttered, and he sighed heavily. "Hey, I'm sorry you are down here, but selfishly, I'm glad I won't be dying alone."

His lip twitched, and an odd sensation fluttered through the folds of my brain as he stifled a memory.

Fine. We could talk about something else. "Um, so Thoth possessed Dana." I glanced at him, seeing a stoic nothing. "Where is Dana when he's in charge?"

Pluck's brow smoothed out as he lost a sliver of tension. "Still there." He fiddled with his shoes, and they solidified enough that laces appeared. "He walled her off from her consciousness much as he did Cameron. It's a nightmare he will likely never free her from, as Thoth will obtain much sway over the university in her name." He glanced at me, green eyes catching the light, reflecting it. "I'm sorry."

"It's not your doing," I said. I put my free hand to the floor and tried to feel something, anything, past the rippled glass. The universe still rang in my thoughts, obviously, since I had used it to make a light, but beyond that? Nothing. "Hey, if we get out of here, could we make him let her go, like we did for Cameron?"

At that, Pluck turned away again. "There is no if," he said softly. "We can't escape, and that's what pains me the most. You didn't have to die. You could have survived."

I pulled my knees to my chin. "I doubt that," I said sourly. "Okay, I wouldn't suffocate, but there is no way I could survive Thoth, especially if he's walking around St. Unoc in a brand-new Dana suit. And certainly not without you. At least it's quiet down here."

Pluck's lip twitched. "I made you dangerous to him."

"I made myself dangerous," I muttered, the light in my hand

glowing stronger as I became angry again. Threads of dark matter lifted into existence, glittering in the light I created until they snarled and knotted about themselves.

Pluck rose to his feet, the motion liquid as he probably evaporated somewhat to do it. "I don't see it that way," he said, voice gaining strength as his own anger swirled through my frustration. "If you hadn't tried to work around the damage he did to your magic—"

"I was not going to stay like I was. Broken!" I interrupted, pushing to my feet as well.

"If Thoth hadn't seen you as a threat, you might be on the other side of the vault and free me as you did before. Now we are both trapped."

"You're blaming me?" The light in my hand burst into a harsh glare, illuminating the snarled threads threatening to tangle about it. "You, sir, have been bottled *twice* in one day because you were protecting me. Stop protecting me!"

"I don't think that's going to be an issue anymore!" Pluck shouted, and I squinted at the harsh glow lighting both of us and the tangled dark matter our anger had pulled into play. "You shouldn't be here! You are not a shadow to be stuffed in a glass vault to die a slow death!"

I stood toe-to-toe with him, so close I could see his edges fraying and feel the universe chime through him as his feet phased into mine. "Hey!" I barked, ticked. "I got news for you, Pluck. It's not going to be a slow death but a fast, painful one as I drown in a room of carbon dioxide. But you know what? I'd do it again in a heartbeat because there's no way in hell I would stand by and do nothing when some wackadoodle is trying to hurt you, *so get over it!*"

"You . . ." Pluck faced me, green eyes wrathful as he lost his grip on solidity. "You are infuriating! Why can't you admit you were wrong!"

"Because I'm not!" I shouted. And then I yelped when the snarled knots of energy around my glowing fingers suddenly organized under an influx of weave I could no longer make. A field formed around the dark matter, snapping into a tight sphere around my fingers and then exploding.

"Pluck!" I shouted as I staggered back, the afterimage the only thing I could see. I froze, my pulse hammering at the sudden dark, and my ankle cramped with cold. "Pluck?"

Here, echoed in our joined thoughts, calming me.

But what was that? I thought, his confusion tracing through mine.

Perhaps . . . he began, and fingers shaking, I cautiously inhaled to bring a new mass of dark matter into existence between my hands, wrapping a thread around my fingers and tightening it until it began to glow again.

"Pluck?" He was at my feet, nothing more than a dark puddle. "Shit, are you okay?"

He pulled himself together, a cobra head rising to consider me. *You made a field,* he thought, his wonder bright sparkles in my mind. *I saw it.*

"I couldn't have," I said, but I'd seen it, too.

The cobra grew, shimmered, and again the man stood before me. "There was a field," he said, taking my wrist in his grip and lifting the glowing thread to shine between us. "You made a field, and it fastened upon your light. Burning your fingers in the process."

Cold cramped my wrist, rising to push the slight pain away. "It had to have been something else," I said, even as I knew it wasn't. "Pluck, I haven't been able to hear the universe echo in my thoughts to weave a field since Thoth broke my wrist. I am listening for it now, and it's not there. No echo, no weave, no field."

My eyebrows rose, and I met his gaze. "But I did hear it echo in yours," I said softly.

Pluck let go of my hand, eyes wide. "You wove a field with the echo in my mind, not yours?"

Hope raced through us both. Pluck looked at the ceiling, and then his hand flashed out, finding my free one.

"Try it again," he said, his words echoing in my mind as if they were my own.

Eyes closed, I exhaled to bring the weft of the universe into play about my hand. As before, there was no echo in my head with which to harness it, and the dark matter tangled and knotted like Darrell's silk on her loom.

Until Pluck strengthened his presence in my mind, bringing with him the ringing of the cosmos. My breath caught as his fizzing shifted, and I watched with my mind's eye, unbelieving as the echo within Pluck wove through the weft between my hands, arranging it, ordering it, giving it structure, tuning it as he once showed me how to tune a stone of moldavite. It was something I couldn't do anymore.

But together we could.

Cold ran scintillating lines through my core, an icy, fractured branching until my very fingertips tingled with dark matter in a hazy, not-there existence. It was Pluck, the edges of the shadow phasing in and out of reality. Behind it, I could feel his awe as he sensed the mass that made me a humming, burning substance, the molecules that I was made of caught in a dance of attraction and repulsion that was stronger and more ancient than the universe itself.

Almost . . . we forgot that we had a reason to escape as our thoughts twined, cool and calm, and certain as we found a new reality, a new balance.

You can do magic. You are whole, Pluck thought, the idea spiraling through my mind as if it were my own. *Make it yours. You can.*

We can, I fizzed, a drowsy lassitude of a faultless connection filling me. It was the perfection found between sleep and wake and it was mine. Ours.

My lips twitched in a smirky smile as I willed the field filled with unorganized dark matter to the ceiling where the vault's sealed intake valve hung in a metal and glass shroud. All I had to do was shift one electron from here to there . . . and . . .

Ah . . . Pluck thought, his sharp warning flicking through me as the entire field of unorganized energy snapped into a tight state that hung for one spin of an electron . . . and then explosively fell apart.

Too much!

A thunderous boom shook the room, throwing me to the floor. I gasped, unable to hear it. My ears rang, chiming in tune with the universe. The floor shook with an unheard sound of impact, and I squinted past Pluck's shadowy form covering me in protection to the huge chunks of glass suddenly half-embedded in the floor in a dangerous circle about us. My light was gone, but the faint glow of moonlight lit the room, shining on the last of the glass shards still falling.

Are you okay?

I didn't know, and I blinked as Pluck dropped away to coalesce into his human form. Brow furrowed, he stood over me. Glass coated the floor, shifting to catch the moonlight when his not-quite-there feet moved.

Petra, he thought again, his lips moving in time with it, and I put my hand in his offered one, letting him help me stand.

"I can't hear anything," I said, neck craned and tears threatening when I looked up, relief spilling into me as I saw the stars past the ragged edges of the broken vault. I had utterly destroyed it, blowing away not just the intake valve but the lung above it, too.

Lock us in a vault, huh? I mused, thinking this time I would be thrilled to take the blame for the destruction. Perhaps it was a good thing that Thoth had damaged every major vault in a fifty-mile radius and they would have to be rebuilt. This was intolerable. Every vault from here on out would have a shadow valve for a quick escape.

If we survive the next few days, Pluck thought, a faint buzzing in my ear accompanying his moving lips. My hearing was coming back, and my hand slipped from his.

"We will," I said, and Pluck dropped his head, glass shards tinkling as his hazy feet phased in and out of them. "Pluck, we will," I promised, and he met my gaze when my surety slipped among his doubt, curling around his worry like flame and turning it to a cold ash. "If you can get me out of this hole, that is."

His lips quirked into a smile and he glanced at the broken ceiling. "Are you good with heights?"

"You mean like flying?" I said, even as my flicker of angst was quashed by his memory. He was soaring over a night-dark forest, black wings silver in the moonlight, but there were two threads of joy twining through it, his and another's.

"I'd like to show you," he said, his mood hesitating when chunks of cement pattered down.

I followed his attention to the ceiling, my lips parting at the trio of faces staring down at us through the ragged hole. A combat hat and the outline of a rifle showed against the lighter darkness of the sky. It was night. We'd been down here an entire day.

"Ms. Grady?" a masculine voice shouted.

Pluck and I had just blown a hole through an impregnable vault. Some guy with a gun wasn't going to faze me. "Ah, yeah?"

The irritating buzz of a military drone became louder, and I jumped, bowing my head when a white-hot spotlight from it slammed into Pluck and me. The shadow darted for the line of darkness, but I stayed where I was, tired, hungry, thirsty, and really glad that someone was up there—even if it was the militia. "Hey, you mind toning the light down?" I called, and Lev's laugh fell over me like a balm.

"Damn, girl!" Lev shouted, and more glass pattered down. "I should have known you'd find a way to bust out. We would have opened it up sooner, but we estimated you had another twenty-four hours of air and we were afraid we might cut you to ribbons if we simply, ah, bombed the place. Hang on. We have a lift."

Green eyes fixed on mine from the darkness, Pluck's head cocked as he looked at the enormous hole in the ceiling and the new hum of activity. *They're going to want a lot in return if you let them believe they saved you.* His eyes closed in a long blink. *You saved yourself.*

We saved ourselves, I thought back, moving to stand with him when someone shouted at me to move clear as the lift was lowered. "Thoth couldn't have caught everyone," I added, and my ankle went cold as Pluck wrapped a tendril about it. Guests of the militia or not, we'd find out who would believe us that Thoth was behind the destruction of St. Unoc's vaults, and then Pluck and I would start a change that would last a thousand ages whether the university or militia liked it or not.

The fool yeth of a shadow had made the tool of his own destruction. Who was I not to use it?

30

I WASN'T SURE WHO WAS MORE RELIEVED—ME THAT I WASN'T GOING TO DIE, OR Pluck that he wouldn't be responsible for it. Our twined emotions buoyed us both as the crane lifted me past the jagged edges of the vault, over the broken room of the lung, and into the night sky. It was dark, but enough dross and moonlight lit the area that I could see the extent of the damage that Pluck and I had wrought. And I wouldn't take credit for this alone. We had done it together.

The lung was completely destroyed, lying open on the sand like a storm-racked flower. Chunks of glass-encrusted metal had flown a surprising distance, landing upright in the desert to look like art installations glittering in the moonlight. Lights played over the trucks and camo-decked tents, and I spotted a news van about half a mile down the road.

You okay? I asked Pluck when the crane swung us under another heavy spotlight and toward the earth. His mood might be good, but his thoughts were troubled. We'd escaped, but doing so had told Thoth we were not helpless—or rather, I was not helpless. It would be harder to pin him down.

I'm fine, he simmered, buzzing with quiet vengeful thoughts.

My stomach hurt when my feet touched the parking lot pavement and three people rushed forward to help me unbuckle—only to hesitate when Pluck hazed to stand at my feet, re-forming as a smooth-skinned hound from hell. Head shaking, he made his ears slap in a subtle warning for them to keep their distance. "It's okay. I've got it," I said, my head going down to free the last buckle, and the harness hit the pavement. "Hey, is there a bathroom nearby I can use?" My makeshift latrine had left much to be desired, and I'd been avoiding the worst.

"Holy shit, girl!" Lev shouted, and my head snapped up to see him striding forward in his militia fatigues. That is, until Pluck flicked an ear and a glob of dark matter splatted inches from his foot.

Rifles clicked from the darkness, and Lev's smile faltered. "Seriously? Stand down," he said, his pace never shifting, but I couldn't see anyone past the circle of light, and it was unnerving. "Good God," the man complained as he came closer and gave me a whack on my shoulder. "You really want to shoot her? After we spent the last twenty-four hours trying to get her out? Someone inform Master Ranger Nodal. I'll escort her up."

Up? Up where? I wondered, then stiffened when Lev leaned in, his gaze worried. "You were down there an entire day," he whispered as he drew me into the dark. "Thank God you blew the roof." He glanced at Pluck padding along beside me, his head in line with my hip. "They were arguing over how to get to you without cracking the vault. Some fool welded the valve shut and coated it with glass. What took you so long? I had to bring Nodal in on this."

"Sorry?" I said, relieved when we left the circle of bright light and I could see again. "Where are Marty and Aasta?"

"Safe." He hardly breathed the words as his hand touched my elbow. "Still at the grotto. That shadow Aasta wouldn't let me take them anywhere else."

"Benedict and Herm?"

He winced, his grip on me falling away. "Ah, safe. Everyone is safe."

Safe, he said, but I wasn't sure his definition and mine were the same.

Pluck's dog shift was turning everyone's head, and whispers were growing in our wake. It was obvious that they knew he was a shadow, and I draped a hand into his presence, remembering the feel of Pluck's weave through the dark matter I had pulled into existence. It was far more energy than I'd ever seen either of us handle on our own, and more malleable than anything I'd pulled from a Spinner lodestone. Shadow magic on steroids. I'd only meant to break the lock, and I had blown a huge hole clear through six inches of glass and a thick plate of steel. Not to mention demolished the building above.

Pluck? I questioned as Lev guided me through the trucks and past what looked like a mess tent.

It was unprecedented, but fulfilling, Pluck thought as he padded beside me. *I suggest we downplay how we worked together lest Nodal become too interested. As far as he knows, you're unable to create a field since Thoth attacked you in Cameron's mind. Let's keep it that way.*

I am unable to create a field, I thought, wondering why Lev was staring at a Jeep in question.

I disagree, Pluck insisted.

"Hey, ah, you got any food and water here, or is it all guns and trucks?" I said, and Lev took his gaze off the vehicle.

"Yeah, we got water. Seriously, how the hell did you get out of there? It was supposed to be empty." He leaned to look past me at Pluck. "Was there dross down there? Enough for Pluck to blow the vault?"

Pluck closed one green eye in a slow wink, a warning fizz bubbling through me. *Give me the credit. Thoth will be easier to catch if he doesn't know you can do magic.*

Crap, he was right. Not only about Thoth, but *I'd* done magic. Sort of. Pluck had been a big factor in it. "Ah, yeah. Pluck figured it out."

"Good job, Pluck." Lev pointed to an aggressive-looking RV painted a flat tan. Mobile command, probably. "But between you and Thoth, Nodal is more set than ever on recruiting shadows to work in the militia. He's especially impressed with Thoth and is sure you can not only bring him in but bring him to heel."

Most military leaders are impressed with the psychotic, fizzed through me, and I snorted.

Lev waited a moment, then, "What did he say?"

I sidestepped a dross drift, missing my stick. "That Thoth is psychotic. Speaking of psychotic, where's Dana?"

"Dana?" Lev questioned, and then his eyes widened. "Oh. Ah. Yeah. Benedict said Thoth was possessing her, but no one believed him because . . . you know." He shrugged.

"Damn right he's possessing her," I said. "It's Thoth's special gift. So, Benedict and Herm are safe, you say? Where is safe?"

"Safe." Head cocked, Lev scuffed to a halt just outside the military-looking RV, and the woman stationed there went in to let Nodal know we were here. "Ben also said that Thoth used Dana's airologist skills to devastating effect. That's unfortunate. It will be harder to convince everyone Thoth is responsible if he can borrow the skills of those he's possessing."

Not to mention make it harder to capture him, Pluck thought, his worry for Benedict and Herm twining through mine.

"Lev, where's Benedict? Is he here?" I asked again, and Lev shook his head.

"He's fine," the man said, but he wouldn't look me in the eye, and I had my doubts. "Nodal has the latest intel."

Nodal's aide was still inside, and I cocked my hip, my urge to find the bathroom suddenly less important than getting a straight answer. The militia had only been here for a day at the most, and dross was already drifting about, snagging on the cacti planted in the medians. "Lev? Where," I said firmly, "are Benedict and Herm?"

Lev turned his back on the military RV. "Your sticks are at the grotto," he said softly. "I'm sorry. Dana still has your lodestone."

"Where is Benedict?" I barked, and he leaned in, eyes narrowed in annoyance.

Lev ran a hand over his chin. He glanced cautiously at Pluck, but the shadow dog had sat back on his haunches, his sort-of-there tongue lolling. Clearly, Pluck was content to let me handle it. "I'm trying to help you," Lev finally said. "Look at it from Nodal's point of view. Pluck busted you out of a facility we have been trying to break into for twelve hours. You destroyed the vault, Petra."

"You'd rather I suffocated?" I muttered. "This wouldn't have happened if the shadow release valves had been installed like the university promised."

"In a vault that no one was using? Listen to me. You are in deep shit. Let me hand you a shovel. While you were down there, Thoth turned the university against you."

My anger vanished and Pluck's ears became sharp. "Is Benedict okay? Herm? What about Cameron?"

"Cameron is fine. Probably," he added, and my worry returned. "I haven't heard from her since Benedict and Herm were arrested. I'm pretty sure Ryan went underground with her and some of the sweepers." Lev's attention went to the RV's narrow door when the woman came back out.

"What were the charges?" I said, but Lev wasn't listening.

"Master Ranger Nodal will see Petra Grady and the, ah, shadow now," Nodal's aide said, clearly nervous as she inched away from the door so we wouldn't have to get close to her.

"Please, Petra," Lev said. "Be nice. I went out on a limb for you. Listen to him. Find out what he wants. Play your cards right, and you might get another lodestone."

Pluck got to his feet and stretched, pretending to be a friendly, happy dog. *It never hurts to listen.*

It was a true enough thought, but I doubted that Nodal would let us walk out of here if I didn't like what he said, much less give me a piece of moldavite. Still, Pluck was waiting, ears pricked in anticipation. "Fine," I muttered. "I'll listen."

"Thank you." Lev flashed me a nervous smile. "Can you maybe put a 'sir' in there? You could use his help and he's got resources."

Pluck padded forward, tail waving. *Resources given can be taken away. Power earned through knowledge cannot.*

Nodal's aide stiffened as Lev passed her and went in. "Master Ranger, sir? I have Petra Grady and Pluck," came his voice, and I rocked forward.

The steps were taller than I had expected, and I used the handrail to almost pull myself in, coming to a quick halt to keep from running into the two other men standing before the desk bolted to the floor. It *was* a modified RV, and I shuddered when Pluck flowed around and between my legs before re-forming as a slightly smaller dog at my side.

Nodal glanced up from his conversation, the lanky, lean man with his straight black hair appearing as if he belonged to the desert. He had traded in his cowboy hat and boots for a pair of fatigues, but he somehow still looked as if he should be on a horse in the late 1800s riding fence, not behind a desk. Eyes sharp, he studied me as he motioned for the two uniformed people with him to leave.

"You too, Evander," Nodal said when Lev didn't move, and I stifled a grimace.

"You wanted some water, right," he said, not waiting for an answer before spinning on a heel and stomping down the stairs. Yeah, I wanted water, but I thought Lev brought it up as a way to get himself back in the room.

"Pluck. Petra Grady." Nodal tidied his paperwork as the door slammed shut. "Have a seat. I was not keen on making a public show here when Lev said you needed help getting out of a supposedly sealed vault, but when Marshal Cameron Owens and then Dr. Strom confirmed you were trapped in it, I thought it worth investigating if only to protect my investment."

Pluck fizzed sourly through me. *Investment?* I didn't sit, didn't move an inch closer to him or the door. "I don't work for you," I said, and he actually laughed, his low voice making it a pleasant sound.

"That last deposit into your bank account says different." Nodal set the papers aside to focus fully on us. "That vault was sealed. I can guess how you got into it as Ms. Vean is an airologist. But I'd like to know how Pluck got you out of an empty shadowproof vault. You can't make a field, and there was nothing down there to work with."

I dangled a hand in Pluck's head, using the chill to ground me. "You seem unusually well-informed." Again I wished for my staff. It would be nice to have something to smack into the floor for emphasis. Not to mention there was dross in here, burning like little suns in the corners.

Nodal's gaze flicked behind me to the door. "Evander told me because he was worried about you."

"You manipulated information out of him," I accused, and the man grinned, totally unashamed.

"I impressed Ranger Evander with the precariousness of your position and my need for all available information to get you out safely." Pushing from the desk, he laced his hands over his flat middle. "That he wants to continue to work with you probably figured into it. So. Ms. Vean has a warrant for your arrest for the recent destruction of the vaults in St. Unoc. Your actions tonight tend to substantiate it."

"That's not Dana," I said. "It's Thoth. Best I can figure, he has possessed her."

The older man's gaze went to Pluck as if adding that particular ability to his résumé. "That checks with what I've been told. I wasn't aware that shadows could do that without leaving the possessor insane."

"Thoth is the only one who can," I said reluctantly, and Pluck's ears flattened. "It's also why he's the devil to catch."

Pluck fizzed miserably, but it was admit to it or we lose everything.

"Sir, where are Benedict and Herm?" I asked, desperate for news.

Nodal glanced at the report at his elbow. "That brings me to my next point." Exhaling, he flipped the top page over. "When Ms. Vean—"

"Thoth," I interrupted, and his eyes narrowed in annoyance. "Sir," I added.

"When Ms. Vean," he started again, "advised a campus-wide search and containment of shadows, both Benedict and Herm were very outspoken, claiming you didn't flee but had been trapped in one of the vaults at Biosphere 2. She put them in custody to shut them up, but not before they divided the entire St. Unoc campus."

Divided? fizzed through me, hope tempering Pluck's bitter mood.

"Benedict has been stripped of any association with the university." He tapped the pages in thought, eyebrows high. "I'm starting to believe you. Ms. Vean doesn't move that fast. Maybe Dr. Strom will come work for me when his wounds heal."

"He's hurt?!" I said, stiffening. "You think maybe you could have opened with that?"

Nodal raised a comforting hand. "Bad word choice," he said. "I meant metaphorically."

I took a slow breath. Not hurt, but being held. Disgraced. Again. Because of me. "And Cameron?"

"AWOL," he said as if it bothered him. "She and Mr. Ryan have disappeared." His attention flicked from Pluck back to me. "So, this is what is going to happen, Ms. Grady."

He doesn't dictate to me, fizzed through us both, but I wasn't sure who was more insulted.

"The world thinks you are dead," Nodal said cheerfully. "That right there is worth having brought my people out here to crack open Biosphere 2's vault. You will do nothing to contradict that. You did not break the vault; we did in trying to get you out. As far as the mundane public knows, someone sealed a door and pressurized lung number two and accidentally broke it. Too much air pressure can do amazing things. The university will be told we broke it in a desperate effort to reach you before you suffocated. Unfortunately we were too late."

"Is that so?" I said, not liking his controlling grin.

"It is. We are arranging a corpse this very moment."

Shadow spit . . . Pluck fizzed, and I was very glad I had no extended family who would think me dead. Benedict and Herm, though, would believe the lie. I had to get word to them. No, I had to get to them.

Let's go, Pluck fizzed, and I forced myself to not look at the door behind me. *There's nothing here to help us and much to hinder.*

"Nodal," I said, again wishing I had a stick. "I don't understand why you're doing this. I can't make a field anymore," I lied. Sort of. "I'm useless."

Nodal set his clasped hands on the desk. "Clearly you are not. I'm giving you a parachute, Petra Grady. Don't cut it from your back. You and Pluck will continue to work with Lev under a new identity. Along with Benedict and Herm if you can convince them. You will be responsible for finding and instructing weavers. You found one; there will be more. With some luck, your abilities may return in time."

Worry for Marty and Aasta lifted through me as Pluck's tail phased in and out of existence. *Finding weavers is my goal, but not to make them soldiers,* he thought.

I could hear a soft, amicable conversation outside at the foot of the stairs, and I forced my hands to unclench. "And if Pluck and I don't want to become the militia's secret weapon?"

Nodal sighed. "Your inability to make a field limits your opportunities. Make the smart choice. You have a chance for something good to come from this."

Thoth has not destroyed everything, echoed in my mind, but I wasn't sure who thought it. If the campus was divided, then someone believed me. Us. And I didn't like how he was talking only to me, as if I was the one making the decisions for Pluck.

"Master Ranger Nodal," I said formally, and the man's smile took on a forced look. "Thank you for your offer. Pluck and I would like some time to think it over."

Nodal leaned forward, squinting at us. "You misunderstand me," he intoned, and tension tightened my gut.

"No, sir. You misunderstand us."

Pluck flicked an ear, the play gone from him as he stood, as still as death, at my heel. Nodal took a breath, but his words remained unsaid when his gaze flicked to the door at the decisive knock. I turned, knowing my face still held my anger when Lev came in, eyes bright and a bottled water in his hand.

"Excuse me, sir. Petra, we're at limited rations, but I found you some water."

I took it, the cold damp from the ice water feeling almost warm after I'd dangled my fingers in Pluck. "Thank you," I said, but he was already gone, having apologized and beaten a hasty retreat before Nodal could reprimand him for interrupting.

Immediately I cracked the top, throat moving as I downed about half of it. It wasn't until I recapped the bottle that I realized Lev had written *thirty seconds* on the top.

Oh, I thought, and Pluck's presence in mine bubbled as he read my mind. *Apparently Lev isn't happy, either. You good to go?*

Pluck's feet hazed in anticipation. *Nodal's offer isn't conducive to finding a balance.*

I took that as a yes. The scrape of Nodal's chair sounded, and I tensed when the man stood. "I'm sorry it has to be this way," he said, clearly done with the carrot and ready to use the stick. "Sergeant Michaels is outside. She will find you a bunk, stay with you until we can find a more permanent situation. You want some time to think about my offer? You do it under my auspices."

"Yeah, I don't think so," I said, and his expression darkened.

"Sergeant!" Nodal bellowed, and then I yelped at the thunderous boom outside, my knees bending to keep my balance when the floor shook.

Pluck evaporated, green eyes glowing from a swirling haze. *I suggest we leave.*

"Grady! Stay put!" Nodal demanded, and I bolted, flinging the door to the RV open and crashing into Sergeant Michaels. The woman pinwheeled backward off the lower step to hit the ground hard, and I ran into the dark.

Flames were rising up out of the broken vault. Somewhere, an alarm began to ring. *What have you done, Lev?*

Look, Pluck fizzed, and I skidded to a halt. A Jeep was racing toward us, Lev at the wheel, the man gritting his teeth in delight as gravel popped from under the tires in his quick stop.

"Get in if you want to live!" he shouted gleefully. The butt of a staff showed beside him, and I yanked myself up and in, holding on when he hit the gas hard and we jolted forward with a roar of the engine. It wasn't my dad's stick, but I'd take it. "I've always wanted to say that," he added. "Buckle up. We've got two gates and a news van to get through."

I reached for the dash, struggling to fasten my belt as he careened around a group of startled men and women. So far, no one was shooting. So far . . .

"Detain them!" Nodal shouted distantly, and Lev looked over his shoulder at the furious man standing beside his mobile command RV.

"Not a chance in hell!" Lev shouted, throwing his militia hat into the dark.

No, I thought with a flash of guilt. He couldn't quit. He was going AWOL.

My shoulder jostled Lev's as he wove through the assembled vehicles to the exit, but I finally got my belt fastened. Behind us, another something blew up, lighting the darkness in a burst of sound and color that faded to leave oily wisps of dross to color the night. "Was that you?" I asked, and he nodded, both hands gripping the wheel as he eyed the vehicles now tailing us through the rearview mirror. "Lev, you can't quit."

"I'm not quitting. I'm refusing to follow illegal orders," he said over the wind noise. "Ah, I hope you have an idea. I really don't want to become Herm's off-grid roomie."

Pluck materialized between us, his great doggy head making Lev jump. *I have an idea,* he fizzed, but Lev couldn't hear him. *Find Thoth and spread his consciousness from one end of the universe to the other.*

"As a matter of fact, I do," I said, hand clenched upon the window frame as I stared at the lights illuminating the gate to Biosphere 2.

Lev stiffened as he studied the pinch point. Beyond it was the main road. "Ah, hold on. We're going off road."

"Off road!" I shouted, one hand flying to the ceiling, the other to the dash. There was no off road, there was only desert. "Lev, it's a Jeep, but I don't know if it's rated for— Hey!" I shouted as he suddenly spun the wheel, never slowing as he drove us into the desert. He hooted gleefully, and gravel clattered against the undercarriage as he made a big U around the roadblock, jostling my teeth almost out of my head when he found the road again. A heavy-weight glass dross bottle slammed into my ankle, rolling about the floor until I pinned it.

The ride smoothed out, and I sat wedged into the seat, unable to take my hands from the ceiling and dash as Lev picked up speed. Behind us, men and women shouted, but no shots were fired. We had made it?

I forced myself to let go of the dash. That stick had bounced to the floor, and I picked it up, feeling stronger for it. *Pluck?* I thought, not seeing him, but I knew he was with us as a snarky amusement drifted about the edges of my fading adrenaline.

Lev stuck his arm out the window and waved merrily at the news van as we sped by. "Hey, I got that bottle from appropriations. It will hold Thoth, won't it?"

I took the bottle from the floor and jammed the ankle-buster into a cupholder. It was too small to be useful in dross collecting, but yes, its thick gauge made it perfect to contain shadow. "It will work," I muttered, not liking that the militia had it.

"Great. I have a way over the border," he said, a hint of worry creasing his brow. "We are both in deep shit. I saw the intel that Nodal is working from. Dana has the entire university board convinced that you and Pluck masterminded everything. Our only shot is to prove that Dana is compromised, and then—"

"No one will believe us," I interrupted, and he flicked off the lights, racing through the desert night and trusting that the armadillos would stay off the road.

"You have half the campus behind you," he said.

"Which half?" I said, but I had a pretty good idea. Sweepers.

"Professor Brown is still at liberty." His expression became introspective in the faint moonlight. There was a drift of dross clinging to his heel, and it bothered me. "And not happy that Dana tried to arrest you in his labs. He knows every sweeper on campus. Better yet, he knows not to confront the university board directly like Benedict did, and is working in the shadows." Lev glanced at Pluck, the wind pulling through his essence like the wind through my hair, and I shivered at the shared sensation of energy stripping from him—not a problem when it was night.

"Ryan is convincing who he can," Lev continued. "And we have a few mages on your side thanks to Benedict." He smirked. "It pays to be the university's most popular instructor, especially when you are in mage jail. And then there's me. Cameron, too, probably."

My pulse quickened and I gripped that trap stick tighter. "You think we can get Benny and Herm free?"

"Way ahead of you." Lev watched Pluck sink down to become

nothing but glowing green eyes and a bad attitude. "Your sweeper friends are already on it. We're meeting at the grotto. All I need to know is if you and Pluck can bottle Thoth."

Pluck? My thoughts carried both of our minds back to how we had been stronger together, with my twisted threads of dark matter and his weave to give it direction. The shadow's mood had shifted since we'd clambered into Lev's Jeep. That a segment of sweepers and mages believed in us had given him a boost of confidence, of hope that we wouldn't have to hide when all of this was said and done.

I'd give us a decent shot, fizzed through me, Pluck's mood shimmering with anticipation.

"Pluck says yes," I said, and then I reached out, fingers burning as I pulled the dross from Lev as I had a hundred times before. Exhaling into the rise and fall of the universe, I brought a mass of dark matter into existence. The threads were twisted beyond belief—until Pluck wove his presence through them and the painful prickles of dross vanished as a field took shape.

Thank you, I thought as I tossed the dross into the night, and Pluck fizzed in satisfaction when it hit a cactus and a budded flower bloomed, pushed into it by the energy released in the breaking dross. I hadn't done it. It was Pluck.

Clearly we could do this. Together.

31

ELEVEN PERCENT IS A DECENT SHOT?" I BARKED, WINCING WHEN MY VOICE echoed over the noise of the splashing fountain. It was nearing two in the morning and the memorial garden was nothing but moonlight and shadows, peaceful apart from us. I was sure if Thoth knew where we were, there'd be blue and gold lights and ugly demands to put our faces on the ground.

Pluck's annoyance fizzed through me. The shadow was currently in his human shift, taking no chances that his opinions would not be heard as we waited for Herm and Benedict. Lev and Cameron sat across from me at the seating nook, that heavy-weight glass bottle and a Waffle House bag on the low stone table between us. "It's better than the five percent I estimated three days ago," Pluck said, his low voice still surprising me.

Lev ate the last bite of his burger, head tilting as he licked the sweet barbecue sauce from his fingers. "I'm in." He glanced at Cameron, and when she shook her head, he pulled the paper bag with the fries closer. "This shadow has to go down, and no one is better suited than us to do it. It won't be pretty, but we'll manage. Eleven percent just means we come out bruised."

Cameron frowned at Lev jamming fries into his mouth. "Our chances go up if we can get Benedict and Herm free, right?"

"Yes."

Pluck's voice was confident, but my breath caught at a flash of memory: his last weaver, dying in his arms. Shadow spit, Pluck had patterned his human shift on him. Guilt, regret, and empathy washed through me, and feeling it, Pluck met my eyes and shrugged. *It was a long time ago.*

Damn. I might get everyone I cared about killed. Effing eleven percent.

"Here." Lev held out the bag to me. "You want these?"

After two burgers, a milkshake, and a folder of fries, I wasn't hungry, but I took the bag, surprised when I found the fries steaming. Lev must have warmed them up. Sure enough, a thin ribbon of dross drifted about his feet, and I sighed when he nudged it into the vegetation that lined our little three-bench nook.

Oblivious, Lev resettled himself. "Once Ben and Herm get here, we are moving." He lifted his eyes to where sky met the old shell of the auditorium. "Not that this isn't . . . nice."

Pluck snorted, the noise sounding a lot like his dog huff.

Benedict and Herm were in transit. The marshal had shown up when Lev and I had arrived, making me wonder if she'd been watching from the shadows. Marty and Aasta had been with her, and the two of them were sitting by the well within earshot as they tried to come to terms with their new situation. Marty wanted to help, but risking her seemed cruel.

"Pluck, I put our chances near eighty with Ben and Herm." Lev crumpled his fry sleeve and tossed it into the empty bag. "We have everything we need, sticks included."

My gaze went to the five balanced sticks propped up against the bench. Now that we had them, they hardly seemed like enough. Sure, Pluck and I had blown off the top of the vault, but I hadn't known what I was doing. It would be too easy to seriously hurt someone, and that wasn't the goal.

"You do your thing," Lev said confidently. "Ben hammers him

with his fire/ice magic. Herm throws the dross we create at him, leaving me to pin Thoth down. Cameron keeps him confused by altering his perceptions."

"That's not how ether magic works, but okay," the woman muttered.

"If we harass him enough, the shadow will evaporate," Lev continued. "When he does, you and Pluck snare him in a field and put him in a bottle."

My gut hurt as I glanced at the lab-grade bottle Lev had lifted. Snaring Thoth would be like catching a feral cat bare-handed.

Clearly worried, Cameron glanced at the well. "Do you think Marty and Aasta could be of some help?"

Pluck shifted on the hard bench, his outline going hazy as his worry fizzed through me. "Ah, I'd rather they stay clear," I said, though a fully functioning weaver/shadow pair would have been helpful. "Marty has a lot to learn, and Aasta is still adapting to her."

"Let them help," Lev said softly. "Marty has been evading Thoth on her own for how long?"

Pluck fizzed possessively in my thoughts. "Hands off. She's not militia," I grumbled.

Lev sighed. "Chances are, neither am I anymore. Refusal to follow 'illegal orders' won't fly unless we pull this off and prove Dana was possessed." Lev hesitated, looking at Cameron now. "I was thinking . . . If you put Thoth to sleep, bottling him would be a snap."

Cameron's eyebrows rose in disbelief. "I can't put a shadow to sleep. I'd have to join my thoughts to his and he'd drop me in a coma again. Which is why I still think we need to free Dana first. If Thoth can use her skills to drop Petra and Pluck into a glass-lined vault, she can do the same thing to him whether he is evaporated or not—if she's free of him."

"I doubt it will work a second time on him," Pluck interjected. "He is forewarned. Additionally, we can't force him to evaporate. It has to be his idea." His gaze went to Aasta sitting with Marty, the two of them talking. "All of these strategies failed hundreds of years ago."

Lev leaned back, eyes narrowed. "You use a lot of big words for a dog."

"Okay." I cleaned the salt and grease from my fingers, silent as a car drove past the walls and continued on. "I hear you, Pluck, and I want to learn from past attempts, but has anyone ever tried to catch Thoth with mage magic?"

Annoyance fluttered against my thoughts. "Not with any effect," he admitted.

Cameron's expression was pinched. "I still say we need to concentrate on Dana. She can clear your name if nothing else. Trust me. The woman knows what's going on. If we can get her free, she will be totally on board and able to bring as many airologists and ether mages and anything else you want to bear. Why are we trying to do this with minimal staff?"

"Because a small footprint can be dusted away easier than a large one," Lev argued. "St. Unoc is already under scrutiny because of the auditorium collapse. We add another national news story, we risk breaking the silence of our existence. It's shaky enough already. Area 52 anyone?"

Cameron crossed her arms over her middle and frowned at him. "This is because you went AWOL, isn't it."

Lev flushed. "I did not go AWOL. I refused an illegal order. We can handle this. The more people that are involved, the more likely it's going to turn into a war by committee. If that happens, Thoth wins hands down."

"Just because you can't work with more than one person . . ."

I tuned them out, my gaze following Pluck's attention to the far gate. His feet hazed to nothing and my expression blanked at his flash of concern. *That car* . . . I thought, tension spiking as the gate creaked open.

"It's Benedict and Herm," Pluck said, green eyes glinting. "They're alone."

My shoulders relaxed and I stood, recognizing Benedict's familiar silhouette when he waved.

"Good." Lev stood as well, clearly pleased. "That makes it six on one. Seven if we can get Thoth out of Dana."

"We are going to have to," Cameron said grumpily. "I don't want to face a shadow wielding an airologist's skills."

The memory of falling through the earth flickered, and then Benedict was before me, his brow furrowed in concern as he pulled me into a heady hug.

"Petra," he whispered, and my arms went around him, eyes closing as I breathed him in, feeling whole again, secure. "You're okay. Pluck got you out?"

"We got out together." I couldn't seem to let go of him, and I tried to stifle my overflowing relief so Pluck wouldn't have to wade through my emotions.

Pluck, though, was as relieved as I was to see Benedict, which was nice all on its own.

Benedict's hug tightened to an almost frightening strength. "I don't think I've ever been more terrified than when you fell through the floor and into the vault," he said. "I knew Pluck would get you out."

"Not half as terrified as me sitting in the dark not knowing what happened to you," I responded, and he let go just enough that I could give him a kiss.

Warmth swirled up as if from nowhere as our lips met, soothing, comforting, and oh so pleasant. It was as sure and strong as Pluck's measured chill, but where Pluck's thoughts held companionship and devotion, Benedict's held love as well—and as I pulled away, a hint of fizzing twined through my thoughts, assuring me that Pluck thought that was a good thing.

Oblivious as to the reason behind my sudden smile, Benedict beamed down, his arms still around me. "I'm fine," he said.

Herm harrumphed, giving my shoulder a pat as he went to stand by Lev.

"I'm glad you're okay, too, Pluck," Benedict said, and the shadow's spiky hair hazed with sparkles.

"You sure you don't want to keep playing dead?" Herm grinned as he stood between Lev and the bench where Cameron was sitting. "It wouldn't be hard to disappear." I shook my head, and he nodded as if proud of me. "Good. I knew you were alive. Even after the news said they called off the search when the militia found a body. Always making up stories to protect the silence. I don't know about you, but I don't feel any safer for it."

"The corpse was real," I said, and his expression faltered. "Nodal wanted me to play dead so they could force Pluck and me to be their secret weapon."

Brow furrowed in accusation, Herm turned to Lev.

"Lev got me out. He didn't think it was a good idea, either," I added, and Herm grunted, mood brightening again.

"Illegal orders," Lev said as he wadded his burger paper into a tiny knot.

"Smart man." Shoulders rolling, the Spinner flicked his gaze to Marty, now coming to sit with us, then to me, his eyebrows rising when I shrugged. "I have a plan if no one else does," the older man said.

"Does it involve Mexico or Canada?" Benedict sighed.

Cameron patted the bench, shifting to make room for Marty as she meekly inched closer. The amulet around her neck was darker than the night. Clearly Aasta was in it. "Is it just you two?" the marshal asked Herm. "I was hoping that some of the sweepers who broke you out . . ."

Her voice trailed off when Herm shook his head. "They weren't exactly subtle. Which is helpful in trying to lay a false trail. They'll be fine if Thoth ever catches up to them. He doesn't care about sweepers."

No, Thoth's beef was with me. *Mostly,* I thought, glancing at Marty and Aasta. I'd made them a target, too, though I couldn't really take the blame for that.

Lev sank back down on the bench. Cameron immediately tucked in next to him. Herm took the bench across from them, where he could see everyone, and Marty sat beside him, the woman looking nervous and yet pleased to be included. Only now did Benedict's hand fall from my waist, and we sat at the third point of the triangle.

"I knew you were okay when they told me the vault blew," Benedict said, and I shifted so our thighs touched. "Pluck, thank you," he added, and the shadow hazed where he stood, his guilt brightening in me.

"Us, not me," the shadow said. "It took both of us to break the vault."

Herm's attention sharpened on me, hope brightening his face. "Us?" he questioned, and Lev grunted, paying attention again.

"Um." I glanced at Marty, nervous for some reason. "Pluck and I learned how to work together as a weaver/shadow pair."

"Petra!" Benedict practically crowed as he jostled against me, and Cameron shushed him. "I knew you could do it," he said, softer but no less enthusiastic as he took both my hands in his. "Didn't I say?"

"We have an experienced weaver/shadow pair, then," Herm said in satisfaction, completely missing my sick expression. Benedict saw it, though, and his enthusiasm dimmed.

"Petra doesn't have a lodestone," Cameron reminded everyone. "And even if she did, we can't stand up to an airologist."

Herm waved a hand in dismissal. "Which is why we have to free Dana first, and not just because she has Petra's lodestone. Any ideas?"

Benedict leaned closer, his hand in mine tightening. "What's the matter?" he asked.

I hesitated, still finding it hard to say. "Um, Pluck and I are up for this, but you should all know that despite what it looks like, I still can't make a field."

"I would argue that," Pluck said. There was a hint of moonlight passing through him, the effect surreal and distant.

"Then how did you . . ." Herm's voice was low in disbelief.

"Pluck makes it." I made a mirthless smile. Pluck's encouragement was bubbling through me, and my ankle went cold. He hadn't taken one step closer, and yet he now stood beside me, feet hazed to nothing so he could wrap a tendril around my ankle. "I supply the dark matter. Pluck weaves it. Gives it direction."

They were silent, and I exhaled to bring a tangled mass of dark matter threads into existence between my hands. "I can, however, make a light." Wrists spinning, I wound a single strand of it around two fingers and pulled it taut. Light blossomed, and Herm swore softly.

"See, I told you," Benedict said proudly as I hunched in my own personal ice age.

"Holy smokes," Cameron whispered. "It's charging my lodestone."

"You're not making dross," Herm said, and I nodded. It felt like a small thing, but in the grand scheme of it all, it was significant. "Light is a waste product. What are you doing with the energy?"

"Ah, nothing," I said, only now realizing why making a light left me cold. If I had a lodestone, I could store it, but as it was . . . *Brrrr.*

Benedict grinned and held out his hand to recharge the lodestone on his ring.

"Balance," Cameron said, voice soft as she settled her lodestone amulet more securely against herself.

"So." Herm chewed on his lower lip. "You and Pluck *are* functioning as a weaver/shadow pair, but Pluck is the one in charge? You are supplying the energy, not him?"

Pluck bobbed his head. "I would not say in charge," he said. "And I don't share Petra's conviction that we can effectively trap Thoth."

"It's this that makes me think we can," I countered, and Pluck fizzed sourly in my thoughts. "Thoth won't expect it."

Cameron tucked her lodestone behind her shirt, and I let the light go out, relieved.

"Mmmm." Herm yawned as he looked at the brightening east. "Our best chance to free Dana will be after sunrise. Thoth's magic utilizes dark matter, which is available twenty-four/seven, and I don't want to rely on Petra's light to recharge our stones. If he knows we need you to keep fighting, he will target you first."

Herm inhaled, hands at his middle. Sensation trickled over me, and I wasn't surprised when a tidy field took shape between his hands. "Last I checked, Thoth was halfway across campus." Herm exhaled and sent the field out. It whooshed over me like a wind, and I swear, my hair moved. "Chasing the sweepers' guild," he finished.

I seldom saw Herm do his water magic, but it was obvious that he had relied on it to stay clear of the separatists—and later, university personnel—who had targeted him. It was lucky, really, that he had the skill to keep my weaver status hidden until Pluck forced us both into society's eye.

Herm frowned, his gaze going to Benedict. "He's not following the sweepers anymore."

Lev looked up, last folder of fries in his hand as Herm sent another field out.

"Shadow spit, he's close," Herm added. "We have to move."

Pulse fast, I looked at Marty. "Take Aasta and hide in the grotto."

"I'm not hiding anymore," she said, pale but determined. "And neither is Aasta."

That's about three thousand years too late, Pluck fizzed.

Benedict scooped up the balanced sticks, handing me one before passing the rest out. "Let her stay."

Lev stood, his lodestone earring glinting. "I agree. She has a stake in this, too. We finish this now."

"What a good idea," came a loud, sarcastic voice from the street, and Herm sprang to his feet. Dana stood at the gate, and Herm moved around the low table to stand beside me, one of my dad's sticks in his hand.

"You think that's just Dana?" he said hopefully, and Cameron shook her head, her expression grim as she found her feet.

"If it was only Dana, there'd be at least six mages behind her to take us in," the marshal said, her own lodestone beginning to glow.

Benedict sidled closer. "I never should have busted the lock on the gate," he muttered when the woman shoved the gate open and strode in, her heels echoing as they trod over the open space below. It had to be Thoth. Dana was confident, but Cameron was right; she never would have come alone. She'd bring witnesses to substantiate our rebellion, and Thoth would not, unable to afford the gossip. Not if he wanted to continue holding power as Dana.

Marty may be of some help, Pluck fizzed, and I glanced at Marty, glad she was behind me. She looked terrified, her hand clenched about her amulet in protection—but she was there.

"That's close enough," Herm said boldly, and Thoth halted Dana, hands loose at her sides and her lodestone glinting in the moonlight. Me being able to make a light wasn't the boon it might be, seeing as it would charge hers as well.

Cameron took a slow breath as she moved out of our alcove. Clustering together was a bad idea, and I sensed Thoth sending out a questing field. The marshal's lip twitched, her fear of him obvious. "You're not getting in my head again, you hear me! You're nothing more than a haze of dross, stinking and ready to break!"

But it looked as if Thoth hadn't been taking care of Dana and an upgrade was needed. The woman was still in the clothes she'd had on yesterday. There were dark circles under her eyes and she clearly had not been allowed to sleep.

Still, Thoth brought her to a halt, his confidence pulling Dana straight as the shadow's disdain poured from the woman. "Still in your war uniform?"

Pluck's heartache flamed through us both, quickly stifled when Thoth swung Dana's arm to awaken the energy in her lodestone ring. The chunk of glass flared, the spell almost visible as the shadow threw it.

"Move!" Pluck shouted as his frantic worry flashed through my mind. It was Dana's magic, not Thoth's, and I shoved Benedict clear as Pluck yanked me the other way.

I hit the ground hard, the staff in my hand bruising my fingers as I refused to let it go. Pluck was a cold, protective blanket, and I struggled to get free of him. The air crackled with Dana's spell, and then I looked up as Benedict gasped. His eyes met mine . . . and then he sank into the ground and vanished—stick and all. "Benny!"

He was gone. Panicking, I scrambled up even as his shout of pain echoed from the well. He was in the grotto.

"Net him!" Cameron shouted, but I ran to the well, skin prickling when Lev pinned Thoth, or Dana, I guess, with a spell, his lodestone sending great streamers of force out to bind Dana to the ground. Herm spun, awkward in his arthritic grace, gathering dross and flinging it at the shadow, his expression twisted in vengeance. Marty was with him, stick in hand as she did the same, determined to have her own freedom from the shadow.

My hands took the brunt of the force as I hit the wall of the well. "Benny!" I shouted down, unable to see anything. "Benny?" I called again, more frantic as I glanced behind me. Cameron had joined the fray, and another wave of energy sparked.

"I'm okay!" Benedict's voice drifted to me from the dark. "I twisted my ankle. I'll be right up!"

"We got him! Pluck! Petra! Get over here!" Herm crowed.

Thoth was down thanks to Lev's earth magic, and Dana's expression twisted up in hate as her face pressed against the pavers—until it went frighteningly slack.

"He's out!" Cameron exclaimed, clearly sensing Thoth leave Dana's body. "Petra! Snag him!"

My breath caught at the haze of gray energy darting to the shadows. Thoth had evaporated. *Pluck!* I thought as I opened my mind, pulling the roar of the universe into me and inhaling to draw a massive wad of dark matter threads to me.

Pluck's thoughts strengthened in mine, weaving through the weft of dark matter to make a net . . . and with a decisive twist of presence, he pulled it from my hands and physically threw it at the shadow.

Scintillating in the moonlight like thought itself, the spell sped across the garden trailing ribbons of energy. "We got him!" I crowed as Pluck's aim was true and it snapped about the shadow.

And we did have him. For about two seconds.

Eyes glowing, Thoth coalesced into his usual human form, shredding the net to mere sparkles. "You should have stayed where you were, rotting," he intoned, then jumped at Cameron, evaporating even as he moved.

"Flaming yeth!" Pluck swore.

Thoth vanished inside the marshal. Stiffening, Cameron went down on one knee.

"No!" I reached out as Cameron convulsed once and her head snapped up, her unnatural intensity landing on me.

"Fools. Five sticks is a myth I started," Thoth said with Cameron's voice as her hand clasped her lodestone and a brilliant glow seeped between her fingers. "It makes it easier to find those who would stop me. No one ever makes five sticks."

It's happening again . . . rasped through me, agony and regret coloring the harsh cold. My gaze shot to Pluck, but the shadow looked as confused as I was. It hadn't been him in my head, and I turned to Marty. Aasta? Was I hearing all shadow voices?

I heard her, too, Pluck fizzed, his wonder genuine.

"He's got Cameron!" Herm exclaimed, and Lev choked, his prepared magic faltering. He couldn't hurt the woman. The arguments, the waiting outside her hospital room: he'd been quietly carrying a torch for her since finding her on the floor of my apartment. Thoth knew it.

"Let go of me, you cretin!" Dana was shouting. "It's me! Get off!"

Herm yelped when Dana backhanded him, the older man handing her a stick when she got up. She was clearly aware, pissed off, tired, cranky, and a hundred percent ready to kick some shadow ass as she got to her feet, hunched and angry.

"Where is he?" the disheveled woman intoned, and both Herm and Pluck pointed to Cameron. "You!" she added, the word almost a curse. She might not trust Pluck or me, but she knew that Thoth was garbage, and her lodestone gave a weak glimmer and hiccuped to nothing. "You used up my lodestone!" Angry, she patted her clothes for a replacement, her eyes alight when she pulled an amulet from her pocket—only to realize it was mine. "I can't use this. This is yours. What did you do with my lodestones?"

"Dana!" I shouted as I wrapped my fingers around nothing and made a light. "Here!"

"You can make a light?" Dana said, clearly shocked as her lodestone flashed with a renewed energy.

I nodded, my motion to catch my lodestone slow with cold when she threw it at me. Cold. I was so cold—until my lodestone smacked into my palm and the waste energy zipped into the ancient glass. The heat of the night slammed into me, and my head snapped up. *Much better . . .* fizzed through me, but I wasn't sure who thought it.

"You can make light," Thoth whispered through Cameron, and then he turned the woman's eyes to Pluck. "I can't allow you to exist," Thoth said through Cameron, moving the woman's hand as he made a spell to snuff us to sleep with Cameron's ether magic.

I took a step back, inhaling to find more dark matter, shocked when a wad of dross hit him/her right across the face. It was Marty, the woman looking scared but determined as Aasta twined a tendril of sparking gray around her heel. Cameron stiffened and, with a cry of outrage, tripped on a raised paver and went down, arms pinwheeling.

"Drive him out!" Herm shouted, and he and Marty sprang forward, a weird laugh coming from the old Spinner as they flung more dross at him until the shadow pulled from Cameron in an ugly black haze.

"It's me!" Cameron shouted when Dana sank her into the ground, but it was too late. The marshal was now in the grotto as well, her pained cry of surprise echoing up from the well.

Thoth coalesced as himself, indignant and angry as he stood on a bench to keep his feet clear of the drifting dross. "Two down," Thoth said, his gaze alighting on Lev.

"Lev! Move!" I shouted, and the light between my hands went out as I brought forth a mass of threads for Pluck to make a field to shield the man, but it was too late and Lev's gathered energy fizzled to nothing as he collapsed.

"Lev!" I ran to him, not knowing why Thoth kept going for my friends, not me—unless he was scared. I fell to a kneel before Lev as Herm continued to bombard Thoth with dross that Dana kept making as she tried to get a spell on the swiftly darting shadow.

"Still breathing," I said as I patted Lev's cheeks. "Pluck, can you break the spell?"

I handed Pluck Lev's stick, and the shadow blinked in surprise. Clearly he'd never considered using one.

We were all again ourselves, but Benedict still hadn't made it up the stairs, and now Cameron was there with him. How were we supposed to act together when he kept dropping into us?

"Petra!" Herm shouted, and I caught the thick-walled bottle he threw to me. "Marty and I will cover him in dross until he evaporates. Stuff him in a bottle!"

Pluck helped me up. *Stuff him in a bottle.* It was what we were down to.

Bottle in hand, I swung my stick in great arcs to gather dross, flicking it at Thoth to keep him distracted. Marty and Herm were doing the same, and my fingers began to burn as the energy threatened to break on me, little discharges prickling up the staff to find me.

"You are like flies!" Thoth screamed under the onslaught, and with a pop, the stick in Marty's hand exploded. The woman cried out in shock, and Herm pulled her behind him. Eyes full of his hatred, Thoth gathered himself to break another.

Now, Pluck fizzed, and I exhaled to gather a mass of dark matter threads.

The night brightened as Pluck poured his thoughts into it, weaving order out of chaos and settling the net over the shadow.

"Pin him! Get the bottle!" Herm shouted as he flung a great, glowing ball of dross, and Thoth jerked clear. The very air flamed behind the shadow, and Thoth spun, snarling as Herm scooped up more dross. Lev wove between them, a spell within his hands as he looked for an opening.

"You will go into a bottle, you fetid worm," Dana snarled, spell at the ready. "Hold him! Pluck, Petra, hold him!" she shouted as the shadow darted to evade Lev's spell. "Hold him!"

But the shadow was in flux and nothing could catch him. Damn it all to hell! How could we get him into the bottle if we couldn't even get a spell on him?

Thoth's lip twitched, and then his gaze shot to where the fire door slammed.

My attention faltered as Benedict and Cameron limped forward. Benedict was grim, and Cameron held her arm close, pain etching her expression. Marty was scared but determined as she moved to stand beside Herm.

"You can't best me," Thoth scoffed, his outline glinting in the moonlight. "The legend of five balanced sticks is only to force out those brave enough to wield them, and not only are you weak and untrained, but you have no weaver."

Benedict's hand clenched in frustration. "Petra is a weaver," he said, and Thoth laughed.

"No, she isn't. Not anymore. If she dares to put her thoughts in mine, I will make her my puppet, same as anyone else."

My pulse quickened and Pluck poured into my mind with the cold of an unending winter. We had lost, and a bitter realization smothered us both. Even Pluck's and my net couldn't hold him, and I looked at Benedict in anguish.

"There is always darkness." Thoth smirked, green eyes sinking to pits as I felt a great massing of threads. "You can't best me. Not alone, not together. Not without a weaver, and they are all . . . utterly gone."

"I'm not gone."

I spun at the tremulous voice as Pluck's shock twined through mine. It was Marty.

Oh no. Get back, I thought, worried for the girl—until I saw emotion flash over Thoth's face: frustration, anger . . . fear?

"You are no weaver," Thoth said, chin high. "You are a pathetic need. No shadow will touch you. Your heart is traitorous and your will thin. I will crush you under my bootheel the very next time you sleep."

He didn't know. He didn't know that Aasta had again risked heartache to bond to Marty.

"You are nothing!" Thoth shouted, and Aasta's form beside Marty flickered with a sickly green light. Vengeance flooded me, shocking in its strength. It was Aasta, and it was all the shadow had allowed herself to feel.

"I am shadow!" Aasta exclaimed, eyes wild with conviction. "And I will see you gone!"

"Marty!" I shouted, and Pluck gasped when I threw my longstick to her. It hit her hand with a solid thump, and the woman spun it to pull dark matter into existence. Teeth clenched, she wove her will through the energy, making a solid net to hold Thoth as Aasta billowed into a haze and flung herself at him.

The shadows dissolved into each other, and I saw through Pluck's eyes as Aasta fastened upon Marty's field, taking it deep into Thoth.

Lev swore, retreating as sparks of sensation flew like shrapnel. A boom of presence lit the night, rocking us all in an unseen wave. Spinning like a mad thing, Aasta and Thoth rolled about the patio, everything they touched fracturing to dust as Aasta struggled to fasten Marty's net around Thoth.

"Now! Do it now!" Marty gasped when the living ball of black lightning crashed into the well and a great slice of the wall dissolved to sand. Pluck's astonishment filled me. Marty's field was about Thoth. She had him.

"Aasta says bottle him," Marty gasped again as she used the staff to keep from falling. "I can't hold . . . him . . ."

And then Thoth twisted his mind through the gaps of Marty's field and escaped.

Marty cried out in pain when a wave of glittering presence pulled from the blackness rolling about the pavers. Two shadows unfurled, one limping and broken, the other having a sparking stillness. "No," Marty sobbed, and Lev grabbed her, keeping her from running to Aasta.

Something prickled over me, icy and cold. *You will not ruin us again . . .*

I shuddered at the rasping cold spiraling through me, the simple words ringing both in my ears and in my thoughts. It was Aasta. It had to be. This presence carried despair where Pluck had hope, guilt where Pluck had companionship, and my shadow sidled closer to me, his worry twining in mine as a hazy shape billowed up behind Marty, enveloping her and eddying in a protective cloud.

It is *Aasta,* fizzed in my mind, Pluck's shock eliciting a flicker of amused chagrin from the shadow in question as the familiar shape of my onetime mentor coalesced before Marty. Not only was it Aasta's words that reached me, but I could sense her emotions as well, her presence zigzagging through mine with a painful harshness compared to Pluck's gentle fizzing.

How . . . I thought, my confusion twining with Aasta's guarded hope. "How can I hear her as well?"

"Because you are not shadow or weaver," Pluck said, his familiar fizzing stronger than the rest. "You're something more, something that can hear the universe echo in all shadows."

He was right. I could hear it echoing in both Pluck and Aasta—and as I gripped my lodestone, the beginnings of an idea began to take form. One weaver, one field. That had been the norm. But I wasn't normal anymore, and I could hear the universe echo in both Aasta and Pluck. A field created from the echo of two shadows would be twice as thick, twice as tight. It might be strong enough to hold Thoth.

We could catch him, not in a bottle that could be opened, but in moldavite. If we could hold him there long enough for someone to break the stone, he would never coalesce again.

Pluck's fear flashed through me as my idea melted into Aasta's mind as well, a haze of warning until Aasta smothered it in a rasping demand. We would do it.

But we'd have to catch him first.

"Pluck! Aasta! A field!" I shouted. Inhaling, I brought forth a mass of dark matter between my hands. A trill of sensation rippled through me as first Pluck wove his presence through the weft of dark matter, and then Aasta. I heard the universe singing through them both as the field formed and Pluck pulled it from me, throwing it at Thoth. It settled over him and sank in, snaring him.

Again. The thought might as well have been from the universe itself as Pluck put his entire will behind it. I inhaled to bring more threads of dark matter into existence to strengthen it, and both

Pluck's and Aasta's thoughts wove within mine, making a field even Thoth couldn't slip through.

Smaller, Pluck thought. *Tell Aasta we have him. Make him smaller.*

But Aasta could hear him through me, and the field holding Thoth began to shrink.

Nooo! The howl dug at all three of us, gouging great rents in our wills as Pluck and Aasta spun the snare tighter, smaller, thicker, working together to keep him from taking solid form and breaking free again.

Heady with an old anger, Pluck's thoughts twined with mine. Aasta's guilt and frustration swirled through us both as we dropped all three of our thoughts into the stone, dragging Thoth's with us. Ice froze my fingers as dark matter poured through me, singing with the echo of the universe, stunning me with the depth of time.

The angry knot of Thoth's mind tried to escape the sparkling lattice, yanked back by Pluck's and my determination and Aasta's guilt-ridden resolve. Together, our thoughts held him.

We have him, Pluck fizzed, his thoughts garbled and rent from Thoth's anger as the shadow rebelled, agony thundering in my head as Thoth turned a great glittering eye of hate to me. *Petra, get out! Hold the net from the outside as I break the stone. You must leave!*

But I didn't know how, and I groaned, feeling myself pulled inside out as Thoth latched on to my thoughts and drew me deeper into the stone with him.

Tell them to let me go, or I will rend you for eternity! Thoth raged.

I shuddered, my psyche curling in on itself. I was somehow both trapped within the stone and standing upon the pavers, holding it. He had possessed me, and I could do nothing as Thoth gouged at my will, leaving it bleeding but not broken. Outside of myself, I could feel my hands shake as I held the moldavite so hard that the edges bit deep and blood smeared the brilliant black stone.

"Petra, let go."

The low, comforting voice was familiar, and I looked up to see Pluck's angular face, green eyes fixed to mine. "I can't," I rasped, and he smiled, fingers prying at mine as he took the stone from me. "If I let go of the dark matter, the field will fall and he will escape."

Let go of your thoughts from the stone, not your hold on the universe, he thought. *Phase. Move your thoughts from the stone. Your mind is not in the stone, only your thoughts. You are already outside it. You only need to phase your perceptions of reality out between the spaces of the stone's reality.*

How . . .

A comforting, warm presence wove through me, suffusing my entire being. *Phase your thoughts through the mass of the stone,* Pluck said, twisting my thoughts sideways and inside out.

She cannot! Noooo! raged in the back of my mind as Pluck shifted my thoughts. I couldn't tell what to let go of, but Pluck I trusted, and I felt tears of agony start at the corners of my eyes as Thoth raked his anger and frustration through my mind until with a ping, everything tilted sideways and my thoughts were free from the stone.

"Now!" Cameron shouted, and I gasped, suddenly falling. My butt hit the stone tile and a wave of dross billowed up and away, burning until it evaporated.

I blinked, staring up at Pluck standing above me. In his grip, my amulet glowed a black so deep I could not focus on it. Satisfaction poured from Pluck, flooding my mind and filling the gouges.

Finish it. The words iced through my mind with the painful grip of an ice cream headache. It was Aasta, the shadow's thoughts raspy and harsh as she stood beside Marty. The weaver held one of my dad's sticks in a death grip, her eyes wide as if she was unsure we were safe. And as I saw my moldavite lodestone in Pluck's grasp, I wasn't sure, either.

It was hazing at the edges. Shadow spit, it was starting to vibrate, a high-pitched whine coming from it as Pluck's fingers grew indistinct, phasing in and out as if trying to match some harmonic. *Or alter one,* I thought as Pluck's grip clenched, his fingers phasing right through the stone until the vibration peaked—and the stone shattered to dust, taking Thoth with it.

"Hey!" Dana yelled, her voice echoing off the walls of the garden, and Pluck eyed her as he blew the last of the dust from his hand. "What did you do that for! Damn it all to hell, he needed to account for what he did!"

"He did," Pluck said, infuriating her even more. It was death to the immortal. Thoth could never coalesce again, divided into millions of shards of glass dust that were already scattering to the wind.

"Huzzah!" Lev shouted, and Cameron jumped, clearly startled since she gave him a smack. "We got him!" the man exclaimed, undeterred as he grabbed the marshal's hands and swung her around in a big swirl much to the disgust of Dana, who had to lurch out of their way.

"Is it over?" I said as Benedict extended a hand, his fingers lovingly gentle as he pulled me to my feet. My voice sounded as it always did, but I felt as if I were someone else.

"Seems so." Benedict's arm went around my waist, and I leaned into him. "Are you okay?" he asked.

"Maybe," I said, watching Herm scoop up the broken pieces of my dad's stick. "Aasta's thoughts are giving me a headache."

Apologies, the shadow rasped, making it worse. Marty was with her, and the shadow's disbelief that Thoth was gone was slowly evaporating into a joyous understanding.

"I'm so sorry," Cameron said, her annoyance at Lev's exuberant howl evolving into a smile. "Thoth is gone, right?" she asked, clearly not sure, and Pluck nodded.

Herm harrumphed as he came closer and handed me the broken stick. "And we have a new weaver/shadow pair," he said, gaze going to Aasta and Marty. Dana was talking to them, and Cameron frowned.

"Excuse me," Cameron said as she rocked into motion. "That woman would blame God for too much sunshine."

Herm chuckled. Giving me a respectful nod, he followed Cameron to congratulate Marty and Aasta.

"Are you sure you're okay?" Benedict tugged me into him, and my eyes closed as I soaked in his warmth.

"Ask me tomorrow," I said, and he chuckled. The reddish wood felt odd under my fingers, sort of spongy. Frowning, I squinted at it, eyes widening when I realized my fingers had sunk halfway into it. Something was wrong with the wood!

The wood is fine, fizzed through me, and my gaze shot to Pluck. The shadow shrugged, embarrassed, and my lips parted. It wasn't the stick that was spongy. It was my fingers. They were phasing. They were half in, half out of reality.

I stiffened, the motion catching Benedict's attention. "What's wrong?"

"Um . . ." I stammered, gaze going to Pluck. He had shown me how to phase my thoughts to get them out of the moldavite. And now my fingers were phasing for real?

Ah, sorry? fizzed through me, and my heart thudded. They were solid again, but what if it kept happening?

Beaming, Lev gave my shoulder a hard whack. "Well, you did it, Grady," he said, ignoring Pluck's dark glare. "You got your new weaver/shadow pair. How come you always have to do everything the hard way?"

Herm laughed, and I slipped my arm around Benedict, leaning on him as we all started for the gate. "At least this time she didn't blow up a building," he muttered.

"Or a military base," Lev added. "Flood the city with ten years' worth of dross. Upend the status quo."

Pluck hazed at my side, making my ankle cold. His thoughts, though, were at peace, and the sensation was better than having sipped tequila all day. I felt good, even if I was likely going to have to play buffer between Marty, Aasta, and Dana. "Benedict, I would knock my own mother down for a coffee."

Silent, Benedict slipped an arm around my shoulders. He sighed, his entire body melting into mine. "Coffee sounds good." He looked up. "Herm? Marty?"

"Hell yes!" Lev exclaimed, and together we walked out of the garden and into whatever came next.

32

SHADOW SPIT . . . MY FINGERS WERE PHASING AGAIN, AND I PUSHED THEM INTO the hard oak floor of the lower auditorium until they were solid once more. "So," I said brightly, my voice echoing on the grotto's dark ceiling. "Since there is no absolute way to ascertain if a shadow is a city shadow familiar with humans, or a desert shadow stumbling in with no previous awareness, let me hear a few options on how to handle the situation when one appears."

The students all looked at the spot of sun behind me, or the far walls lost in shadow, or even the podium standing unused behind me since I was sitting on the edge of the stage, feet dangling. There were only five, and all of them were considerably older than me, transfers from out of state lured by the chance to be a Spinner at the end of the course. It had taken a good two weeks and some help on Pluck's part to convince them I knew what I was talking about. That I hadn't been able to convince even one person from my local sweepers' guild to take my class was kind of a disappointment.

Perhaps I should have kept it upstairs, I mused as I waited for someone to speak up.

Seriously, though. It wasn't that bad in the grotto, the temp pleasant despite the room having no air-conditioning and being open to the air. The seats had been professionally cleaned and the lights in the stairwell replaced. I had made sure that class time would be when the sun was at its highest so the sun coming in the well would be enough to read by. I'd reluctantly accepted the university's offer to teach when I realized I had no paycheck—even if it was an obvious bribe to not file charges against them for wrongful prosecution.

But the memory of the ceiling collapsing on St. Unoc's graduating class was too new, and it was only incoming students who would take the risk. Even the lure of gaining a moldavite stone tuned by Pluck and a rise to Spinner status at the end of term wasn't enough.

It's not the room, it's the resident occupants, Pluck fizzed, and I sent my gaze to the top rows where three shadows sat in their graduating-rez skins, listening. The shadow lounged at my hip as a large dog, his smooth skin sparking where motes of dust landed.

They are being quiet, I thought back. Honestly, that the resident shadows might take an interest was most of the reason I had asked for the room. That, and it felt good down here.

I sighed when it became obvious that no one was going to say anything. They wanted me to spoon-feed it to them, and I pointedly cleared my throat. "The intention of this class is not to teach you a method of shadow interaction but to increase your awareness of shadows' limits, threats, and possibilities. They are individuals with histories far more complex than we can guess at, histories that impact their actions as much as any battle trauma or personal tragedy affects us. Giving you a three-step method implies they're predictable. They aren't. So . . ."

I gestured for someone to say something, glad my fingers were solid in the faint light.

"Talk to it?" someone said, his low voice holding a hint of sarcasm, and a nervous chuckle rose.

I was just glad someone had said something. Sure, the class had been given to me to shut my mouth, but if I failed to increase attendance, they'd cancel it. "Talking is an excellent start," I said, and Pluck flicked an ear, sending a splat of dark matter to land by the student's toe. "But I'd suggest setting your sticks down between you and the shadow before initiating conversation. It not only forms a barrier that they will likely not cross without dire need, but it indicates a willingness on your part to assume he or she means no harm."

"Damn," someone whispered, and then louder, "That sounds risky."

"It is," I admitted, being a product of the same propaganda they were brought up on. "But chances are good that if you 'stumble' onto a shadow, it's been watching you for a time and has gauged you to be a level thinker and not prone to acts born in fear."

"Dr. Grady . . ."

I nodded at the woman with her hand hesitantly raised. It was an honorary title, and embarrassing, but the university had a rule that you had to have a doctorate to teach, so . . .

"You can't transition from sweeper to weaver unless you are a weaver already. Why would a shadow even *want* to communicate with someone like me?"

"Shadows pine for human connection. That's why they often animate rezes to facilitate communication." Damn it, my fingers were phasing again, and I made a fist, hiding them.

You should tell them you can evaporate. They will give you a raise, Pluck fizzed, an eye rolling to the top of his head when he sensed my flash of fear.

I don't need money. I need them to think I'm normal.

I cleared my throat, adding, "Shadows are also known to make mistakes."

We do not. Unless it's underestimating our weavers. Which I have done. I am a foolish yeth.

"But some," I said, ignoring his sparking skin, "are working toward desensitizing themselves to masses of humanity in the hopes of finding weavers again. They have spent eons hiding from us, and change is as hard for them as it is for us." Pluck's ear twitched, and I followed his gaze to the propped-open fire door. Someone was on the steps, and I glanced at my phone beside me. "Ah, watching a sweeper or Spinner and then speaking to him or her is a way to start building trust and move on from their past."

Pluck got to his feet, hindquarters rising first to stretch like a big black Lab. *It's Benedict,* he fizzed in my mind, well aware that every eye was on him.

I turned my phone over to check the time. Class was almost done. It went surprisingly fast from this side of the podium. "Okay," I said, and there was a general gathering of air as they recognized my mood of dismissal. "I'm going to give out some homework for next Thursday." Again, my fingers phased as I thought about Benedict, and I concentrated on making them firm as Pluck told me to get over it and tell everyone. "I want you to find a city shadow taking residence within a rez. Don't approach him or her, but watch from a comfortable distance for ten to fifteen minutes. I'd like a page on what you see and your thoughts on how you think the shadow is feeling." *Because creating a pathway to empathy is more important than creating a dialogue.*

The students gathered their things, clearly uncomfortable. But the lure of a Spinner stone was such that they wouldn't complain.

"A ten-minute observation," I said as I stuffed my phone in my pocket and pulled my long-stick closer. "One page, double-spaced. It won't kill you."

"The shadow might," someone muttered, and I glanced at the fire door when Benedict came in. My pulse fluttered. "What if it tries to talk to me?" my student finished, and I tore my eyes from Benedict, hoping they couldn't tell how besotted I was. *Gaaaawd . . .*

"Then explain who you are," I said, and Benedict rocked to a halt beside the stage, waiting. "That you're part of my class, and invite him or her to join us next Thursday. Chances are good that he or she is looking for an invite."

"Why does a Spinner need to know about shadows?" someone whispered, and my expression blanked.

"You want a Spinner stone?" I barked. "You aren't getting one until you convince me that you understand and can work with shadow. You don't have to trust them. You don't even have to like them. But you *will* understand them, and for that, you have to lose your fear. I'm not asking you to sit next to a shadow-animated rez and buy him or her a cup of coffee. Stay within your comfort zone. At least twenty feet. Are we good? Yes? See you all on Thursday."

No one said anything, heads down and grimacing as they filed out, passing Benedict with hardly a glance. Even the shadows auditing the class had left, their rezes beginning to shriek as they lived out their last few seconds of life over and over until they dissipated and vanished.

Amusement fizzed through me as Pluck made an eerie, slow-motion leap to the floor. Damn it, Benedict was laughing at me, and I slid from the stage when the last student scuffed up the stairs.

"I don't want to hear it," I grumped as Benedict came closer, his smile becoming decidedly fond and loving. "They wouldn't even be here if they didn't want a stone. Not one of them is anywhere near to earning it. Greed, Benedict. That's all it is."

Pluck flicked an ear, phasing out completely to re-form as a person in one of the vacated chairs. "Give them time," the shadow said. "You're dangling magic in front of them and telling them they have to work for it instead of it being their birthright."

Benedict shifted nervously as he watched Pluck, but it was obvious he felt honored that the shadow had taken a human form.

"Hi, Pluck," Benedict said, and Pluck nodded, one knee crossed over the other. Benedict hesitated, then added to me, "I think a little tough love is the only way to get through to them. I like watching you teach. You're a badass."

"I don't feel like a badass," I grumbled, and his arms went around me. They were warm and comfortable, reassuring me that I hadn't made a mistake accepting the university's offer to teach instead of demanding the apology that I deserved.

"So, week three, and you've got them talking to a wild shadow? On their own?" Benedict rocked back, and I felt the loss of his warmth. "Isn't that risky?"

I shrugged. "Possibly," I admitted. "But any shadow that is in a rez is looking for interaction." Pluck bobbed his head, and a sensation of desperation—my desperation—flooded us both. "Benny, I want this new Spinner track to go through. That means I have to fill a classroom. I will never have more than five or six students if I can't convince my own friends to take it. Besides, I'd rather my friends become Spinners than someone I have known only for taking a class or two."

Damn it, my fingers were phasing again, and I took a breath to steady my thoughts. Head down, I pulled my long-stick from the stage and tapped it on the floor until everything felt like it should.

Pluck's eyebrows rose as he stared at me. *Tell him,* the shadow encouraged. *Skills are not shameful.*

How you use them might be. My lip twitched. Seeing it, Benedict put a hand on my shoulder, his eyes searching mine. "Maybe it's your choice of classroom," he said softly.

"The thought had occurred to me," I admitted, my gaze lifting to the last row of chairs by the ceiling. "I wanted to be somewhere that the shadows would feel comfortable joining us, and if someone can't handle the dark, they probably can't handle the shadows."

Benedict chuckled, his hand finding mine and giving it a quick squeeze before he pulled me a step toward the door. "Hey, the repaired vault is ready for your inspection. You want to stop for some lunch before we go out? Taco Train okay? I love street tacos."

Pluck perked up, his skin hazing a faint green. "It's done?"

Benedict beamed as if he'd finished it himself. "Glass is applied. Shadow valve installed. We just need your stamp of approval to open it."

The shadow hazed to nothing, reappearing to stand before us both. "I will do so. Immediately."

I patted my pocket again, reassuring myself I had my phone. The one time I had left it down here, I'd found it drained of power and possessing an entirely new ad bank. "Well, that's got to please the university." I hooked my arm around Benedict's waist, and we started for the stairs. "Three vaults done."

Benedict nodded. "All of which were completed without incident, all of which contain the new shadow escape valve engineered by Pluck and Aasta."

My reputation had been cleared. Even better, both the city and the campus were again clean of dross, leaving only the usual friction between sweeper and mage. Old patterns of dross creation and removal were reasserting themselves, and the sweepers' guild was content they weren't going to lose their jobs. The few mages who had liked working with dross to fix it inert had been encouraged by peer pressure from both sides to resume their regular duties. Life was returning to normal, with the radical changes happening "under the fold," so to speak.

The stairs were brightly lit, and I almost missed the dross waiting there to trip me. I gathered it with the tip of my long-stick, expertly flipping it over my head and back downstairs to deal with later.

Tell him you can phase through glass, Pluck fizzed as he skated up the stairs like a black snake.

And if someone tries to seal us in an old vault again? I thought dryly. *I'd rather they not know we can get out.*

Pluck coalesced into a dog at the top of the stairs, looking like his namesake as he waited for us. *There is that. Okay. Don't tell him.*

We were almost to the top, and my steps slowed. "Benny, I'm fine," I grumped. "I'm okay with where I am and what I can do."

His smile held a hint of pity, and I could have smacked him for it. "I know you miss not being out there."

"Miss being looked down on?" I said. "Being treated like a trashman?"

"It's not like that anymore," he said, and I nodded. Things had gotten a lot more respectful after the mages had to deal with their own waste for a while. The better treatment might also be why I couldn't get my friends to leave the sweepers' guild for the new Spinner track I was trying to develop.

Yes, it had been a bribe to forget and forgive Dana for accusing me and Pluck of blowing up the vaults. But I wasn't going to give out a moldavite stone unless I was sure the person holding it wouldn't freak out over a shadow. Right now, my class was the best option for sweepers looking for a better skill set. Until they found more weavers, I'd have the chance to work with every potential Spinner this side of the Mississippi.

And that, Pluck fizzed, *is how change happens.*

I hid a private smile when we reached the top and Benedict held the door for me. The bright light spilled over me, banishing the chill of the grotto as I waited for Benedict to move so I could lock up.

Clearly winded, Benedict stood before the drink machine, pretending to look over the selections as I keyed in my code to the door and **Petra Grady, weaver first-class** popped up. Again, the rating felt honorary, not earned. But without it, I couldn't teach.

Not that anyone was really learning two credits' worth of anything . . .

The clink of money sounded, and then Benedict punched a button. "All Taco Train has is sugar drinks," he said as the machine whirred and I watched a bottle of water drop to the bin. "You want one?"

"Thanks. Yes, please."

I didn't see Pluck, but I could feel him lurking around. It was hot, and I moved to the shade as Benedict fed the machine more money.

"Hey, I have a lead on some new apartments." Benny hit the button again. "You want me to mention it to Marty?" He shrugged as the machine whirred. "Unless you want her and Aasta living in your building."

"I do," I said. "But ask her. She might appreciate the distance. I have no idea when she will be back, seeing as she's out with Lev again and I was told it was a need-to-know situation." The university wasn't happy that Marty had turned down their free ride scholarship, instead choosing to find more weavers with Lev. But in all honesty, both she and Aasta were far better suited for the field.

Benedict frowned as he punched the button again. The mechanism had jammed, and the bottle of water was just hanging there.

"Leave it," I said, looping my arm in his and pulling him away. "We can share yours until we find another machine."

"Yeah, I suppose."

My ankle went cold as Pluck wrapped a tendril of thought around it. *It's only stuck because it's behind glass,* he mused, and I glanced over my shoulder at it.

"Um . . ." I slowed, and Benedict looked at me when I pulled away from his arm around my waist. "I want to check on that lock. Meet you out front with the car?"

He blinked, then glanced at Pluck beside me, the shadow being very careful to stay within the footprint of the cactus's shade. "Oh, gosh. Yes." He jiggled. "I'll go bring the car around. It's a scorcher."

I leaned in and gave him a kiss. "You're so sweet. Thank you."

His eyes darted to Pluck, and then back to me. "See you there," he said, then spun and walked quickly down the path.

I waited until I heard his shoes on the tile. Exhaling, I gave in and let my hand phase through the vending machine's front. Pluck's pleased fizz held pride and astonishment as I did what no shadow could do. With a nudge, I freed the bottle. It hit the bottom of the bin with a clunk, and I beamed.

"Hey, I forgot. I got a spot under the solar panels," Benedict said, and I spun, my hand twinging as it pulled through the glass.

Benedict froze, his eyes going from the machine to me, my hand now hidden behind my back. "Y-You . . ." he stammered, and I took the water from the bin. Pluck evaporated, his chuckle warming me even though his touch in my mind was blissfully chill. "Ah, did you just . . ."

"No." I cracked the lid and took a sip. "No, I did not." Grinning, I looped my arm in his, pulling us into motion to find his car, a gleeful shadow in tow.

Pluck was right. It did feel better with Benny knowing I could phase. I wasn't a weaver, but Marty was, and though I had a suspicion Lev had been assigned to keep the new weaver from finding her old boyfriend, Marty and Lev would find what weavers existed, bringing them out of the light and into the shadows where they could thrive.

Me being able to communicate with any shadow would give them all a voice until they found their weavers to stand with them again, a good thing when change was often feared.

Balance, Pluck had wanted, and though I had once thought he had meant only a way to eliminate dross, I knew now it was far more than that. Balance also meant a way to find peace through the flood of fear. It would be generations before a true balance of mage, Spinner, and weaver, of light and dark, of fear and understanding, would be found—but being here at the beginning of it, it felt good.

And from the beginning, we could go anywhere.